The Best Boomerville Hotel

Caroline James

Copyright © 2018 Caroline James

Published 2018 by Ruby Fiction
Penrose House, Crawley Drive, Camberley, Surrey GU15 2AB, UK
www.rubyfiction.com

A CIP catalogue record for this book is available
from the British Library

ISBN: 978-1-91255-004-3

Printed and bound in Great Britain by Clays Ltd, Elcograf S.p.A.

This book is dedicated to my wonderful friends, old and new, who celebrate life and are my inspiration.

Thanks too, to the brilliant team at Ruby Fiction.

Acknowledgements

Thanks to the fabulous Tasting Panel
for choosing my book for publication:
Stephanie H, Elena B, Susan D, Debbie S, Melissa B,
Jenny K, Katie P, Sue R, Ruth N and Hilary B.

Thank you!

Boomers

Boomers are people born during the post WWII baby boom and the phrase refers to a noticeable increase in the birth rate. Their current ages are 50–69. As a group they are the wealthiest, most active and physically fit generation up to that time, receiving peak levels of income which now enables them to reap the benefit of abundant levels of food, clothing, housing, retirement programmes and even 'midlife crisis' products.

Chapter One

Kate Simmons stared out of the window of her beautifully appointed home and remembered the words that her mother often said when Kate was growing up. *'Somewhere in the universe, there is someone who will love us, understand us and kiss and make it all better.'* She repeated the words as she gazed across a terrace that led down to a neatly trimmed lawn, where a family of ducks waddled across the grass.

As she watched them approach the inky water, Kate wished that she had a family too, with a loving man by her side. Her mother's words were all very well, but to date no one in the universe had come forward to love, understand nor kiss Kate and make it all better. She visualised a partner, striding across the lawn, his arms outstretched and smile warm as he held up a hand to wave. If only she had someone to share her life, to live with her and be the companion that she yearned for.

She turned from the window and ran her fingers along a shelf of books. The titles leapt from well-read pages, taunting Kate, for she'd always imagined penning a novel but despite having plenty of time on her hands, writing was another unfulfilled dream.

Kate had been ten when she knew that she wanted to live in a schoolhouse full of books; not that she wanted to be a teacher, teaching was the furthest thing from her mind. She loved reading and wanted to be a writer and live in a world where her characters chatted happily and stories were real. But Kate grew up, schoolrooms became a memory and, after her mother's death, life went in quite a different direction.

She peered in a mirror and tugged at curls of long dark hair. At fifty, Kate was pleased with her appearance and, despite all the stress of recent years, knew that she looked younger. Her only regret was that she wished it was a lover's hand caressing her silky locks.

The hollow click of her heels echoed as she turned to cross the tiled hall floor. In the kitchen, a newspaper lay on the table and a headline caught her eye.

Boomers are unlikely to find lasting love!

The journalist wrote with cynicism about the UK's maturing population having the highest divorce rate and their endeavour to seek a happy-ever-after. Kate wondered where the writer carried out the research, for it was hardly rocket science to work out that as people all lived longer, the number of divorces would increase.

She pushed the paper to one side and thought about the article. She still clung to the hope that the maturing single population that she was now a part of had a chance to find true love.

Women of a certain age had it tough these days. Hot on their heels ran the career-driven thirty-somethings, a new breed of women who'd popped up in the race to find a partner and seemed set on the older male. Any eligible male on Kate's radar was spoilt for choice and younger women were stacked like a pack of cards in their quest for Mr Right. This completely buggered up the limited opportunities for any single woman teetering into her fifties and beyond. In Kate's experience, it was nigh on impossible to form a relationship with anyone of her own age and the men attracted to Kate were doddering around on a walking frame or looking for a ride to their next doctor's appointment.

The men she met wanted someone to look after them, to ease their journey into later life. Ideally attractive, she would have a healthy bank balance, be selfless and stimulating in the bedroom and a wizard behind the stove. Especially when it came to being creative with low cholesterol recipes and diabetic meals.

Kate had been a carer to her dad and now she wanted

someone to love and care for her. Similar in age, he would be spontaneous and sexy, fun and attractive and willing to spend the rest of his life worshipping at the altar that was Kate Simmons. Not spending all his effort on women like this know-it-all journalist, who must be decades younger.

But, as Kate got older, there seemed little chance of finding The One.

Outside Kate saw the ducks launch themselves into the pond and paddle around, creating ripples on the silver-blue water. Kate watched the happy family and realised that she'd never felt so alone. She was crying out for a partner to share her home and live between the secure and welcoming walls.

From the moment she'd seen the old schoolhouse in her home county of Wiltshire, she'd known that she had to have it. Slate-grey stone covered a kitchen floor worn smooth by centuries of little feet, tapping idly as they sat at wooden desks. Kate imagined their teacher standing in the very same spot while pupils studied lessons chalked on a board. Logs roared in a wood-burning stove where, in days gone by, the children would have huddled around an open fire.

As she boiled water for coffee, Kate wondered for the umpteenth time what she should do with the rest of her life. The fabulous fifties that everyone raved about seemed lonely and unwelcome and she yearned for some stimulating company to stop her from disappearing into the oblivion of middle age. Kate still felt young, even if the years were catching up. She was fit and healthy despite reoccurring pain in her fingers, which her doctor had diagnosed as the start of arthritis. She prayed that some day soon The One would come knocking on her door. But, in truth, Kate knew that the only knock would be the postman with a catalogue for comfy shoes and hearing aids. If she wanted to run down the road to happiness, she had to put herself on the starting line.

Before it was too late.

Kate sipped her coffee and the buzz of caffeine reminded her that she was still very much alive. She reached for the paper. What she needed was a break; a change of scene to stimulate her into action.

Spreading the newspaper over the table, Kate scanned the holiday section where a variety of adverts offered cruises for the single traveller or writing holidays with a group of women ensconced on a Greek island. Kate couldn't imagine anything worse. She didn't fancy a coach trip, or a walking holiday in the Alps and the thought of a hotel catering for solos filled her with dread. She fancied somewhere that could offer new experiences, a holiday with mental stimulation and a chance to learn with like-minded people. Hopefully, with a few eligible males thrown in too.

Kate sighed. Such a holiday didn't exist.

She finished her coffee and decided to challenge herself with the crossword. Picking up a pen, Kate was about to put her mind to the test when, alongside the puzzle, an advert caught her eye.

Boomers! Give us your body and we'll bring back your brain.
AT BOOMERVILLE.
A luxury retreat for guests of a certain age.
We run courses to enrich the retirement years:
Clairvoyance in Midlife, Sharing with the Shaman,
Write a Best-Seller, Curry in a Hurry & many more.
Come and learn with us at our lovely country house:
Boomerville, Kirkton Sowerby, Westmarland.
For further information contact:
info@boomerville.com

A country house in the Lake District, one of the most beautiful areas of north-west England, had recently opened for guests 'of a certain age' who wished to pursue new interests in the comfort of a luxury hotel. Kate felt a tingle of excitement as she picked up her iPad and found the website.

Boomerville was located on the edge of the village of Kirkton

Sowerby and set amongst the fells, close to the Lake District with the county town of Marland just a few miles away. There were twenty bedrooms, accommodating up to forty guests, and a cookery school with state-of-the-art equipment was located alongside a pottery studio and creative writing classroom. In the meadow at the end of the garden, an old gypsy caravan stood freshly painted and a mysterious tepee could be seen. The restaurant boasted a menu designed by a Michelin-starred chef.

Hotel Boomerville seemed perfect.

Kate thought of her diary and the empty days ahead. What had she got to lose? There were only so many weeds to dig up in the garden and the furniture wouldn't crumble if it wasn't polished for a week or two. She found the online booking form and began to fill it out.

Ten minutes later, it was complete.

Two or three weeks away might help her heal, for sitting around here only made the loss of her beloved dad more unbearable. If her booking was accepted, she could soon be heading north and there was only one way to find out.

Kate pressed the *send* key.

She thought about clothes for autumn in the Lake District and, feeling energised by the turn of events, decided to head upstairs and check her wardrobe. There was a spring in Kate's step as she hurried through the house.

Perhaps there was hope after all?

Hattie Contaldo picked up the newspaper to check her weekly advert. She turned the pages until she reached the holiday section where, alongside the crossword, an advert announced: *Boomers! Give us your body and we'll bring back your brain.*

She read the wording and smiled.

It was perfect. Her target audience always went straight for the crossword and the advert hooked them in. Hattie's marketing campaign, in a series of local newspapers throughout the country, had worked and bookings were pouring in.

Boomerville was a retreat for midlifers, a fresh new concept, and there were lots of enquiries with guests making reservations for rooms and courses at the recently re-opened hotel. As general manager, Hattie was thrilled that the old place was coming back to life. Following refurbishment, Boomerville, previously a residential hotel known as Kirkton House, was welcoming folk from all corners of the country, to relax in luxurious surroundings and enjoy the pleasures of the Westmarland lakes and fells whilst embracing first-hand the updated facilities on offer.

Hattie reached for a mug of coffee and as she sipped the hot milky drink, she sat back and contemplated the notion of a bacon sandwich.

The kitchen door flew open and a calloused hand held out a plate.

'Get yer laughing gear around this lot,' Sandra, the cook, said. 'I've slathered it with ketchup, just how you like it.'

Hattie fell on the warm doughy bread and sank her teeth into locally smoked bacon. The sandwich was scrumptious and she licked her lips with pleasure.

Hattie was in heaven, for Boomerville had given her a new lease of life. The owner, Jo Docherty, had a vision for the business and had closed the original hotel the previous year to re-open it as a centre for men and women who, in midlife, through various circumstances, now found themselves on their own. Unwilling to disappear down the years into old age, Jo hoped that her guests might take advantage of an opportunity to learn new things and take up fresh challenges with others of similar standing. All in the comfort of a country house. On enquiry, guests filled out a booking form, stating how long they wanted to stay and which courses they wished to participate in.

Footsteps shuffled along the carpeted hallway and Hattie recognised the soft-soled step of their oldest guest.

'Morning Hattie!' a voice boomed out.

'Morning, Sir Henry.'

'It's a fine morning for it.' Sir Henry acknowledged Hattie by waving his silver-topped walking cane. His heavily waxed handlebar moustache stood at right angles above jowls that wobbled as he teetered along.

Hattie pushed her plate to one side. She wasn't sure what 'it' Sir Henry Mulberry was referring to and glanced at her computer to see which course he'd booked that day. She noted that he was down for wine tasting.

Hattie frowned. Sir Henry had caused chaos in creative writing last week and the other students had to be calmed at the end of the session. Sir Henry's half-completed memoirs, *Fifty Shades of Sheepdogs*, had upset some of the ladies in the group, although one or two, including Hattie, enjoyed the scintillating excerpts.

'Just like the old days,' Sir Henry said. 'Marvellous to see the place back on its feet. Book me in for a month.'

'I'll be happy to extend your booking.'

'Good girl. Looking forward to my breakfast,' he said and trundled off in search of the first meal of the day.

Hattie made a note on her pad. Guests came to stay for a week or two at a time and many stayed longer, depending on their commitments at home. She wondered how Sir Henry had slipped through the net. His criteria had been way outside the specifics Jo laid down, breaking the rules on age and health, but they'd needed some fee-paying guests when the hotel re-opened and Jo had a long-standing loyalty to Sir Henry. In days gone by he'd stayed at the hotel with clients, spending a considerable sum entertaining the hoi polloi of the booze business.

'Any post for me?'

A deep smoky voice woke Hattie from her daydreams.

'The postman hasn't arrived yet, Lucinda.'

Hattie looked up at a woman leaning on the desk. Lucinda Brown was weighed down with chunky wooden beads and a forlorn expression.

'Have you cut yourself shaving?' Lucinda asked.

Hattie frowned and, wiping her chin, found a large dollop of ketchup.

'I see you're down for a day with the Shaman?' Hattie checked her spreadsheet. She ticked Lucinda's name off the list of participants for Sharing with the Shaman, a course that was run in a tepee situated in the meadow.

'I hope it's better than Clairvoyance in Midlife.'

Hattie listened to Lucinda drone on about the shortcomings of her experiences. The clairvoyance course was an intimate little group who met in an old gypsy caravan and, to date, had been a big hit with guests and non-residents alike. Middle-agers had returned from their sessions with beatific expressions as they floated down the garden, confident that the spirits of their dead granny and Rover the family pet were beside them, whispering and woofing encouraging words from beyond.

Lucinda was probably after a refund. She claimed to be an artist whose work was highly sought after and, after googling her name, Hattie wondered who on earth was daft enough to purchase the paintings that appeared online. She had doubts about Lucinda's financial status and would need to keep a close eye on her account.

'Sharing with the Shaman is right up your street and I can personally recommend it.'

Hattie watched Lucinda's aloof expression change to one of feigned interest and questioned how the artist supported the weight of that much silver draped around her thin wrists. A lick of polish on her talon-like nails wouldn't go amiss.

'The older I get the more ridiculous this all seems,' Lucinda sighed. 'I may indulge with the Shaman but I'll want a credit if his teachings aren't to my liking.'

'I think it will leave you with memories that will stay long after your time here ends.' Hattie smiled and made a note to nip over to the tepee to tip the Shaman off before the course began. Lucinda's welcoming drink might need a dash more magic potion than normal.

Lucinda walked away and Hattie watched her ignore a waiter, on hand to guide guests into the breakfast room. At the conservatory door, Lucinda stopped and placed a cigarette in a holder. She held it high as she set off across the lawn, creating a halo of smoke around her diminishing figure.

Hattie looked at her watch. The morning team was about to take over, which meant that she could take a break. Picking up her empty plate, she headed for the kitchen.

Just enough time for another bacon buttie!

Chapter Two

Jo Docherty stood by a border in the walled garden and reached across a patch of late-blooming chrysanthemums until her secateurs found a bunch of prize salvias. She snipped at the stems and held them out to admire the pretty flowers. Her gardener had found a new species called Blue Enigma, which was far removed from the dumpy scarlet bedding plants she remembered in the mature garden at her parents' home.

Jo placed the blooms in a wooden tray and stepped onto a path.

A puppy hurtled across the lawn and as she pounced on the cuttings, a stem came away. The dog tossed it in the air.

'Bunty, that's very naughty.' Jo bent down to scold but as her hand fell on the silky fur, she smiled. It was impossible to be cross with the adorable chocolate-brown Labrador. The puppy was a gift and statement of affection from the man that Jo had allowed into her life. Bunty wriggled as Jo scooped her up and removed the gnarled plant from the sharp baby teeth.

Walking across the neatly mowed lawn, Jo noted that the croquet set was laid out. The game had been at the hotel for as long as she could remember and was popular with residents and their guests.

A voice called out and Jo looked up. Hattie, her close friend of many years and manager of the hotel, stood in the conservatory doorway.

'I thought you'd got lost,' Hattie said. She tucked her hands into the pockets of a dress that stretched tightly across her ample hips. Ginger curls bounced as she shook her head.

'Just getting some flowers for the house. I'm creating an arrangement for tonight.' Jo walked past Hattie and placed her tray on a table.

On a Saturday night Jo hosted a cocktail party. Canapés

and cocktails were served and it was an occasion for everyone to socialise. Residents looked forward to meeting new guests alongside Boomerville tutors and staff.

'Shouldn't it be on a lead?' Hattie stared at Bunty. She didn't approve of a dog in the hotel.

Bunty was exhausted and snuggled into a box that lay in a corner of the conservatory. She yawned and thumped her tail then rolled onto her back and fell asleep.

'No, the guests love her.' Jo leaned down to caress the pink tummy and tiny brown paws. 'It's good therapy having an animal about the place.'

'The hotel is almost full,' Hattie said as they made their way through to the Green Room, a lounge at the front of the building. 'There's folk checking in today and bookings for dinner from non-residents.'

The restaurant at Boomerville was thriving and it hadn't taken long for locals to learn that Jo was opening up again. The menu had earned many awards in the past and with a revamped set of recipes devised by Jo's youngest Michelin-starred chef son, Zach, Sandra and her team looked set for further success.

'Are you staying tonight?' Jo asked. She knew that her friend wouldn't miss the party. Hattie had her own home in Marland, a stone built property with a view of the fells, but she loved being involved with the business and, instead of driving home to an empty house, often stayed over in Jo's spare room. Boomerville was Hattie's salvation. Single again in her fifties, with family far away, she refused to give in to advancing years and loved having a busy and active job as Jo's right-hand manager.

'I'm going to knock 'em dead with a new dress,' Hattie said, 'but I might lose one or two down my cleavage.' She thrust out her chest.

'Just as long as they settle up before they go missing.'

They'd reached the Green Room and Jo began to arrange

her flowers in an urn on a plinth in the bay window where the view overlooked the gardens at the front of the hotel. A log fire crackled in the hearth and a gilt framed mirror hung above the marbled fireplace, reflecting a brightly lit chandelier. Paintings, depicting scenes of local mountains and valleys, graced the walls.

'Is Pete coming over?' Hattie asked as she flopped down on a chair.

'He might call in for a nightcap.' Jo teased her flowers into an oasis block and snipped foliage into place.

Pete Parks had been smitten with Jo for as many years as she cared to remember, and now, as village gossip had it, they were officially 'walking out'.

'Aye, nightcap and a leg-over.' Hattie smiled. 'He knew what he was doing when he got that daft dog.' Hattie thought about Pete's gift of the puppy, a timely gift when Meg, Jo's faithful canine companion of many years, suddenly departed to the great kennel in the sky. Hattie couldn't remember a time when Jo hadn't had a dog trailing along beside her.

Jo ignored Hattie's comments. 'I'm so glad that we've re-opened, I love Kirkton House,' she said as she tidied the cuttings.

'Better get used to calling the place Boomerville.'

'I'll never get used to that, the name seems wrong in such a gracious old building.' She stood back to admire the room. 'I wonder what John would have thought.'

'Your late husband would have approved of your idea.' In reality, Hattie thought that John would be turning in his grave but went on, 'Personally, I think it will become a posh dating destination for the elderlies and why not? Let there be new life in old limbs.'

A car appeared on the drive and the two women looked out. New guests were due to arrive. Kate Simmons was travelling from Wiltshire and Andy Mack from London. Hattie reached into her blouse and pulled out a lipstick. 'Shall I do the honours?' she asked and smoothed pink gloss over her lips.

'That would be lovely.' Jo plumped cushions and tweaked at a curtain.

Hattie straightened her skirt and sucked in her tummy then bounced across the room. When she reached the door, she glanced out of the window. A member of staff was helping the guest with luggage.

Hattie turned and gave Jo a wink.

'Just like the old days,' Hattie said. 'You never know who's going to walk through that door.'

Kate sat at the dressing table in her bedroom and reached for a jar of moisturiser. She dipped a finger into the creamy lotion and began to smooth it over her neck. The cream felt wonderful, instantly reviving her skin after a soak in a hot bath.

Having checked in that afternoon, Kate had been shown around Boomerville by the manageress.

'Call me Hattie,' the woman told Kate as she pointed out the main rooms of the hotel. They went through a conservatory to a large garden. She took Kate to the studios and asked her which courses she was taking the following week.

'I thought I might try my hand at creative writing. I've always wanted to write.'

'What stopped you?'

'My mum died unexpectedly when I was a student and my writing got put on the back burner.'

'Oh, I'm sorry to hear that.'

'Then business got in the way and my dad got dementia and, to be honest, I never thought I was good enough to write.'

'What's your business?'

'I was in IT and my internet company grew beyond my wildest dreams, but I had to sell it when my dad became ill.'

'Well, let's hope your creative juices flow during your time here,' Hattie said. 'Let me show you the writing studio.'

They stepped into a room where a bank of computers sat on desks along one wall. A wood-burning stove, in a brick chimney breast, was surrounded by leather sofas and armchairs. Books lay everywhere, stacked on shelves and coffee tables. Kate felt drawn to the room and had to stop herself from settling in a chair by the fire.

'Well, this class should give you inspiration,' Hattie said. 'The tutor is very popular and they say that there's a best-seller in all of us.'

She guided Kate across a courtyard, past tubs of late-blooming flowers where flourishing herbs grew in rich dark soil beside the garden wall. Aromatic leaves scented the air as woody stems of thyme nestled under succulent bushes of rosemary and sage. Basil and coriander in pretty pottery containers sat in a window box. Hattie pinched the fresh herbs and nibbled, then opened a stable door and stepped into a bright and airy space. 'We hold cookery classes in here,' she said, flicking a sprig of thyme from her lips.

She indicated that Kate follow.

Individual workstations faced a tutor's bench, each with a hob and oven, fully equipped with all the utensils needed for a busy session. They crossed the tiled floor into a corridor and Hattie pointed out a dry-store area where a brace of pheasant hung from the beams. 'We can arrange for you to go on a shoot, if you fancy it.'

'I've never held a gun,' Kate said. 'I'm not sure that I'd like to kill anything.'

Hattie smiled. 'Early days.'

They'd wandered out to a walled area and Kate took in the sprawling borders bursting with herbaceous plants. Weed-free, they were a riot of colour and she was reminded of her own immaculate garden. Apple trees laden with fruit bowed in an orchard and, as they strolled through wrought iron gates to the meadow at the far end of the property, Kate caught her breath. Wild flowers swayed in the afternoon breeze, their heads held up to the sunshine, creating a glorious mass of colour and scent. She reached out and stroked the silky heads.

'This is the boss's favourite bit.' Hattie pointed out Jo's old gypsy caravan. Ornately painted and decorated with carvings, it had wooden steps and a raised roof with a chimney peeping out. Windows to the side looked out over open fields where, beyond a stile, the River Bevan flowed close by. 'It's perfect for a walk out here,' Hattie added. She looked around and pointed to a tall tepee that stood in the corner of the meadow. Smoke puffed from the top of the cone shaped structure and animal designs and celestial drawings covered the outer canvas layer. 'Come and meet our resident Shaman.' Hattie took Kate's elbow.

Kate could hear soft chants and was curious as Hattie explained that this was one of the more popular courses. She let Hattie lead her towards the tepee.

As they approached, a man's face peered out of an opening in the side. The Shaman wore feathers in a band across his head and his nut-brown skin was weathered. 'Namaste,' he said and fixed his intoxicating green eyes on Kate.

Kate felt a shiver, despite the warmth of the autumn afternoon.

'Been plucking pheasants again?' Hattie asked with a nod to the Shaman's headband. Her palms were touching and with the fingers pointed upwards, she bowed slightly in greeting. Turning to Kate, she whispered, 'He's very popular,' then taking her arm again, retraced their steps back to the hotel.

Kate finished applying her make-up and brushed her hair. She teased the immaculate cut into a flicked-up style, then began to dress. She'd chosen a red crepe cocktail dress for the welcoming party and a pair of matching killer heels.

Satisfied with her appearance, Kate picked up a black leather clutch, closed the bedroom door and, slipping the key into her bag, walked along the gallery to head for the wide staircase that swept down to the hall.

The party was in full swing in the Green Room and a lively

buzz greeted Kate. The room was warm and logs blazed in the hearth. Pillar candles, interspersed with ivy and roses, lined the mantelpiece and cast a flattering light. Kate noted the attention to detail. A waiter came forward and offered champagne and Kate wrapped her fingers around the chilled glass. She sighed with pleasure as tiny bubbles exploded on her tongue. Studying the mix of people who would be joining her on courses, Kate was dismayed to see that most seemed older.

'Don't worry, plenty of young blood comes in from the real world.' As if reading Kate's mind, Hattie appeared. 'They're not all old and doddering.' She spotted Sir Henry across the room and gave him a wave. 'You'll probably have to put up with Sir Henry, and if you need a restraining order, just let me know.'

'Is he staying here for long?' Kate asked.

'He's booked for a month and I've no doubt we'll need a crane to wrench him out.' Hattie smiled fondly at the old man. 'Sir Henry used to stay here when Jo ran the place as a residential hotel. Alongside his brother, Hugo, they were high-spending guests.'

'You've been at the hotel for some time?'

'I've worked here from the very first day Jo opened the doors, nearly three decades ago. I'm part of the fixtures.' Hattie smiled. 'But I love this new concept. It's giving us all a fresh lease of life.'

Hattie began to introduce Kate to fellow guests but when they reached Lucinda, Hattie was called away.

Kate smiled as she acknowledged Lucinda but Lucinda was distracted.

'She's dreadfully common,' Lucinda said as they watched Hattie's ample figure wander through the room. Draped in a wrap-around jersey dress, Hattie's cleavage and curves left little to the imagination.

'I think she's rather sweet.' Kate said. 'She's very attractive and a credit to women our age.'

Lucinda tutted and rolled her eyes with disdain.

'How long have you been staying at Boomerville?' Kate asked.

Lucinda stared at Kate through weary eyes, bruised by blocks of olive-green shadow. 'They've accommodated me for the last two weeks but I may not extend,' Lucinda said, 'not unless something riveting happens. Most of these people aren't my sort.'

Kate wondered who Lucinda's 'sort' was as she took in the happy crowd enjoying their cocktails.

A waiter approached and held out a tray.

'You took your time,' Lucinda snapped and took a flute of champagne.

'What courses are you taking?' Kate asked.

'I'm an artist, darling, I engage with passion and moods.' Lucinda knocked back her drink and reached for another. 'I've told the owner to let me take classes, for some reason there's no art course.' Her gaze travelled up and down Kate's body. 'I want to teach life classes, painting to challenge and stimulate.' Lucinda reached out and circled a finger. 'You have interesting breasts. I'd like to see you naked.' She tilted her head to one side. 'Come up to my room sometime.'

Kate was mesmerised.

Lucinda had walked away and now stood beside Sir Henry. She placed a hand on his shoulder and dipped a thin hip to perch on the arm of his chair. Without looking up, the old boy latched onto her knee, moving his fingers over the soft velvet of Lucinda's tunic, until he connected with bare flesh. Lucinda smiled and leaned in to listen to a joke that he'd told umpteen times.

An attractive woman wearing a stunning silver cocktail dress made her way across the room and appeared at Kate's side. 'Welcome to Boomerville,' she said, 'or Kirkton House, as it used to be called. I'm Jo Docherty, the owner.'

'I think I prefer Kirkton House,' Kate replied and shook Jo's hand.

'Me too, but Hattie says I need to keep up with the times and not be stuffy, so Boomerville it is.' Jo shrugged. 'Can I get you another drink? I do hope that you're looking forward to your stay with us. Some of the tutors are here tonight; I can see James from creative writing and Paul from pottery.' Jo looked around the room. 'I hope you get a chance to meet them.'

The two women began to chat and Kate told Jo about her life. She explained that she'd been studying at university when her mother suddenly died.

'That must have been terrible. How did you cope?'

'My dad rallied because he had me to look after and, after our loss, we became very close.'

'Did her death affect your studies?'

'No, it seemed to make me work harder, as if I had something to prove, and Dad was so supportive when I told him I wanted to start a business.'

'I'm sure he's very proud of you.'

'Oh, he was, but just when we should have been reaping the rewards and enjoying quality time he developed dementia and began to fail. He didn't even know me most of the time. It broke my heart.'

Jo watched Kate's eyes mist over. 'What happened?'

'I sold the business and moved him into my home. I couldn't bear to put him into residential care and I looked after him. But I was misguided; it was impossibly hard and so soul destroying.'

'I'm terribly sorry.'

'It was devastating to watch someone you love and admire become an unhappy and confused soul, trapped in a failing mind.'

'I'm sure you did the best you could.'

'I do apologise.' Kate stopped and looked at Jo. 'This is a party and I don't know why I'm talking about myself so much.' Kate was mortified. Earlier she'd told Hattie about her past and now she was pouring her heart out to Jo.

18

'We all have a story to tell and I hope that your days here will help with your healing.' Jo smiled and touched Kate's arm. 'Be kind to yourself; it takes time to overcome such grief.'

'Thank you.'

'My husband, John, died suddenly. He had cancer and I hardly had time to say goodbye,' Jo said. She was thoughtful as she went on, 'I was so upset that I closed the hotel and it stood like a ghost for nearly a year. I was numb with grief and could barely function.'

'That's hard to believe, looking at the place now.'

'I know, but Hattie and I went on a holiday and, while I was away, things fell into perspective and I knew what I wanted to do. I decided to help people in our age group who find themselves on their own and Boomerville was born.' Jo smiled. 'But here I am talking about myself, tell me about your business. What's your secret to success?'

'I ran an internet dating agency, one of the first to go online. It was successful and I was lucky to sell at the right time.'

'But that's wonderful. You must have worked very hard?'

'Not really,' Kate replied modestly. 'I think a lot of it was luck.'

'The harder you work the luckier you get,' Jo said. 'But what about you, did you find true love?'

'On the contrary.' Kate shook her head. 'I can't tell you how many weddings I got invited to from satisfied clients but I was always the bridesmaid and never the bride.'

'You were probably too involved with the technical stuff.'

'Oh, I was involved all right, with some serious deadbeats, to be honest. Now I've hit fifty the only men interested in me are having hip replacements and trouble with their prostate.' She glanced at Sir Henry who'd turfed Lucinda off his chair and was doddering past on his way to the bathroom.

'Nonsense, don't put yourself down. You're a stunning-looking woman and an eligible man's dream.'

'And the not so eligible. I think I'm emotionally drained after looking after Dad and now I'm probably too old for love.'

'Don't let age hold you back, look at me. I thought my life was over when John died. But I've started a new business and am tentatively stepping into a new relationship. Most importantly, I can't wait to try all the courses we've arranged here. I set this place up with someone exactly like you in mind.'

'So are you saying it's all right to be a boomer heading for old age?'

'Who said anything about old age?' Hattie suddenly materialised. 'Age is just a number.'

'And mine's ex-directory!' the three women chorused and laughed.

'But seriously,' Kate said, 'is there any hope of finding The One at our age?'

'Well, you could begin by getting involved with some new activities and see what happens,' Jo said. 'There are lots of courses to choose from.'

'Lucinda seems disappointed that there isn't an art course.' Kate raised her eyebrows.

'We may introduce one in time, but I wanted to start with courses that offered something different.'

'An hour or two with the Shaman should soon sort you out,' Hattie interjected. 'Our resident Shaman comes highly recommended.' She smiled as she remembered her experience with the Shaman who ran similar sessions from his home, halfway up a hill on the fells beyond the village. Hattie had gone to research prior to the opening of Boomerville and hadn't returned for three days.

Jo turned to Hattie. 'Has our last guest checked in?'

There was one more arrival that day and Jo had been holding dinner in the hope that the residents could eat together on what was, for some, their first night at Boomerville.

Hattie nodded. 'He's settling into room two and getting changed; he'll be down soon.'

'Mr Mack has travelled from London. I expect he'll be exhausted after his long journey but it would be polite to wait for him,' Jo explained to Kate and indicated to a waiter to top up their drinks.

'I've rearranged the seating plan so that Kate can sit next to him, two fresh starters together.' Hattie looked pleased.

Kate nodded to the waiter to pour. She felt an urge to keep drinking. Mr Mack was no doubt charging his hearing aid and rubbing Deep Heat into his arthritic knees. God knows what they would find to talk about and he'd grumble about eating late and upsetting his digestion.

Unexpectedly, a hand brushed across Kate's bottom and startled, she turned.

'Now, let's get you back to your chair, shall we?' Hattie knocked Sir Henry's hand away and, gripping the old man's arm, spun him round. 'Just like a bleedin' nursing home,' she muttered as she led him away.

A dinner gong sounded in the hallway and Kate watched the gaggle of tipsy residents head for the door. Lucinda led the troops and sauntered down the hallway as Sir Henry, energised by the thought of dinner, grabbed a hunting horn from a display on the wall and cantered along behind. 'Tallyho!' he cried.

Staff guided guests to their seats and Kate found herself sitting alongside a widow from Wolverhampton, who explained that having spent a day with the Shaman, she was too exhausted to eat and, leaning back in her chair, promptly fell asleep.

The Shaman has much to answer for, Kate thought and edged her chair away from the empty seat next to her, reserved for the late guest. Mr Mack would probably dribble and she had her dress to consider.

The lights were dimmed and waiting staff appeared. They carried tureens of piping hot onion soup, the rising steam dancing in flames of brandy, adding theatre to the service.

'Sorry I'm late,' a voice whispered through the dimness and a hand reached for the chair next to Kate.

Kate spun around and for a moment wondered if the

Shaman had spiked her drink. She was speechless as she stared at the man before her.

Mr Mack was possibly the most handsome man Kate had ever laid eyes on. Dressed in a dinner suit, immaculate white shirt and neat bow tie, he smiled as he took his place.

'I hope I've not missed anything,' he said. 'Andrew Mack, at your service, but you can call me Andy.' His grin lit up the room as he held out his hand.

In a trance, Kate reached out. Candlelight bounced off his glossy black hair and his dark eyes twinkled.

'K-K-Katherine,' she mumbled as she felt his warm flesh. 'But you can call me Kate.'

Chapter Three

'He burst into the dining room like James Bond.' Hattie chuckled and reached for a slice of toast. 'Even Lucinda sobered up and went into a Pussy Galore routine.' She sat at the table in Jo's house, which adjoined the hotel and was accessed through a doorway leading to the panelled restaurant.

Hattie recalled the previous evening. Andy Mack had certainly made an impression on everyone.

Pete, Jo's partner, looked up. 'Are you going to eat all that?' he asked as Hattie piled breakfast into her mouth.

'Think of your cholesterol,' Jo said.

'It'll be lower than yours, that's for sure.' Hattie reached for a napkin. 'I have the BMI of a baby.' She dabbed at her mouth. 'My appetite merely feeds my beautiful soul.'

'And your hips.' Pete chuckled and ducked as Hattie swiped at his head with a napkin.

'Was there ever a time when we didn't worry about what we eat?' Jo sipped a coffee and flicked through the Sunday papers.

'Not something Andy Mack will worry about,' Hattie said. 'I bet he's got a six-pack you can dance on.'

'He certainly doesn't look his age.' Jo thought about the booking form they'd received from Andy Mack. He came within their boomer category, but at fifty-three looked far too young to be a widower, newly single and retired.

'He ticks all the boxes,' Hattie said, 'but mark my words, there'll be trouble. You won't be able to move in Hair and Beauty tomorrow.' She thought about the flood of requests she'd received that morning from female guests who'd been dazzled when Andy had made his late appearance the previous evening. Even Lucinda had booked a manicure. 'Sir Henry won't be happy,' Hattie continued, 'with a young buck on the loose he'll be well and truly put out.'

'Hattie, you do exaggerate, although I have to say that Kate was very taken.'

'Taken?' Hattie was aghast. 'She was as red as a raspberry from the moment he sat down. No one needs a course on Clairvoyance in Midlife to see which way the wind blows there.'

'Kate is very vulnerable at the moment.' Jo folded the newspapers. 'She's still getting over the death of her father and we need to keep an eye on her.' She reached down to stroke Bunty, who'd appeared from under the table. 'Come on, Pete, it's time we took this one for a walk.'

Pete flicked a scrap of bacon and Bunty wagged her tail as she caught it. He stood and followed Jo to the utility room.

Jo grabbed a coat and handed Pete a pair of wellingtons. He pulled them over thick walking socks. 'See you later, Hattie,' they both called out.

'Aye, you two lovebirds, have a good time.' Hattie watched them slip out of the side entrance of the house and head for the village and fells beyond. She poured herself another cup of coffee and sat back. She loved Sundays. It was the one day when there were no classes and guests were left to amuse themselves. Some got together and went for a walk by the River Bevan or into the Lake District, while others lingered around the hotel and sat by the fire to catch up on the week's gossip. Later they'd dine on a roast dinner, then relax with a good book or perhaps a game of scrabble or chess.

Hattie made a mental note to call her family later. Her two sons had left Marland several years earlier and both were now married. One in the army living abroad, the other settled in Australia having married an Aussie girl he met when travelling. She missed her boys terribly but was proud of the life they'd made for themselves and even though they were far away, looked forward to their phone chats.

She finished her drink and decided that she'd have a bath. The bathrooms in Jo's house still had the old roll-tops, which were deep and a comfortable place to relax. She grabbed the last piece of toast and, selecting the gossip section from the papers, headed up the stairs.

Kate lay in the bubbles of her jacuzzi and wondered what the hell had happened. Had a lightning bolt struck Boomerville the previous evening? For something had rendered her senseless and her heart felt like it might explode. For the first time in years, Kate had feelings. Feelings that were not connected with pain and sadness over death and illness, but those of romance and passion. Suddenly life felt a little bit scary but incredibly exciting too.

She sat up and ran cold water, splashing it on her face. *'You can call me Andy.'* Kate buried her face in her hands as she remembered his words.

Andy Mack sat beside her throughout dinner and his dark eyes had studied her carefully. When he spoke, his hands moved to emphasise a point and Kate noted that they were strong and expressive. She'd been glued to his words as she listened to his story unfold as he explained that he'd been a busy entrepreneur who'd recently sold a chain of clothing stores, following the tragic death of his wife who'd suffered from an incurable tumour on her brain.

Kate had tears in her eyes as she remembered her mother's similar death and, over a glass of port, they swapped stories. They nibbled from a platter of cheese and Kate talked about her father and how devastating his spiralling illness had been. Andy was sympathetic and showed concern. He dismissed his own pain and cheered Kate up by declaring that life had to go on and what better way to start than by enjoying an interlude at Boomerville? Andy said that he hoped for some like-minded company and activities that would distract from his mourning. His friends had told him that life could begin again and, taking their advice, he was determined to find out.

Kate lathered soap across her skin. She had a fluttering

sensation in her tummy and remembered their walk to her bedroom door. Andy asked if they might catch up the next day. Perhaps a stroll on the fells and a drink at the pub? When he kissed her lightly on the cheek, it was all she could do not to crumple and her knees had threatened to give way as she gripped the handle and fumbled about with the key. Andy's steadying hand had assisted and, once she'd said good night and closed the door behind her, Kate had collapsed on a rug, wondering what the hell had happened. A hammer had hit her heart! It had awakened feelings of emotion and need, something she'd not experienced for years.

She climbed out of the bath and reached for a towel. Wrapping it around her hair, she slipped her arms into a robe and stepped into the bedroom where she began to daydream, closing her eyes as she swayed to an imaginary love song.

Andy Mack was too good to be true!

The perfect age, he had money, charm and good looks. Kate hadn't been in the hotel for more than twenty-four hours and already she was planning her wedding. Boomerville would make a wonderful venue, the place where the happy couple met.

Kate opened her eyes and caught a glimpse of her flushed face in a mirror. She flopped into an armchair and told herself to calm down and not be so foolish. She mustn't get so carried away. Clearly, she'd been intoxicated the night before and anyone would look good after that amount of alcohol. Even Sir Henry seemed to have charm and Kate vaguely remembered giving the old lecher a peck on the cheek when he tottered off to bed, aided by two waiters, while Lucinda snored loudly in a chair by the fire.

Kate looked out of her window at the front of the hotel and toyed with the thought of what she might wear if Andy's invitation still stood. There were plenty of outfits to choose from. A shopping trip to Harvey Nichols and Selfridges had ensured that she'd covered all options. She watched a weak sun break through passing cloud where, in the distance, mist shrouded the top of the fells. As Kate stared at the hazy vapour, it lifted to reveal mysterious peaks and she wondered what the day might bring. She'd an urge to walk over the hills, hand-in-hand with Andy, but he'd probably forgotten that he'd asked her.

A puppy appeared from the side of the building and as it reached the drive, Kate saw it skid to a halt on the gravel, where a woman bent down to clip a lead to its collar. A man followed. He smiled as the dog skipped ahead and, wrapping an arm around the woman's shoulder, leaned in to kiss her cheek. Kate realised that the woman was Jo and the man, who was clearly besotted, must be her new partner. She watched the couple leave Jo's house and head for the fells. They paused to cross the road and stroll through the village, then the happy trio disappeared into the mist.

A man, a woman and a dog.

A picture postcard moment, and Kate wondered if Jo had always been so happy in her new relationship, for she was clearly happy now. Her body language spelt out love in capital letters and Kate felt a pang of envy.

Suddenly, Kate had doubts. Had the previous evening been a dream, a trick of her imagination? Andy had appeared out of the Westmarland ether and he'd seemed as drawn to Kate as she was to him. Could it really have happened? Surely there were other female guests who would catch his attention? She must get a grip and not get so carried away. There were lots of women at the hotel. He could pick and choose. Kate was probably just a pleasant dalliance over dinner and his invitation for a walk no more than a chivalrous courtesy as he helped a tipsy woman to her room.

Kate gathered her robe and snatched at the towel around her head. Her hair was already curling into a tight frizz and would look terrible unless she got a move on. She needed some fresh air too, to clear her head. As she rummaged for a hairdryer, Kate vowed that she'd abstain from alcohol all day. It weakened her resolve and had given her a pounding headache.

She searched in her bag until she found a couple of painkillers, and pouring a glass of water, she swallowed them.

She wouldn't think about Andy. He was probably in the breakfast room, charming the walking socks off a bevy of females, all memories of their dinner gone as he lined up ladies for the weeks ahead. Kate turned the dryer to a high setting and, as she got to work, made her mind up to have a drive out. Sunday stretched ahead and Kate determined that she wouldn't set herself up for disappointment.

She pushed all thoughts of Andy to one side.

With normal service resumed and her headache gone, Kate fell back in her groove. She grabbed a jacket and pulled on a pair of leather boots, then picked up her bag and, with a last glance around the room, closed the door and skipped down the stairs. It was a perfect morning and the hall was awash with sunshine as she made her way out of the front door.

She reached in a pocket for her car keys.

'Kate!' a voice called out.

Andy stood by a gleaming Porsche, holding the passenger door open.

Kate felt the keys drop back in her pocket and, trance-like, moved forward.

'I've been waiting for you,' he said. 'I thought we might drive over to Ullswater. It'll be lovely on the lake today.'

As Kate let Andy guide her into the car, she felt a sexual current surge through her body and her heart began to race. She slid onto the soft leather seat and, with trembling hands, clicked her seatbelt into place.

'You look gorgeous,' he whispered and jumped in beside her.

The car roared into life and, as they sped off, Kate stole a glance at the man beside her and felt her resolve melt. Suddenly the day beckoned with promise far beyond her expectations.

Boomerville was beginning to feel right.

'Sir Henry has asked if his brother Hugo can come and stay,'

Hattie announced. Refreshed from her bath and a walk around the hotel, she was back at the table in Jo's house to join Jo and Pete for Sunday lunch. Spooning vegetables onto her plate, alongside slices of lamb and a crisp Yorkshire pudding, she continued, 'Sir Henry says he can bunk up with him in his suite, as it has two big beds and a good-sized sitting room.' She reached for the gravy and poured lashings over her dinner, then began to tuck in.

Pete asked Jo for mint sauce and she pushed a pretty cut-glass bowl across the table.

'Hugo Mulberry must be getting on a bit,' Jo said.

'I thought he was dead,' Hattie replied.

'He's a few years younger than Sir Henry and I suppose we should consider him.'

'Aye, I wonder if he's still as nimble.' Hattie remembered the days of Sir Henry's shoots at the hotel, when she'd spent a great deal of time being chased around the kitchen table by Hugo, fending him off with a rolling pin, all of which seemed to excite the younger brother. 'I hope he's grown out of his upstairs-downstairs fetish.'

'You probably encouraged him,' Jo said.

'Nope, but I added another fifty quid on his bar bill for putting up with it. The things I did to help your business.'

'He might be quite entertaining. I liked Hugo. Did you know that he used to be a member of Parliament?'

'I rest my case.'

'Didn't they have a nanny when they were growing up?'

'She was the subject of Hugo's fantasies.' Hattie remembered late night conversations in the bar with the brothers.

'Perhaps we could get him involved with the writing class. I could suggest he begins an autobiography, he must have had an interesting career in politics.'

Hattie rolled her eyes. 'Be it on your own head.'

'Some of the ladies might find him an entertaining guest.'

'Or enjoy watching paint dry; he's as boring as his brother.' Hattie reached for a roast potato.

'If he shared a room with Sir Henry, it would be another decent revenue stream.'

Hattie stopped eating and considered Jo's financial argument. 'I'll get the other bed made up.' Hattie was on a profit-share bonus and suddenly Hugo's booking looked attractive.

'I remember the old days and shooting parties,' Jo said. 'Sir Henry was always so keen to impress his clients.'

'Aye, all expenses paid with the hotel booked for the start of the shooting season.'

'Do you remember the cars?' Jo looked up from her meal and stared at Hattie.

'How could I forget?' Hattie was thoughtful. 'The drive was awash with chauffeur-driven Range Rovers.'

'Henry and Hugo and all their cronies would fall out of the hotel, guns at the ready.'

'It was a bleedin' miracle they didn't shoot themselves.'

'The bar takings broke all records.'

'Happy times.' The two women shook their heads as a wave of nostalgia swept over them and they thought about the good old days when the hotel was in its infancy.

'I always thought you had a soft spot for Hugo?' Jo had finished her meal and placed her serviette on one side.

'He was a fine-looking man.' Hattie was thoughtful. She remembered a late-night encounter with Hugo, long after the guests had gone to bed. Tired of fending off the nightly chase around the kitchen table, Hattie had succumbed to Hugo's affections and they'd ended up in Sandra's pantry. Hattie could still recall the pungent aroma of strong farmhouse cheese and freshly made chutneys, as they'd tumbled from shelf to shelf. In the morning, Hugo had the hangover from hell and barely looked up from his breakfast. Hattie was sure that he'd forgotten the incident as she waved the shoot off to the moors and she'd never spoken of it since.

Not even to Jo.

Suddenly, Bunty bounced out of her box and began to

scrabble at Pete's leg. He cut a tiny slice of lamb and fed it to the puppy.

'You're spoiling that daft dog,' Hattie said, pleased for the distraction.

'It's Sunday, let her have a treat.' Pete stroked Bunty's head.

Gravel crunched on the drive outside and the three diners looked up. Peering out of the window, they stared with interest as a car cruised to a halt. The driver raced around to the passenger side to open the door.

'The name's Bond,' Hattie said as Andy assisted Kate out. 'My, he's one smooth operator.'

'They seem to be getting along very well.' Jo watched Andy take Kate's hand. 'I hope she's not letting her heart rule her head; her emotions are all over the place.' Jo began to gather the plates. 'But they do make an attractive couple.'

Hattie observed the new guests as Andy opened the front door for Kate and they disappeared into the hotel. He had good manners and his looks were head turning, but Andy didn't impress Hattie.

'Pudding anyone?' Jo appeared from the kitchen with an apple crumble and jug of cream. 'The apples are from the orchard; Alf picked them this morning.'

Alf had been their gamekeeper when the hotel was open for shooting parties and now helped out with maintenance and repair around the building. Jo considered Alf to be part of the backdrop of the business and relied on him to ensure that the hotel kept a high standard. 'He says there are plenty on the trees.' She began to portion the dessert.

'Bring it on.' Hattie beamed. She loved her food and a traditional Sunday meal was one of her favourites.

A large helping later, Hattie pushed back her chair, straightened her skirt and loosened a button on her blouse. She announced that she was going to have a walk to check on the guests. 'You two can put your feet up. I'll make sure the place is still standing and Sir Henry hasn't set fire to anything.'

Sir Henry had a penchant for cigar smoking and Hattie had threatened to boot him out if he persisted on smoking surreptitiously when he thought no one was watching.

'Thanks,' Jo said. 'I do feel a little bit tired and we have such a busy week ahead.' She yawned as Pete cleared the table.

Hattie reached into her cleavage and, finding a lipstick, smoothed gloss over her lips. She waved at Jo and Pete, then disappeared through the adjoining door from the house that led into the hotel.

Pete and Jo watched Hattie retreat.

'Let's hope that no one's misbehaving,' Pete said.

'Well, if they're not, they soon will be.' Jo smiled, secure in the knowledge that her business was in Hattie's capable hands. 'And talking of misbehaving.' She leaned in to kiss his cheek and, as Pete chuckled and reached out to grab her waist, they hurried up the stairs.

Chapter Four

Monday morning at Boomerville was a hive of activity and the hotel buzzed with life. For the tutors, the beginning of a new week meant an early start and they were busy in the studios preparing courses for the days ahead. Guests, rested from a relaxing Sunday, had risen promptly to make their way to breakfast and now chatted over bowls of cereal and fruit followed by a substantial Westmarland breakfast from the buffet. Sausages sizzled in warming trays, alongside locally-cured bacon and freshly prepared eggs, and waiting staff worked hard to ensure that everyone had their breakfast on time, ready for the day ahead.

In the reception lounges, non-residents, excited at the prospect of a stimulating and fulfilling day, gathered for coffee and shortbread. As they introduced themselves they discussed which of the day's activities they'd be participating in. The creative writers listened with interest to the would-be clairvoyants, whilst prospective potters anticipated elaborate creations and dreamed of TV appearances on *The Great British Pottery Throw Down*.

The laundry was bustling and two housekeepers gossiped as they loaded their trolleys with fresh cotton bedding and thick fluffy towels. Miniature bottles of luxury toiletries were piled high alongside complimentary biscuits, fresh from Sandra's kitchen and stacked in pretty tins. With the hotel fully occupied the ladies were keen to make a start and discover what shenanigans had taken place over the weekend. No doubt Sir Henry had concealed a stash of cigar butts and his suite would need fumigating. Lucinda would still be asleep with an empty bottle of wine under her pillow, snoring loudly beneath her quilt with a chaotic assortment of sketches, paintings and artist's paraphernalia scattered untidily around her room.

In the kitchen, Sandra was busy. As head cook at the hotel, she'd worked with Jo for more years than she cared to remember and was delighted that the old place had re-opened. She'd had the pleasure of training Jo's youngest son, Zach, who was always in the kitchen when he was growing up, shadowing Sandra as she prepared time-honoured recipes. Zach had gone on to catering college and spent stints abroad at Michelin-starred restaurants, returning to Kirkton House to work alongside Sandra and gain stars of his own. She was intensely proud of her protégé who was now paving a successful career as a celebrity chef in London.

Sandra smiled as she thought of Zach's handsome young face. He was the image of his father, with dark Romany looks and mischievous twinkling eyes. Zach combined entertaining cooking skills with a cheeky charisma and it was no wonder that his TV career was booming. Sandra was proud of the new menus that she'd helped him create and, as she sat at her table, she wrote out orders for the forthcoming week while two young commis chefs set to work. Occasionally, Sandra looked up as pots and pans rattled in the stillroom where Gerald, the porter, ran his dishwashing facility with military precision as waiting staff emptied trays of clutter from the breakfast service.

'Have you got your TV set up for later?' Gerald called out. Zach's cookery show had a regular slot on a prime-time channel and an episode was due to screen that evening.

'Aye, I'll be glued as usual,' Sandra said and, easing her weight off her stool, set about her day.

As the hotel hummed with life and occupants began their day, Hattie and Jo sat in reception with a tray of coffee and biscuits beside them. Hattie dunked shortbread into her drink and bit into the soft buttery bake, while Jo studied the bookings on a computer screen.

'Every place is taken on the courses,' Hattie said. She peered over Jo's shoulder and studied the packed timetable. 'Some guests are extending their stay for another week or booking to come back in the spring.'

'This is far more lucrative than I imagined.' Jo sipped her coffee and smiled. 'The courses sell easily, there's such a large demand.'

'Aye, you wouldn't think us old 'uns had the energy. I think your boomer brainwave is going to pay off.'

'As long as everyone benefits from their time here, it's not about the money. I want them to leave with energy and enthusiasm for the years ahead.'

'Oh, what does that matter?' Hattie said. 'As long as they leave and your bank account is bulging.'

'That's not what Boomerville's all about.' Jo frowned. 'I don't want our age group to think that they're past it with nothing to look forward to and no purpose in life.'

Hattie yawned. She let Jo drone on about the merits of opening the doors to a middle-aged audience and the benefits to be had. If Jo wanted to polish her halo and be nominated for a sainthood from her boomer brothers and sisters, Hattie would let her, but there were far more important fish to fry. Hattie's fingers were itchy. It was ages since she'd had a bit of fun and she didn't hold with Jo's nonsense that it was hard at their age to find a bit of nookie. On holiday in Barbados the previous year, Hattie had enjoyed a glorious fling with a local, Mattie, who was equally enamoured with Hattie, and had been there to tickle her fancy whenever she felt the need.

But Mattie was four thousand miles away.

Hattie thought of her handsome island man. She'd experienced pleasures far beyond anything that murky old Marland had to offer and one night with Mattie was worth all the months of missing him. But the flames of passion still fuelled a glowing ember in Hattie's heart and she didn't intend to let it go out.

Boomerville for Hattie was fun. Never mind all the energising and restorative courses that were booked up for weeks, it was the people that made the place and Hattie loved being involved. Since they'd re-opened the doors, she'd never once thought about her age or worried about getting older. The job provided her with an ample income but more importantly, it kept her young. There was nothing better than being amongst folk and enjoying yourself and if it happened that a bit of bedtime action came along, then Hattie was all for it. It was as good as any tonic wine or live longer, life-enhancing potion. Nothing put a spring in your step faster than a romantic tryst or two and Hattie's antennae were tuned to all possibilities.

'I wonder what James Bond got up to last night?' Hattie said as she checked application forms into a folder.

'If you're referring to Andy Mack, I'm sure he was early to bed; he'd had a long walk with Kate during the day.'

Hattie rolled her eyes heavenward. She sometimes wondered what planet Jo lived on and wished that she didn't see the world through rose-tinted glasses for the majority of her day.

'Judging by the look on his face when I last saw them, I'd say he didn't get a great deal of sleep.'

The previous evening Hattie had enjoyed chatting to guests as they sipped their after-dinner coffee. She'd kept a wide berth from Andy and Kate, who were snuggled on a sofa by the fire, only interrupting to replenish their drinks. Hattie knew when to let well alone and could see that there was enough passion smouldering between them to launch a rocket. She'd discreetly said goodnight and had no doubt that housekeeping wouldn't need to make the bed in Andy's room that morning.

'We've a new guest checking in and I'll go to the station to pick him up this afternoon,' Jo said.

'Why don't you send a taxi?'

'It's Bob Puddicombe and I want to meet him myself.'

Hattie nodded her head. Bob was Zach's London agent, heading to Boomerville for a short break. Hattie quite understood why Jo would want to lay on VIP treatment for her son's boss.

The women looked up as guests wandered by and, as Hattie drained her coffee, a tall man with a distinguished wave of thick dark hair, greying at the edges, stopped at the desk and leaned in.

'Morning, James,' Jo said.

'Good morning, I wonder if I could have a word?'

Hattie stood up. She had a feeling that she knew what was coming. James Bryne taught creative writing. He was a likeable and talented teacher, popular with his students. Hattie thought James attractive too, in a studious sort of way. The previous week, Sir Henry and Lucinda, fresh from a morning of wine tasting, had rolled into an afternoon session and caused mayhem in James' class.

Hattie gathered a clipboard and eased out of the office. 'I'll go and gather the strays,' she mumbled as she heard James ask Jo about the house rules on sobriety during classes.

Closing the door, Hattie bustled into the hall. Jo could mop-up Sir Henry's mess. Hattie decided to have a quick check around the place to make sure that everyone was where they were meant to be. With only a few arrivals that day, Hattie could leave reception duties with Jo until the day team turned up but first, she'd go and say hello to Sandra.

Finding the kitchen door open, Hattie stepped in. The commis chefs were busy chopping vegetables and didn't look up. In the stillroom, Sandra was deep in conversation with Gerald, discussing the merits of an HD screen to view Zach's TV show, and on a stainless-steel table, within arm's reach, a row of freshly baked shortbreads sat in a neat pile. The delectable smell of crisp buttery biscuits was irresistible.

Hattie licked her lips and dived in.

Kate was in her bedroom. She was naked as she clambered out of bed to rummage through the items on a drinks tray, placed on an oak console table beneath the window. She had a raging thirst that only a cup of hot milky tea would quench and as

Kate waited for the water to boil, she searched for something to eat. A pretty tin sat by the kettle and she picked it up and eased the lid to reveal a stack of home-made biscuits. She broke off a piece and crammed it in her mouth.

Kate was absolutely ravenous.

The biscuit melted in her mouth as she brewed her tea and, wrapping her hands around the welcoming drink, she sat down on the bed to enjoy it. Glancing at the disorderly pile of sheets, Kate hoped that Andy remembered to ruffle his bed linen when he got back to his room. The ladies in housekeeping would be alert to every detail of Boomerville's guests' behaviour and Kate was sure that there was plenty for staff to relish. But as she thought about the night she'd spent, Kate wondered if she cared about gossip? For Andy's walk of shame a few moments earlier, as he gripped Kate's bathrobe around his naked body and clutched his clothes, would not have gone unnoticed.

She placed her cup on the floor and, lying back on the rumpled duvet, placed her cheek on the cotton pillow where a trace of Andy still clung to the fabric. Closing her eyes, she breathed deeply, savouring the smell of lust and excitement.

Kate Simmons had a man!

She felt like shouting out loud. For she'd just spent a most exhilarating night of passion and it was tempting to jump up and throw the windows open to scream out to the world. In the biblical sense, she reasoned; whether anything long-term came out of the relationship would remain to be seen. But right now she couldn't care less. Sex and Andy Mack was a match made in heaven and Kate wanted more.

Much more!

Feeling a chill on her naked skin, she nestled into the billowing cloud of bedding and as she succumbed to the warmth that enveloped her body, Kate thought back to their time together the previous day.

It had been a glorious morning and Andy had driven to Ullswater where they'd parked by a river, then walked over a bridge to a steamer waiting to take passengers on a cruise along the lake. As it headed to Glenridding Pier a few miles away, the boat ploughed through the crystal water and they stood by the rails and stared up the valley to the Gateway of Helvellyn, England's third highest mountain. Mist rose to reveal streaking white waterfalls that gushed down the peaks and crevices, while a brisk wind whipped the swell into white horses that danced across the glassy lake.

Kate's hair flew across her eyes. She shivered and Andy reached for her hand to tuck it into his own. But her shiver was of anticipation and had nothing to do with the weather.

Having disembarked at the pier and wandered around the former mining village, they'd followed a path back along the lake where sun filtered through the trees, dappling the water with light. They stopped at a waterfall to admire the dramatic drop as red squirrels scampered up and down the mossy hillside, in and out of bushes. Hand-in-hand, they'd walked through the woods where leaves crunched underfoot as they chatted and Andy quoted Wordsworth: 'I wandered lonely as a cloud that floats on high o'er vales and hills.'

It was a perfect day, topped off with a pub meal. When they arrived back at the hotel, tired yet elated from their outing, they'd settled by the fire in the bar and, after a restorative brandy, it seemed the most natural thing in the world for Andy to follow Kate up the stairs and along the galleried landing to her bedroom. When he reached to turn the key, he'd raised an eyebrow and Kate had nodded.

Kate wriggled under the duvet and felt herself colour. Down in one date! Was that the way to behave at her age? She threw her legs over the side of the bed and wandered into the bathroom then stepped into the shower. But as the water gushed over her body, she closed her eyes and knew that she didn't give a damn.

It was years since she'd felt like this.

Andy made her feel alive and not just between the sheets.

After all, they had a great deal in common. Both had sold successful businesses and were of similar age with mutual interests. They'd even booked the same writing course. Over lunch she'd told him more about the difficulties she'd experienced with her father and he held her hand and said she was an amazing woman to have given so selflessly for so long. She mustn't feel guilty if she enjoyed herself; it was time for her to have some happiness and take advantage of the opportunities that came her way.

For the first time in years Kate felt excited. Andy had woken long forgotten feelings and she was determined not to feel guilt for making the most of it.

She was going to enjoy every minute of her time at Boomerville.

Chapter Five

Jo pulled a wrap around her shoulders as she opened the conservatory door and stepped out. The morning sky was mostly cloud and a chill breeze blew through the garden where a flurry of leaves whipped across the lawn, piling on the path and steps leading up to the meadow. She wondered if Alf was out and about and hoped that he'd remember to clear the autumn debris; she didn't want anyone slipping and could almost hear Hattie whispering, 'Where there's blame there's a claim.'

Jo was heading to creative writing. She wanted to speak to James. It had been difficult to give him time earlier as the phones were ringing, several guests had queries and Hattie had buggered off just when she was needed. She opened the gate to the courtyard and headed for the studios where James would be preparing for his class. Jo wanted to catch him before the session began.

'Hello, James,' Jo said. She closed the door and shrugged off her wrap, laying it on a nearby chair.

'Hi, Jo,' James replied. He was busy placing writing equipment on a table that stood in the centre of the room. 'Thanks for coming over.'

'I'm sorry, it was busy at the desk and it seemed inappropriate to have a discussion with guests milling around.'

'Yes, I understand.' James opened the door of the stove.

'That will be a welcome sight for your students.'

'And a welcome sight for me.' He thrust several logs on the glowing embers, coaxing the fire into life. 'I love the setup here at Boomerville, it's a credit to you.'

James remembered the hotel from the old days when he'd known it as Kirkton House. It had been a treat to dine in the restaurant and he'd enjoyed many meals with Helen, his ex-wife. It was her favourite venue to celebrate family birthdays and anniversaries. When the hotel reopened, James had jumped at the chance to tutor courses. He'd taken early retirement from the college in Carlisle where he'd taught English and it was a refreshing challenge to work with students of more mature years. The studio, a former stable block, was full of character and a perfect environment for creativity.

'Have you got time for a coffee?' James asked as Jo moved over to the fire.

'Yes, I'd love one, thank you. It's very fresh out there today.' Jo held out her hands and rubbed them together as she stared into the welcoming fire.

In the small kitchen, James flicked a switch on a high-tech machine and watched steaming coffee flow into two mugs. He carried them into the studio where Jo was perched on a sofa by the stove.

'I'm sorry about Sir Henry and Lucinda,' Jo began. 'I promise that I'll have a word with them.'

'I didn't want to mention it. The old boy is very likeable and I'd enjoy having him in the class,' James said, taking a sip of his drink, 'but preferably when he's not half-cut with Lucinda hanging drunkenly off his arm.'

'I hope it wasn't too disruptive?' Jo sipped her coffee.

'One or two students complained, which is why I had to mention it, but on the whole most of the class seemed to enjoy the show.' James smiled. 'They make quite a double act.'

'Don't they just,' Jo agreed. 'I've known him for years. Sir Henry was a guest in days gone by when the hotel was Kirkton House and I felt duty bound to accommodate him when we reopened as Boomerville.'

'I'm sure he'll benefit from his time here.'

'Hattie thinks I'm too sentimental and we'll end up with him treating the place as a nursing home.' Jo placed her empty mug on the hearth.

'Hattie will have her reasons but in the meantime, I'm very happy to work with him, just as long as he is sober.'

Jo glanced at her watch. 'Look at the time, I'm holding you up and your students will be here any moment.'

'Thanks for coming over.' James picked up Jo's wrap. He held the door as she draped it over her shoulders.

'Have a lovely day,' Jo said and with a smile was gone.

Kate ran across the courtyard just as the coach-house clock struck ten. She'd been so busy daydreaming about Andy that she'd not noticed the time and now she was late for her writing class.

Flinging the door open, Kate saw several pairs of eyes turn in her direction. 'I'm so sorry. Am I late?' She faltered nervously in the doorway. Her hair was a wind-swept tumble and she pushed the tangled locks behind her ears.

'Good morning,' James called out, 'do come and join us, we're just about to start.' He felt the stiff breeze that followed Kate in and saw that it was catching at paper and pencils.

'Oh dear, I'm so sorry,' Kate apologised as she stared at the class, who were scrambling about to retrieve their writing tools.

But James didn't hear her apology.

He was poleaxed and stared at the gorgeous creature who'd fallen into his class. For a moment, time seemed to stand still and he wondered why he hadn't noticed her at the cocktail party on Saturday. She must have been surrounded by admirers and hidden from his sight. He should have stayed on for dinner instead of disappearing home after drinks. The woman was tall and curvy, with long muscular limbs and her skin peachy on a face that seemed ageless. He was hypnotised by the changing colour of her eyes as they adjusted to the light, rimmed by thick lashes. James felt a deep-seated emotion as his heart lurched and he watched Kate toss her hair until it fell softly to her shoulders. He melted when she turned and her anxious eyes met his.

'I didn't mean to be late,' Kate said.

'No problem at all,' James replied and waved an arm mechanically in the direction of the class. 'Do join us.'

Kate closed the door and placing her bag down, found a seat. She realised that she was next to Andy and tried not to meet his eye as she felt colour flood into her cheeks, the memory of their passionate lovemaking still fresh.

James watched everyone shuffle to make space for Kate. He noted that she smiled and her cheeks were flushed when a man pulled out a chair and helped her settle in. James frowned and wondered who the man was, for the two were clearly familiar.

Kate tried hard to concentrate as she heard the tutor introduce himself. His name was James Bryne and he explained the content of the course. A single name badge sat in a box on the middle of the table. Kate reached out and pinned it to her shirt.

'Hello, Kate,' Andy whispered and Kate felt his hand run along her thigh. His fingers created ripples of pleasure as they stroked the soft skin beneath her skirt and she wondered how on earth she was going to get through the session in such close proximity. Taking a deep breath, she attempted to focus on James' instructions.

The class were to write in longhand for the next twenty minutes, writing a memory of their favourite childhood toy. James explained that they were to let the words flow and not stop to think about the content.

The only content that Kate could summon up was X-rated and suitable for a porn magazine not a middle-aged writing class. She closed her eyes and forced pictures of teddy bears and fluffy bunnies into her mind but images of Andy's naked form pounding into her own submissive body soon took over. She glanced sideways and saw that Andy was writing. Words appeared with a flourish as he concentrated and Kate could see that he'd already covered half a page.

Grabbing a notepad and biting hard on her pencil, Kate forced herself to focus.

As everyone settled to the task, James took a seat nearby and discreetly observed. The new set of pupils looked a mixed bunch but he knew that you could never tell at this stage. Expect the unexpected, he told himself. James took a deep breath and tried not to stare at the woman who'd arrived late and awakened such feeling. He squinted at her name badge and could see that she was called Kate.

A clock on the wall ticked. It was an old fuse clock, of the type found in a schoolroom, with a circular face and wooden surround and James enjoyed the sound as it methodically echoed the passing minutes.

He looked up. It was time for the class to stop writing. James noticed that Kate was nibbling the end of a pencil and seemed lost in thought. Sun streamed through the window and caught the sheen of her porcelain skin and he wondered what it would feel like if he reached out to stroke her cheek. His stomach fluttered and again, he was startled by the attraction.

Kate sat back. She gripped her notepad and wished that she was hotfooting it across the courtyard, not waiting for her work to be read. She dreaded anyone reading the nonsense that she'd written and wished that she'd been able to put something interesting together instead of a garbled memory that would be mortifying when told to others. She heard James ask how they felt about the writing exercise and as the class joined in, Kate looked at Andy. His replies were interesting and stimulated discussion. Many of the women were spellbound and hung off his words.

James asked the class to share and Kate felt sick as she listened to the polite applause as each student stood and read their work to the group. All her insecurities about writing came flooding back. 'That's wonderful,' she heard James say. 'You've all done well to express yourselves and it's been enlightening.'

Kate's cheeks began to burn and she felt herself grow tense.

'And finally, we've one more piece to share.' James indicated that Kate stand up and as she gripped the table and forced herself to her feet, Andy reached for her chair to assist.

'Kate,' James said, 'would you like to read your work from today's lesson?'

Chapter Six

Hattie came out of the kitchen and wandered through the bar. She was wearing her old duffel coat, which lived on a peg in the stillroom, and with a pocket full of biscuits, she munched happily as she headed out of the conservatory. Picking up her pace to keep warm, she ran across the lawn to a door in the wall, beyond which lay the pottery studio. She'd done her rounds, was eating her elevenses and, with an hour or two free, decided to sit in on the class.

Wind blew across the garden, whipping wayward leaves into a dense carpet. Damp, slippery and dangerous for those not so light on their feet.

In the shadow of the wall, handyman Alf was occupied.

'This weather will keep you busy!' Hattie called out. Alf was having difficulty gathering debris into a huge sack and huffed and puffed as he fought against the gusts. 'Jo will want those leaves cleared. We don't want anyone falling.'

'Tha' wants to watch tha' doesn't get swept away.' Alf snarled and hurled the sack into a wheelbarrow then stopped to roll a cigarette. He struck a match and leaned into the barrow for shelter. Cupping his hands around the flame, he dragged deeply. 'In a hurry?' Alf asked as he watched Hattie fiddle with the latch on the door.

'Can't you give this some oil?' Hattie grumbled as her fingers probed the metal.

'Aye, 'tis on my list.' Smoke trailed past Alf's bushy eyebrows and danced across the lawn. He placed the rollup on his lips and with a grunt reached down to hoist the barrow up. 'I'll see thee,' he said and set off to dump the contents on a compost heap at the end of the garden.

The latch had been on Alf's list for as long as Hattie could remember and she shook her head as she watched him stagger down the path. He stopped to open the gates to the meadow where smoke puffed out of the top of the tepee. Hattie knew that the Shaman had a full house which, she thought, should make dinner conversation interesting for those with any energy left to rock up for the main meal of the day. She noticed that the curtains were closed on the gypsy caravan and as ominous dark clouds rolled down from the fells, eerie shadows clawed across the countryside and shrouded it in darkness.

The spirits are out in force! Hattie thought.

She tried to recall who was participating in Clairvoyance in Midlife that morning and remembered that Hugo Mulberry was joining his brother today. Hattie hoped that 'Nanny' wasn't making her presence felt from the great nursery in the sky. Hugo would be a handful if past history was anything to go by and Hattie made a mental note to have a rolling pin on standby in the kitchen. There would be no repeat of their pantry experience. Hugo would be old and doddery these days and Hattie preferred her fun wrapped in a younger parcel.

The latch gave and moments later, Hattie stood on the step of the pottery studio to peer through the windows. She was miffed to see that two bud vases she'd made during a practice workshop had been removed from the sills.

Jo had said they resembled phalluses.

Hattie reached for the door and thrust it open. 'Morning, Paul,' she said. 'I've come to have an hour with you.' She threw her clipboard to one side and unbuttoned her duffel coat then dug her hand in the pocket. 'Biscuit?' she asked.

Paul, the potter, shook his head and a quiff of thick hair fell over his forehead. He was sitting at a wheel with a lump of wet clay in his hands. He pulled it into a long length and looked nervous as he studied Hattie.

A group of students gathered around the wheel to watch their tutor demonstrate the skill required for making mug handles. Hattie shrugged off her coat and, grabbing an apron, tugged it over her chest. She went to join them.

Paul was the owner of Petheriggs Pottery, located a few miles away. He'd been making his bespoke range of dinner and kitchenware for many years but competition from other potters in the popular tourist area had made life stressful and Paul was glad of the opportunity to teach at Boomerville.

'That's a nice length,' Hattie said and gave Paul a wink. She'd known the attractive divorcee for many years and had encouraged him to run the classes.

Paul's clay instantly dropped in a wet heap onto the stationary wheel. Several students giggled as he retrieved the clay and began again. When he was confident that his instructions were clear, he dispersed the students to their own tables to begin work.

Hattie plonked herself on Paul's stool and rolled up her sleeves.

'Let's show them how to do it. We'll soon have those babies full of tea.' Hattie nodded towards a line of mugs waiting for handles, and began to pummel her clay.

Paul sidestepped Hattie and went to help his students.

The air was tense as everyone focused on the task in hand. They held up their clay and with sweeping downward movements, slowly pulled it into shape.

'Keep it well lubricated,' Hattie called out to a timid-looking couple that were working as a team. 'Nice and slow.'

The process was time-consuming and the students were deep in concentration. The room was silent and they all worked hard as handles began to form.

But Hattie was bored. She looked around the room and frowned. Her handle was nothing like the neat shapes that now graced the sides of the mugs.

Paul, sensing Hattie's discomfort, made his way back. 'This can happen to a beginner,' he said as he looked at her thin gooey mess. 'Part of the process is to keep going until you get the length and thickness you require.' He cupped the clay in Hattie's hands. With his eyes focused and mind set on rescuing the handle, Paul dipped his fingers in a bowl of water and guided Hattie.

Hattie sat very still. Paul's warm fingers entwined with her own and she stared into the potter's gorgeous green eyes, succumbing to his kneading and stroking while the handle took shape.

'You see, it's easy when you have a technique,' Paul said and handed Hattie a mug. 'Now hold it firmly and guide it in.'

The final hold was a hold too far and as Hattie grabbed the mug with one hand and held up a length of drooping clay in the other, she lost her balance and fell forward onto the wheel. Scrabbling about with her feet, she hit a button and electricity shot through the wheel causing it to spin madly. Hattie lunged forward to steady herself and grabbed Paul but this sent them both flying across the room. The astonished students flung their half-finished mugs to one side and raced to rescue their tutor.

As Hattie emerged from under a pile of wet and broken pottery, she struggled to her feet. 'I think I'll go and check on the cookery class,' she said as she smoothed clay from her fingers. 'Shout if you need anything.' Her cheeks were burning as she removed her apron and tossed it to one side. Embarrassed and keen to be gone, Hattie retrieved her coat, popped a biscuit in her mouth and ploughed through the mayhem to make her way out.

The students were open-mouthed as they stood beside their dazed tutor.

'Don't make a meal of things,' Hattie mumbled as she looked at Paul and without a backward glance she headed to the hotel.

'Bloody hell, Hattie,' Jo exclaimed, 'it'll be a miracle if he doesn't sue us!'

Jo, who had been in the hotel at the time of the pottery incident, had rushed to the studio after an anxious student appeared at reception to say that their tutor seemed to have had a funny turn.

Half an hour later, Jo was helping Potter Paul into the back of an ambulance.

The paramedics were reassuring, confident that he was only suffering from shock and not a heart attack as initially feared. Jo had anxiously watched the medical team hit the blue lights as they sped off to A & E.

'I can't help it if he lost concentration.' Hattie was peeved. 'You've no idea how arousing pottery is. It could have happened to anyone.'

'Strangely enough, it didn't happen to any of the other students, nor anyone in the previous classes.'

'Must be something wrong with the wheel. It's lucky health and safety isn't breathing down your neck.'

'Well, you've certainly put a spoke in the potter's wheel, God knows when he'll be back.' Jo glanced at the timetables. 'I haven't a clue what I'm going to do with six traumatised potters for the rest of the week.'

'Send them to see the Shaman; an hour or two in the tepee will erase their memories.'

'Let's hope Paul's fingers are just bruised and not broken.'

The front door bell rang, summoning a member of staff, and a porter hurried past to help a new arrival with their luggage.

'Oh heck, it's Hugo.' Hattie leaned over the desk to peer down the hall where their new arrival was heading her way.

Sir Henry, who was sitting in the bar with Lucinda, heard Hattie. 'Is that my brother?' he said. 'Send him in here. He'll be ready for a livener.'

'Bleedin' hell, I'm trapped.' Hattie opened the kitchen door to make her escape.

'Oh no you don't,' Jo said and she grabbed Hattie's arm. 'You've got some brownie points to make up and Hugo always had a thing for you.' She shoved Hattie out through reception and into the hallway to greet their new guest. 'Go and say hello.'

Hugo Mulberry strode into view. Smart and dapper in country tweeds, he looked fresh despite his long journey.

'Hugo, how wonderful to see you again.' Jo pushed Hattie forward. 'I hope you've had a good trip.'

'Blasted train was packed, a man can barely read his paper on those damn tilting things.' Hugo was clearly not suited to the high-speed west coast trains and Jo wondered if he'd prefer steam.

'Your brother is waiting for you in the bar.'

Jo guided Hugo along the corridor where Hattie stood by the window in an attempt to blend into the curtains.

'Hello, old girl,' Hugo said when he saw Hattie and reached out to pinch her cheek. 'You're still a damn fine filly. How are you?' A slither of dry clay came away in his hand.

Hattie watched Hugo wander into the bar. She was surprised that he was so sprightly. Clearly the years had been kind.

Lucinda sat beside Sir Henry on a straight-backed couch. She wore a silk tunic, buttoned high at the neck. Her legs were crossed to reveal ox-blood coloured stockings with matching pixie boots and she leapt up to tower over Hugo as he was introduced.

'Do you paint?' Lucinda asked, her bangles clanging as she shook Hugo's hand.

'Daubed a couple of coats on Nanny's walls a long time ago.' Hugo stared at Lucinda as she slithered back into her chair. 'Never been one for the artistic brush.'

'Then you must learn.'

'Then you must teach me.' Hugo winked.

'I'll be holding classes soon,' Lucinda confirmed. 'Jo is arranging a studio. It's bound to be popular.'

Jo and Hattie looked at each other with raised eyebrows but before Lucinda could elaborate, Sir Henry insisted that Hugo join them for a drink.

'I'll sort everything out,' Jo said to Sir Henry as Hattie sloped away. 'Hugo's luggage has gone up to your room. Now, what drinks can I get you?' She fussed around the guests, making sure that they had everything that they needed.

'What's all this about Lucinda holding art classes?' Jo asked Hattie. She'd found her in the kitchen, regaling Sandra with her tale. The cook was all ears as she pushed a bowl of hot soup across the table. Hattie began to tuck in and Jo watched her spread butter over a chunk of crusty bread.

'Nothing to do with me,' Hattie said, 'but I think it's a cracking idea.'

'Do you think you might go and get changed?' Jo frowned as a lump of dry clay from Hattie's fingers fell onto the table.

'All in good time,' Hattie replied. 'My nerves are shattered, I feel weak.'

'Well, I suggest you gather your strength, ready to show Hugo around the hotel.' Jo winked at Sandra.

'Do I have to? Can't you do it?'

'Nope, you've a penance to pay for the potter.'

'Shite,' Hattie said, but as she glanced around the kitchen her eyes fell on a rolling pin and she made a mental note to pocket it. Finishing the soup, Hattie held out her bowl for more. 'Set it up, Sandra,' she said, feeling revived. 'I feel a show round coming on.'

Kate was having a panic attack. It had been a mistake to sit next to Andy and her brain had refused to concentrate and participate in the morning's tutorial, where students had been asked to write about a favourite childhood toy. Her thoughts strayed persistently to the previous night and with her lover within touching distance, Kate could only think of one thing. It had nothing to do with childhood toys.

But now James was asking everyone to read out their work and Andy had risen to his feet to give a glowing account as he recalled memories of a neat little pedal car. His words tripped poetically off the page and when he'd finished the class applauded enthusiastically.

'And finally, we've one more piece to share.' Kate heard James say. 'Kate, would you like to read your work?' He indicated that Kate stand up and as she forced herself to her feet, Andy, ever the gentleman, reached for her chair to assist; several female students nodded in approval as he blinded them with a smile.

Kate gripped her notepad and stared at the line she'd scrawled across the top of the page. She'd wracked her brains to think of a toy and remembered a moth-eaten rag doll that her mother had made when Kate was young.

'Er, it's called "Rag doll".' Kate squirmed as she looked at the expectant faces. She lowered her head and began to mumble. 'I had a little rag doll, its name was Peggy Sue, I didn't really love it 'til I was forty-two.' She felt a flush spread across her face. 'It's a work in progress.'

Kate sat down. She was mortified and wanted the ground to swallow her up. Where the hell had that nonsense come from?

There was silence and everyone stared at Kate.

Suddenly the door burst open and Hattie bounced over the threshold with Hugo hot on her heels. Thankful for the diversion, Kate grabbed her bag and raced to the ladies' room.

'Let's take a break,' James said as he stood to welcome the newcomers. He'd noticed Kate's distress.

'Another literary genius joins us,' Hattie announced and introduced Hugo. She stood back as the two men shook hands. 'Hugo has just arrived at Boomerville and would like to start his time here with one of your classes.'

'Penned a few ditties in my time.' Hugo stared at Hattie's chest.

'I'd be happy to welcome you to the group,' James replied. 'Would you like to join us for coffee?'

'Got anything stronger, old boy?'

'We won't be stopping, thank you.' Hattie grabbed Hugo's arm and led him towards the door. 'I'd like Hugo to catch an hour or two with the Shaman before lunch.' The old codger was persistent and driving Hattie mad. She'd had enough of his wandering hands and leering eyes as she'd shown him around

Boomerville and intended to shove him in the tepee to let the Shaman work his magic.

'Happy writing everyone,' Hattie said and guided Hugo to the door. 'Remember, pencil power!'

'Nice to meet you, Hugo,' the class chorused.

Kate had returned and looked around for Andy, who was sitting by the fire. He was surrounded by a gaggle of women and looked comfortable in their company. She was hesitant to join them.

'Would you like a coffee?' James asked.

'Yes, I'd love one.' Kate turned. She was grateful to be rescued and hoped that a dose of caffeine would jolt her out of her stupor and enable her to join in and not make such a fool of herself.

'It's quite intimidating to begin with,' James said, noting that Kate was distracted. 'But we'll sit at separate desks for the next session. Some people feel more comfortable with their own space.' He followed Kate's gaze to the group by the fire. The object of her distraction was holding court with a besotted group of women. Andy Mack was certainly a charmer and the would-be writers hung off his words.

'I liked your rag doll,' James said.

'I'm afraid I wasn't concentrating. It was a stupid thing to write but I didn't know what else to say.'

'Did you really have a rag doll?'

'Oh yes, my mother made it for me when I was young but I hated it. The doll's eyes were huge and scary and I used to hide it in a cupboard. Mum always retrieved it and placed it at the foot of my bed.'

'So it was hardly conducive to a good night's sleep?'

'I had nightmares all the time; the damn thing seemed poised to attack.'

'Why did you keep it?'

'I didn't have much from my childhood.' Kate fiddled with the handle on her mug. 'I found the doll in a trunk, years later.

It was hand-stitched and I suppose I finally came to appreciate how much effort Mum had put into making it. I was a student when she passed away.'

'And you finally forgave her for leaving you.'

Kate stopped fiddling and was wide-eyed as she looked at James. 'How very astute,' she said. 'I never thought about it like that.'

'Were you close to your parents?'

'I was an only child. I looked after my dad until he died, he had dementia in his later years.'

'That must have been very hard.' James looked into Kate's eyes and the passion he'd felt earlier leapt into life. He longed to reach out and touch her, to stroke her face and assure her that the world was a safe place. But before she could reply, they were interrupted.

'Back to school, my lovely.' Andy appeared beside them and wrapped a protective arm around Kate's shoulder. 'My memoirs are calling and yours need brushing up.' He pulled her towards him and Kate looked at him with adoring eyes.

The spell was broken and James had the urge to punch Andy, very hard on the nose. His fingers balled into a fist as the couple moved away.

James regained his composure and felt annoyed for feeling such emotion but there was something about Andy that grated and James found it hard to warm to the man. He turned to the students and gave instructions on a writing task to be completed in the hour and a half left. With their heads bent over notebooks, he left the class and went into the kitchen to rinse and dry mugs.

James stared out of the window and thought about Kate. A few innocent words had unearthed long buried feelings and he knew that this was the beauty of these sessions. He hoped that all of the students would dig deep and discover treasures that might enhance their life in some way. Kate was obviously complex and vulnerable and he'd felt a magnetic pull to protect her, for she was clearly besotted with Andy. James' instinct suggested that Andy was trouble but as he closed the cupboards and neatly folded a tea towel, he told himself not to be so stupid. It was only day one of the course and anything could happen. It was wrong for a teacher to form personal opinions and he was being paid to do a job.

He closed the door and tiptoed back to his desk. The class were engrossed and no one looked up. James read the quotes written on chalkboards displayed around the walls and his gaze fell on one by Oscar Wilde:

The true mystery of the world is the visible, not the invisible.

He turned to the students and realised that Andy was staring at him. James felt a shiver of foreboding and wondered if, on this occasion, Oscar was right.

Chapter Seven

Jo stood on the station platform at Marland and looked up at the arrivals board. The London train was due at any moment. She tucked her hands into the pockets of her quilted jacket and watched with interest as people began to gather belongings and got ready to board the train, which completed its journey in Glasgow.

She was meeting her friend, Bob Puddicombe, who had booked a stay at Boomerville and Jo was anxious that everything ran as smoothly as possible, for he was an important person in her life. As a media agent in London, Bob specialised in the representation of celebrity chefs and Jo had made his acquaintance when Zach, her youngest son, had signed to his agency. It had been odd for Jo to make a connection so fast, for she had few close friends and finding Bob had been like a lottery win.

Jo trusted Bob completely and knew that Zach, who could be wild unless tamed, was in safe hands. From a child, Zach had always been a wizard in the kitchen and had grown up drop-dead gorgeous to boot. The young man, known as The Gypsy Chef, was making waves on the hospitality scene and having inherited his father's Romany looks, enjoyed a successful cookery series on television. He'd won a reality TV show, *Jungle Rock*, which had sent his profile soaring and his cookbook, *Foraging with the Gypsy Chef*, looked certain to top the charts at Christmas. Zach was one of Bob's most successful clients and Jo knew that the success of her precious son was down to Bob's meticulous professionalism.

Jo walked along the platform beside a length of track that snaked past a commercial depot where goods carriages lined the sidings, beneath hoardings advertising holidays in Westmarland. As she looked into the distance, searching for the train, Jo imagined Bob to be sitting in a first-class compartment, meditating throughout the journey, for Bob was of a spiritual leaning and lived his life according to the words of his idol, the Dalai Lama.

The station manager announced that the London train was approaching and Jo hurried back to the main platform. As the wheels slowed and the mighty engine cruised into Marland, the brakes sighed and the train stopped.

Jo caught sight of Bob, who waved as he stepped down onto the platform. He placed his Louis Vuitton messenger bag around his shoulder, grabbed the matching cases and beamed as Jo ran towards him.

'You made it!' she exclaimed and hugged him.

'Finally.' Bob smiled and returned the embrace.

'The car is just outside, let me take a case.' Jo reached out.

But Bob would have none of it and insisted on carrying his own luggage. 'I don't want you to break a nail, darling,' he said.

They bustled through the crowd and came out of the station, where Jo's shining black Range Rover was parked. 'Nice wheels,' Bob said as he jumped in and Jo started the engine.

Bunty was asleep on the back seat and looked up when she heard Bob's voice. Giddy with excitement, she threw herself onto his lap and began to lick his face.

'Oh my, the little princess is growing,' Bob said as he held his head high in an effort to avoid the puppy's probing tongue. 'Wait 'till you see what Uncle Bob has brought for you.' He stilled the squirming body with gentle stokes and turned to Jo. 'Harrods' doggy department is cleaned out.'

'I hope you haven't been spoiling her.'

'That's why I'm the dog-father, it's as close as I'll ever get to babies.' Bob planted a kiss on Bunty's soft fur. 'Now, sweetie, do tell. What's the gossip and who's shagging who?'

As Bob listened to Jo and the miles sped by, he thought of the opening party a few weeks ago when he'd been shown the programme for the forthcoming activities. He'd made a promise that he'd be back to try some of the classes. Jo had turned a fading old hotel into a retreat for the future and Bob was looking forward to his stay, confident that time away from the hustle and bustle of London would realign his chakras and set him up for the busy season ahead. He put his faith in prayer and meditation and liked to interact with his yin and yang to maintain the harmony and balance of his demanding life.

'I can't wait to try a session with the Shaman,' Bob said and reached for the prayer beads wrapped around his wrist. He stroked the smooth surface and closed his eyes. *'Au, Nama Shiva,'* Bob whispered.

Jo glanced at her friend and smiled. When he opened his eyes, she continued to tell him all about Boomerville and everything that had happened since the hotel re-opened its doors. 'We've some very interesting guests,' she said, 'I think you're going to enjoy your stay.'

'Darling, I can't wait to meet everyone.' The car slowed and came to a stop by the front door of Boomerville. Bob hopped out and, placing Bunty onto the ground, reached into his bag. 'Here we are, princess,' he said, 'try this on for size.'

Hattie was in reception and heard a commotion at the front door. She glanced at her watch. Jo was due back from the station with Bob Puddicombe, who would need to be checked in and shown around the hotel. Dragging herself away from a plate of scones and jam, she dabbed crumbs from her mouth and went into the hallway.

A moving object, resembling a Christmas tree bauble with four legs, pounced across the threshold and pounded down the corridor.

'Bleedin' hell,' Hattie said and shook her head. Bunty was dressed in a pretty new coat festooned with flashing lights and around her neck was a heavily jewelled collar. 'That outfit won't last five minutes on the fells.'

'Lovely to see you again, darling.' Bob wrapped Hattie in a hug. 'Is Mr Caribbean here?' Bob raised his eyebrows.

'Nope, winter in Westmarland isn't his cup of tea, far too cold for him.'

Jo unzipped her jacket as she followed, then took Bob's arm. 'Let's get our guest settled in,' she said and turned to Hattie. 'Judging by the amount of jam on your chin, I take it that we're in time for afternoon tea?'

'Aye, I'll get some organised.' Hattie stuck out her tongue to lick at the jam. 'You've had a long journey. Can I get you a livener with your scones?'

'As long as it has bubbles,' Bob said.

'I'll catch up with you shortly,' Jo gave Bob a peck on the cheek, 'I need to check the kitchen. Hattie will look after you.'

Hattie led Bob into the Red Room where a fire roared in the grate. It was a chilly afternoon and he rubbed his hands together at the welcome sight. A group of guests looked up and Sir Henry waved his cane in greeting. 'I say,' he said and turned from Hugo and Lucinda, 'another new face in our midst, pull up a pew, old boy.' He indicated that Bob join them.

'I'd like you all to meet Bob Puddicombe.' Hattie plumped a cushion and Bob sat down beside Lucinda.

Hugo, who was mellow after a session with the Shaman and a hearty lunch, stretched out his arms and sat up. 'Are you one of the Portobello Puddicombes?' he asked and leaned forward to study Bob's face.

Hattie could see that Bob hadn't a clue what Hugo was blabbering about and waited for Hugo to explain.

'Fine family, the Puddicombes, all daughters, of course.' Hugo raised a heavily whiskered eyebrow. 'Great gals with thunder thighs that could grip a thoroughbred for hours.' He looked at Bob and smiled. 'Petunia Puddicombe was the most accomplished female rider the hunt ever had and any friend of Petunia is a friend of ours.'

Hattie shook her head. Hugo was waffling as usual and she could see that Bob was mystified. He'd obviously never heard of the Portobello Puddicombes, nor any woman called Petunia.

'This is Lucinda Brown, an artist,' Hattie said to Bob.

Bob reached out to shake hands with Sir Henry and Hugo and turned to Lucinda who'd tilted her head to one side and lowered heavily mascaraed lashes over eyes that studied his every move. Lucinda smiled and raised her hand in greeting, chunky bangles clanging along her scrawny arm.

'I was one of the first guests to arrive,' Lucinda said. 'I'll be taking art classes soon, you must book one.'

'I'm happy to make your acquaintance,' Bob said and took Lucinda's hand. The skin was icy and felt as dry as old leather.

'You have interesting bone structure.' Lucinda made a circle with her finger. 'I'd like to paint you.'

Hattie looked on. She was interested to see what Bob made of his fellow guests and as she watched his anxious face, called out to a waiter, 'Better make it two bottles.' She skilfully opened the champagne and poured everyone a glass. Hugo's hand was perilously close to the edge of her skirt; as she leaned over, she flicked a linen napkin sharply across his fingers and then, with a deft shake, smoothed it over his knee.

'Cheers!' Everyone raised a glass. 'Here's to a happy stay.'

'I can't wait to begin my classes,' Hattie heard Bob say as she placed the bottle in an ice bucket and tidied the table, placing coasters under glasses. Lucinda picked up a plate of scones and held them out.

'Not for me.' Bob looked at the scones. 'I don't want to spoil my dinner.'

'Or your figure.' Lucinda put the plate down.

Bob drained his glass and held it out for a refill. Hattie could see that Lucinda had edged too close as bangles rattled and her hand came to rest on Bob's knee.

'I like a well-turned-out man,' Lucinda said and traced the herringbone pattern on Bob's trousers. 'Firm legs as well as a fine face, perfect for life classes; you must let me paint you and perhaps we could have some time with the Shaman, just you and I?'

Hattie sensed Bob's distress and leaned in to rescue him. 'The Shaman is very busy at the moment. Bob will want to settle in and make himself familiar with Boomerville before he begins any sessions.'

'By jingo, the little fella is lively today,' Sir Henry suddenly announced.

Bunty appeared from under a seat and began to bounce up and down as Sir Henry teased her with his cane. She pranced around on the rug to the amusement of the two elderly brothers.

Hattie shook her head in disgust. Grown adults rendered stupid by a puppy that should, in her opinion, be out in one of the kennels at the back of the hotel. But at least Jo had removed the ridiculous jacket and jewel-studded collar and the animal could be recognised as a dog and not a performing puppet.

'She'll make a fine gun dog.' Hugo tickled Bunty's neck then stroked her tummy as she lay on the rug, paws up, basking in the attention.

'Good breeder too,' Sir Henry said.

The brothers gazed at the dog.

'Do you remember our shoots?' Hugo said and Hattie could see that he was thinking about days gone by when, in the company of friends, they'd strutted across the fells, dressed in Barbours and breeches with their faithful canine companions by their sides. Geared up for a day on the rugged Westmarland moors, they'd watched their dogs race ahead of the beaters.

'We bagged many a brace when the birds were in season,' Sir Henry said as he too remembered heading back to the hotel, happy and exhilarated, to enjoy an evening of frivolities, safe in the knowledge that the dogs were being cosseted in Alf's luxurious kennels.

'Do you shoot?' Sir Henry bellowed. The old man's mouth was full of scone and he sandblasted his corduroy clad legs. Hattie dusted the coating of crumbs and tucked a serviette securely over his knees.

'Er, no, can't say that I do.' Bob was thoughtful. The only

thing he'd ever shot was the best part of a bottle of absinthe with his partner, Anthony, at a birthday celebration. Having lost consciousness for the following two days, he'd vowed never to drink shots again.

'The Portobello Puddicombes always shot.' Sir Henry looked to his brother for confirmation.

Hugo nodded his head. 'Petunia shot her mother, damn near killed her as I recall, nasty mishap on the moors, devil of a job to keep it quiet.' The brothers turned to the fire and stared into the flames.

Hattie could see that Bob was wondering what on earth he'd let himself in for. The old men must appear deranged and Lucinda, under the delusion that she was a sexual temptress, was determined that Bob be smitten by her charms. She stepped in to help.

'Bob, Jo needs you to check in, can you go to reception?'

'Oh, thank you,' Bob replied but as he placed his empty glass on a table, Lucinda grabbed his arm; as her flesh brushed against his jacket, he got a whiff of perfume and winced.

Patchouli oil, circa 1980.

'Will you join me in the tepee?' Lucinda whispered.

Hattie tapped Bob on his arm. 'Jo's waiting.'

Bob glanced at the group, then muttered an apology and hastily left the room. 'Where's Jo?' he asked.

'Down here.' Hattie led him along the hallway.

'Is everyone barking mad?' Bob said when he found Jo, who was checking the menus for dinner.

'Welcome to Boomerville.' Jo smiled. 'You'll soon get used to them.'

'That artist woman is bonkers.' Bob closed his eyes and stroked his prayer beads, caressing the smooth stones circling his wrist.

'Shall I book you a session with the Shaman?' Hattie asked.

'The old boys are off their rockers.' Bob ignored Hattie and ran his fingers over his bald head. 'What on earth have you let me in for?'

'Don't worry, in a couple of days it will all feel completely normal.' Hattie took Bob's arm. 'Let's get you settled in and then you can meet the rest of the residents.'

'Dinner's at seven,' Jo called out.

'I might have mine in my room,' Bob replied and with Hattie in pursuit, stomped off.

Jo fiddled with her paperwork and thought about Bob. He loved a drama and was relishing every moment of his arrival at Boomerville, no doubt taking note of the characters and storing up gossip to share with Anthony. She began to sort out table arrangements for dinner and wondered where she should seat him on his first evening. It was important that it went well. She looked at the list of names and decided that Kate would make a perfect dinner partner for Bob, even though Jo would have to find a new dinner companion for Andy. But there was no shortage of women who would kill each other in the crush to bag a seat next to their handsome guest.

Satisfied that arrangements were in order, Jo checked her watch and was pleased to see that she had time to take Bunty for a walk. Grabbing her jacket, she closed the door to reception as Hattie headed down the hallway.

'He's all unpacked and comfortable with a cup of Earl Grey,' Hattie said. 'Says he's going to meditate before dinner.' Hattie inclined her head towards the Red Room where Sir Henry and Hugo were dozing by the fire. 'Might be best to give that lot a wide berth this evening?'

'All sorted, Bob is sitting next to Kate.'

'That won't suit James Bond.' Hattie peered over reception and looked at Jo's seating plan.

'I think it's time that Andy met Lucinda.' Jo winked.

'Do you think the lovebirds can bear to be parted?'

'Well, we're about to find out.' Jo smiled and with a wave, went off for her walk.

Chapter Eight

The writing class had finished for the day and Kate decided to take a stroll. A chill in the air, a harbinger of autumn, was sharp and crisp and soon cleared her head as she walked across the courtyard into the garden, zipping her quilted jacket and pulling on a pair of gloves.

Writing longhand in class all day had strained muscles in her fingers that were tired from years of perpetually tapping on a keyboard. Kate felt a stabbing pain and thrust both hands deep into the warmth of her pockets. The discomfort was worrying and she wondered what she was going to do to stop the spread of arthritis.

Opening an iron gate, Kate stepped into the meadow. She looked up and saw the tepee where puffs of pale grey smoke rose from an opening at the top. A breeze carried the swirling matter towards the fells. She could hear faint chanting coming from inside the tepee and the vibrating sound reminded Kate of a swarm of bees. She paused to listen.

'Namaste,' a voice called out.

Kate spun around and was startled to see the Shaman standing before her.

'Will you join us?' he asked and moved a length of brightly covered canvas to one side, indicating that Kate step into the dark abyss beyond.

Despite the warmth of her jacket, Kate felt a shiver run down her spine. She could hear voices and the chant was getting louder. 'I'm just taking a little exercise,' she said. 'I've been cooped up in a classroom all day and thought that I'd take a walk to unwind.'

'I will help you to relax.'

'That's very kind,' Kate mumbled, 'but I think I'll pass for now, perhaps later in the week?' She didn't want to offend the man but had no intention of venturing into the tepee.

The Shaman looked down. He placed his palms together as if in prayer and bowed slightly. 'You will come when the time is right,' he said.

Kate felt her feet turn to stone. 'What is it that you do in there?' she asked, rooted to the spot.

'I heal and you have pain.'

The man looked up and Kate was captivated by his shining eyes. 'Pain where?' she whispered.

He held out his hands and Kate stared at the long fingers. She was mesmerised as he reached out to take her hands in his own. His skin felt hot and a burning sensation rippled through her flesh. Her bones cracked and, shocked, Kate pulled away.

'You can heal my fingers?' She pushed her hands back into her pockets.

'I just did.'

A drum was beating in the tepee and the Shaman lifted his head to listen. He swept his cloak around his body and with a nod, was gone.

Kate was speechless.

Falling leaves began to tumble from interlocking branches lining the edge of the meadow. They fluttered down like multicoloured rain in the cool autumn air, which carried an aroma of musky perfume. The potent smell drifted towards Kate and she stared as a woman, head shrouded in a long scarf, reached out to unhook the canvas doorway of the tepee. Heavy bangles circled a bony arm and rattled as the woman closed the inner world of the Shaman from the outer.

An owl screeched and the eerie cry shook Kate from her stupor. She forced her feet to move and hurried through the meadow to climb over a stile and scramble onto damp green fields and walk along a well-trodden path.

Kate knew nothing of Shamanism and couldn't explain the scene she'd just experienced. In the back of her mind she recalled that it was an ancient mode of spiritual healing. A Shaman being the medium for the spirits. But Kate felt uncomfortable. She didn't believe in spirits of the mystic kind and right now the only spirit she wanted was a large gin with a dash of tonic. Whatever went on in the tepee was no concern of hers.

She picked up her pace as the wind blew and tried not to think about her feelings when the Shaman took her hands in his. Instead she focused on the writing class, which, to her surprise, she'd enjoyed immensely. James, the tutor, was encouraging, even when she felt that she'd made a complete fool of herself with her rag doll rant. He'd listened, offering constructive comments and she'd been inspired to write on. James was easy to talk to and by the end of the session, Kate knew that she was looking forward to the rest of the course. Andy had sat next to her and she'd watched his fingers grip the body of his expensive fountain pen as it moved confidently across his page. She'd longed to reach out and hold his hand but Andy had been immersed in his writing and oblivious to Kate. He'd occasionally looked up and smiled, much to the delight of the female writers, alert to his every glance.

Andy certainly attracted attention.

Kate turned to retrace her steps and wondered if she should be concerned? She'd slept with the most eligible man in the building and there didn't seem to be a woman on his radar who wasn't attracted to his good looks and charm. Kate knew that she'd have to be on her guard if the relationship was to progress. But, she reasoned, Andy was so attentive and they had much in common; she shouldn't be paranoid. Surely it was best to enjoy the experience and see where it went? Her stay at Boomerville was exactly what she needed and to have a gorgeous man thrown in was a bonus. She was a long way from her lovely old schoolhouse but so far, she hadn't missed it one bit.

Clouds gathered in a dark squall and Kate felt rain on her face. A storm was brewing and she cursed. Her hair would be soaked and she'd have to hurry if she was going to get back in time to be ready for dinner. She pulled on her collar and as the hotel came in sight, looked up and saw the tepee. As twilight fell, it cast menacing shadows and Kate thought about the Shaman. A warm sensation had crept over her hands and as she hurried through the meadow, the tips of her fingers tingled. She stopped to stare at her hands in disbelief. The pain was gone. Had his healing worked? Did the Shaman really have magical powers? Kate shivered and shook her head. It was all a lot of nonsense; surely she was imagining things?

The rain was falling heavily and like a bunny returning to a burrow, Kate longed to be back in her cosy room. She ran into the garden, relieved to see the welcoming lights that shone from the conservatory. With relief, Kate flung the door open and stepped into the building. She shook off her jacket and placed it on a rack to dry. A gilded mirror hung to one side of the room and Kate leaned in to straighten her wayward hair.

But as she studied her reflection, she gasped.

The Shaman appeared behind her. His eyes shone and he seemed to be shaking his head. Kate spun around. She clasped her hand to her mouth to stifle a scream but the Shaman had disappeared.

There was nothing but an empty room and Kate was alone. She stared out of the window where shafts of moonlight glistened on the rain-soaked lawn and told herself that she really mustn't go out on the fells on her own at this time of night. The light must be playing tricks! For the Shaman was far away in the tepee.

What she needed was a hot bath and a stiff drink. Kate sighed and, feeling cross for letting her imagination run away, hurried through the hotel and up to her room to get ready for the evening ahead.

Andy sat by the window in his room. Evening had closed in and as light drained, shadows danced across the pale walls. He stared out at the garden where the moon hid behind a dense layer of cloud and rain began to fall, ricocheting on the conservatory roof below.

On a nearby table a decanter of malt whisky sat on a silver tray and he reached out to pour a generous measure. The window was open and a draught crept over the sill but, as Andy sipped the whisky, he felt a warm glow.

Things were working out perfectly.

He picked up a packet of cigars and tipped one out then peeled the cellophane wrapper. The tobacco was rich and he held it to his nose. There was only one thing that complimented a good cigar and excellent whisky and that was a wealthy woman. He flicked a gold lighter and drew heavily, then puffed smoke through the window. As he watched it drift into the twilight and disperse over the conservatory roof, he thought about Kate. She'd gone out earlier and he waited for her to return.

Andy sighed contentedly. He couldn't believe his luck. Within hours of his arrival at Boomerville, everyone had soaked up his fictitious story and there was genuine sympathy for the grieving widower, who'd lost his wife so tragically.

Cancer was powerful in many ways.

He rolled the whisky across his tongue then let it slide slowly down his throat and thought about Kate's welcoming creamy white thighs and how he'd rolled his tongue around their innermost secrets. An experience that had been thoroughly enjoyable, unlike many in the past. Only the thought of a deep and plentiful bank account, belonging to the grateful recipient of Andy's attention, had enabled him to ply his amorous performance to the string of rich, ageing and desperate women that he'd ruthlessly hunted down.

He remembered the advertisement for Boomerville, which he'd come across by chance. Andy didn't normally read the newspapers but earlier in the week, with nothing better to do, he'd sat in a station waiting room and idly attempted a crossword. The advert glowed like a rainbow and he knew that he'd found an untapped pot of gold. His booking had been accepted and on his very first night he'd met Kate Simmons. He hadn't even had to wade through boring encounters and conversations with eager females anxious to make his acquaintance.

Kate had been served up on a plate and from the moment he laid eyes on his prey he was determined to snare her. Single and rich, she was absolutely gorgeous.

He thought of some of the women he had bedded over the decades and winced. There was only so long that you could keep up a performance and as the years crept on Andy found it increasingly harder to satisfy women who held no charm. Only the thought of their ample funds diminishing magically into his own swelling account kept him going – that and the help of a little blue pill and a line of Bolivian marching powder.

But there was no need for Viagra and coke with Kate Simmons in his bed.

She'd succumbed very quickly and he'd had no trouble in rising to the occasion. Sex with Kate was a pleasure and he found himself enjoying her voluptuous body; she had curves in all the right places and breasts that were still firm and inviting. The experience was so enjoyable that he'd struggled to keep away from her all day and it was all he could do not to hustle her into the kitchen in the writing studio and ravage her over the sink. He imagined lifting Kate's neat little dress and removing her lace knickers and felt himself grow hard. The thought of pounding into her within earshot of that pompous English teacher made him groan with anticipation.

He chuckled at the thought of the boring boomers with their withered fingers, penning hot romance. Andy had been charming all day and there wasn't a woman in the class who wouldn't drop their droopy old drawers if he gave the word.

God help him! He took a slug of the whisky. With luck, he wouldn't need to spread his charms further afield than Kate. A week or two of careful surveillance would enable him to access her accounts and source her funds and with his usual cunning, he'd slip away before Kate had time to wonder what had happened to her money.

Andy poured another drink.

Cigar ash had fallen onto the carpet and he ground it into the thick pile with a well-polished loafer. The problem with his lifestyle was that he continually had to finance it and work, in the conventional sense, was alien to Andy. At school, his teachers had despaired of his inability to focus and the young student spent all his time running schemes amongst his fellow pupils to earn money, which mostly paid off. The product of a single-parent family, Andy had been brought up by his mother who often supplemented their benefits by offering benefits in kind to a trail of men who never lingered. He'd left home and reeled from one job to another until one day, working as a deckhand on a yacht in the south of France, he'd been seduced by a wealthy heiress. She'd showered the handsome young employee with gifts and money in return for sex and confidentiality, but as their time together increased, became careless. When her husband discovered the relationship, Andy escaped to the French Riviera where he perfected his talents as a gigolo and his life rapidly improved. Time after time, he accumulated illicit funds that would have set him up for life, had he been able to resist the urge to spend nights at the gaming tables of some of the world's top casinos.

His playground until the money ran out.

Then it was back to the drawing board and the trawl for his next victim. So far, he'd never had any difficulty finding a new income stream and had travelled the world on the proceeds. Women were incredibly gullible and never came after him. Their shame gave Andy control and he skilfully covered his tracks. Who needed a steady job and regular hours when you could live like a king? With no commitments, he could shag his way into the most prestigious circles with a few concocted stories and a bag full of charm.

Andy chuckled as he knocked back his drink. It was so easy! Middle-aged women were desperate for a final fling and he was happy to provide it.

A figure moved across the lawn and he leaned forward. Kate was running and by the look of things, was soaked. He flicked the butt of his cigar out into the dark and rubbed his hands together. She'd welcome a long hot bath, a bottle of champagne and his gentle caress.

He reached out to close the window but as he leaned forward, another shape moved through the darkness and caught his eye. A man in a long cloak appeared from the shadow of the conservatory and looked up. He stared at Andy and glared, then disappeared into the darkness. Andy slammed the window and it rattled in its frame.

Another Boomerville weirdo! he thought and, leaping to his feet, went to find Kate.

Chapter Nine

Hattie lay in a bath in Jo's house and closed her eyes. Hot water trickled from the faucet and she was tempted to grab a few winks as scented foam billowed over the roll-top edge of the freestanding tub.

Hattie enjoyed a soak in the deep and comfortable bath, with a generous lashing of Jo's expensive oils. It was a one-way trip to relaxation heaven and following her afternoon with Paul the Potter, she felt the need for a restorative rest. The man had magic in his hands and he'd rubbed and caressed Hattie's willing body, treating her to all the skills that he used when moulding soft, moist clay, manipulating the motions into orgasmic proportions that produced enough explosive energy to fire Hattie up for the best part of three hours.

Exhausted, Hattie soon drifted off to sleep. Her gentle snores purred around the lofty room as she languished in the warm enveloping water.

Suddenly, the bathroom door flew open and Hattie opened her eyes, startled.

'Have you slid down the plug-hole?' Jo said as she stood in the doorway. She held a large fluffy towel in her hands. 'I brought this from the airing cupboard. It's still warm.'

As Hattie sat up, water gushed over the rim of the bath and pooled across the wooden floor. Bubbles lay several inches deep and Bunty, who'd followed Jo, paddled through the damp mess.

'Bloody hell, Hattie, this lot will be leaking down to the living room!' Jo leapt across the bath to turn the tap off. 'Did you have to fill it so full?' She stared at Hattie's face. It was caked in white goo. 'Is that a mud-pack?'

Hattie grabbed a flannel as Jo leaned in closer to inspect the daubs of substance hardening on Hattie's cheeks.

'It looks like clay on your cheeks,' Jo said, looking puzzled.

Not the only cheeks covered in clay! Hattie thought and with haste, dabbed at her face.

'I've got some very good news,' Jo announced. She reached for a chair and sat down.

'Astonish me.' Hattie screwed her eyes up and scrubbed at her skin.

'Potter Paul has been in touch and his class can resume from tomorrow.'

'Aye, that's cracking,' Hattie replied and thought about the class he'd taught her that very afternoon. It had made mug handles look like child's play. In the blink of an eye they'd moved swiftly on to maintaining a firm erection in a medium far more interesting than clay.

'Thank goodness he didn't suffer any lasting injuries when you spun off the wheel. He says his hands are working perfectly. It's such a relief.'

'That's grand.' Hattie remembered the recent relief Paul's hands had administered on her willing parts.

'Are you all right? You seem very distant.'

'Aye, right as rain.' Hattie flung the flannel to one side and stepped out of the water. 'Bleedin' hell! What's that?' A bubble bounced across the floor and she leapt back in the bath.

'It's only Bunty.' Jo scooped the puppy onto her knee. 'Now you've soaked the floor again.' Jo stared at the water seeping into crevices. 'You used a lot of face-pack; there's clay everywhere.'

'Got to keep myself beautiful.' Hattie wrapped her body in the thick towel and tentatively stepped out of the bath. 'Does that mutt have to follow you everywhere?' She glared at Bunty, whose head peeped from a shroud of bubbles as she licked her way out.

Jo scooped the dog under one arm and stood up. 'Don't be late for dinner.'

'Don't worry, I'll be there. I'm ravenous. I can't imagine where I've got my appetite from.'

A little while later, Hattie hurried through the hotel and, reaching the hallway, took the stairs two at a time. She felt energised from her afternoon with the potter and now, under strict instructions from Jo, had been sent to ensure that Bob was revived after his journey and ready for dinner.

She stood outside his bedroom door and gently knocked. 'Only me,' Hattie called out, 'do you need a hand with anything?'

The door opened and Bob appeared.

Hattie could see that he'd taken a considerable amount of time with his appearance and she was impressed by the cut of his suit as he strutted across the landing and skipped down the stairs to the hall where he caught his reflection in the mirror above the console table.

'Fifty-something isn't so bad.' Bob straightened his tie and smoothed the palm of his hand over his head.

'It's a shame Anthony couldn't join you,' Hattie said.

'His job is too demanding to take time off at this time of year,' Bob replied. Anthony was the manager of a theatre in Chipping Hodbury. 'But it gives me plenty of time to catch up with Jo, I've been looking forward to it.'

Hattie was aware that Bob and Anthony had homes in London and the Cotswolds and Bob's office was in the heart of the West End. His life was an eclectic mix of business and social affairs and combined with a deep faith in his spiritual leanings, Bob had found his true path. His middle years were so far proving to be his best. But everyone deserved a rest and she knew that his batteries needed recharging.

'Very smart,' Hattie said, 'you look extremely handsome.'

Bob spun around. Hattie was wearing a mid-calf emerald-green dress that clung tightly to every inch of her body. 'Gorgeous dress, sweetie,' he said. 'It would look even better if it fitted.'

'You're just jealous of my voluptuous curves and sexual appeal.' Hattie ignored Bob's sarcasm and took his arm. 'Have you seen the sainted one?'

'If you mean Jo, no I haven't, but I'm far more concerned that I'll run into that horse-faced eighties throwback with wandering hands.' Bob glanced nervously down the hall. 'For God's sake don't put me anywhere near her.'

'Ah, you mean the lovely Lucinda.' Hattie led Bob into the Green Room, where a waiter poured drinks. 'Don't worry, we've partnered her with a very charming dinner companion.' She passed a cocktail to Bob. 'Here, get your gob around this before the battle begins.'

The room began to fill as guests arrived to relax and chat about the events of the day. The aerobics class had enjoyed a session of Nifty Fifties and members' cheeks glowed from their afternoon exertions.

'Do you enjoy exercise?' Bob asked Hattie as they skirted the group and found a seat next to the Mulberry brothers, in chairs by the fire.

'My favourite is a cross between a lunge and a crunch,' Hattie said as she made Bob comfortable. 'I call it lunch.'

Pottery students were buzzing with the news that Paul would soon be restored to the helm of their wheels, whilst the would-be novelists discussed their class. They thought that James was a motivating tutor and writing longhand had been inspirational. Sir Henry and Hugo had been on their best behaviour in Curry in a Hurry. After sharpening up their knife skills they were looking forward to Heaven-Sent Bread the following morning.

'Sandra has a marvellous wrist action,' Sir Henry said as he knocked back a sherry. 'Had me chillies chopped before you could say, by jingo!'

'I remember Cook, pounding away on the kitchen table at Raven Hall,' Hugo said and thought fondly of the kitchen in his family home. He looked at Hattie and picked up his spectacles to read the menu. Placing them on the bridge of his nose, he sighed. 'Such powerful hands.' He stared longingly at Hattie as she leaned in to top up his glass.

'Settle down, your glasses are steaming up,' Hattie said, then turned to Bob who was staring at her cleavage.

'What on earth have you got down there?' Bob whispered. A wooden knob peeped out of the front of Hattie's dress. 'Has it got batteries?'

'Damage limitation,' Hattie replied in a conspiratorial voice. 'If Hugo's fingers come near me, he'll have this to grapple with.' She produced a mini rolling pin and Bob swerved away.

'Crikey, I wouldn't put it past you.' He looked at Hattie with new admiration.

'Unfortunately, it turns the randy old devil on.'

'A childhood fetish?'

'Naturally. Nanny, the cook, his governess.'

Dinner was announced and the residents gathered to head into the restaurant. Hattie introduced Bob to Kate and could see that he was delighted to meet his dining partner. He held her chair out as she sat down.

'I was beginning to think I was the youngest here,' Hattie heard Bob say as he shook out a linen napkin and placed it on his knee. 'Surely you don't qualify for Boomerville?'

Kate smiled. 'That's very flattering, but I can assure you that I more than meet the criteria.'

On the other side of the room, Hattie took Andy's arm and led him to a table where Lucinda sat, waiting to meet her dinner companion. She fluttered her eyelashes and stretched out her arm and Hattie saw Andy recoil as he shook the artist's hand. Hattie turned and, with a smile, joined Jo by the dining door where they stood to observe their guests.

'Double-oh-seven's firing blanks,' Hattie said as she watched Andy pick over his starter while Lucinda prattled on.

'I think he fired them all before dinner. Room service took champagne up to Kate's room at six o'clock.'

'Charged to her account?'

'Actually, no, it's gone on his tab.'

'There's a surprise.'

'Don't be so judgmental, he seems like a charming man.' Jo picked up a bottle of chilled white wine. 'Do you want to pour the red?'

Hattie watched Andy gaze over at Kate's table where his bedfellow was giggling and flirting with Bob. 'Aye, no problem,' she said and grabbed a bottle of Merlot.

Sir Henry and Hugo were enjoying the company of a group of locals who'd participated that day in Boomers Re-Boot, a strenuous activity course in the grounds of the hotel.

'Hattie, old girl,' Sir Henry called, 'what say Hugo and I knock up a Balti for this lithesome lot?' He looked around the table. Robust-looking women of good farming stock, faces still flushed with exertion, giggled as Sir Henry continued. 'A little bit of Indian heaven? Do us all good.'

'I think that's a cracking idea,' Hattie said as she poured the wine. 'We could have a theme night. I'll talk to the boss.'

'The last days of the Raj,' Sir Henry said.

'Happy times.' Hugo nodded.

'For One Night Only the Boomerville Balti! Gentlemen, brush up your naans in Heaven-Sent Bread,' Hattie said. 'I'm sure these ladies would be happy to come back and join us for an evening of Indian cuisine.'

The boot-camp boomers nodded eagerly.

'Did I hear you correctly?' Jo grabbed Hattie by the arm as they met to replenish the wine. 'We're turning the hotel into a Balti palace for the evening?'

'Bloody brilliant idea. Open it to the public and you'll be bursting at the seams.'

'But Henry and Hugo can't peel a potato; they've been spoon-fed all their lives.' Jo was aghast.

'Don't let them anywhere near the menu, just let them think they've contributed or you'll have a Delhi-belly outbreak faster than you can boil an egg.'

'Well, it might not be such a bad idea.'

'The craft class can knock up some outfits and the Shaman can do a few mystical Indian tricks. Get everyone involved, it's got winner all over it.' Hattie beamed.

'We can look at the diary in the morning and set a date. Go easy on the Merlot, most of the residents are half-cut and we haven't served the main course yet.'

Kate sat in the Red Room with Bob and felt a comforting glow as they stared at the fire where logs crackled in the hearth, blazing cheerily. Dinner had been delicious and Bob's company entertaining. She'd told him about her life and how she'd thrown herself into studies to create the opportunity to start her business and ultimately purchase her beloved old schoolhouse. She'd asked about Bob's life and been fascinated by his tales of dealing with high profile clients.

'They're just like the rest of us,' Bob said, 'but life in the limelight can change people and sometimes I have to be strict in my guidance and ensure they don't go off track.'

'Is Zach a good client?' Kate asked, keen to hear about Jo's youngest son. His menus were one of the highlights of Boomerville and she told Bob that *Foraging with the Gypsy Chef* was one of her favourite programmes.

'That boy is a master in the kitchen,' Bob was discreet. 'He's handsome, charming, makes brilliant TV and has fans all over the world.' Bob thought about the scrapes he'd dragged Zach out of and the continued effort it took to keep the celebrity chef away from the press and incriminating headlines.

'I think you must be a wonderful agent. I'd love to be a fly-on-the-wall in your life.' Kate was riveted by Bob. She wanted to know all about his relationship with Anthony and what had kept them together as a couple.

'A loving home,' Bob said. 'We adore our country house. It's our refuge, a place to unwind with close friends. You must come and stay.'

'I'd love to,' Kate said, 'and I hope you'll visit my home too.'

Bob had sympathised as Kate spoke of her parents' deaths and Kate was glued to Bob's words as he told her about the business world of celebrities and all the mischief that went on behind the scenes.

They were so engrossed in each other that they didn't see Andy approach.

'Ah, there you are,' Andy said.

Kate's eyes lit up. 'Bob, can I introduce you to Andy Mack.' She wriggled along the sofa to make room.

Bob held out his hand. 'Charmed to meet you. Do join us.'

'God, it's a relief to get away from that dreadful woman.' Andy slid alongside Kate. 'I can't tell you how much I've missed your company.'

'You've met Lucinda.'

'What an old crone.' Andy shook his head. 'I thought I'd never get rid of her.' He laid an arm across Kate's shoulder.

A waiter served coffee and Kate listened to the two men as Bob and Andy discussed Lucinda. She looked adoringly at Andy. His sex appeal oozed and she felt that she could drown in the pools of his incredibly dark eyes as she snuggled into his trim and muscled body, longing to reach out and stroke the thick black hair, slightly greying at the sides, which gave her lover a distinguished look that sat well on a man of his height.

'It's past my bedtime.' Bob finished his drink and put the empty glass on the table. 'It's been a very long day. I'll say goodnight.' Bob leaned over to kiss Kate on the cheek. 'Sleep well.'

'Oh, we will,' Andy said and moved closer to Kate. Her body shivered with anticipation as his warm lips brushed her ear and he whispered, '*Of that, I have no doubt!*'

Chapter Ten

Jo stood in the kitchen of the creative writing studio and watched James pour freshly brewed coffee. It was early and his class wasn't due to arrive until the clock in the courtyard struck ten. She wanted to have a word, for James looked tired when he'd arrived that morning and Jo wondered if all was well.

'Let's sit by the fire for a moment or two,' Jo said and led James to a sofa. She opened the stove and threw a log onto the embers.

As they sat back and sipped their drinks Jo thought about Helen, James' ex-wife. Jo had known her for years and remembered her flamboyance. She was a colourful sight when they came into the restaurant at Kirkton House for family celebrations, always dressed in elaborate creations, inspired by her art, with her adoring husband in tow alongside their sons, who hung off their mother's every word.

'Is everything all right?' Jo tentatively asked. 'You seemed distant today when you passed me in reception.'

'Sorry, Jo,' James said, 'I had a very late night.'

Jo wondered if Helen was creating problems again and remembered how James had been devastated when she left. It had been the talk of Marland for many months as James was seen to bury his pain and forge a new life as a single parent.

'How are the boys?'

'Tom is working in London and Jack beginning his final year at university in Leeds.'

'Do they still visit Helen in France?'

'Yes, when they can,' James said and stared at the fire, lost in his own thoughts.

Each year the boys had spent part of their summer holidays with Helen and her new partner in France. But despite the countryside, glorious weather and the relaxed attitude to alcohol, James knew that Helen drank to excess and would cause scenes, and her sons were always keen to return to the safe and happy environment that he'd created.

'Do you want to talk about it?' Jo sat forward. James was very subdued and she was concerned. A biting wind rattled the windows and leaves swirled along the cobbles as heavy rain began to fall. She looked out at the herb garden, which was taking a battering as the deluge pounded delicate fronds of dill and coriander and water puddled on the rich dark soil.

James sank back into the sofa, grateful for the comfort of the log burner, where flames glowed beyond the smoky glass. He turned to Jo and sighed. 'It's Jack. He turned up last night.' He began to explain his concern.

Having suddenly announced that he was in a committed relationship with a girl he'd met at university, Jack had told his father that he wanted to get engaged and married as soon as his exams were over. James had been staggered as their discussion deepened.

'We drank far too many beers.' James rubbed his eyes and thought about the empty case by the bin his kitchen.

'I wouldn't worry about that,' Jo said. 'Drink numbs the senses and Jack probably needed courage to share his news, while you required patience to accept it.'

She listened as James went on to explain that he thought it crazy for two young people to make such a commitment. With careers to consider and life to be lived, surely they could wait? He explained that this wasn't what he'd expected of Jack at all and he stared into the fire, as if searching for answers. 'Her name is Desiree. I didn't even know that he had a girlfriend.'

'Well, at least he had the decency to come home and tell you and not announce it by text.' Jo thought of the electronic missiles she'd received from her own sons over the years.

'Helen will hit the roof when she hears news of the engagement and Jack is frightened of his mother.'

Jo knew that Helen had a temper and remembered scenes in

the restaurant when, after several glasses of wine, she would flare up if anyone voiced an opinion that didn't match her own. Helen would most likely blame James for a lack of parental responsibility and be apoplectic at the thought of her baby tying the knot at such a young age, all memory of abandoning her sons completely erased.

Jo heard James sigh.

'I think the sooner I get it over with and tell Helen, the better,' he said. 'Sorry to have off-loaded.'

'Don't apologise, I wish I could be of some help.'

'You have been.' James smiled. 'Just by listening.' He stood and picked up their mugs. 'But I mustn't take any more of your time.'

'Good luck with Helen. She may have mellowed.' Jo gave him a peck on the cheek, but in her heart, knew that it was unlikely and James would have many more battles ahead. 'Give me a shout if there is anything that I can do.' With a sympathetic smile, Jo left James to prepare for his class.

Kate turned into the courtyard to see Jo bracing herself against the wind as she stepped out of the writing studio to run across the cobbles and disappear into the kitchen. Kate glanced up at the courtyard clock. She was early for her class and as she opened the door and stepped into the cosy warmth of the room, she saw James sitting by the fire.

'Gosh, it's wild out there,' Kate said and shook off her wet jacket to place it on the back of a chair. 'Mind if I join you?'

James moved along the sofa and Kate sat down. He looked tired but smiled, clearly pleased to see her.

'Are those biscuits?' Kate asked and pointed to a tin on the table.

'Help yourself.' James leaned forward and opened the tin and watched as Kate took a shortbread. Her neat white teeth sparkled as her tongue licked traces of sugar from her moist pink lips.

James stared with fascination as she bit into the biscuit.

Drops of rain glistened on Kate's hair and he was shocked to find that he longed to reach out and stroke the soft locks. He wondered if she'd spent the night in the arms of Andy Mack. The glow in her eyes, as she stared at the fire, answered his question and anger welled in the pit of his stomach. He was jealous! The bitter feeling was akin to the pain he'd felt after Helen walked out, for she too had glowed at the thought of a lover. James hardly knew Kate, but as he felt her presence, so close to his own, he wanted to reach out and pull her into his arms.

'You're miles away, penny for your thoughts?' Kate said.

James sat up. 'Sorry, I've a lot on my mind.' He silently scolded himself. This was crazy. He was getting carried away with illicit thoughts about a student, something he'd never allowed himself to do.

'I hope I can contribute today.' Kate felt anxious as she thought about her participation in yesterday's class.

'Your contribution is completely worthy and the most important thing is that you feel worthy of yourself.'

As lovely as Kate was, James knew that he must be professional and focus on her writing path; after all, he may uncover a talent, and wasn't the ethos of Boomerville to encourage new learning to enrich the later years?

'I've always wanted to write, but never thought I was good enough,' Kate said. 'I'm scared that people will laugh at me.'

'The only way to find out is to commit and the only way to do that is to sit down and begin.'

'Point taken.' Kate grinned. 'I intend to, hence my early start, but what about you? Couldn't you sleep?'

James looked into Kate's eyes and, in moments, words were tumbling over themselves. He picked up where he'd left off with Jo and told Kate that he was worried about his youngest son and Kate learnt about the pain James and the boys had suffered when Helen abandoned them. He explained that she'd been a beautiful young woman when he'd met her, with vitality and charisma that charmed anyone. James had been staggered when Helen agreed to marry him.

'You must have been very young.' Kate was fascinated.

'We were. Students who knew very little of life, we both left university with first class degrees, mine in English and Helen's in art. We couldn't wait to set up home together.'

'Did you find jobs?'

'I got work teaching at a sixth-form college and Helen continued to paint.'

'Was she talented?'

'Yes, very. She worked on commissions, mostly for friends, which supplemented our income but she didn't know what to charge and never made a great deal.'

Kate listened as James explained that they were delighted when Tom, their first-born arrived followed by Jack two years later. But the responsibility of a family fell heavily on shoulders that had led a bohemian life and Helen stopped painting.

'I knew that Helen had begun to drink. She wasn't cut out to be a mother and seemed to resent the children, as though they were the reason she couldn't paint. I didn't know how to handle it.' James sighed. 'When an opportunity to holiday in France with girlfriends from university came along, she seized the chance. I was fearful of her going but thought that the break would do her good and she'd come back to us a better mother, having had some time to herself.'

'So, what happened?' Kate asked.

'I watched her pack her easel and oils and a suitcase of clothes as the boys asked where Mummy was going. She never looked at us as we stood on the doorstep and waved her off. She climbed into her friend's car and disappeared.'

Kate held her breath. She knew what was coming.

'She never came back,' James said.

Two weeks later James learnt that Helen had fallen in love with a much younger man. Life on a vineyard, in the heart of the Charente, surrounded by fields of swaying sunflowers and heady lavender, with an ardent lover by her side, had far more appeal to the thwarted artist than semi-suburbia, on a housing estate in Marland, with a middle-income husband and two demanding children.

James looked up. He seemed astonished that he'd told Kate, a complete stranger, about his problems. 'I'm so sorry. I don't know why I'm burdening you.'

'I think you're a brilliant dad.' Kate spoke softly. 'Jack must think the world of you and have confidence that you can handle Helen and make her see that it's your son's right to make his own choices.'

'I hope you're right,' James said. He must be supportive to his son who'd simply fallen in love at an early age and wanted approval from a mother who behaved erratically. She was still his mother and Jack craved her love.

'Are you worried that Helen won't understand?'

'She has violent rages, fuelled by her love of booze.'

'That makes it difficult.'

'She terrifies the boys when she starts ranting and yelling; it's as though she blames them for making her leave.'

'Perhaps Tom and Jack may believe it was their fault that she left; had they not been born she wouldn't have started to drink.'

'Oh, goodness, I hope not, they were just little children.'

'Maybe she's guilt-ridden because she's a crap mother. It's a shame they can't sit down and talk it out.'

'I've tried to get them together but Helen is difficult.'

'Perhaps life in the Charente isn't all she expected it to be?'

'Quite possibly.' James sat up. 'Look,' he said, 'I shouldn't be telling you all this, I really mustn't burden you with my problems.' He was anxious to change the subject. Kate would think him a hopeless wreck if he continued to pour out his troubles. 'What did you say your business was?'

'I didn't.' Kate smiled. 'But I ran a dating agency and it sort of went hand-in-hand with listening to people's problems and helping make them right.'

'Have you thought about writing a romance story?' James reached for a biscuit. 'You must have a wealth of material.'

'I was very good at matching others and sorting out their problems but absolutely useless at sorting out my own; all my relationships went wrong.'

Kate felt James study her face. 'Did your parents have a happy marriage?'

'When my mum died of cancer, my dad was never the same again. He started drinking and despite the fact that he tried to cover it up, I knew how broken he was inside. He missed her terribly. I tried to be the perfect daughter and he was a great help to me, supporting me when I started my business. When he got dementia, I cared for him until he died, but I could never compare to my mother.'

'Perhaps you were too like her?'

'Possibly, I never thought of that.'

'You can't be responsible for his actions; after all, he chose to drink, not you.'

'Likewise with Helen. She chooses to drink and has a difficult relationship with her sons, not you.'

Their eyes locked. It took every ounce of willpower for James not to reach out and take Kate in his arms.

'Things have a way of sorting themselves out,' Kate said and stood up. 'I'm glad we've had a chance to chat but if you'll excuse me, I'm going to spend a little time on my own, working on an idea I have.'

James watched her walk away and hoped that he hadn't said too much. He'd never confided in a student and knew that it was wrong. He was amazed that she brought out such feelings of need, feelings that he'd suppressed for years and now found difficult to control.

He sat down at a table and pulled his laptop towards him. The screen flickered and James stared blankly. His head was filled with an image of Kate and Andy passionately entwined in her bed.

Things have a way of sorting themselves out …

No wonder an idea had miraculously evolved in a head that was blank the previous day! Kate was doubtlessly penning pages of romantic prose in a happy-ever-after. James sighed with frustration and decided to focus on a subject that he could do something about. He logged onto his email.

Hi Helen, he wrote, *we need to have a chat about Jack and I'd be grateful if you'd get in touch*.

James pressed *send*. He wondered how long Helen would take to reply and began to rehearse the conversation. He was thankful that it wouldn't be a face-to-face meeting as she spent all of her time at the vineyard and rarely returned to the UK. She was volatile at the best of times but this news would send her temper soaring. James knew that Helen would be against the relationship. She'd always insisted that her sons travel and experience life.

Not marry at a young age, like their parents.

Enough, James told himself and pushed the laptop away. His students were due in class. James glanced at Kate and saw that her head was dipped and her fingers flying, her face a study of concentration as words cascaded onto the page. Whatever her idea, it had clearly come to life. He decided to let Kate carry on while the words were flowing and moved silently around the room in preparation for his class.

Kate was oblivious. In the safe and cosy atmosphere of the studio, she seemed to have found her writing muse and as James arranged notes for the students and piled logs onto the fire, he hoped that he'd helped inspire whatever magic was happening.

Chapter Eleven

The next morning there was an excited buzz in the Rose Room, where residents gathered for breakfast. Bright sunshine burst through the French windows, latticing light across tables as staff moved around, topping up cups and taking orders. Guests munched on muesli and whispered over plates of crispy bacon and lightly poached eggs.

Lucinda reached for a jar of gooseberry marmalade. A smug smile crept across her lips as she spread the thick sweet substance over her toast. She broke a piece and popped it into her mouth.

At last, she had her own class!

Today, she would endeavour to bring creativity into the lives of a group of guests who would be inspired by her talent. She thought back to the day that she read the advert for Boomerville in her local paper. She'd been blinded by the vision that this was her path, the route to her future and a journey that she had to make. Lucinda had no money and scraped a living by teaching and selling the occasional painting. She lived in a shared house with a handful of other eccentric creatives on the outskirts of London and led a bohemian life, but as the years progressed she knew that she needed some form of security as she got older. Boomerville had come like a bolt out of the blue, a sign that she must follow and, acting on instinct, Lucinda filled in the booking form, reserved a seat on a train and began to pack.

Now, as she sat in the dining room, she thought about her finances. Her money was running out. She urgently needed a job or a wealthy lover.

Lucinda smiled to herself as she finished her breakfast and tossed her napkin to one side. She'd been working on her options since her arrival a couple of weeks ago and had high hopes for both. Today would accelerate her mission. A pop-up art class had been announced for that afternoon and Lucinda was to be the tutor.

As she made her way out of the room, she glanced at the other diners and knew that those lucky enough to have booked a place were wondering what the subject matter would be and whether Lucinda was a suitable instructor.

Finally, she was going to be put to the test.

Jo returned from her morning walk with Bunty and as she went into reception was surprised to see a queue by the desk. 'What's going on?' she asked.

'The life class is a sell-out,' Hattie said.

'What life class?' Jo pulled out a chair and sat down as Hattie told disappointed residents that the class was now full but they'd be running another very soon.

'I thought I'd mentioned it.'

'I think I'd have remembered.' Jo drummed her fingers on the desk and waited for Hattie to explain.

'Lucinda's been banging on about art classes and I thought it might be a good idea to see what she's made of. I've arranged a pop-up.'

'Pop-up?'

'Aye, there's an empty studio where the kennels used to be. We might as well make good use of it.'

'But there's no heating in there and it's cold.'

'I've told everyone to layer up.'

'And what exactly is Lucinda teaching the budding artists to do?'

'Oh, I don't know, paint bowls of fruit, that sort of stuff. You should be pleased. We've got six outsiders all paying top price for the privilege, plus twelve residents. It's a cracking earner.'

'What's Lucinda getting out of it?'

Hattie fiddled with the diary. 'I said we'd come to an arrangement on other classes, offset it or something.'

'Well, I don't suppose it can do any harm; it will bring new people to experience Boomerville and might have a ripple effect.'

'Like a tidal wave.'

'I'm going out with Pete and we were thinking that we might have a night away,' Jo said. 'Are you free to keep an eye on things?'

'Aye, don't you worry about a thing, leave it in my capable hands.' Hattie spun on her chair. 'You go and have a good time.'

'Pete wants to go to an auction of old farm machinery. It's near Skipton and there's a lovely little hotel close by.'

'Crackin', it will do you good to have a night off.' Hattie frowned. 'You'll be taking the mutt with you?'

'Of course, the hotel is dog friendly. Bunty will be made welcome.'

'That's all right then.' Hattie had no plans for pooch sitting.

'I'll go and check the day's menus and make sure that Sandra has everything she needs.' Jo stood up and opened the kitchen door. 'We'll be heading off soon. Call me if you need anything.'

'Only in a dire emergency. There's nowt special happening, so get off and enjoy yourselves.' Hattie waited for the door to close then spun on her chair and punched the air.

Perfect! Jo's timing couldn't be better. She turned to the switchboard and placed a call to Lucinda's room.

'All sorted,' Hattie said. 'The class starts at two and it's full.'

She listened to Lucinda's instructions then hung up. Placing another call to housekeeping, she arranged for portable heaters to be placed in the old kennels. The new art studio would be freezing without any heating. She'd find Alf, then have a wander over there and get him to tart the place up a bit. Hattie sat back and twirled a pencil in her fingers as she thought about the afternoon ahead.

She could hardly wait.

Kate finished her tea and pushed her chair back from the table. She'd enjoyed a delicious breakfast of poached eggs and, fortified for the morning, was keen to get to class where her new project was progressing well.

She'd left Andy in bed.

He'd seemed reluctant to get up and it was all she could do not to climb back in and snuggle next to him under the cosy duvet. Kissing him tenderly on the forehead, she hung a 'Do Not Disturb' sign on the door and crept out.

As Kate wandered through the conservatory, she wondered if they ought to share a room, for they'd certainly spent every moment of their spare time together and Andy had suggested that it would make sense not to be creeping along corridors in the early hours. Boomerville might miss the revenue that two rooms provided but the hotel was busy and an extra room would be occupied in no time.

But Kate was hesitant. It was early days in the relationship and for no reason that she could justify, part of her held back.

She grabbed her jacket from a hook and stepped into the garden. There was time to have a quick walk before she went to class. She couldn't wait to start writing and as she thrust her hands into her pockets and picked up her step, her thoughts were filled with storylines and characters.

Her muse was demanding that morning.

Kate knew that something special was happening at Boomerville. She'd come alive again and couldn't wait to start each day. As she paced through the garden, the wind smacked, and uplifting gusts gave her the urge to run along the path. An inner happiness was filling her with enthusiasm for life. It reminded her of the days when she'd started her business, when there were never enough hours and she'd loved every single moment as she plotted and planned and watched her dreams become reality. Now, having been dormant for far too long, that feeling was back. Boomerville was helping and meeting Andy was the icing on the cake. It made her feel special. Sex was good for her soul and to experience love with a man who made her heart leap at his touch was something Kate had feared would never happen.

But something else was happening too.

Writing classes had reignited her creative side and James was a wonderful teacher. His enthusiasm encouraged Kate to explore the magic that flowed through her fingers where thoughts became sentences. He gave her confidence to face her fear and try her hand at the written word.

A story that had been in her head for years was sprouting. A sapling where new shoots led Kate along its spiky path, with twists and turns creating potential in her novel. Originally titled *The Dating Game*, her imagination had surprised her. Expecting to write prose of romance and happy endings, Kate found that a darker side had emerged and the genre had changed as well as the title. With a one-word addition, *The Deadly Dating Game* was born. James encouraged her to not be in fear of a plot that developed quite differently from the one she'd begun. He taught her how to build a strong outline and plan the framework so that all she had to do was fill it in and, in time, write the story.

Kate kicked at piles of leaves and strolled through to the meadow. She wished she'd put a notebook in her pocket; a plot idea was on her mind and she longed to write it down. She closed her eyes in an attempt to commit it to memory and was startled when she heard a voice.

'Namaste.'

Kate stopped. She'd almost reached the Shaman's tepee but he was nowhere to be seen.

'Namaste.'

With a start, Kate realised that he was standing right behind her.

'Oh, you made me jump!'

'Your hands are better?'

'Er, yes, I think they are.' Kate wriggled her fingers in her pockets and realised that she'd had no pain whatsoever since their last meeting.

'So now you can write.'

'How did you know?'

'I just know.' His green eyes glinted.

'Thank you,' she whispered.

'Be careful, there is evil around you.'

Mesmerised, Kate stared. His eyes had become murky pools and she was uncontrollably drawn. She felt herself being pulled into the dark depths and staggered back, rubbing her eyes with her hands. When she looked up, the Shaman had disappeared. A tingle ran through her fingers, spreading a warmth through her hands and, after the moment of panic, she felt an inner calm.

But the Shaman was a mystery. His ways were odd and she had no longing to learn more about Shamanism than was necessary.

Kate checked her watch. She must hurry or she'd be late. She turned to head back to the hotel and as she walked, she thought about his words. What was all that nonsense about evil? It was confusing and impossible to fathom. She felt a shiver and decided that it might be a good idea to find another route for her walk.

Ahead, a group of students gathered to unlatch the gates that led from the garden to the meadow and as they came in sight, Kate saw that some were heading for the tepee and others to the gypsy caravan. Kate smiled and pleasantries were exchanged.

'Enjoy your day!'

Boomerville, at times, felt like a holiday camp and wherever she went, Kate was met with happy people and smiling faces. It was a recipe for feeling good and no wonder the courses were so busy. The place seemed full of the elixir of life and maturing adults, like Kate, were clearly enjoying their stay.

But there was something about the meadow that she couldn't explain. The atmosphere changed whenever she walked through the pretty pasture and as smoke puffed from the tepee, tumbleweed blew across her path. Kate hurried away and vowed not to participate in sessions there, nor let her superstitions get the better of her.

She turned into the courtyard.

James stood by the window of the studio. He smiled and waved when he saw her approach and Kate visualised the welcoming fire and hot coffee and hoped that James had time to chat about her work before class began.

She was happy and life at Boomerville was all that she had hoped it would be. *Thank goodness she'd found it!* Kate crossed the cobbles and, returning the greeting, hurried to her class.

Chapter Twelve

In his comfortable suite overlooking the garden, Andy stood in his dressing gown and watched Kate hurry across the lawn and turn into the courtyard. She had a smug look on her face as she headed to her writing class.

He sighed, for he wasn't feeling quite as bright and cheerful as his bedfellow.

Andy couldn't be bothered to dress and the thought of a morning's tutorial did nothing for his mood. He was bored rigid by the poker-faced teacher and already tired of pretending that he enjoyed penning pointless tales whilst discovering his creative self. Unlike Kate, who'd blossomed since she'd been at Boomerville and was enjoying all that was on offer.

He thought how effortless it all was for people with money to spare.

With an abundance of pleasures at their fingertips, they could embrace whatever took their fancy. But he had to work hard for whatever he got. It wasn't easy pandering to the attention of a demanding woman, even one as lovely as Kate. When they made love, he was spurred on by the thought of her bank account and the only assets he was really interested in were her savings. The sooner they got a room together, the sooner he could start to delve into her private affairs, for he was keen to be off to warmer climes.

Andy never liked to stay in one place for long and the one and only time that he'd been caught for his underhand behaviour was when he'd become too comfortable in a relationship and landed up in jail. But three years for robbery at HM Prison, Pentonville had advantages. His cellmate, who'd been convicted of fraud at a major bank, had been a font of knowledge when it came to hacking and had taught Andy the finer details of computer scamming.

A quick leaner, Andy honed skills in jail that had been invaluable and now he had the ability to hack into most things and disperse the contents into a web of untraceable accounts, all registered to fictitious names that ultimately flowed back to him. He was anxious to get access to Kate's laptop. It was the perfect time to dig deep into her accounts, while she was engrossed in her new environment and oblivious to the realities of life.

Andy puffed on a cigar and wondered what he would do to pass the day. Kate wouldn't come up for air once she started writing. She'd told him that she'd begun a novel which seemed to be writing itself and all she had to do was turn up to the page and the words came tumbling out. Perhaps he should join another class, widen his scope and see what else was on offer at Boomerville? There were plenty of well-heeled guests who might easily be blackmailed into parting with some cash.

He blew rings of smoke out of the window and considered his options. The crazy artist hadn't a bean but the wealthy old brothers were sitting ducks. There must be a scam he could pull. The flashy gay was no dumb bunny and Andy got a bad vibe when he was around.

He'd need to keep Bob at arm's length.

Andy yawned and contemplated breakfast. He decided to shower and dress then wander down for a bite to eat. Kate wore him out and he needed to conserve his energy. A day perusing the papers was in order and he'd watch the world go by as he sussed out his fellow guests. Perhaps he'd check out the weather in the Caribbean. It was turning cold here and Andy planned to be financially replenished and heading off before winter really kicked in.

Stubbing his cigar out on a saucer, he flicked the butt out of the window to join the collection on the roof below and stared at the watery-blue sky where wispy vapour trailed from the engines of a high-flying jet.

He imagined sitting in a first-class seat. *I'll be on that plane soon*, he thought and watched the soaring giant head high in the sky, far away from the fells below.

With a smile, Andy turned to begin preparations for his next victim.

Chapter Thirteen

Hattie stood in the hastily refurbished building that for years had been used to home generations of canine guests. Wooden cages with metal grilles had long gone, leaving an open space with thick stone walls and a smooth quarry-tiled floor. Two large windows faced the sunny courtyard and as Hattie closed the stable door against the chill, she rubbed her hands together. 'Blimey, there's a sharp nip in the air,' she exclaimed as she studied the room and decided what to do.

The girls in housekeeping had rounded up a selection of oil-filled radiators, which were stored in the cellar in case of emergencies. They'd been placed around the room and Hattie ran a length of cable to connect the power. A tall arc lamp stood in a corner and after plugging it in, she dragged it to the centre of the room then stood back to contemplate the positioning. She'd whipped it from the pottery studio, where it was used to light a cabinet displaying finished work. Potter Paul would miss it and might come searching, but for now, it was perfect for the art class.

'Where's tha' want these?'

The door burst open and a face peered above a stack of chairs on a trolley, which wobbled on the courtyard cobbles.

'Set 'em up in a circle,' Hattie said as Alf staggered into the room. She reached into a box and pulled out a pile of artists' pads, complete with a selection of pencils, charcoals and pastel crayons and, as chairs were unloaded and positioned, placed the objects on each seat.

'Nip into the Green Room and get the chaise,' Hattie said. 'We could do with some wall art too.'

'Leave it with me,' Alf replied and made his way past with the empty trolley. 'I've got just the thing.'

Satisfied that everything was ready for Lucinda and her budding artists, Hattie stepped into the courtyard and closed the door. She hoped that Jo had set off with Pete and with only an hour to go before Lucinda showed everyone what she was made of, Hattie hurried to get ready.

Kate sat at a table in the writing studio and stared at her notebook. James had set a tutorial and, together with the rest of the class, she was working her way through his instructions. But her heart wasn't really in the lesson and she longed to get on with her novel. She was fired up with ideas for the story and keen to set them down. She looked up and studied her classmates; they were a decent crowd and she enjoyed their company.

Andy had decided to give the session a miss and Kate was pleased. It was too distracting to have him close by.

She watched James as his students worked on the task that he'd set. He stared at the screen on his laptop and looked concerned and Kate wondered what he was thinking about.

But James was oblivious to Kate as he digested the content of an email that had appeared in his inbox, for Helen was on her way to Westmarland.

On receipt of his message, she'd telephoned and after he'd explained Jack's situation, burst into a fit of temper criticising James' lack of parental skills. He'd heard her gulp wine as she ranted. It had been impossible for James to understand what she was saying and he'd ended up disconnecting the call.

Now, she'd decided to respond in writing.

James, I am very disturbed by your news and thought that you would have more sense. To encourage Jack is absurd and surely our own pitiful relationship speaks volumes. We cannot allow history to repeat itself. Jack must get over this infatuation; he needs to travel and see the world, not marry in haste and make the mistakes that were ours. He is too young. Alors! If you are not prepared to deal with the situation, I must take it into my own hands and visit. I need to speak to him personally, face-to-face. I will make

arrangements to travel and let you know in due course.
Jusqu'à ce qu'on se rencontre. Helen.

James sighed. The last thing he wanted was for Helen to come roaring across the Channel and cause mayhem, but unfortunately it looked as though there was no way of stopping her.

He'd made things worse and now could only hope that she wouldn't just turn up. Deciding that he'd better let Jack know, he began to write a new email.

Hey, Jack
Just a heads-up. Your mum and I have discussed your news and she is so pleased that she has decided to pay us a visit. It would be good for us all to get together and meet your future wife and I'll be in touch as soon as we have Mum's travel dates.
Love, Dad.

He must make sure that he met with Helen first, to calm the situation. He wracked his brains for a solution on how to get Helen on board and happy about the union.

The courtyard clock struck twelve and Kate stopped writing, then stood up and went over to James' desk. She touched him on the shoulder. 'You seem engrossed,' she said.

James turned and saw that the class had broken up and people were moving about the room.

'Why? What time is it?'

'It's break-time. You seem distant?'

'I'm so sorry, I was miles away.'

'News from abroad?' Kate raised an eyebrow.

'Only an act of God would stop this confrontation,' James replied. 'Helen is heading this way.'

'Oh. I see.'

'Sorry, shouldn't bore you.' James closed his laptop. 'Have you had a good morning?'

'Yes, it's been very positive. Having another class member read my work is useful.'

Everyone had been given a section of work by a fellow student, to read and write a critique.

'Don't take it too seriously at this stage; it's only intended to get you to think from another perspective.'

'I understand,' Kate said. 'I can't wait for the afternoon session.'

For the second part of the day, James gave his students an opportunity to work on their own pieces or do more exercises and Kate chose to work on her novel, taking a seat by the window, making notes on a pad as she typed.

'Let me know if you want to chat any time before Helen arrives. Two heads can be better than one.' Kate touched James' arm again before moving away.

He watched her circulate with the other students and wished that he could reach out and pull her into his arms. Problems with Helen would disappear into oblivion when buried in the warmth of an embrace that he longed for. Kate had an aura of calm and kindness, combined with a bewitching twinkle and he imagined her luscious body lying across his bachelor bed. Her skin would be soft like velvet and her limbs strong as they wrapped around his body.

Stop it!

James was horrified that he'd let his thoughts run so freely, especially during a class. He stormed into the kitchen and poured a black coffee, wishing that he had something stronger to add to the steaming liquid. He stared out of the window where Alf was wheeling a trolley along the cobbles. James thought about Helen and shuddered at the thought of her arrival. Would she be inebriated and impossible to reason with? He blamed himself for her drinking and thought that he should have done more to stop her all those years ago, when it became apparent that it was getting out of hand.

A flurry of movement in the courtyard made James look up. Alf was buckling under the weight of an object on his trolley, which was covered by a sheet. James thought he should go out and assist the handyman but Hattie appeared and beckoned Alf to hurry. She grabbed two tapered wooden legs, sticking out of the sheet, and together with Alf clattered along the cobbles. Hattie's breasts and bottom bumped along and James was fascinated as he watched Alf push and Hattie pull, until they reached the building that had been the former kennels.

They disappeared inside.

James wondered what they were up to and wanted to go and investigate but his break was over and his students were waiting. With a sigh, he ran his mug under the tap and, leaving it to drain, returned to his class.

Bob was in his bathroom. He was looking forward to the art class that afternoon and as he stood at the sink and lathered soap over his hands, he stared at the mirror.

'What does an artist wear?' he asked his reflection and, tilting his head from one side to the other, visualised a cotton smock with jaunty cravat and soft felt hat cocked at a rakish angle.

He reached for a towel and dried his hands and, folding the soft fabric neatly, placed it on a radiator and stepped into his bedroom. He opened the wardrobe and flicked through the outfits. With nothing fitting the occasion, he chose casual slacks, a shirt and a cashmere sweater then added a liberal splash of cologne and hurried out of his room.

He didn't want to be late.

As he passed the Red Room he noticed Andy, Sir Hugo and Henry, sitting by the fire.

'Be along in a jiffy!' Sir Henry waved his cane.

Bob held up a hand in acknowledgement and continued on his way. He marvelled at the constitution of the brothers. They'd packed away the best part of two bottles of claret and a three-course meal at lunch and instead of slipping into a peaceful oblivion for the afternoon, would forgo their snooze to partake in yet another class. With Lucinda running the art class for the first time, everyone was curious to see what she had to offer and Bob could understand why the brothers remained alert. They were hardly likely to miss out and deny themselves a valuable source of gossip for discussion over dinner.

Earlier in the day, Bob had enjoyed a morning in pottery and, under Paul's careful tuition, was now the proud owner of a handcrafted mug, which he would decorate and glaze. He was proud of his work and hoped that it would impress his staff in London. He intended to make more and by the time he got back would have a set of personalised pottery as a gift for the team.

He stepped into the conservatory and opened the door. The wind had a keen bite and as Bob hurried into the courtyard, he wished that he'd put a coat on.

A sign hung off the wrought iron gates: **Art Class – This Way**.

An arrow pointed towards the last building and Bob raced on until he reached a stable-style door. He grabbed the handle and stepped in.

'Close the door!' Lucinda commanded. She stood in the centre of the room and struck a pose.

Barefoot and dressed in a long white robe, she ignored the no smoking rule and held a cigarette holder high in one hand, whilst resting the other, bangle encased, on her bony hip. Smoke rings rose towards the ceiling and Bob fanned his hand. He was startled by Lucinda's blood-red lipstick and kohl-lined eyes. Her skin looked blue in the dimly lit, icy-cold room and Bob shivered, wondering if they would be painting scenes from a morgue.

Chairs were placed in a circle and as he sat down he picked up a selection of drawing implements, including an artist's pad, which he balanced on his knee.

'There's plenty of blankets if anyone feels the chill.' Lucinda pointed to several rugs in a corner, piled beside a heater from where a distinct smell of old damp fur wafted.

It was freezing.

Bob looked around and saw that the group appeared

mummified, with only arms and heads sticking out of layers of canine-smelling blankets. Some doodled on their pads as they waited for the session to begin. A thin layer of dust lay on the windowsills and floor and as Bob studied pictures on the walls he realised, to his surprise, that they were covered entirely with photographs of dogs.

Stuck to every nook, cranny and expanse of brick were images of hounds of all breeds. Retriever Labradors with bright eyes and wagging tails stood proud, alongside handsome beagles and bulldogs. Bob was open-mouthed as he stared at dogs of days gone by, when the hotel was full of shooting parties and this room was a five-star doggy kennel, housing them all. He knew that Alf, Jo's handyman, had been her former gamekeeper in charge of the dogs and Alf clearly had an obsession. His smiling face was captured in many photographs as he grinned for the lens, crouched beside his doggy friends, including West Highland Bella and Winston Royal of Windsor, fine examples of pedigree canines who'd tramped the local moors with their masters, before returning to Alf's care in the comfort of the kennels at Kirkton House.

Bob scanned the walls and his eyes were wide when he saw that Bunty was also honoured. Alf's show must go on and the pretty puppy had been captured, sitting on the lawn, dressed in a familiar jewelled collar.

'Stop daydreaming!' Lucinda snapped. She threw a rug in Bob's direction. 'Put this over your knees and pay attention.'

Bob hastened to do as he was told. He tried not to recoil as ancient hairs from the coats of many a fine gun dog stuck to his cashmere sweater and slacks.

Lucinda paced the room.

'Today's lesson will be an opportunity for self-expression,' she said, scowling as the door opened and Sir Henry and Hugo, in full winter gear, trundled in. Waving her arm at the last remaining seats, she waited while they settled.

'I want you to react to your inner feelings and put down on

canvas what you are about to see.' She motioned to the centre of the room. A white sheet covered a lumpy object on a velvet-covered chaise longue. There was an excited murmur as students, confined by their layers, struggled to sit up and take a closer look.

'I cannot teach creativity where it does not exist and this is your chance to show me what you can do.' Lucinda picked up a brush from a large pine easel. 'I too will be creating an image and discussion will follow the session.' She walked over to an arc lamp and turned it on. Light pooled over the chaise. 'You must draw what you see and I want absolute silence for the next hour.'

Budding artists shuffled and coughs could be heard as nervous throats were cleared.

Taking her position by the chaise, Lucinda reached for the sheet and tugged. As the cover fell away, Bob's hand flew to his mouth as he tried to stifle a gasp.

The room was silent as the students stared at their subject.

The naked figure of a full and comely woman reclined across the chaise longue. Her heavy breasts and exposed body left nothing to the imagination as she leaned back on the smooth velvet. She held a bunch of plump black grapes, which barely covered her pubic area. Bob reached for his pastels but his hand had begun to shake and the tremble jolted his fingers.

Suddenly, his sketching tools tumbled from his lap to scatter across the floor.

He glanced at the other open-mouthed students and, mortified with embarrassment, fell to his knees. As Bob scrambled to retrieve his pencils, he looked up and found that he was inches from the woman's face.

Eyeball to eyeball, they stared.

Without moving a muscle, nor distorting her features in any way, Hattie looked at Bob and gave him a knowing wink and as Bob crawled slowly back to his seat, he was sure that he heard her whisper,

'Eat your heart out, Mona Lisa!'

Chapter Fourteen

'I cannot believe that you did this!' Jo was furious. She stood before Hattie in reception and hurled a copy of the *Westmarland News* across the desk. Jo and Pete had extended their break to two nights and now, on her return, Jo glared at Hattie. 'What possessed you?'

Hattie glanced at the headline.

Boomers Enjoy Nude Sessions at Boomerville!

A painting of a naked woman, with the Westmarland fells and River Bevan meandering in the background, sat alongside an article announcing that renowned artist, Lucinda Brown, was in residence at Boomerville, a local hostelry that held creative workshops.

She'd produced her first local portrait, whilst staying in the North West.

'Renowned artist?' Jo pointed to the paper. 'Since when did Lucinda lay claim to that title?'

'Oh, it's just the local rag, pumping up a story to create a headline.'

Hattie scanned the article. She'd worked hard to get the journalist, a pimply-faced lad who'd been at school with her sons, to cover the story. The promise of a slap-up dinner at Boomerville with his equally spotty girlfriend had clinched the deal. Hattie stared at the portrait and smiled. Lucinda had done a bloody good job of catching a likeness and to use artistic licence and add a local background was pure genius. Hattie had visions of herself prostrate across posters, cards and notelets.

They would fly off the shelves.

'You can stop looking so pleased.' Jo was angry. 'I leave you for five minutes and the hotel becomes a den of iniquity; there are drawings of you plastered everywhere. Sir Henry and Hugo have been out in Marland looking for a frame shop for their own dubious efforts.'

Hattie thought of the crazy collection of drawings that had been displayed after the art class. Everyone was proud of the first work to come off their pads and over several bottles of wine and much praise from Lucinda, an area had been cleared in the Red Room to exhibit the drawings.

Hattie, naked as the day she was born, with the exception of a diminishing bunch of grapes, which had provided a snack during the life class, had been drawn from all angles. The class had shown a variety of styles and the results were impressive.

Jo rounded up the drawings and placed them in a stack on the desk. 'Bloody hell, Hattie, did you really need to put the grapes there?' She held a canvas to the light and stared into the drawing.

'The portrait is in the painter's eye. I never moved a muscle.'

'You could have kept your legs together.'

'I did.'

'Hell fire.' Jo squinted as she examined another drawing. 'Is that a rolling pin?'

'Lucinda said I needed props.'

'I hope that doesn't get in the papers.'

'Oh, come off it, Jo, it's hardly *Hello!* magazine.' Hattie threw the paper to one side. 'Let's face it, there's nowt interesting in the news around here other than the price of sheep, this will give the place a bit of publicity, mark my words. You should have a viewing gallery. They'll be queuing to come and see our artists at the coalface. Your food and bar takings will double. Be positive about it; I've done you a favour.'

Jo sighed. Hattie was probably right. The waiting staff had been run off their feet all day with visitors arriving for morning coffee, lunches and afternoon teas and the restaurant was fully booked that evening.

'Well, I suppose it wouldn't hurt to create a small display.'

'That's my girl!' Hattie grabbed Jo and held her in a bear hug.

'Have you asked Lucinda to do any more classes?' Jo pushed Hattie away.

'Yes, and she's booked up for the next month.'

'Permanently in situ then?'

'Afraid so.'

'Shall we have a livener?' Jo asked.

'You took the words right out of my mouth.'

'I wish it had been the rolling pin.'

'Keep up, Jo, the punters love it.'

The two women stared at each other and Jo began to laugh.

'Oh, Hattie, what on earth am I going to do with you?'

'It's what would you do without me that you need to worry about.' Hattie took Jo's arm. 'Anyway, I think I make a wonderful nude.' She picked up Lucinda's painting from the top of the pile and opened the door. 'I think this should be displayed in the bar.'

'It might put people off.'

'Are you mad? They'll be knee-deep as they queue to see it. You should name a cocktail after me.'

'Now, there's a thought.'

'The Boomerville Bend Over.'

'That's your next life class.'

'Lucinda's Leg-Up?'

'Not on your life.'

'Each to their own,' Hattie said. 'Lucinda clearly has talent and is the queen of our financial canvas. I say she stays in residence as long as she likes.'

Hattie reached up and, moving several liqueur bottles to one side, placed Lucinda's portrait on the middle of a shelf. She grabbed a bottle of wine and poured two glasses.

'To Queen Lucinda,' Hattie said. 'Long may she reign.'

Bob was exhausted. He lay on his bed and ran his fingers over the droplets of smooth stones that formed bracelets around his wrist. An hour's meditation had helped with his fatigue and in a while he would go for walk before he changed for dinner.

The workshops had proved stimulating and so far, his participation in cookery, pottery and Lucinda's life class had whet his creative juices and given him a taste for subjects outside his normal working box. He'd been terrified at the sight of Hattie, displayed on the chaise with mountains of pale flesh quivering almost as much as his shaking hand, but he'd steeled himself and, putting pencil to paper, had begun to draw. He was proud of his effort and thought that his 'Study of a Woman on White' had been a worthy runner-up, when Lucinda judged their work.

He swung his legs over the side of the bed and stretched, then walked over to the window.

It was late afternoon and the light was fading but as he glanced at the drive below he could see Andy. He was standing by his Porsche, checking his phone. Bob felt a deep dislike for Andy and he couldn't understand why the feeling was so strong. The man had been perfectly charming in Bob's company and other guests all spoke highly of the handsome widower.

Including Kate.

Bob thought of the wealthy entrepreneur. She had a warmth that attracted company and Bob failed to see why she had never married nor hooked up with a life partner who was worthy of her attention. How strange it was that some women of a certain age struggled to find love and ultimate happiness.

Bob thought of his own relationship with Anthony that had stood trials at times, but survived. These days the pair had a mantelpiece of invitations to gay weddings and blessings. Friends of similar age were mostly settled with a partner and, like Bob and Anthony, content with their lot. But Kate had much to lose if she fell into bed with the wrong man and as far as Bob could understand this had happened on several occasions.

He felt uneasy as he stroked the beads on his bracelet and began to utter a soothing chant. His instinct told him to keep an eye on Andy.

In the meantime, he had a call to make before he went for his walk. Anthony would want a word-by-word account of Bob's newly-found talents. He turned from the window and reached for the phone.

Jo studied the paperwork spread out on the table. Her extended break with Pete had put her back and she needed to catch up. She'd had a meeting with her accountant that afternoon and the overall outcome was positive. The financial forecast that they'd put together, following the first few weeks of trading, showed that Boomerville had the makings of a very profitable business. The old place had needed a large amount of investment to create the new studios and upgrade the previous hotel; maintenance was ongoing but, fortunately, borrowings were non-existent.

When Jo's husband, John, died suddenly, he'd left her with a comfortable amount of capital which had enabled her to revamp the buildings and relaunch her business as Boomerville. Jo looked over to a desk in the corner of the room, where a collection of framed photographs was grouped. In the centre was a picture of John and Jo on their wedding day. His handsome face beamed as he looked into his bride's eyes and Jo felt a lump in her throat.

She'd never loved anyone as much or as totally as she'd loved her Romany man and knew that she probably never would. Their romance had been all consuming and had stayed that way throughout their marriage, as they embraced the birth of their beloved son Zach, a half-brother for Jimmy, Jo's son from her first brief marriage.

Jo's eyes travelled to photographs of her sons.

Jimmy, tall and handsome, silhouetted before a Caribbean sunset, where he ran a fashionable bar in Barbados. Zach, mischievous and grinning from beneath a mop of dark wavy hair, holding a copy of his best-selling cookery book. She was immensely proud of her offspring and knew that John would be too, for he had loved Jimmy as much as Zach and treated his sons as equals.

But, after all the pain of loss, when she least expected it, love had blossomed again for Jo. Cupid had reached out and shot his arrow, wrapping her with affection from an admirer who'd stood in the shadows for years, waiting for his opportunity.

Pete had been in Jo's life for almost as long as she could remember.

When she was a young mother with an unpleasant divorce still fresh, Jo had bought Kirkton House and risked everything she had on building a business. Pete, a local garage owner, had been one of her strongest supporters and frequented the restaurant with family and friends.

They'd led lives in their own ways, Pete in an unhappy marriage, where he'd stayed loyal until his wife's death, and Jo, blissfully married to John. When both lost their partners, Pete's persistence to be with the one he had always loved eventually weakened Jo's defences and in time, she'd allowed him into her life. He'd never replace John, but Pete was kind and loving and would walk to the end of the earth for Jo if he had to. She felt lucky to have him in her life, in whatever form their relationship took. She felt good with Pete around.

After all, what was life without love?

Jo reached for her papers and gathered them in an orderly pile. She studied the figures, which showed healthy occupancy levels as some residents, booked for only a week, extended their bookings or booked to return at a later date. She thought about the people who'd arrived at Boomerville in search of something but with little idea of what that might be. Divorce, death and being single could be so unsettling on lives that had been full and rewarding. When the clock was ticking down, society slotted the more mature into categories many didn't wish to fill, and Jo hoped and prayed that Boomerville would bring fulfilment to the folk who passed through her doors. Life *could* begin again at any age and Jo vowed that she would do everything she could to help.

Bunty stirred in her box.

The slow beat of her tail pounded into life and in moments the puppy was up and skipping around. She found an object peeking out from a pile of toys and hurled it high, encouraging Jo to play.

'Come here, my beauty,' Jo said and Bunty grabbed her new toy as Jo scooped her onto her lap, gently easing it from the dog's mouth.

Bunched into a ball was a short length of pink coloured fabric, threaded with bright gold silks. Jo spread it out on the table and smiled. Hattie had wound the cloth around her body in an effort to create an Indian-style outfit to cover her ample chest, and in a fit of temper had rolled the fabric and thrown it on the floor. 'It makes me look like pork sausage!'

Hattie's efforts to enthuse Jo into making plans for a Balti evening had fallen flat and she'd stormed off. Now, as Jo stroked Bunty and looked at the cloth, she decided that she must show enthusiasm and support Hattie in her effort to bring variety to Boomerville. The event would be fun.

'Come on.' Jo placed Bunty on the floor. 'Let's go for your evening walk, we've some planning to do.' Jo grabbed a coat and soon the pair were heading out of the house and into the garden where, in the distance, smoke puffed from the tepee. 'I think we'll visit our favourite Shaman,' Jo said as Bunty shot ahead. 'I'm sure he'll want to add his blessings to the Balti evening.'

Chapter Fifteen

Andy made himself comfortable in the Red Room. He sat in a chair by the fire with the day's news spread on a nearby table and smiled at the two elderly men sitting on the opposite side of the fire. Sir Henry and Hugo, having enjoyed a liquid lunch, were discussing Lucinda's art class.

'Marvellous session,' Sir Henry said.

'I thought it would be all fruit and flowers,' Hugo replied. 'I'd no idea we'd get a full-frontal.' He looked at Andy and asked, 'Will you be joining us for future classes?'

'No, art's not for me.'

Sir Henry reached for his cane and leant heavily as he stood. 'Excuse me, gentlemen,' he said, 'call of nature.'

Andy watched the old man move slowly out of the room. He looked at Hugo. 'I prefer a bit more excitement online.'

'Never had much to do with computers,' Hugo said. 'Always steered away; I had a secretary to deal with that sort of thing.'

'Really? You should get up to date, it's how the world works these days. There's everything you could possibly want online and you can use one here. I understand that there's a class that teaches the basics.'

'What's the benefit then?' Hugo raised a bushy eyebrow.

'Chat-rooms, making contacts, that sort of thing.'

Hugo looked puzzled but Andy had piqued his interest.

'It's easy to find a bit of action, if you know what I mean.' He leaned forward and made a crude hand-gesture.

'I say, old son,' Hugo said, sitting up, 'do you mean what I think you mean?'

'All very discreet of course, no one can trace anything.'

'But there would be a full class of beginners?'

'I can help you use a computer out-of-hours.'

'Not sure I'd know where to start.' Hugo frowned.

'I could show you and make sure nothing is traceable.'

'I'd be interested in giving it a go. Keep abreast of things and all that.' It was Hugo's turn to wink.

They heard voices in the hall. Guests were heading to the lounges to relax after classes. Hugo leaned forward and, in a conspiratorial tone, whispered, 'Can you set something up?'

'It would be my pleasure.' Andy picked up his paper. 'Go to the IT class this afternoon and I'll meet you later.'

Like taking candy from a baby! With a grin, he sat back to relax for the rest of the morning.

The computer room was dark and empty. The current group of IT enthusiasts, eager to learn how to silver-surf, had ended their day by mid-afternoon and were now enjoying afternoon tea in the Green Room.

Mature students, who'd bypassed new technology, were enthralled with the opportunities offered on the internet and the vast amount of information so readily available. Over mouthfuls of warm scones spread generously with jam, they chatted and shared websites and didn't notice Hugo, a new member of the group, slip away.

Hugo hurried through the garden. His brother was taking a pre-dinner nap and there was time to grab an additional hour on a computer. He doubled-back to the classroom in the courtyard and smiled when he saw Andy waiting by the door.

'All ready for you,' Andy said.

'Managed to get a key?'

'No problem.' Andy strode ahead of Hugo and, turning his back, used a specially adapted tool. Within seconds, the door was open. He flicked a light, then pulled out a chair for Hugo who shrugged off his jacket and sat down.

'I've found a site that will suit you.' Andy logged onto the open network and a screen popped up.

'I say, old chap ...' Hugo's mouth dropped as he stared at the images.

'Use the cursor and see if there's anything to your liking.' Andy was surprised that Hugo was able to easily negotiate the website and he pulled up a chair.

Hugo's eyes lit up. The website was a winner!

That afternoon, while Hugo was at the IT class, using images that he'd copied from several risqué sites, Andy had built a site and uploaded it to a temporary server. Adding captions to encourage Hugo, the website was custom-made to fulfil Hugo's earthy fantasies but little did he know that he was the only voyeur.

'Do the ladies ever interact?'

Andy smiled. This was easier than he'd anticipated. 'If you read the small print it tells you to post a photograph and then you can start an online chat.'

'How the devil can I do that?'

'There's a camera on my laptop.'

Hugo looked puzzled. 'Camera?'

'It might be better if you used my laptop in the privacy of your room.'

'Damn decent of you. Would you mind?'

'We men must stick together.' Andy stood up and slapped Hugo on the back. He'd heard footsteps outside and was keen to clear their browsing history. 'Let me log off for you.'

Hugo grabbed his jacket and watched Andy's fingers fly over the keyboard. In seconds the screen was blank and all data removed.

'Probably best if we set this up when Sir Henry is otherwise engaged.' Andy ushered Hugo out of the room.

As they stepped into the courtyard, the pair collided with Bob.

'I didn't know there was a class at this time of day,' Bob said. 'I was taking a stroll before dinner.'

'Hugo left his jacket, we came back to get it.'

'Yes, it was forgetful of me.' Hugo held out a pile of tweed, giving Andy an opportunity to lock the door with his illegally adapted key. Another valuable trick he'd learnt in prison.

'It's nippy out here.' Andy turned to face Bob. 'Make sure you button your coat.' He took hold of Hugo's elbow and walked away.

'Do you think he suspects?' Hugo asked as they hastened along.

'Not at all. Would you like to meet up again tomorrow?'

Strike while the iron is hot!

'Henry has booked us on the Indian dinner outing but I can always cry off.'

'Me too.' Andy remembered that there was a trip arranged to a local restaurant and many of the residents would be out for the evening. 'I'll bring my laptop to your room.'

'Now, that's something to look forward to.' They'd reached the hotel and Hugo made a beeline for the bar. 'Care to join me for a bracer?'

'I don't mind if I do; I'll have a large scotch.'

As Hugo ordered their drinks, Andy looked at the clock above the bar and realised that he hadn't got long. He'd arranged to meet Kate in her room for a pre-dinner drink and whatever else was on offer. He thought of her creamy white skin and inviting smile and decided that it would be good to celebrate his successful day. With the additional con nicely in place, Andy felt a surge of excitement. He wouldn't need the help of a line of coke, nor a little blue pill to satisfy Kate and he might even enjoy the experience.

Hugo appeared with two large drinks. 'Cheers,' he said. 'To excitement!'

Andy returned Hugo's toast, his dark eyes shining. 'To excitement,' he replied, 'in whatever form it may take.'

Chapter Sixteen

A new morning dawned over the rooftops at Boomerville, where the vibrant greens of late summer were now replaced by the drama of autumn. Gold, red and orange leaves tumbled along footpaths surrounding the garden and unlike previous days, recent cold winds and rain had been set aside by mother nature and a brilliant sun burst through in a fanfare of colour and light.

Guests were taking advantage of the unseasonal weather and many cast their overcoats to one side as they enjoyed a post-breakfast walk within the sheltered walls. One or two had picked up croquet mallets and knocked a heavy wooden ball across the lawn, cheering loudly when it found its way through a hoop.

Jo and Bob, who were also enjoying a brisk constitutional, joined in with the cheering and Bob clapped as a ball whizzed by, to tunnel through two hoops, before hurtling with a splash into the pond. Bunty teetered on the edge and woofed at the water where the ball had disappeared.

'Extra points for a dunk?' Bob asked.

'Another job for Alf,' Jo said. 'People discard the most unusual things in the pond, the pump was blocked last week.' She watched a guest roll up a sleeve in an attempt to retrieve the ball.

'Are you going on the dinner outing tonight?' Bob asked as he skipped up the steps, taking them two at a time.

'I was going to leave Hattie to sort it out.'

'Is that wise?' Bob remembered the art class.

'She can't come to much harm at the Bengal Balti.'

'I wouldn't be too sure.'

'Then perhaps I will join you all.'

Hattie had laid on a courtesy coach to transport residents and the cookery students were hoping to pick up ideas for their

Taste of the Raj evening, which Jo had confirmed would take place soon.

'I went to see the Shaman last night,' Jo said.

'How exciting, darling, did you learn anything?'

'To be honest, I didn't linger; he wanted me to vape with him and offered something that smelt very strange.'

'Electronically?'

'God no, he threw a brownish weed on some red-hot stones and as he started to inhale his eyes lit up and he began to chant. I thought it was time to leave.'

'Sounds like fun to me; we really ought to go along to one of his sessions.'

'Yes, you're right. I shouldn't endorse the class if I haven't experienced it. Guests who go to his sessions say they feel like they've gained a new lease of life. Hattie did one before we opened Boomerville and I asked her to research the Shaman's course.'

'Did she enjoy it?'

'Hard to say. She went missing for three days and came back with an eagle tattooed on her bottom. She couldn't sit down for a week.'

'The eagle has landed.' Bob giggled.

'He may not take flight again.' Jo thought about the weary old eagle who would end his days in the soft folds of Hattie's slowly drooping posterior.

'Well, I'm up for it,' Bob said. 'I'm having a marvellous time at Boomerville and I think your business is pure gold. You're putting a new spring in everyone's step.'

'Oh, I do hope so. I just want everyone to be as happy as I am. I love what we do here.' Jo turned to call out to Bunty. 'But we should be getting back, classes are about to start.'

'I thought I might have a dabble at creative writing,' Bob said as Bunty scampered ahead.

'Good idea, the students love James. He's a great tutor and you might pick up a new skill.'

'He is rather dashing, never mind the writing; I could sit and gaze at him all day.'

'No flirting with our tutors, please.'

They'd reached the steps and Jo took Bob's hand as she negotiated the incline.

'I can keep an eye on Andy Mack in class today,' Bob said.

'Hattie calls him James Bond. Do you think he's dashing too?'

Bob stopped. 'I get a very bad feeling about him.'

'Really? I think he's a sweetie and Kate is very smitten. Do you think Boomerville might get its first engagement in the coming weeks?'

'I think she needs to be wary.'

'Oh, I don't think so, they seem a perfect match.'

'Well, we'll see.'

They crossed the lawn. With classes about to begin, it was empty of guests. Jo took a last glimpse of the fells as she turned to go into the hotel. Patches of bracken had turned to bronze and a smoky haze gave the countryside an ethereal feel.

How she loved this place! Westmarland had magical qualities and Jo hoped that it would cast its spell on everyone who passed through her doors.

'See you later,' Bob said, and with a wave he headed off to the courtyard.

'Enjoy your classes.'

Jo scooped Bunty under her arm and went in search of Hattie, to begin their day.

Kate took out her laptop and set it on a table under the window. The view followed the slope of the courtyard where beyond an open door leading to the end of the garden, the fells were framed in a cameo image. For a moment, she was lost in the mist that rose under the morning sun, curling its way through the rise of the hills.

'You're deep in thought.' Bob stood alongside and followed her gaze.

'It's so beautiful here,' Kate said. 'I want to leave the class and go walking.'

'Oh, don't do that, I hear that you're making progress with a novel.'

Kate turned. 'Sorry Bob, I was miles away. Yes, I've started to write and I have to admit that I'm loving it.'

Bob watched Kate's eyes light up as she told him about her book. He didn't listen to the intrigue of the plot as his thoughts strayed to an earlier conversation. If Jo's mission was to help and motivate people, Kate was a shining example of a Boomerville success. The woman had found her mojo and whether she had a best-seller in her or not, Bob could see that Kate was benefitting tremendously from her time at the hotel.

'So, what do you think?' Kate looked expectantly at Bob.

'Er, I think it's a winner,' Bob mumbled. He hadn't a clue what Kate was talking about. 'Get it finished as soon as you can.'

'Do you really think it has potential?'

'Fabulous plot, darling, let me throw a launch party for you in London.'

'Oh, that's light years away. I'd have to write and finish the manuscript and find a publisher.'

'Well, I have contacts; give me a copy when you've finished.'

Bob thought of the many events that Anthony hosted at his theatre for authors and publishers. It was never what you knew in the business, more who you knew and how to get to them.

James joined them and welcomed Bob to the class. 'It's great to see you,' he said. 'The morning is generally a tutorial with students free to do their own thing in the afternoon. I help wherever I can.' James looked at Kate. 'This lady is an inspiration; showing us what one might get out of the course. She's begun a novel.'

Bob had a tingly feeling in his wrist and reached out to stroke his prayer beads as he watched James speak about Kate. Kate, meanwhile, had opened her laptop and began to arrange her notepad and pen, oblivious to the adoration that shone from her tutor's eyes.

The man is besotted! Bob thought as he watched James. Bob felt like an intruder as waves of desire vibrated in an aura so strong that he had to steady himself by holding on to the back of a chair.

'Come and sit down and we'll get started,' James said and indicated that Bob join the class. As Kate turned, James held out a chair and made sure that she was comfortable.

The plot thickens, Bob thought as he watched the performance. How interesting! The tingle in his wrist began to subside and he muttered a prayer to his own precious gods as he looked forward to the day ahead.

Hattie sat in reception and stared at a list of names pinned to her clipboard. The outing to the Indian restaurant that evening was popular and she had limited the number of seats. Boomerville would be half-empty and Sandra, whose menu and the satisfaction of her diners was a matter of great pride, had cursed Hattie for stealing the residents away.

Hattie could hear the sounds of pots crashing beyond the kitchen door.

Biddu, Hattie's friend and the owner of the Bengal Balti in Marland, had promised a banquet fit for a king and Hattie smiled in anticipation as she thought about mountains of tender meat falling off the bone into an aromatic sauce. She leaned back in her chair and closed her eyes. Images of sweet onions gently sautéed with garlic, turmeric and garam masala swirled through Hattie's imagination as she licked her lips and mentally dipped a soft, warm naan into a dish of delicious Balti then into her welcoming mouth.

'You look like a goldfish.' Jo leaned over the desk and stared at her friend. 'Can you close your mouth or are you hoping for breakfast by osmosis?'

Startled, Hattie sat up.

'Bleedin' hell, Jo, you nearly gave me a heart attack.' Hattie's clipboard fell to one side. 'Do you have to creep up on folk?'

Jo ignored her. No point in explaining to Hattie that she was on a reception desk, a public place that required an alert member of staff.

'Have you had anything to eat?'

'I had a snack earlier but I'm giving the kitchen a wide berth. Sandra is cursing me.'

Hattie, having polished off the buffet in the Rose Room when the breakfast guests had departed to their classes, pulled a face and rubbed her tummy.

'I'll go and order a bacon buttie,' Jo said and turned to open the kitchen door. 'Coffee too?'

'Aye, plenty of sugar. I'm feeling weak.'

Hattie pulled her chair under the desk and picked up a pen. She began to check that everyone had paid in advance for their meal and transport that evening.

'Just Sir Henry to cough up,' Hattie said when Jo returned. 'I'm surprised that Hugo isn't going. I thought the dinner would have been right up his street.'

'Perhaps he prefers Sandra's cooking,' Jo replied. She placed two mugs of coffee on the desk.

'Good job some bugger does!' A hand curled around the door as Sandra held out a plate stacked with bacon sandwiches. 'This'll keep tha going 'til your Indian nosh tonight.'

The door closed with a bang.

'I think you might have upset her.'

'State the bleedin' obvious, why don't you.'

'What's the transport tonight?' Jo asked.

'William's Wheels.' Hattie dabbed at a trail of tomato ketchup on her chin.

'I thought he retired years ago?'

'Aye, but he's bringing a vehicle back to life as a favour for me.'

In days gone by, William's company had been the transport

of choice for the Westmarland elite and many an outing to the races at York and Cartmel, or a social county event, had been catered by William's fleet.

'His coaches should be in a museum.'

'Like most of our residents,' Hattie said as she eyed the last sandwich. 'Are you eating that?'

'No, you go ahead.'

Hattie continued to munch as she perused the total revenue for the trip. 'We'll make a decent profit tonight, so never mind lost money in the dining room. Biddu has given me a cracking deal on the Balti.'

'Well, as long as William gets us there and back safely and the guests have a memorable meal.' Jo picked up the mugs and plate. 'Don't forget to do a list for the wholesaler for our Indian evening; it'll come around quickly and I don't want to leave everything to the last minute.'

'Got your outfit?'

'No, I'm not sure what I'll wear.'

'We'll be like a couple of Bollywood Belles.' Hattie grinned. 'I can see this as a regular event.'

'I'm not sure Boomerville is ready for that.'

'I might set up a couple of belly-dancing classes to warm everyone up.'

Jo sighed. Hattie's imagination was running wild as usual and there was no saying where it might go. 'Let's just enjoy the evening tonight, then plan carefully ahead.' She turned to go into the kitchen.

'We certainly will plan carefully,' Hattie whispered with a smile.

Chapter Seventeen

Andy ignored a knock on his bedroom door and puffed on a cigar gripped between his pearly teeth as his fingers flew across the keys on his laptop. Housekeeping could wait. He had no need of a maid to clean his room. Not unless she was nubile, sexy and willing, with a spare hour to indulge in the fantasies he was creating for Hugo on the screen.

For Hugo was like putty in his hands.

Earlier in the day, they'd managed another session on Andy's laptop and tonight he'd set it up for Hugo to use in his room, while Sir Henry went out on the dinner trip. Hugo was competent with the website now and eager to participate more.

Andy sat back and blew smoke to spiral through the open window as he thought about plans that would soon reach a conclusion. Hugo would be ripe for the picking with two or three more sessions. The trap was set and the old boy would fall straight in. As for Kate, her finances would peel open as easily as her lovely long legs. He only needed an hour or so on her computer and he'd crack the passwords to her accounts.

But finding the opportunity to delve into Kate's private affairs was proving more difficult than Andy had expected. She carried her damn laptop around all the time, using every opportunity to pen her ridiculous novel. He could sneak into her room when she went on a walk and hope that it was there, but there was no certainty that she'd be gone long enough.

Nor could he time her return.

What he really needed was to arrange accommodation for both of them. It made sense to be sharing now that they were sleeping together, not sneaking about the corridors at all hours.

But so far, Kate had avoided the subject of room sharing and to complicate matters further, she was a light sleeper and he'd have to find an opportunity to slip a couple of sleeping tablets into her nightcap. If she was comatose it would clear the way for a nocturnal trip into her bank accounts. He needed to crank up the chase and go all out to win Kate's total affection. A few clues to her financial status would ease his forensic search when the time came to hack her computer and with enough alcohol, pillow talk might glean this.

Andy could almost taste the rich pickings and the Caribbean was calling. Fantasy was soon to become reality and with Kate and Hugo's dosh nestling safely offshore, Andy could sit back and take life easy.

Until the money ran out and his next victims came along.

A knock on the door disturbed him. The handle turned and Andy spun around.

'Oh, I'm sorry, I thought you were out.' A middle-aged woman appeared.

Andy looked at the weathered face and long white overall. Housekeeping didn't live up to his fantasy. He waved his hand in dismissal then threw his cigar out of the window. The cleaner could wait. He had a website that needed final touches and an old man to entice. If he was finished by lunchtime, he would seek Kate out and over a glass of chilled wine blind her with charm then send her back to her writing with a head full of promises and a heart full of hope.

And soon, stored neatly in his memory, a list of her accounts!

Andy decided to select a suitable outfit for the day and dressed carefully in a smart cotton shirt and navy trousers, then rummaged around in a drawer until he found a pair of diamond cufflinks, a gift from a previous lover. The gems were dazzling.

He looked in the mirror and struck a pose.

With both hands cupped around the cufflinks, Andy made the shape of a gun with his fingers and pointed it in the air. The reflection reminded him of James Bond and the gems felt good.

Diamonds Are Forever!

With a knowing smile, he clicked the gun.

Chapter Eighteen

Darkness descended on Boomerville and only a sliver of light lit the sky, where the silver crescent of the new moon sat in a mass of inky black cloud. Evening traffic wound its way in a steady stream through the village and past the entrance gates to the hotel. A coach had slowed, causing weary commuters to pause on their homeward journey and with a flash of neon, the coach indicated and turned onto the driveway.

The old Marland transport vehicle was emblazoned with large gold letters on each side, announcing the name of its owner, *William's Wheels*. It cruised to a halt and the driver, complete with uniform and hat, silenced the engine.

Hattie appeared at the front door and waved. She had a grin as wide as the moon and stood resplendent in a sari, which was wrapped around her waist and draped across one shoulder, baring her midriff, as it fell softly to the ground.

'Charabanc for Boomerville!' the driver called out and leapt onto the gravel. 'Didn't recognise thee,' he said, when he saw Hattie and moved forward to plant a kiss.

'Look out, Willie,' Hattie said. She jumped back to avoid William's rough embrace and pointed to a red dot in the middle of her forehead. 'You'll smudge my bindi.'

'Thought you'd cut tha' self.'

'Very funny,' Hattie said. She touched the dot with her finger and frowned as a waxy red substance came away on her skin. Hattie knew that lipstick was not the dye of choice used by Hindu women for their bindi spot but she'd needed to improvise.

Residents, who'd been waiting in the hallway, poured out of the hotel and, as they wrapped scarves tightly and buttoned their coats, Hattie stood back and beckoned them onto the coach. 'Form an orderly queue, there's plenty of room for everyone.'

William doffed his cap and helped the ladies climb up and into the elderly vehicle while Sir Henry, wrapped in a muffler and sporting a trilby, held up his cane and called out, 'By jingo, that's a beauty!'

'The finest in my fleet.' William paused as Sir Henry admired his coach. 'She's a 1946, AEC Regal.'

'Daimler chassis?'

'Aye and a five-cylinder diesel engine.'

'Brush coachworks, one of the best they made.' Sir Henry's eyes glazed. He was back in the heydays of his youth, when together with his brother, motor vehicles and engines were a passion as they roared around the family estate.

'Never mind all the chit-chat,' Hattie said as she helped Sir Henry find a seat then plonked herself on the front row beside William.

'I didn't realise that it was fancy dress.' Jo appeared on the steps.

'Just getting everyone in the party spirit.'

'Aren't you going to be cold in that get-up?'

'Got two pairs of long johns hidden under here.' Hattie swept her sari to one side to reveal thermal clad thighs. 'Come on, Lucinda!' Hattie called out as the artist grabbed a handrail unsteadily. 'Smacked off her tits,' Hattie whispered to Jo. 'She's been in with the Shaman all afternoon.'

Lucinda, wrapped in an old blanket that she'd taken from her art class, weaved down the aisle and fell onto a seat next to Sir Henry. She grinned foolishly and took the old man's hand.

'Waggons roll, Willie!' Hattie said.

The coach moved off and Jo gripped her seat as Willie thrust his vehicle forward and hit the accelerator with a polished boot. In his youth, he'd been known as Whirlwind Willie, and in their younger days, a ride with Willie had been a big part of the thrill of a day's outing for Jo and Hattie.

'Should we have a sing-song?' Hattie said.

'Have you brushed up your Indian repertoire?' Jo asked.

'Only thing I know is "Vindaloo" by Fat Les.'

'Perhaps you should save it for the way home.'

Hattie reached down and pulled out a box from under her seat. She fumbled with the lid. A spicy smell wafted down the coach, combined with the strong smell of diesel.

'Just going to hand these out.'

'What are they?'

'I got Sandra to knock some appetisers up, whet everyone's appetite.' Hattie stuffed a samosa in Willie's mouth as she passed.

Jo watched as Hattie began a belly dance. Faces lit up as guests, eye level with Hattie's wobbling belly button, tucked in to a handful of spicy treats.

Kate was in the second row and as Hattie began to lead everyone in a chorus of, "Boom Shack-A-Lack", she slipped out of her seat to sit beside Jo.

'This is a great outing,' Kate said and bit into an onion bhaji.

'Yes, it makes a change for everyone to get out for the evening.' Jo was watching Willie crank through the gears and winced as the old cogs squealed.

'I haven't had an Indian meal for ages.' Kate licked her lips and searched for a tissue in her bag.

'Well, prepare yourself for a feast,' Jo said as she braced her body against the lurch of the coach which Willie had forced to career around a bend at speed. 'Hattie regularly frequents the Bengal Balti and I am sure they'll roll the red carpet out tonight.'

'How lovely. I had a very light lunch so I'm looking forward to dinner.'

'Is Andy not joining us?'

'No, he doesn't like spicy food, says it upsets his stomach.'

'I'm surprised, a well-travelled man who looks the picture of health.'

'We met at lunchtime and he promised he'd wait up for me.'

'You seem to be getting along very well.'

'He's great.' Kate beamed. 'Everything I could ask for. I can't believe that he's come into my life. I certainly never expected anything like this to happen.'

'Good looking, single, intelligent and rich.' Jo gave a thumbs-up.

'I keep waiting for the bubble to burst.'

Kate thought about the conversation she'd had with Andy earlier. He'd been attentive as always, wanting to know how her writing was progressing and when she'd asked him how he'd passed his morning, he'd replied that he'd been looking at his investments and had asked Kate if she was confident that her money was working and what sort of accounts she held. Unused to sharing her confidential affairs, Kate had changed the subject and had been pleased when it was time to go back to class.

'I hope you're enjoying your experience at Boomerville?' Jo broke into Kate's thoughts.

'Yes, it's perfect.'

'How's the novel coming along?'

'Very well. I thought I was going to write a slushy romance but it seems to have taken a sinister twist and I don't know where the dark thoughts are coming from.'

'How interesting, crime is one of my favourite reads,' Jo said. 'Imagine, a best-seller that was born at Boomerville.'

'I don't know about a best-seller, getting it written will be a challenge, but I've wanted to write for years. It's amazing to think that I've started a manuscript and, with luck, will eventually complete it.'

'Well, I'm very thrilled for you. You've found love and in writing, embarked on something that gives you a great deal of satisfaction. My work is done.'

'I couldn't have begun to pen a novel without James.'

'He's a great teacher, isn't he?'

'The best. He's inspired me in so many ways.'

'I wish he could find someone to share his life,' Jo said. 'He had a rough time with his ex-wife and had a family to raise on his own.'

Kate thought about James and wondered if he'd heard from Helen. She was due any time and from what little information Kate had gleaned from James, she sounded like a force to be reckoned with. Kate hoped that James could make Helen see sense and accept their son's wishes. He was such a decent sort of man and Jo was right, James would make a wonderful partner for the right woman; he deserved to find happiness in love.

The two women stared out into the darkness and the winding road ahead as Willie wrestled with the mechanisms of the old coach.

The miles flashed by and a sign for Marland appeared in the gloom.

'Nearly there!' Hattie boomed as Willie eased off the accelerator and coaxed the vehicle into the town. Hattie grabbed the back of Willie's seat and leaned in to show him where to park. 'Toot your horn,' she said and in moments, Biddu appeared on the restaurant steps.

He leapt back as Willie swerved to a halt.

'Thank God.' Jo let out a sigh as the tyres on Willie's coach burned into the road. Her hands were clenched in her lap and she flexed her fingers as she stood. Willie's driving certainly hadn't improved over the years.

'Biddu, me old mucker.' Hattie grabbed her sari and ran down the steps into the warm embrace of their host.

'Miss Hattie, how beautiful you look.'

'I didn't want to let you down.'

'We are honoured to receive you and your guests to our restaurant.'

Hattie stood with Biddu on either side of the coach door and helped the boomers to disembark.

'Welcome,' Biddu said and shook everyone's hand.

'I hope the Balti banquet is up to your usual high standard.' Hattie ushered the last folk off the bus and linked her arm through Biddu's. 'I'm absolutely starving.'

'I am sure that your evening will be full and memorable,' Biddu said and, with a beaming smile, escorted Miss Hattie into his restaurant.

James gripped a glass and poured a slug of whisky from the bottle of malt on the table in his living room. He'd just received a call from Jack and the explosive news that his youngest son had imparted merited a strong drink.

Jack had sounded anxious.

'Hi, Dad, I've been meaning to give you a ring. I wasn't sure when was the best time to, sort of, catch you.'

'Hello, Jack, it's good to hear you. Are you okay?'

'Um, I, er … we … need to talk.'

'I meant to say, last time we spoke, that Desiree is a very pretty name.'

'She's West Indian.'

'I can't wait to meet her.'

'She's pregnant.'

'Pregnant?'

'Yes, Dad, we're expecting a baby. We've just found out that Desiree is pregnant.'

James took a deep breath and sat down. He forced a note of cheer to his voice. 'Congratulations, Jack. You're going to be a fantastic father.'

'I'm terrified, Dad. I've really fucked things up.'

'Do you love her?'

'From the bottom of my heart.'

'Then there's nothing we can't sort out and you know that I'll help you.'

'Her parents will kill me.'

'Does Desiree love you?'

'Absolutely; we don't ever want to be apart.'

'Then her parents will get used to the idea and will love you as much as I'll love Desiree.'

'But what about Mum?'

'Leave your mum to me.'

'Thanks, Dad.' Jack stifled a sob. 'Thanks for being there for me.'

'Will you bring Desiree to meet me? Jump on a train and let's have a weekend together. I'll sort your fares out.'

'Are y-you sure?'

'Of course. I can't wait to see you both.'

'She'll be happy to hear this.'

'Not as happy as I am. It will all be okay, I promise. There's nothing we can't figure out and the sooner we make some plans the sooner you two can start to look forward to your future.'

'Oh ... that's great, brill, you're sick, Dad, really sick.'

James was thankful that his grasp of English slang helped him understand that Jack had paid him a compliment.

A cool dad.

It felt good. Perhaps he'd handled the call better than he thought.

But now, as James contemplated things, he felt anxious. A baby? Jack's news was shattering and James feared that he had a very rocky road to travel with his youngest son. He'd help Jack as much as he could but, remembering his own naivety, knew that it wasn't going to be easy. And how was Helen going to take the additional news? Her reaction to the fact that she was going to be a grandmother wasn't to be underestimated. Jack was making the same mistake that they'd made all those years ago and Helen would blame James.

But Tom and Jack had never been a mistake to James.

True, he'd never planned to have kids with Helen so early but James loved his sons with a passion and his life had focused on being the best dad that he could be, especially when Helen left. He had loved his sons from the moment they were born and had enjoyed their growing years, even when he was exhausted from work and coping with running a household on his own.

James frowned.

He hated arguments and knowing that Helen was going

to arrive any day made him anxious. She loved nothing more than a drama and would make a meal out of this latest episode, when all he hoped was that she'd be strong for Jack in his hour of need and not have the world revolve around herself.

Oh, well, what the hell, James thought as he prepared for bed. Tomorrow was another day and he had a class to teach. He felt that he was making good progress with the current group of students and was keen to know how Kate would develop the plot of her novel. Andy seemed to have stopped coming to the writing class and James was delighted. He'd been a hindrance and many of the women students barely paid attention when Andy was in the room. His absence was a bonus and allowed James more time with Kate when Andy wasn't constantly breathing down her neck.

If only James was breathing down Kate's beautiful neck!

He carried his glass into the kitchen and, as he drained the contents and placed it in the sink, he told himself that he must stop thinking about her. It achieved nothing. For Kate wouldn't so much as glance in his direction while Andy was on the scene. But as James climbed the stairs to his lonely bedroom, he knew that Kate would dominate his thoughts and be a major part of his dreams and with a frustrated sigh, he got ready for bed.

Chapter Nineteen

The following morning, residents at Boomerville who'd been out to the Bengal Balti the previous evening were animated as they ate their breakfast.

They'd much to discuss with those who'd stayed behind at the hotel.

Andy, who'd decided to get up, sat in the Rose Room and listened to the gossip which escalated as it whipped around the tables. He'd heard the original version last night when Kate knocked on his door a few moments after midnight. She'd arrived at the hotel with the other Balti diners after a hair-raising return trip on the coach. Willie had pushed the old engine to break-neck speed on the journey back to Kirkton Sowerby and the journey left Kate in need of a stiff drink. Andy welcomed her into his room and as she flopped down on his bed, feigned an interest as he poured them both a whisky.

He buttered a croissant and spooned marmalade onto the warm folds of pastry then summoned a waiter to refresh his coffee.

'Joining me in the art class, old boy?' Sir Henry raised his cane when he saw Andy. Hugo followed behind.

'I may,' Andy replied. 'Will it be an interesting session?'

'I didn't think anything could top the last class, but who knows what could happen today,' Sir Henry said. 'Let's hope there's more models lined up to whet our artistic appetites. Lucinda is a woman of many talents.' He chuckled as the brothers were shown to their table.

Hugo sat down and, placing a napkin onto his knee, gave Andy a conspiratorial wink. Hugo's session on the internet the previous evening had clearly been a success.

Andy sipped his coffee. Little did the old fool know that the 'woman' Hugo had been baring his soul to by way of email chat on the fabricated website was none other than yours truly, and with the help of the webcam on the laptop, a very incriminating set of photographs were ready to be printed off.

It had been far easier than Andy anticipated.

With photos of a well-endowed woman named Helga, copied from a porn site and dressed in a variety of uniforms from a nanny to a cook, Andy, alias Helga, had begun a dialogue chat with Hugo and Hugo had been very explicit, not realising that the camera had recorded his every move during the session. When Andy collected the laptop later that night, Hugo had answered the door in his dressing gown. Gone was the bizarre outfit that he'd worn for his chat with Helga and Hugo hadn't had the sense nor the knowledge to realise that he'd been framed. Andy had little doubt that Hugo would want to repeat the sessions and as he had time to humour the old man's fantasies, he thought that he might let things run for a little longer. After all, he had yet to crack Kate's accounts and it would be better to run both operations to a satisfying climax at the same time.

A hush descended and Andy looked up. Lucinda was making her way through the Rose Room.

'The Queen of Bengal, I salute you!' Sir Henry called out and one or two guests began to clap as Lucinda tossed her head back and ignored them all.

'Fine filly,' Sir Henry said with a sigh as he watched Lucinda's defiant back. 'I was worried about her last night when they took her away, but thank the Lord, she's back in the bosom of Boomerville.'

Jo sat in reception and held her hands over her face. 'You have no idea how embarrassing it was to find myself in a police station at that time of night.' She rubbed her tired eyes. 'Lucinda didn't seem in the least perturbed that she'd been arrested.' Jo had had very little sleep the previous night and her head was throbbing.

'Oh, don't get your knickers in a twist,' Hattie said, rocking gently in her chair.

'Knickers in a twist?' Jo was incredulous as she stared at Hattie. 'One of our guests lights up a spliff, leaps onto the buffet table, takes off her clothes and you say, "Don't get my knickers in a twist?"'

'She put her foot in the biriyani Balti, it was the best dish of the night, I was looking forward to a portion.' Hattie sighed. 'Biddu was mortified; it will take his wife hours to get the stains out of the cloth.' She remembered Lucinda kicking up her bare toes as lashings of dark red sauce splashed around the restaurant.

They both stared ahead.

'It was a pity that the local plod was in for a takeaway,' Hattie said. 'A few moments later and she'd have got away with it.'

'Constable Harry could hardly ignore a stoned woman when she offered him the biggest joint of cannabis his county has ever seen.'

'Shame he confiscated it.'

'He was going to charge Lucinda with lewd behaviour too. I don't know what possessed her to take off her clothes.'

'Good job I whipped me long johns off and managed to cover her up in time.'

Lucinda had gesticulated wildly and added to her embarrassing antics by prancing around the restaurant, stoned and half-naked.

'She's spending too much time with the Shaman,' Jo said, 'and that article in the newspaper must have gone to her head.'

'She's become a celebrity. The guests loved it.'

'Thank goodness I know Harry from the old days,' Jo said. 'He used to come to Kirkton House with the rest of the local force for their Christmas parties.'

'So you talked him out of pressing charges?' Hattie raised her eyebrows.

'Yes, thank goodness. He was very decent about it and let her off with a warning.'

'Ah.' Hattie smiled. 'A favour for an old friend.'

'Well, I wouldn't put it like that.'

'Hmm.' Hattie was thoughtful. She knew that Harry-the-Helmet, as the constable was known to his colleagues, was probably more concerned with the look she'd given him as he led Lucinda away.

Harry and Hattie went back a long way.

With a knowing nod, Hattie had mouthed the word, 'Truncheon,' and watched the fear sweep across Harry's face as he lowered Lucinda into the back of a squad car. The officer of the law had been in Hattie's embrace on many occasions and had many uses for his truncheon and most of them were unconnected to his police work.

Harry was very aware that one word from Hattie and his marriage would be over.

'Aye, always good to have friends in high places.' Hattie stood up.

'I do hope that Lucinda behaves from now on,' Jo said. 'She seems to be causing chaos.'

'The residents love it. Where else would you get such stimulation at their age?'

'I hope she doesn't stimulate anyone in her art class today. I see it's fully booked again.'

'She's promised to do a bowl of fruit and a basket of vegetables.'

'With a naked Sir Henry strategically placed?'

'The old boy would catch his death of cold.' Hattie yawned. It had been a late night and she was tired. 'I hope Willie got home in one piece,' she said, and stretched out her arms.

'Which would be more that the majority of our residents.'

'They had a ball.'

'Of course they did.' Jo shook her head. 'Death defying speed, racing through the countryside in the dead of night, in a cloud of diesel fumes that could kill you. I've never seen so many inhalers in use at one time. We're lucky there were no broken bones or asphyxiations.'

'Aye, it was a real white-knuckle ride.' Hattie grinned. 'Good old Willie, he knows how to keep the punters coming back for more.'

'If anyone can walk this morning.'

'Will you please take a chill-pill?' Hattie stared at Jo. 'Your residents are having the time of their lives. Those that have only booked a week or two, have booked ahead to come back for more. They never know what's going to happen next and are loving each moment of every day. You don't get this sort of excitement in suburbia. We're giving everyone a new lease of life.'

'Well, that's what I always intended, but not like this.' Jo scowled.

'Get a grip,' Hattie said. 'Everyone's happy and Boomerville's bank account is bulging.'

'Hmm, I suppose you're right.'

'I'm always right. Now I'm off to see the Shaman to see if he can come up with some entertainment for our Indian evening.'

'Could you ask him to stop supplying the residents with his aromatic herbs?'

'Yes, Jo, of course I will.' Hattie gave Jo a hug then opened the door of reception and made her way through the hotel. She'd have a look in at the art class and see what Lucinda was up to before she went to visit the Shaman.

Hattie glanced at her watch. It would be break-time any minute, she thought, and she'd not had a peek in pottery for a day or two. Potter Paul might have fifteen minutes to spare.

With a smile as wide as the walled garden, Hattie headed across the cobbles to the studios.

The Shaman could wait.

Chapter Twenty

In the dark depths of the mysterious tepee, Bob and the Shaman sat cross-legged on cushions and stared at each other. Bob was mesmerised by the man's green eyes and hypnotic yellow irises.

'Journeying is a diverse tool,' the Shaman said. 'It can enhance your spiritual growth and help you to connect with your cosmic guardians.'

He turned to a pile of stones that lay on a white-hot charcoal bed and tossed a handful of dried herbs and twig-like sticks across the surface. They watched as the sticks began to shrivel, creating a pungent smoke.

'Breathe,' the Shaman whispered and reached out his hands, as if to caress the smoke and guide it towards Bob.

Bob could feel his eyes beginning to smart as the acrid smell burnt the inside of his nostrils and he longed to stand up and thrust his head into the fresh air. But the Shaman held his gaze and soon, Bob's body became a powerless tool. His shoulders relaxed and any tension he was experiencing magically disappeared, as if soothing waters had bubbled up from the River Bevan and rippled through the meadow to wash over him.

'Concentrate,' the Shaman ordered and Bob obeyed. 'Allow your altered state of consciousness to access the hidden reality of the spiritual world.'

Bob, who was used to meditation, closed his eyes and let his thoughts wander. He thought about the uncomfortable aura he experienced whenever he was near Andy. As he became aware of his heightened senses, this seemed to manifest and an image of Andy, swathed in a dark cloak, swirled in his thoughts.

'There is a power amongst us that threatens,' the Shaman said. 'You must call on your guardian spirit to guide you from this evil.'

Bob breathed deeply.

He was enjoying the session now and sat with a beatific smile on his face, feeling far away from any evil, and wondered if his guardian spirit had popped out for a break during his last few days at Boomerville. The smoke was the sweetest thing he'd ever smelt and suddenly the world was a wonderful place. and he had the urge to reach out and embrace Andy's ghost-like presence.

'You must practice divination and act on your instincts; you are a receptive organ and the spirits will guide you.'

Bob was very happy to let the spirits play with his receptive organ and guide him anywhere they wanted and as he sat with his palms turned upwards on his lap, he smiled and began to raise his arms to embrace the swirling apparition.

'It is a sign!' the Shaman shouted and Bob wobbled. Shocked by the tone, he opened his eyes.

'You're not listening to your messenger.' The Shaman threw more herbs on the coals. 'He calls to you. There is work to be done, at this place and beyond, and souls to be protected.'

The smoke in the room thickened and as the Shaman wafted, Bob took deep breaths and felt a sense of relief, for his guardian spirit was no doubt hoofing it over the hills at that very moment and heading Bob's way to help him.

Together with the Shaman, he began to chant.

The vision of Andy, swirling in the background, grew fainter and the Shaman whispered, 'You have the power, use it wisely.'

At that moment, Bob felt that he had enough power to fly to the moon and back and wondered why he had waited so long to come and see the Shaman.

Forget about pottery and art, this was by far the very best class he'd taken.

Hattie ran across the courtyard and darted through the door to the garden. She brushed her hand across her skirt where two chalky palm prints were tattooed to her bottom. 'Damn!' she exclaimed and rubbed at her rear in an attempt to remove them.

Lucinda, who was strolling across the grass, called out, 'You're looking very flushed. Have you got a temperature?'

Hattie wanted to tell Lucinda to get stuffed but as the artist was surrounded by a group of students who were spending the afternoon outside, with their canvases in one hand and paint brushes in the other, she smiled and gave the group a wave.

'Everyone having a good time?' Hattie asked. She noted Sir Henry and Hugo sitting on a bench, both wrapped up in overcoats and scarves. Sir Henry held a brush at arm's length and appeared to be studying proportions before applying the brush to his canvas.

'We've been working on our landscapes,' Lucinda said and swept her arm out to the distant hills. The students looked frozen to the bone and one or two were shivering. 'I was expecting you to join us.'

'Sorry, but I got held up.' Hattie felt the cold too and wished that she'd had time to put her knickers back on instead of stuffing them in her pocket when Paul's class returned from their break, seconds from finding their tutor in a position that had nothing to do with his course.

She moved forward and peeked at the students' work. 'Lovely art, gosh what wonderful scenes.' She studied the daubs of paint on canvasses, held rigid in arms numbed by the Westmarland cold. 'I think everyone should head for the bar and have a hot toddy.'

At Hattie's invitation, bedraggled and weary artists suddenly found a new lease of life and Lucinda was shoved to one side as they stampeded across the lawn. Brushes flew and one or two dropped their canvas. Hugo helped Sir Henry rise to his feet and they hastened along behind.

'Bloody cheek,' Lucinda snarled. She lit a cigarette and, placing it in her holder, dragged deeply. 'I spend all afternoon sharing my skill and knowledge and just look at them, they can't get in the bar fast enough.'

'If they stay out here any longer they may never see a bar

again,' Hattie said. 'Get yourself in there too and I'll be along in a mo.'

Lucinda glared and blew a cloud of smoke into Hattie's face.

Hattie ignored the insult and, pinching her fingers to her nose, moved away. She could see that the tepee was operational, as silvery puffs, drifting from the top, wafted across the sky.

The Shaman was at home.

She needed to have a word with him about their Indian evening and perhaps, as Jo had instructed, she should mention that he needed to tone down the recipe for his herbs.

Hattie raced down the path and as she turned the handle on the wrought iron gates that led to the meadow, she saw that the canvas flap on the tepee had been flung to one side.

Bob skipped out.

He glanced around then leant down to grab a handful of wild flowers, which he began to toss, one by one, into the air.

Grinning foolishly, he started to dance.

'Bleedin' hell,' Hattie muttered. 'He's smacked off his face.'

She watched Bob prance up the steps of the gypsy caravan before pausing at the top. Placing the last of his flowers between his teeth, he pirouetted on one foot then flung out his arms and started to tap dance down the steps.

Curtains parted on the windows of the caravan and several faces peered out. A woman wearing a headscarf and hoops of gold in her ears smiled and waved at Hattie. Her skin was bright orange and as Hattie stared at the apparition she wondered if Hair and Beauty had a spray-tan offer that week. 'Nothing to worry about, Queenie,' Hattie called out. 'Carry on with your session.'

Queenie, a Romany friend of Hattie's who read Tarot cards at the annual horse fair in Butterly, nodded and gave Hattie a thumbs-up and Hattie returned the greeting. Queenie's readings for Hattie had been astonishingly accurate over the years and she'd been the ideal candidate to take clairvoyant classes. 'She probably saw this coming,' Hattie mumbled to herself as she turned to look for Bob.

Hattie found him dancing around the meadow. Jo was going to have a fit and Hattie couldn't let Bob go back to the hotel in this condition. Damn the Shaman and his herbs. She must do something.

'Oi!' Hattie called out. 'Fred Astaire! Get your dancing feet over here.'

'I'm singing in the rain.' Bob sang as he twirled over to Hattie.

'And I'll be singing in the sin bin if you don't get your act together.' Hattie shoved one arm under Bob's shoulder and tried to head him off and away from the caravan. But Bob was not to be stopped and, pushing Hattie to one side, broke into a repertoire of song and dance from all his favourite shows. Kicking his legs in the air and striding across the meadow, he belted out a medley.

'And all that jazz!' Bob sang.

'You're in bleedin' Marland not Chicago.' Hattie tried to grab Bob but he twirled away.

'Raindrops on roses and whiskers on kittens.' Bob held up a finger and Hattie looked around. He clearly thought that he had an audience. 'Bright copper kettles and warm coloured mittens …'

'Look, Bob.' Hattie grabbed his arms. 'There are no brown paper packages tied up with string and these may all be a collection of your favourite things,' she said, waving her arms vaguely, 'but it's time to get you safely back to your room.'

Bob shrugged Hattie away and ran to the gate.

Bursting through, he hooked his thumbs around a pair of imaginary braces and line-danced down the garden. 'Oh what a beautiful morning, oh what a beautiful day.' Bob arrived at the top of the steps and his chorus reached a climax. 'I gotta beautiful feelin' …'

A group of guests enjoying a game of croquet on the lawn looked up as Bob achieved full throttle. They held mallets and one struck a ball in the direction of the hoop nearest the pond.

But the player, distracted by Bob, mis-hit and sent the heavy ball speeding across the path where it hit a stone and bounced up. Hattie heard a whoosh as it sped in Bob's direction.

In a split second, she pushed Bob out of the way.

Bob heard the players call out and as Hattie lunged, he turned and missed his footing and fell headlong into the pond. Hattie skidded to a halt and gravel flew in all directions, pebble-dashing the guests.

Time seemed to stand still as Bob started to sink into the water.

'Help him!' Hattie screamed and everyone dashed to the pond to pull Bob out. He lay motionless, with eyes closed, and Hattie fell to her knees. 'He needs the kiss of life,' she cried and began to rip his shirt open to begin chest compressions.

'Everythin's goin' my way!' Bob woke up and Hattie fell back.

He looked around and smiled at the crowd, then jumped up and began to wipe at his wet clothes. 'Has it been raining?'

Hattie pulled herself to her feet and stared at Bob. 'Are you all right?' she asked. A lump had appeared on Bob's temple. He must have hit his head when he landed in the pond.

'Where am I, sweetie?' Bob looked vague.

Thank God! Hattie took his arm. He had a concussion, which could be put down to the fall and would explain his bizarre behaviour. Hattie knew that Jo would murder her if she thought the Shaman had been overdosing the guests again.

'He's fine,' Hattie told the anxious bystanders, 'just a little incident which can easily be sorted out.' She grabbed Bob's arm and led him away. 'Finish your game and we'll all go and get ready for dinner. There's hot toddy in the bar if anyone fancies a drink.'

The croquet players held up their mallets and formed a salute as Hattie and Bob staggered into the hotel.

Hattie looked back and sighed. Another bleedin' day at Boomerville!

Chapter Twenty-One

Jo woke early on Saturday morning. Harvest festival was being celebrated in the village that weekend and she decided that she would put together a box of fruit and vegetables from the garden to take over to the church.

She turned to Pete.

He was still asleep and she kissed him softly before slipping out of bed. A lump moved from under the bedcovers and Bunty plopped onto the floor. The puppy shook herself and skidded across the polished boards to land by Jo's feet, where she began to wag her stumpy tail.

'Shush,' Jo whispered, 'don't wake him.'

She scooped Bunty into her arms and carried her into the bathroom and placed her on a wicker chair while she dressed. Bunty was anxious to be off and, gripping a sock in her mouth, began to tease Jo as she watched her mistress pull on a pair of jeans and slip an old T-shirt over her head.

'I'm ready,' Jo said and tugged at the sock then tiptoed out through the bedroom and along a corridor until she came to the top of the stairs.

Loud snores reverberated from the floor above, where Hattie occupied the guest room. The rhythmic sound vibrated through the old building and Jo hoped that guests in rooms on the other side of the walls were sleeping as soundly as Pete.

She skipped down the stairs and found a jacket and boots in the utility room and, opening the back door, braced herself against the chilly morning. Bunty, ecstatic to be out, raced ahead.

'Tha's makin' a fine lil' dog!' Alf called out as he repaired a pane on the greenhouse window, which rattled about in the wind. He knelt down to rub Bunty's head. 'No breed as fine as a Labrador,' he said. Bunty rolled onto her back and her legs thrashed with delight as Alf's rough fingers tickled her pink tummy.

'She's a little treasure.' Jo smiled fondly.

'Is tha' wanting the crates filling?' Alf nodded towards a stack of old apple boxes piled along the outhouse walls.

'Yes, we could take half a dozen down to the orchard,' Jo replied.

'Want a hand?' a voice called out. Bob, cosy in a cashmere jacket, jogged across the lawn. 'Is there something I can do to help?'

'How are you?' Jo asked and looked anxiously at his temple where a bruise had spread. She reached out and gently touched the darkened skin.

'Oh, I'm fine, darling.' Bob waved her hand away. 'It's nothing, just a little lump. I've finally got some sense knocked into me.'

'But you were so unlucky to fall into the pond.'

'My own fault, I missed my footing. No harm done.'

'I think you're taking it very well.'

'Your poor guests were mortified. The croquet players thought they'd killed me.' Bob frowned. 'Funny though, I haven't a clue where I was before it happened.'

'Hattie said you'd been out for a walk.'

'Then I need to be more careful where I'm walking.' Bob grinned and, grabbing Jo's arm, linked it into his own. 'Now what are you up to with those boxes?'

The trio headed off to the orchard with Bunty trotting alongside. Alf produced a ladder and Jo stepped up.

'Mind tha' footin',' Alf said as Jo climbed and grabbed a branch. He gripped the ladder to steady her.

'Hold this branch for me, Bob, then pull it down so I can reach the apples.'

Bob reached up and, dragging the bough down, held on tight. In no time at all they'd filled one of the crates.

'Tha's blackberries in the meadow,' Alf said as he folded the ladder and placed it against the garden wall.

'We could get a punnet or two,' Jo said.

'My favourite fruit.' Bob grinned and they set off again.

In less than an hour they were in the hotel kitchen with their crates bursting. Sandra looked up with interest when she saw the seasonal offerings and Alf, seeing Gerald, the porter, disappeared for a chat about the workings of the industrial dishwasher.

'Select what you want and I'll take the rest over to the church,' Jo said to Sandra.

'Can I come too?' Bob asked.

'Of course, I'd welcome your company.'

Sandra chose her produce and Bob made a show of arranging a selection of fruit and vegetables. When Jo was happy that it made a good display, Sandra held the kitchen door ajar and they picked up the box to head off to the village.

'We plough the fields and scatter,' Bob sang as they walked across the courtyard. Jo, who had Bunty on a lead hooked around her arm, joined in and together, they headed for the church. 'The good seed on the land, but it is fed and watered by God's almighty hand.'

From the open window of his room, Andy leaned out. He could hear singing and, recognising the words of the hymn, thought that it was time for God's almighty hand to start reaching out in his own direction. He longed for a cigar but knew that there was little chance of lighting up, for Kate was asleep in his bed and if there was any scent of smoke, she would wake.

Her laptop was on a chair, underneath a pile of clothes and Andy felt his fingers itching to open the notebook and hack his way into its secrets. But Kate would stir soon and catch him in the act. Tonight, he decided as he watched her body move gently with each soft breath, he would grind a couple of sleeping tablets and mix them in a nightcap. When he was sure that she was out cold, he'd begin his nocturnal investigation.

Andy sat back. He was tired. Tired of the pretence and effort that it took to be Mr Nice Guy all the time. Kate was exhausting both in and out of bed and he was sick of listening to her rave about the merits of Boomerville and how much the residents were benefiting from their time there.

His funds were running low and Kate was expensive to keep

in the style that she expected. Suspicions would be raised if he stopped picking up their bar tabs or paying for meals and his regular order of flowers for her room was an expense he could do without. The weekly account at Boomerville was draining his funds and the Porsche, standing idle on the drive below, was a rental costing a fortune. Very soon, his money would be depleted.

Yes, Andy decided, it was time to start making a move. Hugo was ripe for the plucking and the photographs he'd collected of the old boy in many incriminating positions were already printed off and sitting in a large brown envelope, hidden in Andy's wardrobe.

The ex-MP would be mortified if they fell into the wrong hands.

Although he was no longer an active member of the Conservative party, Andy knew that Hugo had recently been vetted for nomination to become a life peer, a position that demanded the highest standard of propriety. The press would have a field day if the photographs came out, but Andy knew that would never happen as the Mulberry family would cough up enough readies to ensure that the prints never made the light of day.

Kate stirred. She opened her eyes and patted the covers. 'Why don't you come back to bed?'

Andy looked at her sleepy face where a smile formed on soft pink lips as she pushed her tousled hair to one side.

'It's Saturday, there's no need to rush anywhere,' she said and pulled the duvet back.

'I was thinking of going out for a drive.'

'We could do that later?'

'I thought you'd be writing today.'

'It's good to have a break; I can pick up again tomor

'I feel that I need to get out of here for a bit.'

'Well, should we go for a walk around the lake?'

'Yes.' Andy suppressed a sigh. He longed to ge
hotel to find a pub on his own and have some tim
all the idiots who constantly plagued him at

Kate was fast becoming as irksome as the rest. 'That would be lovely.' Andy pasted a smile on his face. He knew Kate wouldn't be satisfied until he got back into bed. 'Cup of tea?' he asked, and clicked the kettle.

'Mmm, please.'

Andy reached into his dressing gown pocket and felt for the little blue tablet nestling in the soft folds. Just time to swallow it and pep himself up before he got back into bed, where a performance would be expected. He made their tea and took a sip then, with no more reason to delay, turned to Kate and carried her cup and saucer over to the bedside table.

'On its way, my darling,' he said, through gritted teeth. 'Anything for you, my beautiful girl.'

Hattie stood in the bay window of the Green Room and watched the world go by. She'd enjoyed a lie-in that morning and, after a restorative breakfast, had checked all the bookings, happy that everything appeared to be in order. Saturday was a quieter day at Boomerville with guests checking out and many of those remaining venturing out to the tourist attractions in the area. Lucinda had taken a party of artists to see an exhibition at the grass-roofed heritage centre and gallery near the town of Marland. Situated in a former quarry, there were a variety of entertainments to be found there and Hattie knew that some of the party would drift off to the 3D cinema to watch one of the re-runs of James Bond movies that were being shown over the weekend.

At that moment, Hattie watched Boomerville's very own James Bond, who was holding the front door open for Kate. He reached out to take her hand and guide her across the gravel into his waiting car.

Andy Mack.

Hattie shook her head as she watched his slick performance. wondered why the man got under her skin, for he was ther than Hattie's favourite Marland toffee and Kate was clearly besotted. As the car roared into action and moved towards the gates, Hattie saw Kate turn and wave. She smiled and blew her a kiss. Hattie returned the wave, noting that Andy glanced up but completely ignored Hattie as he turned onto the road and sped away.

'Creep,' Hattie muttered. She walked out of the room and went to the front door.

It was a perfect autumn morning and the sun was bright as cars tootled along the road outside the hotel. Hattie opened the door and strolled across the drive. From her position by the hotel entrance she watched several vehicles turn into Kirkton Sowerby village, where a fete to celebrate the harvest festival was taking place on the green. Pedestrians mingled, families chatted and, together with a variety of four-legged pets, made their way across the grass to the activities. Colourful banners were strung across the many stalls and pretty bunting hung from the trees as villagers, eager to buy home-made bread, cakes and novelties, queued as they waited for a turn on the tombola.

Hattie watched the crowds and saw a man in a long dark coat edge his way through the gathering. It was the Shaman and he held a package in his hand. She prayed that he wasn't contributing to the cake stand. A couple of his cupcakes in the wrong mouths and there would be carnage.

She saw Potter Paul standing behind a stall.

He was selling his wares and some of his students had offered to help out. Hattie toyed with the idea of going over but there'd be no chance of getting him on his own.

She rubbed her eyes and yawned.

'Are we too early for a livener?' Sir Henry called out.

Hattie turned and saw the brothers standing by the door. 'I thought you'd both be at the fete,' she said and followed them into the hallway.

'Not on your nelly.' Sir Henry went into the Red Room and, spying a pair of comfortable chairs either side of the fire, made his way over.

'Henry doesn't like that sort of thing,' Hugo said and sat down beside his brother.

'Coffee and brandy?'

'Lovely,' the brothers replied.

People had begun to drift over to the hotel to enjoy morning refreshments and the reception rooms were filling as guests took their seats. Hattie gave the order to a waiter, then sat down beside Sir Henry.

'So,' she asked, 'are you enjoying yourself at Boomerville?' The old boy had looked pale and tired in the last few days, unlike his brother who looked perkier than ever.

'Having the time of my life.' Sir Henry raised his cane and smiled. 'Haven't stopped since I got here.'

'Perhaps you should take things a bit easier this weekend, put your feet up?'

'I don't want to miss anything,' Sir Henry said.

'I'll make sure you don't,' Hattie said and moved a pile of magazines from a nearby table as their drinks arrived. 'But you need to look after yourself.' She poured the coffee and placed it beside him.

'Bless you.' Sir Henry smiled and took Hattie's hand.

For once she didn't draw back and, as Hattie stared into the watery eyes, she realised that she was extremely fond of the old man. After all, she'd known him for years and he'd always been polite and charming in her company. A touch boisterous at times, but Hattie knew that she'd egged him on, and now, in the latter years of his life, she felt pleased that he chose to spend some of his time at Boomerville.

Hattie gave his hand a reassuring squeeze and he smiled gratefully. A wave of affection flooded over her and she felt an overwhelming sense of pride that she was part of the Boomerville experience. Jo was right in her vision, Hattie thought as she comforted Sir Henry. It was good to be alongside people as they found happy paths in later life.

'Drink up,' Hattie said, 'we want you on top form for the

cocktail party tonight.' She watched Sir Henry pick up his cup and saucer with shaking hands. 'There are guests arriving today and the restaurant is fully booked for dinner, so you'll have some new faces to mingle with.'

'Splendid,' Sir Henry replied.

Hattie gently took his cup and replaced it with the brandy. 'That's more like it,' she said as she watched him take a sip. Colour was restored to his cheeks. Hattie stood and as she turned Hugo's hand brushed against her bottom. She slapped him away.

'Still in fine fettle,' Hugo said as his eyes ran up and down Hattie's body. 'Any time you fancy a canter out.'

Hattie sighed. She wished she'd got the rolling pin tucked into her cleavage for she'd whip it out to deal with Hugo's roving hand. She had to give him credit for he never gave up, but recently Hugo seemed to be frisky at all times of the day and she wondered what he was up to, for something was definitely perking him up. She decided to leave the brothers to their drinks and, making sure that they were comfortable, placed the morning papers by each of them, threw a log on the fire and made her exit.

As she walked into the hall, the door flew open and Bunty, with a neckerchief of colourful streamers knotted around her collar, burst across the threshold, followed by Jo and Bob.

'Greetings,' Bob cried and smacked a kiss on Hattie's cheek. 'How are you today, dear Hattie?'

Hattie thought that Bob's fall in the pond, combined with the Shaman's herbs, had clearly unbalanced the man. He was far too full of bonhomie. She much preferred him when he was grumpy.

'Fair to middling, thank you.' Hattie stood back.

'We've had a lovely time at the fete,' Jo said.

'So I can see.'

Jo held out an armful of fresh vegetables and several packages of cakes.

'Like bringing coals to Newcastle.' Hattie scowled as she examined the offering. 'Sandra will be pleased.'

'I have to support the villagers and these are for me and Pete, not the hotel.'

'Look at what I've got,' Bob said excitedly. 'Just look!' He thrust a wooden staff into Hattie's hands. It was short and thick and beautifully carved with mystic symbols on one end.

'The Shaman gave it to me.'

'Fascinating,' Hattie said and examined the object.

'He says it's a symbol of authority, a tool for my spiritual journey and will help guide my path.'

'It'll come in handy on the tube when you get back to London.' Hattie handed the staff back to Bob.

'I think it's beautiful.' Bob lovingly ran his hands over the smooth wood.

'Anything happening here?' Jo asked.

'No, nowt, all quiet on the western front.' Hattie glanced into the Green Room where Hugo had his head in the *Financial Times* and Sir Henry was sound asleep. 'The restaurant is fully booked. James Bond has taken Miss Moneypenny for a spin and Lucinda is out with the artists. Everyone else seems to be doing their own thing.'

'Excellent,' Jo said. 'I'm going to see Pete. I'll catch up with you at dinner tonight.' She leaned in and gave Bob a kiss on the cheek.

'See you later,' Hattie and Bob chimed and watched Jo disappear down the hallway with Bunty following behind.

'Time for my elevenses,' Hattie said and rubbed her tummy.

'I think I'll have a nap,' Bob replied. 'I feel the need for a little meditation.' He caressed the Shaman's gift.

'Aye, you head off on a spiritual journey, just be careful you don't sleep on your staff.'

Hattie watched Bob climb the stairs, then made her way on her own spiritual journey to the kitchen and a plate of Sandra's shortbreads.

Chapter Twenty-Two

Jo sat in her dressing room and looked at her reflection as she dabbed a light foundation across her cheeks. 'I wish I could smooth the years away,' she said and touched the fine lines that crinkled around her eyes.

'You're beautiful,' Pete whispered. He stood behind her and held her shoulders, then placed a kiss on her neck. 'As gorgeous as ever.'

Jo looked up and reached for his hand. 'You're still full of charm.'

'Only for you, my love.'

'Let me finish here, I'll be down shortly.'

'Aye, I'll go and feed little 'un.' Pete gave Jo another kiss then headed off for the kitchen, where Bunty could be heard tossing her bowl across the tiles.

Jo brushed gloss on her lips and fiddled with her hair and, satisfied that she was ready, stood up and slipped into a long red dress. The dress had a tightly fitting bodice and fell from her waist into silky swirls. It was ages since she'd worn it but she wanted to feel glamorous that evening and it seemed a perfect choice.

Boomerville had exceeded all her expectations in the weeks since opening and Jo had decided that, as a thank you to her residents, she would spoil them with a complimentary champagne toast at dinner. Sandra had made a special cake, steeped in rum and layered with tropical fruits, and it would make a perfect accompaniment.

Jo was pleased that Pete had agreed to join the guests for dinner. He normally kept a low profile around the hotel and spent his days with numerous hobbies from tractor restoration to sponsoring aspiring motorbike riders, a sport he'd always been passionate about. Jo knew that he was happy to be with her whenever her schedule allowed, and she managed to find plenty of time these days with Hattie at the helm of the hotel.

She reached into a jewellery box and rummaged about until

she found a necklace, a thin gold chain with a pretty little diamond that nestled on her neck. It had been a gift from John and she smiled as she fastened the clip. A photo of her late husband sat in a silver frame by a lamp on her dressing table and Jo picked it up. Jo stared at his image and thought that her handsome Romany would be proud of the woman he'd loved.

Very gently she replaced the frame, turned off the light and went to join her guests.

The weekly cocktail party was underway with a full house at Boomerville. Many of the residents were now familiar, having shared tutorials, meals and social times and they mingled with tutors and new boomers who'd arrived that day, chatting about everything from pottery classes to the state of the weather.

Jo circulated and caught up with the news. It was a useful time to gauge how everyone was getting along and to ensure that they were making the most of their time under her roof. She made sure that newcomers had someone to talk to and were beginning to feel at home.

Andy and Kate sat by the fire and greeted Jo.

'Have you had a relaxing day?' Jo asked.

'Andy took me to Butterly,' Kate said. 'What a gorgeous little town. We had a walk by the River Bevan, then tea and cake in the Lemon Drop Café.'

'That's one of my favourite walks; I often take Bunty for a stroll by the river.'

'Excuse me, ladies,' Andy said and stood up. 'I'll be back in a mo.'

Jo and Kate watched Andy disappear out of the room.

'Everything all right?' Jo asked.

'Yes, he's probably gone to the bathroom. We drank gallons of tea today.' Kate laughed.

'How's the book coming along?'

'Most days it's writing easily but there are others when I seem to stare at the page.'

'Writer's block?'

'James says you just have to plough on when that happens. It doesn't matter what you write, something will eventually stick and you'll soon be back in the groove.'

'Sounds like good advice. Does it work?'

'Yes, it does. James is a good teacher.'

'He's coming in for dinner tonight.' Jo glanced at her watch. 'A table booked for three, with his son, Jack, and his girlfriend, Desiree.'

'Oh, that will be nice. I'd love to meet them.'

'I've known Jack since he was a small boy,' Jo said. 'James is a great father. It can't have been easy bringing sons up on his own but the boys are both lovely young men.'

They chatted about the classes and an upcoming exhibition that Hattie was planning to showcase the students' work.

'Sorry to abandon you, ladies.' Andy returned and put his arm around Kate's waist. 'Can I get you another drink?'

'Not for me,' Jo said. 'I just need to check on the kitchen. I'll catch up later.'

'She's a nice woman,' Andy said as they watched Jo walk away.

'I think she's an inspiration. Boomerville should be rolled out; it would have a terrific following in counties around the country. She could even go global.'

Kate began to talk about the merits of Jo's business but Andy wasn't listening. Having slipped up to Kate's room to make sure that he could find her laptop, he'd discovered it under layers of clothing in the bureau and was satisfied that he would locate it easily later that night. In the meantime, he looked wearily at the mature faces and decided that he might as well try to enjoy dinner.

Hattie was talking to Pete in the bar. Bob had joined them and to Hattie's surprise was holding his own in a conversation about motorbikes, a subject he seemed to know something about.

'It's Anthony's passion,' Bob said. 'No one expects a couple of queens like ourselves to don helmets and leathers but come Sunday in the Cotswolds, Anthony can be found careering around corners at top speed with me clinging to the back, chanting my head off.'

'What does he ride?' Pete asked.

'A Harley-Davidson, only the most iconic brand for my husband.' Bob smiled. 'He imported it from the States.'

'You should bring it up here,' Pete said. 'I'm a member of the owners' club and there are lots of meetings in the area. I'd be happy to ride with you.'

Hattie was fascinated. She saw Bob through new eyes, never having imagined his highly precious ego astride such a powerful machine. It just went to show that you should never judge a book by its cover, she thought, as she left the men to chat.

Hattie was planning to stage an exhibition of work by the boomers and was lost in thought as she went into the hallway. She was considering who to invite and thought that the local press might cover the event; perhaps the Mayor of Marland might attend too.

James had arrived and Jo was welcoming his family. She ushered them into the bar and called out, 'Hattie, would you be kind enough to take a drinks order?'

'My pleasure,' Hattie said and fussed around the party until they were settled and comfortable.

'Who's the pretty girl?' Hattie whispered as she slid alongside Jo behind the bar.

'Her name is Desiree and she's about to become James' daughter-in-law.' Jo opened the wine cooler, checking to make sure that there was plenty of chilled champagne. 'You remember his youngest son, Jack. They're getting married.'

'Aye, but I haven't seen him in ages. He's a grand looking lad. She's not from round here?'

'James said her family is from London.'

'Lovely features, pretty eyes.' Hattie fiddled about with glasses and ice as she poured a measure of gin for James and watched Desiree look lovingly at Jack as he chatted with his dad.

'Time to call the residents in for dinner.' Jo looked at her watch.

'Right-o, boss. Let service begin.'

James followed Hattie as she guided them into the restaurant. Jack and Desiree went ahead and, as they linked arms, James thought that they made a lovely couple.

They'd arrived the previous evening and James had liked Desiree from the moment she stepped off the train. She'd beamed when she greeted him and her smile lit the platform as she held out her arms in a warm embrace. The girl was no shrinking violet and radiated a confidence that made James think his son had chosen well. Whatever difficulties they might have to face, his intuition told him that they'd work together and now he looked forward to the challenge.

As they got in the car, Jack had asked about Helen and if she would be getting in touch to arrange to meet Desiree. James tactfully explained that he wasn't sure what Helen's plans were but would let Jack know when she made contact.

James ducked his head in the low doorway as they went into the Panel Room. He smiled as he recognised some of the residents who were on his course. But as his eyes travelled around, he suddenly stopped. Kate was sitting at a dimly lit corner table, where a candle flickered, highlighting the glow of her cheeks.

She looked up and saw James.

His heart lurched. She was so beautiful! James felt a magnetic pull and it was all he could do not to move forward and sit beside her. Kate gave him a wave and James smiled. But the smile fell away when he saw Andy, who had turned to stare at James.

The man's eyes were cold.

'You can stop for a gossip later.' Hattie took James' arm. She led him through to the Rose Room where Jack and Desiree were already seated. 'Bon appétit,' Hattie said and stood back to let a waiter take over. 'Enjoy your dinner.'

Jo looked around the restaurant. The resident boomers were coming to the end of their main course in the Panel Room, the smaller of the two rooms used for dining. She saw that Sir Henry was sitting next to Lucinda on a table of six with Hugo and members of the art class. Kate and Andy had a cosy table in the corner, while Bob sat at the head of a table of potters, with Pete at the other end listening attentively as they discussed fettling and flatware and how to crackle a glaze.

'All shipshape, boss,' Hattie said. She stood beside Jo and watched the diners. 'Sandra's ready with the cake and the lads are on standby with bubbles.' Hattie glanced over at two waiters who were pouring champagne into fluted glasses.

'I'm going to make a speech.'

'Aye, well don't go on for too long. This lot have a tendency to fall asleep if not constantly stimulated.' Hattie looked at Hugo who, catching her eye, blew her a kiss.

'The outside diners don't need to hear it but make sure they all get cake and champagne when they've had their main course.'

'Leave it with me,' Hattie said.

'Ladies and gentlemen,' Jo began and Hattie banged a fork against a glass. 'Could I have your attention for a moment.'

'Keep it down in the kiln!' Hattie nodded towards Bob and the room hushed as conversation trailed off.

Expectant faces turned to Jo.

'I just want to say a huge thanks,' Jo began. 'You're a special group of people because you're the first guests to have come to our newly revamped hotel. Sir Henry and Hugo remember us from the days when we were purely residential but now, with the very recent addition of many courses and classes to stimulate and entertain, Boomerville is a brand-new place which we hope will give you all a new lease of life and purpose when you leave us.'

'Hear, hear!' Sir Henry called out and held up his cane.

'This was a massive experiment. I had no idea if it would work or not. But with Hattie's help and encouragement over the last few weeks since opening, it seems to be doing just fine.' Jo turned and smiled at Hattie who had taken a little bow as waiting staff placed glasses of champagne on everyone's table.

'We may be getting older, but we're just getting better and you, as a group, are proving this. Anything is possible if we have the courage to try new things.'

'Well said, darling!' Bob cried.

'We have talent pouring out of our studios from budding authors to artists and creatives experimenting in a host of new projects. Who knows where all this will lead.'

'Especially if you take a trip with the Shaman ...' Lucinda drawled.

'So please raise your glasses in celebration and a toast to yourselves.' Jo beamed at the group. 'You are all official members of the First Boomerville Club, and I hope that you'll spread the word and go on to very great things.'

'Cheers!' the boomers cried out. 'To the First Boomerville Club!'

Jo and Hattie were engulfed as guests shuffled to their feet, pushed back chairs and raised their glasses, then moved around the room to congratulate each other and embrace.

'Bring the cake out?' Hattie asked above the noise as she ducked and dived, conscious that Hugo had left his seat and was heading in her direction.

'Absolutely,' Jo said and turned to Sandra.

Resplendent in a fresh white jacket and chef's hat, Sandra held a magnificent cake on a large flat board. It was modelled in the shape of the hotel with sugar caricatures of Jo and Hattie either side of the front door. A large sparkler was placed to one side, which a waiter lit as Sandra stepped into the centre of the room.

'Hurrah!' the residents called out and began to clap their hands.

What happened next happened so quickly that in the ensuing melee it was difficult to establish exactly what had gone wrong.

Suddenly Sandra, who had been pushed from behind, let go of the cake and it flew across the room. The cake landed on Lucinda who'd knelt down to talk to Sir Henry and, as it broke into a shower of fruity pieces in the old boy's lap, the sparkler ignited Lucinda's hair.

'Bleedin' hell!' Hattie cried and, grabbing an ice bucket, upturned it on Lucinda's head. The crowd gasped as Lucinda, with chunks of ice and a deluge of cold water pouring down her face, fell onto Sir Henry.

Hugo, who leapt up as the cake made its aerial descent, caught the figurines. 'Gotcha!' he roared, shaking the quivering models of Jo and Hattie in each hand.

Behind Sandra, a woman, unknown to the onlookers, began to scream obscenities in French.

'Où est ce batard?' she cried, forcing her way through the astonished boomers, peering into their faces with a maniacal stare. 'Où est-il?'

In the Rose Room, James felt his body tense.

He recognised the cry coming from the commotion next door. 'Stay where you are,' he ordered Jack. 'Look after Desiree.' He flung his napkin to one side, pushed back his chair and ran into the Panel Room.

'It's all your fault!' the woman cried out as she saw James. 'Why,' she slurred, 'why can't you let him 'ave 'is freedom? He's too young to be sh'tied down!'

As she lunged for James, with lightning reactions, Pete and Andy leapt to their feet. They pinned her arms behind her back and held on tight.

Helen blinked and glared at James.

Hattie, who had leapt to Lucinda's aid, stopped what she was doing and hissed, *'Get her out of here!'*

Jo was helping guests back to their seats and when she saw James she called out, 'My house, through the door behind you!'

James pitched forward. Helen was staggering and he picked up her feet as Pete and Andy propelled her ahead. In moments, they'd manhandled her through the Panel Room door and into Jo's lounge.

Jack stood in the restaurant and stared at the door as it closed.

'It's all right, Jack,' Jo said softly and touched the young man's arm. 'Let your dad deal with it.'

Jack looked at Jo. His eyes were full of pain as he turned and went back to Desiree.

'More drinks for everyone,' Hattie said and, with a hefty tug, removed the bucket from Lucinda's head. She winced as the smell of singed hair wafted across the room.

'I shall sue!' Lucinda yelled. She was purple with rage. 'Just look at my hair!' She pulled at her straggly wet locks, which were considerably shorter on one side.

'I think it rather suits you, old girl.' Sir Henry chuckled as he flicked the last of the fruit cake off his lap. 'Damn fine cake,' he said and popped a piece into his mouth.

As the disturbance died down and normal service resumed, guests returned to their seats and desserts were served. Lucinda, with a full bottle of champagne on the table before her, sat with Sir Henry. He stroked her knee in a comforting way, as she tied back her hair and gazed into his eyes.

'She's too pissed to remember,' Hattie said to herself. 'And we can send her to Hair and Beauty in the morning.'

Jo appeared and stood beside Hattie. They gazed around the room. 'Did that really just happen?' Jo asked.

'What?' Hattie said. 'Was there an incident?' She reached out and tucked her arm into Jo's. 'Welcome to the First Boomerville Club.'

Chapter Twenty-Three

As a new week began at Boomerville, James arrived early to prepare for his class. He busied about, placing notes on the table in the centre of the room. The morning's session would cover what James considered to be the first essential steps to writing. How to get into the proper mindset and the secrets of staying focused.

If only he could find the proper mindset to deal with his ex-wife! James knew that he needed to be completely absorbed in his work, anything to take his thoughts away from the events at the weekend.

For Helen had been out of control.

She'd been drinking all afternoon on her journey to Westmarland and James learnt later, from his local taxi driver, that she'd staggered off a train and into a vehicle at Marland station. Finding no one at James' house, she'd let herself in. James cursed himself for never changing the locks and imagined her searching around. She'd discovered a telephone number that he'd jotted on a note by the phone. It read, 'Table for three at eight', and it wasn't rocket science for her to work out where James was. Taking the same taxi again, as well as a good quantity of his whisky, she'd arrived at the restaurant, hell-bent on making a scene.

Thank God it had been dealt with swiftly but the damage had been done.

Jack took one look at his mother, as she was being manhandled away, and left with Desiree. James followed later when he'd calmed Helen down and Jo kindly offered a spare room for Helen to sleep it off.

The following morning they'd spoken on the phone.

James told Helen that Jack didn't want to see her. Jack wanted her to sober up and accept the fact that he was going to get married. When James told Helen that there was a baby on the way, she'd been silent.

Eventually she spoke.

'I'm going back to France,' Helen said. 'Tell Jack that I love him and hope that he'll bring Desiree to meet me.' James was confused. One moment she was against the relationship and the next she'd accepted it. Perhaps it was the booze causing her erratic behaviour.

James drove the young couple to the station and in the car park as they unloaded their bags, Jack held Desiree's hand and turned to his father.

'Mum needs to sort herself out,' Jack said. 'Don't worry, Dad, it will work out fine.'

James watched them walk away and as they turned to wave, he felt immensely proud as he stared at his son and future daughter-in-law.

The optimism of youth, he thought, as he placed the last of the notes on the table.

The door of the studio opened and Kate appeared. 'Morning,' she said. 'How are you today?'

'Where do I begin to apologise for my ex-wife's behaviour?'

'Oh, don't worry about that.' Kate took her coat off and hung it on a peg. 'I'm early. Is it all right if I make a coffee?'

'Help yourself.'

'You look like you could do with one too.'

'It would be most welcome.' James moved around the table and flicked a lamp on. He tossed a couple of logs in the stove and pushed a stack of books to one side. 'Let me help you,' he said, reaching out to take their coffees as Kate flopped down onto the sofa.

'God, I'm tired,' Kate said and yawned. 'I don't know what's got into me.'

'Late night?'

'No, not really.'

'Perhaps things are catching up with you?'

'What things? I feel better than I've felt in years but for some reason all I've wanted to do in the last twenty-four hours is sleep.'

'Maybe you've been working too hard on your novel.' James was concerned that her eyes were puffy and she seemed lethargic.

'Hardly, the writing brings me alive and I thrive when I lose myself in my words.' She sat up. 'I'm sorry, you must have had a wretched weekend and all I can talk about is me.' She turned and put a hand on his arm. 'How are you?'

'Oh, I'm all right, but I felt badly for my son.'

'I take it Helen and Jack didn't talk?'

'No, I'm afraid not.'

'Well, you did your best.'

'I hope so. Helen has gone back to France but she seems to have accepted the fact that Jack is settling down and I told her there's a baby on the way.'

'Well, that's a positive.' Kate picked up the coffee and handed James a mug.

'I wish she'd stop drinking.'

James could smell Kate's perfume. Her body was inches away and he yearned to put his arm around her shoulders and pull her close.

'Some drinkers tend to drink to cover up unhappiness. How do you know that she's happy? Is her relationship working?' Kate asked.

'I've no idea but she chose her life and I can't mend her. I have to protect our sons.'

'Did she always drink?'

'Yes, sometimes too much, but I never considered it to be a problem. She was an artist, she mixed in Bohemian circles, she loved life but was frustrated by the confines of a family and routine.' James drained his mug and placed it on the table.

'How are the young couple?'

'Jack is going to finish university and get his degree. Obviously, that won't be possible for Desiree.'

166

'Where will she go?'

'She has family in London. I hope they're understanding. She wants to resume her studies when the baby is born.'

'And then?'

'Jack will get a job and support his family.'

'Will they get married?'

'They want to but it's an added expense now that there's a baby on the way, but I'll help them.'

'It'll work out.' Kate put her mug down and took his hand. 'You're a great dad. If Jack's anything like you, he'll be fine.'

James felt comforted and the warmth from her fingers reassured him. He looked into her eyes and suddenly felt that he was whole again, a man who could cope with anything as long as this woman was by his side. He placed a hand on top of Kate's.

'Thanks,' he said. 'You seem to know all the right things to say.' With his free arm, James pulled Kate towards him and felt her body give. Her lips were inches away. 'Kate ...' he whispered.

She pulled back, snatching her hand away, twisting out of his embrace.

'Oh God, I'm so sorry!' James stood up. He was mortified. 'I don't know what came over me.' His brain raced, what the hell had he done? She was a student, for heaven's sake!

'It's all right, really.' Kate grabbed her bag. 'It's not your fault.'

'It was unforgiveable.' James wound his hands together, agonised by his action.

'Class is about to begin.' Kate glanced at the clock above the stove.

'Yes, of course, we must get on.' James paced the room and then stopped. 'Kate, what can I say?'

'You're upset, you had a crazy weekend, it's understandable. You don't have to apologise, please.' She reached out.

The door burst open and crashed against the wall.

Kate flinched and James turned to see who'd come into the room.

'Good morning.' Andy stepped forward. 'I thought I might join you today.' He looked from one to the other. 'Not disturbing anything, I hope?'

'Not at all.' James pulled out a chair. 'Make yourself comfortable. I'll get you a coffee.' He glared at Andy.

'White with one sugar.' Andy ignored the chair and walked over to the fire where two mugs sat side-by-side on a low table. 'Very cosy,' he said and, throwing himself onto the sofa, tapped the seat beside him. 'Come over here, beautiful, I want you next to me.'

Kate slowly crossed the room. She sat a little distance from Andy and stared at his face. The fire cast shadows over his dark features and for a moment she saw a menacing look in his eyes.

'Get closer, my darling. Let's show lover boy where your heart really lies.'

Andy reached out and pulled Kate into his arms. He traced a finger along her neck and across her shoulder and kissed the top of her head.

James came in with the coffee and looked at the couple by the fire.

Locked in an embrace, with their heads resting together, they stared into the stove, where flames danced behind the smoky glass.

What a fool he was.

Any hope of Kate having feelings for him had been dashed and the cameo image before him, of a couple very much in love, was a testament to his own stupidity.

James sighed. He would never get it right.

Hattie tried to keep up with Jo. She wrapped her duffel coat around her body and pulled on the toggles, twisting them into the leather fasteners as she jogged across the lawn.

'Crikey, Jo, can you slow down!'

'Sorry, I didn't realise,' Jo said. 'I am amazed to see you out in the fresh air.' She stopped and waited for Hattie to catch up.

'Fresh air is good for the complexion,' Hattie said and thrust her hands into her pockets as she slipped into place beside Jo.

'I'm glad to have your company. Pete was up early. He's gone to look at an old tractor in Kendal.'

'Boys' toys.' Hattie was dismissive.

'So, to what do I owe the honour of your company?'

'I thought it would be good to have a few minutes on our own.'

'What have you done?'

'Nothing. Why are you always so suspicious?'

'Because you're always up to something.'

They walked up the steps by the pond and Jo waved at Alf who stood in the greenhouse. He held a hammer in one hand and looked puzzled as he picked up a nail and examined a wooden bench. They watched him bring the hammer down, missing the nail and landing sharply on his thumb. Both winced as Alf let out a curse.

'And you worry about me,' Hattie said.

'I worry about all of you.' Jo grimaced as Alf's expletives got louder.

Bunty scurried along the grass, her nose glued to the ground as a baby rabbit ran out, crossing her line of vision.

'I think James went over the top with his apologies to Lucinda,' Hattie said. 'He can't help his ex-wife's behaviour.'

'I thought it was a very nice gesture.'

'Flowers, chocolates and a fancy new hair-do.'

'James is one of life's good guys.'

'Unlike Helen, she's as mad as a box of frogs.' Hattie shuffled her wellingtons along the gravel path. They'd reached the gate and Jo undid the latch.

'Helen wasn't too bad when she'd sobered up.' Jo ushered Hattie into the meadow and waited for Bunty to catch up. 'Very subdued, in fact. She hardly spoke in the car when I gave her a lift over to James' house.'

'How did they greet her?'

'Sadly, Jack wouldn't even come to the door. At the moment it seems that he doesn't want his mother's input into any aspect of his life. He wants her to stop drinking.'

'That's understandable.'

'I guess she had it coming but I hope that she's happy with her life in France. It would be nice to think that things had worked out for her with her younger lover.'

'Not something you can do anything about, Jo. Stop trying to rescue the world.'

'I know you're right. They'll sort it out.'

'I wanted to ask you about Sir Henry,' Hattie said.

'Ah, you've got me out here to tell me that he's popped the question?' Jo laughed. 'I thought Hugo would have got in first.'

'Very funny. It's not me he's interested in. Haven't you noticed the way he looks at Lucinda these days? Although I'd like a title.' Hattie smiled. 'Lady Hattie would suit me.'

'What are you concerned about?'

'He doesn't seem to be himself. I wondered if he should see a doctor?'

'We're not a nursing home.'

'I know. It's just that the old boy is quieter than normal.'

'Well, if he's ill, he'll have to go home. I'm not here to take care of the elderly.'

'I'm just saying.'

'Do we need to let his family know that he's under the weather?' Jo was concerned.

'No, I mentioned that to Hugo and he said not to worry anyone.' Hattie shrugged. 'Maybe Henry is just tired.'

'Let's keep our eye on him over the next day or two and then make a decision?'

'Aye, all right, if you think so.'

Bunty had followed the scent of the rabbit and was scampering around in the long grass. She circled the tepee and disappeared under the steps of the gypsy caravan.

'Busy up here today,' Hattie said and nodded towards the caravan, where a class, led by Queenie, was in progress.

The door was closed and the curtains were drawn.

'Is there anyone there?' Hattie whispered in a haunting voice. She closed her eyes and held out her fingers. She moved an imaginary glass around an imaginary Ouija board. 'Has anyone got a message for me?'

'Namaste!'

'Bleedin' hell!' Hattie exclaimed and opened her eyes as the Shaman walked around the side of the caravan. 'You made me jump.'

He held a wooden rattle in his hand and a bunch of sage in the other.

'I'm glad that we've caught you,' Jo said. 'I've been meaning to have a word.'

'There is one amongst us who is full of sadness.' The Shaman spoke softly and Hattie frowned as she leaned in to listen. 'We need to purify and cleanse the building of bad spirituality.'

'What do you mean?' Jo looked puzzled.

'There is an evil presence.'

Hattie yawned.

The Shaman was stating the blindingly obvious. You didn't need a rattle and a couple of twigs to work that out. Look no further than Hugo, Andy and that lunatic Lucinda. Bob fell into the same category too. Hattie stuffed her hands in her pockets and, leaving the Shaman and his odd thoughts to Jo, wandered over to the caravan.

Hattie sat on the steps. She'd found a toffee in her pocket. It was one of her favourites and she unpeeled the sticky sweet and popped it in her mouth. Birds twittered overhead as Hattie gazed around the meadow, the sun warm on her face. A crow swooped down and came to rest on a stone sundial. It flapped its wings and walked around then settled in one spot.

Hattie eyeballed the crow. It tucked its brilliant blue and green wings in neatly as it returned Hattie's stare. The bird was motionless, eyes beady, its dark pupils encased in a pure white iris.

'It is a messenger of the gods.' A voice spoke out from inside the caravan.

Hattie recognised Queenie's voice. She sat up and cocked her ear towards the door.

'Who is the message for?' another voice asked.

'For one who has lost their loving partner.'

A woman began to sob. 'It's me,' she said. 'It's my Arthur. He's come back to talk to me.'

'The messenger says that you are in a safe place, a good place to learn and recoup and get ready to go back out into the world.'

Hattie looked up. She wondered if the messenger was reading a line from the Boomerville marketing brochure.

'Arthur wants you to be happy and move on, take what you learn here from the many opportunities and go forward into a new life.'

Hattie was tempted to take notes. The messenger should do their copywriting.

'And how will I know that it's Arthur?'

'He will come to you in the form of a crow.'

'Oh no he won't.' Hattie jumped to her feet and began to clap her hands. 'Be off! Go on, scoot!'

The bird watched Hattie and uncurled its wings. As it lurched forward, Hattie ducked to avoid a collision. She crouched down as the bird flew up and circled around the caravan.

'Oh, I can feel him!' the woman in the caravan called out. 'It's my Arthur. I know he's near!'

Suddenly, a shape leapt out from beneath the caravan and, shocked, Hattie jumped back. She lost her footing and fell to one side.

'Bleedin' hell, Bunty!' she yelled. 'I thought you were old Arthur coming to take his loved one home.' She fanned her face and lay back on the grass.

'What's going on?' Jo raced towards the caravan and reached out to pull Hattie up. 'Are you all right?'

'Aye, fine, it's like an episode of *Most Haunted* out here. Do you think we could get back to the hotel?'

The caravan door flew open and six faces peered out. They stared at Hattie as she staggered to her feet.

'Can we help you?' a voice yelled.

'No, thanks, Queenie, everything is fine,' Hattie said. 'Just having a spiritual stroll.' She brushed at her duffel coat with one hand. 'But there's someone up there who'd like to say hello.'

The faces looked up as the crow coasted on a rising column of smoke, drifting over from the tepee.

'It's my Arthur!' the woman cried out and, with a swoon, collapsed back into the caravan.

'Leave them to it.' Hattie took Jo's arm and marched her back down the garden, where they could see the Shaman walking around the hotel.

'I've had a word and told him to not use so many strong herbs,' Jo said.

'I'm sure he'll make a note of that and take heed.' Hattie shook her head as they stood to watch the Shaman shake his rattle whilst waving a bunch of burning sage in the air.

'Well, that should get rid of a few unwelcome spirits,' Jo said with a giggle as they ran to the back of the building.

'I can think of a few welcome ones,' Hattie said as she burst through the conservatory. 'Let's get the bar open.'

Chapter Twenty-Four

Andy ran up the staircase at the back of the hotel and walked down the corridor to his room. He couldn't be bothered with the afternoon writing session; watching the idiot teacher gush all over Kate was beyond boring.

Putting his key in the lock, he flung the door open and threw himself down on a chair. He couldn't wait to get cracking on his plans. It had taken all night to access Kate's accounts and he'd had to go heavy on sleeping medication to ensure that she didn't wake and find him hacking into her laptop. Once he'd cracked the codes he needed, it wasn't hard to work out her passwords. To make things even easier, she had a list of all her accounts neatly stored in one file. He'd copied everything on an external backup and now he could download it to his own computer and decide when and where he would move her money.

Andy rubbed his hands together and reached out to pour a large malt whisky and, as he took a slug and let the fiery liquid slide down his throat, he felt a contented glow.

He was going to enjoy this.

But there was no hurry. Kate was eating out of his hands and he might even suggest they get engaged to keep her infatuated until the end. When he was ready, and the timing right, he would sneak away and set off in the Porsche to head for the nearest airport.

He put his drink down and went to the wardrobe, where a locked briefcase sat beside a neat rail of polished shoes. He pulled it out and placed it on the desk, then flicked the combination until the lock opened. Several passports lay in rows beside a selection of driving licences and identity cards.

Who should he be next?

He picked each one up and glanced at the photographs.

He was a master at disguise and could easily reinvent himself. A wad of cash, bound in neat bundles, was fast diminishing but there was enough left to help him on his way. Once he reached his destination, the money he transferred from Kate, after being processed through his tangled web of untraceable accounts, would be sufficient to set him up for many years to come. He may even buy a property somewhere warm, with a steady stream of young women to brighten up his days.

Andy unwrapped a cigar.

He peeled the cellophane back and rolled the smooth dark tobacco between his fingers. Cutting one end, he lit the other and wandered over to the window to look out. A man in a long dark coat was walking around the building. He seemed to be shaking an object in one hand whilst waving a handful of smouldering twigs in the other.

The man looked up and their eyes locked.

For the first time in many years, Andy felt fear ripple through his body. The last time he'd had that feeling had been when he'd heard the sound of a lock closing on a thick metal door, isolating him in a cold police cell to await his fate. He'd vowed then that he would serve his time, learn as much as he could and never return to that lonely hostile place. He wouldn't be put behind bars again.

No woman would ever have power over him.

As he stared at the man, he began to smile. Everyone in this place was barmy. There were too many nutcases wandering around and paying top dollar to do so. Gullible people who believed in all this claptrap. Andy shook his head then turned his back and went to pour another drink.

Revenge, for all the wrongs against him, was a dish best served cold and he was ready to put his latest scams into action.

Chapter Twenty-Five

Kate felt exhausted but she couldn't explain why. She sat in the writing class and stared out of the window where Alf was tidying the herb garden that bordered the courtyard. She could almost smell the aromatic leaves as she watched him trim and stake wayward fronds of rosemary and thyme and sprawling oregano with its sweet pungent smell. Kate thought of her own garden at the schoolhouse and hoped that it wasn't too overgrown. She never left it for so long but a neighbour had reassured her that he'd keep an eye on things.

A clock chimed and she turned to see that Bob had closed his notebook and was placing his pen in its case before putting both in his document bag, which he zipped tightly. Stretching his arms out he looked around and saw Kate. He gave her a wave.

Kate waved back then closed her laptop and stored it in her tote bag and, as she fastened it securely, she yawned.

'You look all done in, darling, like me,' Bob said. 'Do you fancy a quick drink?'

'Why not? Where would you like to go?'

'The pub over the road's open. We could head there for a change.'

'That sounds lovely. Let me get my coat.'

Bob buttoned his jacket and wrapped a scarf around his neck and was waiting by the door for Kate when James wandered over.

'Did you enjoy the class?' James asked.

'I thought it was very instructive, especially the bit about staying focused,' Bob said. 'You made some very good points, which I'll put into practice when I get back to work.'

'I'm glad you enjoyed it.'

'We're going to the pub,' Bob said. 'Will you join us?' He

nodded over to Kate who was chatting to another student as she slipped her arms into her jacket.

'Er, no, thanks. I'd better be getting off, got a lot to do at home.'

'Just as you like.'

Bob watched James. The man seemed troubled and Bob thought that a drink would have done him good. 'Ready when you are, darling,' he said to Kate and, taking her elbow, led her out of the studio.

They walked over the cobbles arm-in-arm and, when they reached the road, stopped to wait for the traffic to clear. The King's Arms was quiet but welcoming and Bob soon located a cosy corner of the snug, next to a coal fire.

'This is nice,' Kate said as she watched Bob carry their drinks to the table.

'Have you enjoyed the class today?'

'Yes, but I found it hard to concentrate, I don't think I contributed.'

'I thought that James seemed a bit distracted. It's not like him, he's usually on the ball.'

'He has a lot on his mind.' Kate took a sip of her drink.

'Yes, of course, it was quite a family upset at the weekend.'

'It must be a worry.'

'Andy was on good form.' Bob smiled and waited for Kate to respond. She looked puzzled.

'When he leapt in with Pete to harness Helen,' Bob explained. 'They had her out of the restaurant before anyone realised what was happening.'

'Oh, yes, I'd forgotten.'

Kate wrapped her hands around her glass and smiled at Bob. How she wished that she could confide in someone. Her emotions were all over the place and she couldn't work out why she felt so tired. It had been such an effort to get through these last two days. She looked at Bob's kind face as he observed the early evening drinkers and wondered if she had the courage to talk to him. One moment everything seemed so perfect and the next she didn't know which way to turn.

'How's the book progressing?' Bob asked. 'I love the name of your manuscript. *The Deadly Dating Game* will be a cracker.'

'I seem to be making some progress, despite feeling so tired,' Kate replied. In truth, she was making great progress and the words were writing themselves. It seemed that she had only to turn up at the page and another few pages rolled off her keyboard. Her fingers were like pistons as she tapped out the story and at the end of the day her hands were mobile and pain free. Despite all the typing, her arthritis had magically disappeared.

Bob finished his drink. 'Fancy another before we go back?' he asked.

'Why not?' Kate handed her glass to Bob. 'Let me get this one.'

'Not at all, my treat. You keep comfy and warm by the fire.'

As Bob headed to the bar, Kate wished again that she could confide in him. But what would she say? That she had grave misgivings about a man she'd only just met but behaved as though she had known forever? Sleeping together, dining, eating, working, walking, socialising and being with him as if he was a long-term lover. Kate felt sure that many boomers were placing bets on when the happy couple would name the day.

She couldn't put her finger on it, but something had changed.

It was only subtle, but Andy's demeanour had cracks and she wondered if they'd soon open and become a crater. Perhaps she was being foolish? After all, it was his reaction to James that had thrown a spotlight on her doubts. Men couldn't hide jealousy and Andy clearly thought that she had romantic feelings for James. She was just being stupid to worry. But James had declared how he felt and Kate's heart had missed a beat when he'd tried to kiss her. She should never have put the poor man in that position; he was upset over his wife, worried about his son and vulnerable, to say the least. Comfort from any woman would have caused that behaviour and she felt guilty that she'd led him on. James was a decent man with so many good qualities and if Andy wasn't on the scene, Kate felt sure that she would have responded.

She sighed. She really must pull herself together and stop imagining things. She was tired and blowing things out of proportion. A good night's sleep, in her own bed, and she would be as right as rain in the morning.

'Here we are.' Bob put their drinks down. 'I felt naughty and got us a bag of crisps too.' He held the bag out.

'Just what I needed.' Kate reached to dig in. 'Thanks so much. You're an absolute star.'

Bob lay in his bath and wriggled his toe under the running faucet. The water was warm and comforting, easing the aches in Bob's middle-aged limbs. He splashed a handful of bubbles over his body and thought about the day's events.

He'd been late for Heaven Sent Bread, the morning session in the cookery school where Sandra, formidable in a starched white jacket, had stood ramrod straight, behind a long pine table with a razor-sharp knife in her hand. 'This is Bob Puddicombe,' she'd announced as Bob tumbled through the door. 'He's going to join us today.' A group of expectant faces had turned from the demonstration to stare at Bob.

'There's room for one more over here, old boy.' Sir Henry waved his cane to indicate that Bob pull up a chair.

'Get yourself an apron and scrub up.' Sandra motioned with the knife towards a row of hooks and a sink. Bob did as he was told and in moments, encased in cotton, was sitting with a pencil in his hand and a work folder resting on his knee as a delicious aroma of freshly baked bread drifted across the room.

'Has anyone made bread before?'

Several hands shot up.

'Cook has one of those electric things,' Hugo said.

'If you mean a bread-maker, you can leave the class now.' Sandra glowered. 'All our bread is made by hand, there are no machines, additives or chemicals in this kitchen.' She waited for Hugo's response and when there was none, placed her hands on her hips and looked around. 'Now, who knows what to do with fresh yeast?'

Bob hadn't the foggiest but as the tutorial began Sandra showed the eager cooks how to make a variety of breads using her well-practised recipes and Bob was engrossed. Flour and water was transformed with a few basic ingredients and the kitchen table began to fill with dough of every description from simple Irish soda bread and English muffins to focaccia sprinkled with sea salt and topped with olives. Sandra mixed, pounded and baked and instructed the students to join in.

Sir Henry and Hugo worked on naan and as one shaped, the other sprinkled poppy seeds before carefully placing their dough on baking trays, ready for the oven.

'Nothing to it,' Sir Henry said to Bob. His face was puce and his moustache drooped. He began to spin a naan on the end of his cane. 'I hope Hattie has set a date for our Balti night.' The naan spun off and Bob saw it hurtle towards Sandra.

Sandra caught the twirling object and threw it in a bin. 'Not until your naan is perfect. That was like a lump of lead.'

As dough rose in the ovens and turned caramel brown, Sandra piled the bakes into baskets and placed them on the table. The class tucked in and Bob joined with the bakers as they sampled each other's recipes and made notes. He reached out and tore a handful of warm focaccia and as he took a bite, the delicate flavour of rosemary melted on his tongue. Bob sighed with pleasure as he nibbled the soft dough.

It was heaven sent bread indeed! Bob thought, as he remembered the class while steam rose from his bath and he felt his body relax as water continued to trickle from the tap and bubbles rose around his shoulders.

The afternoon session in the writing class had been most

enjoyable too and Bob found that lessons he was learning in the tutorials could easily be applied to his every day working practice. James' session on staying focused was a lesson well learnt. At work, Bob often sat in his Captain's chair in the office, swinging from side to side as he watched the world go by on the street below. His clients kept him busy but London could be distracting and there was never a dull moment when he gazed down the length of Wardour Street to the hustle and bustle of city life, where magnets of temptation by way of wine bars, pubs and coffee shops stood alongside designer shops and boutiques.

But there was never a dull moment at Boomerville. Bob thought about Andy and sighed. He'd endured him for the best part of the afternoon, followed by drinks with a very subdued Kate and Bob had an inkling that trouble was brewing. He'd sensed tension in the studio and James seemed distracted, glancing at Kate as she worked on her novel, while Andy charmed the ladies and raised points that irritated and frustrated James.

Bob reached for the soap and began to create a lather. His hands tingled as he wriggled his fingers, like a second sense sending out an alert. Perhaps he *was* a little bit mystic? He was sure that the Shaman had said there was a power amongst them that threatened, and Bob should act on his instincts, but he couldn't remember if he'd dreamt these words. His memory was dim when he tried to recollect. Perhaps he should book another session in the tepee and tune into his guardian spirit and, with the Shaman's help, see what the governor up above had to say.

The soap slid into the water and Bob yawned. He reached for his necklace of prayer beads and stroked the smooth stones. The tingling eased and his eyes felt weary and, as water continued to drizzle into his bath, Bob drifted off into a peaceful, happy sleep.

Chapter Twenty-Six

Hattie and Sandra sat at a side table in the kitchen. Their heads were locked over a pile of cookery books, spread out on the stainless-steel surface, as two commis chefs busied about in the background, getting ready for the evening ahead. Hattie flicked through the glossy pages and saw photos of Rick Stein racing around India in search of the perfect curry, while Sandra read up on Madhur Jaffrey's rich dark dahls and fragrant kormas, selecting recipes that would be suitable for their Taste of the Raj night at Boomerville.

'You'll have to have a class on the morning of the event so the cookery students can produce one or two recipes,' Hattie said. She licked her lips as she studied spiced fish and slow-cooked biryanis. 'Let them think they've contributed to the meal.'

'I hope environmental health aren't due a visit.' Sandra made notes in her kitchen diary. 'The Mulberry brothers' contribution could be a problem.'

'No need to worry about that, I'll sort it.'

Hattie had already decided that she'd ensure the students' food never reached the restaurant tables. She'd package their offerings and tuck them into her freezer at home. 'Just make sure you replicate what they make.'

'The boss has agreed then?' Sandra looked up.

'Yes. We've settled on a date and you've not got long.'

'When is it?'

'Friday.'

'Eh? But that's only days away and there's mountains of work to be done!' Sandra's face coloured and she thrust her notes to one side. 'I'll never manage all that.'

'I've asked Biddu to help you.'

'Biddu?'

'Yes. He says he's happy to get out of the restaurant for a bit. It will make a change for him and as long as Lucinda keeps well away, you'll have Baltis and bahjis bouncing out of the pots before you've time to search for your sari.'

'Well, I'm not sure about that.'

'You'll be writing your own curry cookery book soon.' Hattie closed her book and slid off the stool. 'Let me have a menu, when you can.' A tray of almond fingers, fresh from the oven, sat cooling on a side table. Hattie reached out and popped two in her pocket. 'Something to keep me going,' she said. 'See you later.'

'Aye, be on your way, I've got dinner to get ready,' Sandra grumbled as she piled the books to one side. 'Just as long as you're not naming the evening Biddu's Boomerville Balti.'

Hattie ignored Sandra's whinges and left the kitchen.

In the conservatory, several guests were relaxing after their classes. They looked up from books and magazines and smiled as Hattie entered. Outside, the light was fading and autumn sunshine bled into a rhubarb sunset as the day began to close. Bunty was asleep in her basket, her tail thumping and nose and paws twitching as she dreamed of racing rabbits and muddy fields.

Lucinda reclined on a sofa beside Sir Henry, whilst Hugo sat opposite with a copy of *The Times* on his knee, folded back to reveal the crossword. Hattie joined the group and licked crumbs off her lips as she munched on Sandra's baking.

'I say, Hattie, here's a clue for you,' Hugo said, his pen poised. 'Looks after a child while the parents are out. Five letters?' Hugo grinned.

'Nanny,' Lucinda and Sir Henry chorused.

'Exactly.' Hugo winked at Hattie then filled in the clue.

'That's the only nanny you'll be getting next to,' Hattie said as she stared at Hugo and shook her head. She wondered if she should have picked up her rolling pin.

'Don't be such a spoilsport,' Hugo said. 'You and I could have some fun together.'

'Have you had a nap?' Hattie ignored Hugo and turned to Sir Henry. 'I hope you haven't been overdoing things today.'

'No, my dear,' Sir Henry said. 'I've been in the capable hands of our lovely Lucinda.' He looked fondly at his companion.

Hattie placed the last of the biscuit in her mouth and turned to look at Lucinda. As she stared at the woman beside Sir Henry, she almost spat it out.

Lucinda was unrecognisable.

Sporting a new hairstyle and with her slightly singed, uneven tresses slickly coiffured and swept back in a chignon, Lucinda looked positively sophisticated. Her nails were neatly filed and painted pale pink and gone were the clanging bracelets and loosely flowing beads. In their place hung a string of pearls that lay on the collar of a woollen twin-set. Lucinda sat with her knees together and her ankles neatly crossed.

'Are you cooking?' Lucinda asked and smiled at Hattie.

'No, just having a nibble.' Hattie brushed at the sugar on her chin.

'Got to keep your strength up,' Lucinda replied. 'You girls work so hard.'

'I'd like a nibble too,' Hugo said and looked hopefully at Hattie.

'In your dreams.' Hattie dismissed Hugo and took a last glance at Lucinda, who gave a little wave, then turned to leave the conservatory.

'See you later,' Lucinda called out.

Hattie ran into the restaurant and, ignoring staff who were preparing for the evening, slipped through the door to Jo's house.

Jo and Pete sat at the table enjoying a cup of tea.

'Have you seen Lucinda?' Hattie gasped.

'What's she up to now?'

'She's done up like a dog's dinner. I hardly recognised her.'

'Is she going out?'

'No further than Sir Henry's room, I shouldn't wonder.'

Hattie put her hands on her hips and shook her head. 'I think she's making a serious play for the old boy. I hardly recognised her. She's dressed like a reincarnated Lady Mulberry.'

'Lady Lucinda.' Pete chuckled. 'You missed your chance.'

'There's still Hugo,' Jo teased.

'Oh, bog-off, the pair of you.'

'Andy and Kate, Henry and Lucinda, Hattie and Hugo!' Jo said. 'We could have a triple wedding. What an advert for Boomerville that would be.'

'Aye, I told you it would become nowt more than a knocking shop, never mind your high-brow classes and culture.' Hattie was miffed. 'Don't count on any weddings; it will all fall apart, mark my words.'

Pete joined in with the teasing and Bunty, having woken and followed Hattie, appeared and began to bark.

'The damn mutt is following me ...' Hattie cursed and closed the door.

'Shush, quiet,' Jo said. She tilted her head to one side and frowned as she reached down to silence her dog. 'What's the matter little one?' She scooped Bunty onto her lap.

'What's that noise?' Pete said and Hattie and Jo stopped talking to listen too.

They could hear a man wailing.

The door flew open and everyone stared at the figure who stumbled into the room. With a towel gripped around his waist and prayer beads bouncing off his naked torso, Bob hurled himself towards Jo.

'Sweetie, something terrible has happened!' Bob cried.

'It's all right, calm down.' Jo placed Bunty on the floor and rushed over to Bob.

'What on earth have you been up to?' Hattie asked and grabbed the towel, which had slipped from Bob's body and threatened to expose what little was left unseen.

'My bath has overflowed and I think the ceiling is about to come down in the Green Room!'

'I'm on it,' Pete yelled and ran from the room.

'I was meditating and fell asleep. I forgot the tap was running,' Bob sobbed.

'Nothing we can't fix,' Jo soothed. 'Hattie, could you get a robe for Bob?'

'Aye, I'll magic up a builder too.'

As Hattie stomped up the stairs, she glanced back.

Jo had guided Bob to her rocking chair and Bunty was licking his wet feet.

Hattie sighed. 'Bonkers,' she said to herself. 'Boomerville bonkers, the lot of them!'

Chapter Twenty-Seven

Kate stared at the screen on her laptop and typed the last few words of the chapter. She was engrossed in her writing and, with the help of the outline she'd prepared, now knew exactly where the plot was going and how the book would end.

The Deadly Dating Game was flowing. Her main character had depth and Kate was pleased with the way things had developed. It gave scope for a series and she had to stop her mind from racing ahead, planning the next story.

Kate smiled. The novel she'd yearned to write was born and although she knew that she still had a considerable amount of work to do, she was thrilled that she was achieving something she'd always wanted.

As Kate relaxed in a comfortable chair beside the fire in the Red Room, she wondered why she'd agonised for years, for the writing process hadn't been as painful as she'd anticipated. Inspiration at Boomerville had triggered all her natural instincts for words and, once started, with guidance from James, she was managing to achieve a goal she'd always thought impossible.

She put her laptop to one side and looked out through the windows where clouds drifted across a forget-me-not blue sky. It was a perfect autumn day and Kate felt at peace with the world. The hotel was quiet and the tranquillity welcome. Many of the residents were attending classes and others, at Hattie's suggestion, had gone out early, on a shopping trip to Carlisle.

Kate heard voices. Jo and Alf were in the hall discussing a small leak in the ceiling earlier in the week and with the paint now dry, the room was ready to put back in use.

Jo stood in the doorway and, seeing Kate on her own, stopped to check that all was well. 'Can I get you a drink or something to eat?' she asked.

'Morning, Jo,' Kate replied. 'I'm fine at the moment, but thank you.'

'No classes today?'

'No, I've been writing.'

'How's it going?' Jo perched on the arm of a chair.

'There's a great deal to be done.' Kate frowned. 'Even though I've masses to do, James says writing the book is the easy bit.'

'That's interesting,' Jo said, 'why does he think that?'

'Editing and re-writing can take just as long and then of course there's the trawl for a publisher. It may never see the light of day.'

'I doubt that. A woman with your experience will treat it like a business and bring her product to market like any other.'

'If it's good enough.' Kate thought about the long lines of books on her shelves at home. Wouldn't it be wonderful to see her own work alongside? Even better, she imagined the book in a bookshop window, at an airport shop or online as a download.

'I'll be off,' a voice called out and Alf poked his head around the door. 'Tha's all done and dusted.'

'Thanks so much. I do appreciate your hard work,' Jo said as Alf doffed his cap.

'Is the room ready to use?' Kate asked.

'It just needs a clean.'

'Was there much damage?'

'Hardly any. Bob tends to exaggerate; anyone would think the place had been flooded out. It was a tiny leak.'

'Is it ready for your Taste of the Raj evening?'

'Yes, thank goodness and the restaurant is fully booked tonight. All the residents are looking forward to it.'

'How's Bob?'

'He was mortified. The leak trickled onto a painting, causing minor damage, but I'm sure we can have it restored. I'll find a replacement. Accidents happen.'

'I'd better make a move.' Kate began to gather her things. 'I'm meeting Andy and we're going for a walk.'

'It's a perfect day for an outing. Are you going anywhere nice?'

'He says it's a surprise.'

Kate picked up her tote bag and tucked her laptop inside. Andy had been in particularly good spirits and she was looking forward to the walk. Any doubts about Andy had diminished in the last few days and Kate had scolded herself for being worried about a couple of careless remarks he'd made. After all, everyone had faults and she'd probably over-reacted.

Kate knew that she was fortunate.

She had the man of her dreams on her arm and in her bed and had begun to write. Things she'd always yearned for. Boomerville was her salvation and she'd come a long way from the lonely days at her schoolhouse. Soon, she hoped, she would be sharing her home with Andy and the place would come to life. Her dad would be happy for her. The emotional turmoil and pain of his dementia was lifting.

'Got your outfit for tonight?' Jo asked.

'Yes, I asked Hattie to find something that will work for me.' Kate smiled. 'Andy isn't too keen on fancy dress but he's a good sport.'

'I know he doesn't like spicy food. I've asked Sandra to tone some of the sauces down.'

'He'll be fine. It's going to be a lovely evening.'

'I hope so. Hattie has put a great deal of effort into the preparations.'

There was the sound of an engine revving and gravel crunched as a coach pulled onto the driveway outside.

'Looks like she's here now.'

Kate and Jo went over to the window where a coach from William's Wheels juddered to a halt and Hattie trotted down the steps. She had armfuls of packages and placed them on one side. Willie hopped out of the driver's cab and raced around to help Hattie assist the passengers. Boomers, also weighed down with packages, chatted excitedly as they trooped into the hotel and called out goodbye to their driver.

'I'd better make a move. This lot look like they need refreshments.'

'Have fun,' Kate said. 'See you later.'

Jo was in reception checking the guest accounts. Bills for the week were up to date and earlier she'd printed off and placed them in envelopes, to leave in the residents' rooms.

She liked to distribute the accounts herself and, as a personal touch, Jo added a handwritten card of thanks, which she would place on a coaster on the desk in each room. The pottery coasters had been made by Potter Paul and were embossed with the Boomerville logo.

Jo picked up a basket and filled it with envelopes. Bunty looked up and wagged her tail.

'No, you stay here,' Jo said and reached down to stroke the puppy. 'I won't be long.' She hooked the basket over her arm and closed the door, then headed into the hotel.

'Going shopping?' Hattie called out. She was halfway up a ladder at the entrance of the restaurant, draping a garland of paper flowers across the doorway.

'Just taking the weekly accounts to the residents.'

'Nice end to the week, slapping that missile down on their desks. It will put them in a good mood for tonight.' Hattie jingled a brass bell as she pinned it to the garland.

'It's the same every week, Hattie, no one seems to object and I like to keep the accounts up to date.'

Alf wore his cap back-to-front and had a hold on the ladder. He steadied Hattie as she came down. 'Where's tha want it now?' he asked as Hattie picked up a box.

Jo stood back and watched the pair reposition themselves. 'I'll leave you to it,' she said.

'See you later,' Hattie, who was back on the ladder, mumbled through a mouthful of pins. She leaned precariously on Alf's head to hook a wallhanging onto a beam.

'Be careful you don't damage anything,' Jo said, and went on her way.

Andy wore leather gloves as he picked up a neatly stacked pile of photographs and tucked them into a large brown envelope. He removed the sticky seal and ran his fingers along the closure then placed the envelope on his desk and stuck a label to the front.

Private & Confidential
For the attention of Hugo Mulberry

The envelope was to be delivered today and, as the weekly accounts were doing the rounds that afternoon, Andy decided that a double delivery was in order. He would drop the envelope off later by pushing it under the Mulberry bedroom door when no one was about.

In the meantime, he had Kate to contend with.

Andy had promised to take her out for a walk, stating that their destination was a surprise and now he wracked his brains as he thought about suitable locations.

He tore the gloves off and moved to the wardrobe where he pulled out his briefcase, then turned the combination until the lock slid back. Rummaging through a side pocket, his fingers fell on a small leather box and, flicking it open, he looked at the contents. An emerald surrounded by diamonds, set on a platinum band, twinkled as he held it to the light.

Andy stared at the ring.

He'd found it on the dressing table in a suite on the Queen Victoria cruise liner, the night before the ship docked in Santiago. The woman he'd been screwing had slept, having drunk one of Andy's drug-laden nightcaps which led to her comatose slumber, as her husband, who knew nothing of his wife's indiscretions, gambled through the night in the casino. Andy had managed to take a considerable amount of jewellery and cash too, confident in the knowledge that the woman's illicit fling with Andy would never come to light. He was long gone in the morning when the ship docked and the delights of South America soon covered his trail.

Andy tucked the box in his pocket.

It was worth putting the ring on Kate's finger, anything to keep her happy in their final days and a small price to pay when compared to the spoils to come. He closed the wardrobe doors and began to get ready. Warm clothes and a decent coat. It was cold out despite the sunshine and as he dressed he hummed a happy tune. Soon he'd be in balmy climes wearing thinner garments, far away from this godforsaken joke of a hotel.

Happy days indeed!

Kate walked across the hotel driveway to her car. She opened the boot and reached into a canvas bag for her walking boots. The boots were muddy from a previous walk and holding them in one hand she moved over to a border and began to bang the soles together. Clods of hardened soil fell onto the flowerbed.

'Namaste.' A voice whispered and, startled, Kate spun around.

The Shaman stood under a canopy of arching branches that flowed from a willow tree in the corner of the garden. Camouflaged by his dark clothing, Kate was surprised as he stepped out and bade her good day.

'I didn't see you there,' she said. 'Do you always creep up on people?'

'Your fingers?' the Shaman asked, ignoring her question. He stared into Kate's eyes. 'You have no pain?'

'Well, no, actually there isn't.'

'Your words?'

'My words? Do you mean my writing?'

The Shaman nodded.

'Er, yes, thanks, my writing is excellent, for some reason I seem able to put pen to paper.' Kate felt silly. *Why was she telling him all this?* But unable to stop she went on. 'I've always wanted to write and now, since I've been here, suddenly the words have flowed and in time I may have a book.'

'There will be more.'

'Well, that's good to hear. I was thinking only this morning that I could expand my stories into a series.'

'Your heart?' the Shaman interrupted Kate.

Kate was puzzled. She frowned as she looked at the weathered face. 'My heart is good, thank you. Never been better, every beat a bonus.' She knew that she was babbling nonsense but couldn't stop herself. 'In fact, it's a very happy heart. The happiest that it's been in a very long time.'

'There is danger.'

'Danger?'

'There is a power amongst us that threatens.'

'Oh, right-o, I'll keep a look out for it.'

'The spirits are with you.' The Shaman held up a heavily carved staff and drew a circle in the air around Kate.

'Kate, darling, are you ready?' Gravel crunched and Andy appeared. 'Why are you standing here, staring into space?'

Kate turned to look at Andy. 'I'm just cleaning my boots,' she replied. She peered under the branches of the willow but the Shaman had disappeared.

'Come on.' Andy took the boots. 'I've got a surprise for you.' He grabbed her hand. 'I think you're going to like it.'

Chapter Twenty-Eight

Boomerville looked magnificent. Dressed for the occasion by Hattie and her helpers, the old building was resplendent and shone with the atmospheric light of a multitude of lanterns and lamps as guests arrived for a night of Indian cuisine at Boomerville's Taste of the Raj evening.

'Amazing what you can get from the pound shop,' Hattie said to Jo as they walked through the hotel.

The rooms looked rich and exotic, decorated with lengths of brilliant gold and ruby red fabric, hung in swathes around the walls and festooned with garlands of paper flowers. Gentle notes of a melodic sitar floated down the corridor as Hattie pushed a beaded curtain to one side, and tiny bells, strung through several rows, tinkled as they went into the cocktail bar.

Hattie's sari, still fresh from the Balti night at Biddu's, was draped across her shoulder and secured at her waist. Her bare arms were covered in bangles. 'Borrowed them from Lucinda,' Hattie said as she held out her wrist. 'She doesn't wear them now she's gone all Camilla Parker Bowels.'

'I think you mean Bowles,' Jo corrected Hattie and stared at a set of intricate patterns covering Hattie's skin. 'What's that on your hands?'

Hattie splayed her fingers and admired the outlines. 'It's mehndi, an Indian form of body art. I got the Shaman to do it.'

'Have you got it anywhere else?'

'I might have.' Hattie lifted up the skirt of her sari where her heavily decorated feet peeped out from the hem of her long johns.

'How far does it go?'

'Never you mind.'

'I hope it washes off.'

'Make sure you get a bindi.' Hattie stared at Jo's forehead. 'We want everything to be authentic.'

Jo had no intention of having a bindi. She'd seen Sandra apply one to Hattie earlier that afternoon and was doubtful that cochineal was a suitable substance to use on the skin.

'Oh, darlings, isn't this marvellous?' Bob ran towards them, clasping his hands together. 'I feel like I'm an Indian Prince.' He wore a collarless silk shirt above a length of white fabric, draped and knotted around his legs. 'Do you like my dhoti?' Bob pointed at the pyjama-like trousers. 'I got it in Nepal.'

'Very nice,' Hattie said and stared doubtfully at the nappy-like garment. 'Your turban makes you look very distinguished.' She reached out to straighten the layers of cloth that made up Bob's headwear. It was one of several that she'd hired for the male guests when she found the turbans in a fancy-dress shop in Carlisle.

Jo had kept her outfit simple.

She wore a sharara, a palazzo-style flared trouser that fell softly to the floor, the bodice a bell-sleeved blouse. She ushered Hattie and Bob into the reception room as boomers and guests from around the county gathered for pre-dinner drinks.

'Don't worry, I can liven the drinks,' Hattie whispered to Bob as they stepped into the Green Room, where trays of mocktails, known as sharbats, were being passed around. Hattie whipped her sari to one side and, reaching for a pocket in her long johns, produced a mini flask of vodka, which she poured into Bob's glass.

'Delicious,' Bob said as he sipped the fruity concoction. He looked up and nodded to a space above the fireplace. 'I love the replacement painting.' The leak from his bathroom had slightly damaged a landscape and it had been replaced with Lucinda's painting of Hattie lying naked on a chaise. 'You've given yourself a bindi,' Bob giggled. 'Jo will have a fit.'

'It's only a sticky,' Hattie said. 'It looks quite effective, eh?' She grinned as she admired the image of herself.

'I've been on a strict diet of humble pie since I damaged the ceiling,' Bob said.

'Well, come off it immediately. It was miniscule damage and I think my replacement painting looks wonderful there.'

They turned to the room, where Sir Henry had risen to his feet.

'The Queen!' Sir Henry boomed and held up his drink. 'Long may she reign.'

Several people stood to attention and joined in the toast. Lucinda, elegant in a long silk dress that flattered her slim body, held up her glass. She patted her neat chignon that was decorated with tiny flowers. Gone was the heavy green eyeshadow and layers of thick mascara and she wore pearls at her neck and wrists. The pancake makeup had been replaced with a tinted moisturiser and her lips were pale rose. She sat by Sir Henry and held onto his arm.

'Blimey, Lady Lucinda scrubs up well,' Hattie said as Jo re-joined them. She couldn't believe her eyes as she watched the eccentric artist fawn over Sir Henry.

'It's good that she's teaching classes.' Jo watched Lucinda smile politely as Sir Henry told a joke. 'I don't think Lucinda has a bean to her name.'

'She soon will have, if her advances to Sir Henry come off.'

'I'll let her stay for free if we need to. It's time I offered a bursary of sorts to boomers who can't afford the fees.'

'If she's our resident artist now, you won't need to.'

The event was in full swing and with all the guests having arrived, the atmosphere was lively. Jo looked on as everyone complimented each other's outfits. The men had identical turbans, worn at lopsided angles, above a variety of long cotton shirts and loose-fitting trousers. One or two wore heavily embroidered jackets. The women mingled in makeshift saris and kaftans and their costume jewellery glittered in the candlelight.

'Dressed for excess,' Hattie said.

'I thought the invitation read, dress to impress?'

'Not at Boomerville. There's only one way to dress.'

Biddu appeared and announced that dinner was served. Hattie broke into a Bollywood-style belly dance and indicated that everyone should follow suit.

Jo stood to one side as giggling boomers sashayed behind Hattie to disappear into the restaurant, and as Jo watched the merry troupe she crossed her fingers and hoped that no one put their hip out or dislocated a knee.

Kate was in her bedroom where she could hear the sound of revelry from the reception rooms below. The Taste of the Raj evening was gathering momentum and she heard diners dancing down the corridor on their way to their Indian banquet.

She wore a towelling robe and stared at an elaborate outfit, laid out on the bed.

The lovely emerald green sari that Hattie had kindly collected in Carlisle was a subtle match for Kate's hair and skin and the fabric shone with bright threads and pretty patterns. It was perfect for the night ahead.

But Kate wouldn't be wearing it.

Since her meeting with the Shaman that afternoon, Kate had been overwhelmed by an unpleasant feeling and after the outing with Andy that followed, she needed some personal space. She would feign a headache. Anything to get out of the festivities.

She had to have time to think about the events that had taken place that afternoon.

Andy had driven her to Ambleside. He'd parked the car and led her along a walking route that followed a fast-flowing beck through a pretty valley. They were surrounded by arable farmland that stretched out to limestone uplands in the distance and there wasn't a soul about as they wandered along the pathways. As they approached an old packhorse bridge, Andy led her to the centre. He stopped and reached for her left hand. With a swift movement, he produced a ring from his pocket and slid it onto Kate's third finger.

'Kate, shall we get engaged?' Andy asked and gripped her hand.

Kate stared at the jewels that glittered on her finger, mesmerised by the large emerald as it dazzled in the afternoon sunshine.

'The ring is perfect.' He smiled. 'It suits your hand.'

The stones felt heavy, the platinum band tight. Kate could hear Andy as he told her how expensive the ring was and how he'd had it especially made but his words were distant, drowned out by water, which thundered below the bridge.

A shiver shot up her spine and pain raced through her fingers.

There is a power amongst us that threatens …

Kate could hear the Shaman's words!

She pulled her hand back and looked up. Andy was glaring at her. His eyes were dark and for the first time since their meeting, Kate felt afraid as she stared into the menacing black pupils. He reached out and gripped her arms and as they stood on the narrow bridge, Kate was pinned by the strength of a man that she suddenly realised she didn't know at all.

'I can't take the ring.'

'Why not?'

Kate felt his grip tighten.

'I just can't.'

Andy's face was close and Kate could feel his hot breath on her skin. His breathing quickened, coming in short bursts as he glared. 'Don't be silly, darling, you know it's what you want.'

Kate was terrified. She glanced around but there wasn't another soul to be seen. They were completely alone. She knew that she had to think fast and not upset him further or, with one push from his overpowering grip, she would be in the water below, pounded against the rocks in the icy current.

'It's just so sudden,' she began, 'and so unexpected.' She

looked into his eyes and forced a smile. His lips quivered and Kate prayed that he would believe her. 'Let's go back. We've got so much to talk about.'

Moments seemed like minutes as they stared at each other. Kate held her breath as she counted the seconds, every fibre of her body craving release.

'Of course, my love.' Andy suddenly let her go. 'I've surprised you and you didn't expect it.'

Kate pulled away and reached for the ring to wrench it off her finger, but realised that it would further antagonise him if she were to return it now. Her arms hurt where he'd held her and her fingers ached with pain. Andy grabbed her arm and, tucking it through his own, propelled her back on the path to make their way back to Ambleside. Kate forced herself to be jovial and kept their banter light. He seemed to accept their engagement as a matter of course and didn't refer to the subject. Andy was courteous and entertaining as they drove along the winding roads of Westmarland and Kate played along, hoping that he wouldn't sense her withdrawal and sudden change of heart.

But as Kate stood by her bed and thought about the events of the afternoon she knew that she was frightened. She'd seen a different side to his character and the glamour had fallen away.

Why on earth hadn't she seen it before?

Andy had never wanted to talk about his wife and Kate had put it down to grief but now realised how little she knew about him. Any conversation about his past had been diverted to the future and their time together. She hadn't wanted to share a room with him, her gut instinct had been to keep things separate and now, she wondered why she'd felt that way? The ring lay on her dressing table, the huge stone like an eye, watching her every move. Kate knew that she had to return it. Sooner rather than later.

The shock of the afternoon had exhausted her and Kate decided that she would cry off for the evening and spend the night on her own. She needed to sleep on things and think about how to work everything out. Andy had to be told but she suspected it wasn't going to be easy. From the way that he'd looked at her, Kate was certain that he was a man who didn't take no for an answer and wasn't used to being turned down.

Kate picked up the sari and, folding it neatly, placed it to one side. She'd run a bath and then call Andy; perhaps he'd gone to the party and was waiting for her? No doubt he would search her out soon but she would stand firm and be adamant that she spent the night alone.

She walked to the door, turned the key in the lock and slipped it into her pocket, then moved across the room to the windows. As she reached out to tug on the curtains she noticed a figure in the shadows by the willow tree below. She leant her head against the glass and peered through the darkness but the figure had disappeared.

Kate pulled the curtains and went to run her bath.

Andy stared out of the window in his room. The lawn below was lit with coloured lanterns laced along twisting vines that spread along the garden walls. In the distance, he could see a bonfire in the meadow. Yellow licks of flame illuminated the tepee as they streaked upwards, shooting meteorite-like sparks to explode in the cold night sky.

A group of men stood on the lawn. Dressed in boiler suits and gloves, they wore protective goggles as they made their final checks for the firework display, which would take place after dinner.

Andy held a glass of whisky and thought about Kate.

He knew that she was going to turn him down. She may be prolonging the process and didn't have the guts to come out with it, but he'd sensed a complete change in her feelings as they stood on the bridge and it had been all that he could do not to push the stupid bitch in the water.

He took a slug of the drink and felt it burn down his throat. Suddenly his plans looked as though they may have to be changed. He could keep his relationship with Kate going for a little bit longer but the clock was ticking and he knew that she'd soon make her decision. Not that it mattered; he fully intended to up the ante with Hugo and deliver the photos that evening. A cover note gave instructions for money to be paid immediately into a detailed account.

Andy was in no mood to wait and Kate's accounts were his next target.

The phone on his desk rang, breaking into the silence, and he moved across the room to answer it.

'Hello?'

'Hi, Andy, its Kate.'

'Hello, my beautiful girl, are you ready for the party?' His tone was soft. 'I can't wait to see your gorgeous body in a sari. I might not be able to control myself.' Andy's voice purred down the phone.

'I'm sorry but I have the most terrible headache,' Kate said, her voice faltering as she tried to explain. 'I don't want to spoil your night but I think it could be a migraine. I need to lie down.'

'My poor baby, let me come over and rub your brow.' Andy rolled his eyes and glanced at his watch. The brothers would have gone to the party and he needed to deliver the photos. God willing she'd get off the phone soon.

'No, really, I just need to get some sleep.'

'Well, if you're absolutely sure that there's nothing I can do?'

'I'm certain.' Kate sighed. 'I'll catch up with you tomorrow.'

'All right, my darling, just call me if there's anything at all that you need.'

'Thank you, I will.'

'I love you,' Andy whispered, 'my fiancée.'

But Kate had disconnected the phone.

Bitch! Andy threw the phone to one side and looked at

the envelope addressed to Hugo. Screw the party. If Kate was having a night off from the festivities at Boomerville then he could too. He would push the photos under Hugo's door then return to his room and hack into Kate's accounts. If he worked quickly, he could move most of the money. It was Saturday tomorrow and she was unlikely to spend more than the meagre amount he'd leave, if indeed she spent anything at all. He could be off by Sunday at the latest, inventing an emergency event that would call him away.

His drink stood on the windowsill and he walked across the room to retrieve it. As he drained the glass, he saw something move across the patio beneath his room. Light from the conservatory fell in a beam catching the tail end of the dark shape and Andy peered into the darkness to see what it was. A carved stick moved towards him and took on a ghostly appearance as it shook up and down in the air.

Fireworks, he thought, as he remembered the team of men working earlier. With a shrug, he turned from the window and slipped his hands into his gloves, then picked up the envelope and stole silently from his room.

Chapter Twenty-Nine

The Taste of the Raj evening was underway in the restaurant at Boomerville and the setting had been transformed. Guests stared in wonder at dozens of tea-lights floating in pretty glass vases surrounded by flower petals and smoking incense and a stunning arrangement of hydrangeas and orchids, which lay along a mantelpiece illuminated by a gold candelabra. On the tables, place cards sat in elephant-shaped holders and tiny crystals were scattered over the damask cloths, creating a rainbow pattern in the soft light.

Bob looked around and smiled. He was having a wonderful time.

He adored the opulence of the evening and felt completely at home. Having journeyed to India on many occasions, he had engaged with the culture and considered the vast country to be the cradle of the human race. Bob found it an extraordinary nation, a spiritual place as well as a land of contrasts with a cacophony of exotic sounds that stayed in his memory long after his visits ended. Now he sat happily with his fellow diners, enjoying the company of Sir Henry, Hugo and Lucinda. Students from the cookery class sat with them and all were complimenting each other on their contribution as endless courses of Indian delicacies were served.

'Best naan you've ever tasted,' Sir Henry said as he dipped a handful of soft dough into a mild passanda sauce. 'Took me all morning to make these.' He pointed at a pile in the centre of the table.

'Not as good as my samosas.' Hugo stuffed a tiny vegetable filled parcel into his mouth.

'Pass the poppadums, please,' Lucinda said to Bob.

Bob pushed a plate stacked high with thin, crisp-like pancakes towards Lucinda. He was staggered by the woman's new demeanour. Polite and well-groomed were words he would never have used when referring to the ageing artist, but gone was the wild, untamed and scary creature that had haunted the corridors of Boomerville when he'd first arrived. In its place was a woman who'd transformed herself beyond recognition and Bob was certain that he knew the reason why.

For Lucinda and Sir Henry were certainly an item.

It was clear to all that they now spent every moment together and Bob had no doubt that Sir Henry ventured on many a nocturnal visit to Lucinda's room. Well, good luck to them, Bob thought, as a dish of kebabs arrived. They will never have these days again, so why not make the most of them?

'Everyone enjoying themselves?' Hattie was circulating around the room and stopped to check on Bob's table.

'Splendid night, old girl.' Sir Henry raised his glass. His cheeks were ruddy and his turban had slipped. Lucinda leaned in and, with a loving touch, gently straightened the headdress.

'Tuck in, plenty more to come.'

As Hattie moved away, she scanned the room. There was no sign of James Bond and his partner and she wondered where on earth they might be. She'd gone to a great deal of trouble to pick up an outfit for Kate in Carlisle and was certain that she would have stolen the show and won the 'Best Dressed at Boomerville' prize of the night. Hattie looked for Jo, who might know where the couple were, but could see that she was chatting to James in the Rose Room. He was dining with a group of females from his class. Clad in a variety of odd-shaped kaftans and acres of silk wound into saris of all shapes and sizes, the literary harem hung off his every word.

Hattie decided to leave Jo to it and went through to reception. She'd give Kate a ring and see where she'd got to. She picked up a phone and dialled Kate's room.

There was no reply.

Puzzled, Hattie unlocked a cupboard and ran her fingers

along a line of keys until she found a duplicate. Tucking it into the fabric at her waist, she headed along the corridors until she reached the stairs. She started to climb and when she reached the top, Hattie stepped onto the gallery and turned towards Kate's room. But something made her stop and, tilting her head to one side, she heard footsteps in the corridor leading to the back of the hotel. Hattie knew that all the guests were downstairs and, curious to see who was about, tiptoed in the direction of the receding steps. As she approached Sir Henry and Hugo's door, she saw the shadow of a figure on the far wall as it turned the corner and hurried away.

James Bond!

Hattie wondered what on earth Andy was up to. The brothers' door was firmly shut and nothing looked out of place. Hattie crept further along the corridor. She heard a door close and a sliver of light appeared from the frame around Andy's room. Damn, she'd missed him! Hattie cursed under her breath. She turned to retrace her steps and when she reached Kate's room, stopped and listened again. There wasn't a sound and Hattie wondered where Kate could be. Taking her key, she slipped it into the lock, turned the handle and slipped into the room.

'Who is it?' Kate called out in the darkness.

Hattie fumbled for a light and flicked it on.

Kate sat up in bed and held the sheet across her chest. Bewildered, she frowned as her eyes adjusted to the light and she recognised Hattie.

'Gosh, Hattie, what on earth are you doing?'

'You didn't come down to the dinner and I wanted to make sure that you're all right.' Hattie stared at Kate. The woman looked anxious. 'Is everything okay?'

'I thought you were Andy.' Kate sighed and sank back on the pillows.

Hattie sat on the edge of the bed as Kate raised one arm and brushed a strand of loose hair away from her face. She wore a silk nightdress with shoestring straps and Hattie was horrified to see faint bruising around her arm.

'Kate, what on earth has happened?' Hattie reached out and gently touched the finger-shaped shadows.

'Oh, it's nothing.' Kate winced and pulled away.

'Has Andy hurt you?'

'He held me a little too tightly.'

'But he's made bruises.' Hattie reached for the sheet and pulled it back to reveal both of Kate's arms. 'It must have been a very tight grip?'

'He wants to get engaged.'

'And you don't?'

Kate shook her head.

'So he hurt you.'

Hattie could feel her blood boil and it was all she could do not to thunder down the corridor and wrench James Bond from his room to give him a taste of his own medicine.

'Please don't say anything. I can sort it out.'

'But surely you don't want anything to do with him?'

'I must give him his ring back.' Kate nodded towards the dressing table where the emerald ring lay on a pottery coaster.

'Do you want me to stay with you?'

'No, Hattie, I'm fine, truly.' Kate took a sip of water from a glass by the bed. 'Please don't let me spoil your evening.'

'Can I tell Jo?'

'No, I'd rather you didn't say anything to anyone until I decide what to do.'

'Very well, but I'm keeping an eye on things and you can rest assured that you're safe.' Hattie stood up.

'Thank you, I appreciate your concern.'

'We'll talk in the morning?'

'Yes, of course.'

'Call me if you need anything at all.'

Hattie fussed around Kate, folding and tucking the covers. She refreshed the water and turned on a lamp by the bed.

When she was sure that there was no more that she could do, she whispered goodnight and crept out of the room, locking the door behind her.

'James bloody Bond!' Hattie cursed and went back to re-join the party.

Hugo slipped away and went up the stairs to his room. His brother had sent him on a mission and entrusted with the important deed, Hugo was determined to follow it to the letter.

He put his key in the lock of the door to their suite and turned on the light. As he stepped into the room, he looked down. A large brown envelope lay on the thick carpet and Hugo bent to retrieve it.

Private & Confidential
For the attention of Hugo Mulberry

The weekly hotel bill, he thought and placed the envelope on a chair. Moving over to a desk, Hugo opened a drawer and searched around until he found a small leather box. It was engraved in gold and he ran his fingers over three raised initials.

E.M.M.
Elisabeth Mary Mulberry.

Hugo opened the box and looked at their mother's ring. A large ruby set on a cluster of finely cut diamonds. The stone had come from Burma, purchased when Henry and Hugo's father, a major in the army, was serving there. It was a treasure he bought for their mother and commissioned to be set in a ring.

Now the heirloom would grace Lucinda's finger. For tonight, his brother was going to propose and Hugo had been entrusted with this much-loved piece of family jewellery.

He slipped the box into his pocket and closed the drawer.

Noticing another envelope on the desk, propped up on a

pottery coaster, Hugo wrenched it open. It was the bill for the brothers' stay at Boomerville. Hugo moved it to one side. Nothing could be paid without Henry's agreement and signature. Their finances were joint. Years ago, Hugo lost a fortune on a reckless property deal and since that time Henry had insisted that he controlled the purse strings to the family fortune.

Hugo looked in the mirror and straightened his turban then picked up the key and headed for the door. His eye caught sight of the brown envelope that was still on the chair. Curious, he picked it up and slid a finger under the seal to rip it open.

Several photographs fell to the floor and as Hugo stooped to retrieve them, he could hardly believe his eyes. A man sat on a bed wearing a variety of outfits, from a large towelling nappy and bonnet to a tightly fitting lace corset with sheer black stockings. His bushy pubic hair poked out of a silky red thong. With a rolling pin in one hand, he held a long black dildo in the other and next to him on the bed a cucumber and melon could be seen. Hugo stared in horror as the images became more explicit. His hands shook in shock and his heart hammered for it was quite obvious that the man in the photographs was none other than Hugo himself, caught in the most compromising of positions.

A neatly typed note fluttered onto the carpet and Hugo grabbed it.

The note contained details of a bank account and a demand for a large amount of money. It was to be paid in the next forty-eight hours or, the blackmailer threatened, the photographs would be sent to the press.

Hugo imagined the headlines:

Here We Go Round the Lord Mulberry Bush.
New Peer in Porno Pics!

The family would never get over the shame! Henry would have a heart attack if he thought that his brother was soiling their good name and he could kiss goodbye to his peerage. What the hell was he going to do? Hugo closed his eyes and tried to quell his rising fear.

Suddenly he had an idea. He must tell Andy! He would know how to deal with it and maybe find out who the blackmailer was. Yes, of course! Andy would help him. Hugo stuffed the photographs back in the envelope and shoved it under the chair. In the meantime, he decided, he must act as if everything was normal and not spoil his brother's night. Patting his pocket, he made sure that the ring was safe, then opened the door and stepped into the corridor. As he hurried along the hallway, he reached for his handkerchief and wiped beads of sweat off his brow.

Nothing must spoil his brother's evening, Hugo muttered, nothing at all!

Hattie stood outside, watching the guests gather in the conservatory with many spilling out onto the patio. Grouped together for warmth, most wore coats and having had a wonderful dinner now looked forward to the fireworks that were about to begin. She saw Sir Henry and Lucinda take seats at the front of the crowd, while Hugo slid onto a chair alongside. A waiter handed out blankets and hot toddies.

Hattie watched Hugo and noted that he seemed on edge. He was talking to Andy and kept glancing from side to side. *James Bond has decided to put in an appearance!* Hattie thought cynically as she watched the two men, heads together, deep in conversation. Andy stepped back and stared at Hugo incredulously. Hugo was shaking his head as Andy began to pat his arm, as if to reassure, and Hattie wondered what on earth was being discussed.

'Everything seems to have gone very well.' Jo came alongside Hattie and wrapped a shawl around her shoulders. 'Here, keep warm, the fireworks are about to start.'

Hattie wondered what fireworks were brewing between

Hugo and Andy but Hugo was now helping Sir Henry to his feet.

Suddenly, Hugo started waving his arms in an attempt to silence the crowd.

'What on earth …' Jo said as she watched Hugo reach into his pocket and pass something to his brother.

'Ladies and gentlemen!' Hugo called out. 'Can I have your attention for one moment, please?'

The crowd hushed and people leaned in to catch Hugo's words.

'It is my greatest pleasure to tell you that love has blossomed here at Boomerville.' Hugo smiled at his brother who was helping Lucinda to her feet.

'Bleedin' hell,' Hattie said, 'he's going to propose …'

'Shush, I can't hear.' Jo nudged Hattie and strained to catch Hugo's words.

'Henry, old boy, I'll hand over to you.' Hugo beamed at his brother.

Sir Henry moved forward and, leaning heavily on his cane, began to get down on one knee.

'Christ, he'll never get up again.' Hattie moved forward but Jo held her back.

'Lucinda, my dearest Lucinda,' Sir Henry croaked as he teetered on one knee, 'will you do me the greatest honour of becoming my wife?' He looked into Lucinda's eyes.

Time seemed to stand still and the crowd were silent as they waited for her answer.

'Oh, dear Henry,' Lucinda cried, 'of course I will, yes … Yes!'

As if on cue, a flurry of fireworks shot into the sky and rockets exploded, sending cascading confetti of brilliant white stars to float earthwards behind the happy couple.

'How utterly romantic!' Jo cried out and clasped her hands to join in with the cheering and clapping as everyone circled around to give their congratulations.

Hattie stood on her tiptoes and watched anxiously as

Sir Henry was helped up and onto his feet. The old boy had turned quite pale.

Concerned, Hattie pushed through the crowd.

'Let me through!' she ordered as she made her way to Sir Henry's side. He seemed to be leaning heavily on Lucinda. Oblivious to her fiancé, Lucinda held out her sparkling ring as fireworks continued to light up the sky.

'I say, old girl,' Sir Henry began as Hattie reached his side, 'wouldn't happen to have a glass of water? I'm feeling a little bit faint.'

'Move back!' Hattie yelled. 'Get something for him to sit on!' She shoved the crowd away and, thrusting her arms under Sir Henry's, gently eased him onto a chair.

'Is something wrong?' Jo knelt beside Hattie, who'd removed Sir Henry's turban. As his eyes began to close, Hattie gently wiped beads of perspiration from his brow with one end of her sari. Hattie could see that his colour was fading and his lips had turned blue.

'Someone call an ambulance,' Hattie said. 'For God's sake get some medical help.'

'I'm on it!' James called out and reached for his mobile phone.

Lucinda had fallen to one side in a faint and Bob, having caught her, began to fan her face. Hugo stared at his brother in horror and as Sir Henry's breaths became shorter, he staggered back in disbelief.

Another chair was quickly found and Hugo eased into it, his shock clear to all.

Jo put her arm around Hattie's shoulders as she watched her friend stroke Sir Henry's face.

'Come on, stay with us you daft old codger.' Hattie spoke kindly with reassurance but tears were pouring down her cheeks. With trembling fingers, she gently loosened the buttons on his shirt and eased the cane gripped in his hand.

Stricken, Hattie turned to Jo and whispered, 'Let's hope we're not too late.'

Chapter Thirty

Sir Henry Mulberry died at six-thirty the next morning. Following his collapse at Boomerville, he was rushed by ambulance to the emergency department at Marland hospital where medical staff endeavoured to save his life.

But Sir Henry never regained consciousness and as dawn rose over his beloved grouse moors and the haunting woofs of his dearly departed dogs called from their heavenly kennels, the old man slipped quietly away.

Lucinda, who was hysterical, had been sedated and James, on hand to help in any way that he could, had taken her back to the hotel where he'd woken Kate and told her the terrible news. He asked if she might sit with Lucinda. Kate was pleased to do something useful, given the circumstances, and together they assisted a drowsy Lucinda up the stairs to her room.

In his final hours, a small group had gathered around Sir Henry's bed.

Hugo, with his head resting on Hattie's shoulder, sat on one side with Bob and Jo on the other. Hattie held Sir Henry's hand and stroked the paper-thin skin, while Bob sang a soothing chant. They all knew that the clock was ticking down. The beep from a monitor had stopped and his shallow breaths could no longer be heard.

A nurse padded gently across the room to check the patient's pulse. She stroked her fingers over his eyelids then neatened the sheet across his chest as the assembled group held their breath.

'He's gone,' she said softly. 'I'm so sorry.'

Hugo put his head on his brother's chest and began to weep. He lay there for some time until Hattie, placing her hands on his shoulders, gently peeled him away.

'Come on, Hugo dear,' she said. 'It's time to leave.' She eased him off the bed and hooked her arm around him. 'Let's go and get a nice hot cup of tea.'

Jo leaned in and kissed Sir Henry's forehead and Bob followed suit. With tears in their eyes, Bob gripped Jo's arm and they all silently stumbled out of the room.

They sat in the relatives' room and thanked the medical team and Hattie immediately took control of the formalities. She'd made a call to Henry's son when they arrived at the hospital and now made another to tell him that his father had passed away and that there was no need for anyone to rush to the hospital in Marland. Hugo was on hand and would take care of everything.

Hugo hadn't spoken and seemed dazed as the little procession walked out of the hospital into daylight, where Pete was waiting with his car to take them back to Boomerville.

'Nice and gently, old son,' Pete said as he eased Hugo onto the back seat and helped Hattie slide alongside. 'Soon have you home.'

They set off on their journey as the sun rose over the fells. Clouds drifted lazily in a pale blue sky and birds soared above.

Sir Henry's life had ended and a new day was born.

'Life goes on,' Jo whispered as she watched the world come awake. She stared out of the car window and thought back to the old times at Kirkton House when the two younger brothers were on their finest form – handsome and charismatic and smartly dressed for a day's shooting on the moors. There had been many weekends of fun at the hotel with the Mulberrys and their guests and Jo had enjoyed their company, little knowing at the time the value of those moments.

Now they were just a memory.

Boomerville had never been intended as a place for the elderly but she hadn't thought twice when Sir Henry got in touch again. She'd been delighted to welcome him back and he had spent his final days at Boomerville, where he was happy and had found a new lease of life, and Jo was humbled and knew that she'd done the right thing.

She dabbed at her eyes as Pete drove slowly and as they arrived in the village he eased the car across the drive. It came to a stop by the front door where guests and staff, waiting in silence, had gathered to see the party back.

The Shaman stood in the shadow of the willow tree and closed his eyes, as if in prayer. He raised his staff and made a circle and several crows began to circle overhead. Little was said as Hugo was helped out of the car, followed by Hattie, Jo and Bob, but hands were shaken and shoulders touched as everyone paid their respects.

'How's Lucinda?' Jo asked James as she came into the hallway.

'She's sleeping,' he replied. 'Kate is with her.'

'I think we all need a drink,' Hattie said as she led Hugo to a chair in the lounge and Bob organised brandy for everyone.

With her glass in one hand and Sir Henry's silver-topped cane in the other, Hattie moved to the centre of the room.

'We've lost a dear friend and brother today,' Hattie began, 'and right now this is very painful.' She had tears in her eyes as she continued. 'But Henry was a man who loved life and he wouldn't want us to be sad.' She paused and looked at Hugo. 'I know that each and every one of you will be there for Hugo and Lucinda, who will need our love and support in the days to come. So let's raise our glasses in tribute.'

Hattie looked around the room at the solemn faces.

'Ladies and gentlemen, please be upstanding for Sir Henry Mulberry, a fine man, our dearest friend and valued guest and our very first boomer at Boomerville.'

Chapter Thirty-One

Kate had been sitting by Lucinda's bed for several hours. The doctor had prescribed a heavy sedative to calm the hysteria that had overtaken her the night before and now, after tossing and turning, Lucinda slept peacefully.

Sunlight filtered through a gap in the closed drapes, catching at shadows in the room. It felt watery and cold and Kate shivered as she sat in the silence. Several times she thought she saw the Shaman hovering in a corner or standing by Lucinda's bed. Kate knew that she was probably delirious from lack of sleep and worry but his ethereal presence carried no fear.

James tiptoed in and out of the room during the night, bringing Kate cups of tea and sandwiches, sitting companionably next to her as Lucinda slept and Kate was grateful that he was there.

She'd stood to smooth the bed covers and tuck a shawl around Lucinda's shoulder, when a gentle tap came on the bedroom door.

'Can we come in?' Hattie whispered as she peeped into the room. 'Jo's with me.'

The two women crept in.

'How is she?' Jo asked.

'Fitful,' Kate said. 'She's been restless but is sleeping now.'

'One of us needs to be here when she wakes.' Hattie looked at Lucinda, whose hands rested on the counterpane, Sir Henry's ring gleaming on her finger. 'She must be told straight away.'

'I'm happy to stay,' Kate said.

'No, you've had no sleep.' Jo touched Kate's arm. 'You look drained. Hattie and I will take it in turns.'

'But you've both been up all night too.'

'We can sort it.' Hattie looked at Kate. 'And you have things that need to be done today.'

'The two of you go, I'm happy to stay with Lucinda,' Jo said. 'Please, I insist.'

As Kate and Hattie left the room, Jo sat down on a chair by the bed and closed her eyes. The room was quiet and she felt exhausted. She melted into the cushions and longed to put her feet up to grab a few moments' sleep. Her eyelids felt heavy and tiredness was taking over.

Her head fell to one side and she began to nod off.

'I know that he's dead.'

The voice startled Jo and she jerked her head up. Lucinda's eyes were open and she stared straight ahead.

Jo sat up and, taking Lucinda's hand, whispered, 'It was very peaceful.'

'Our time together has been snatched away.'

'But you made lots of happy memories here as you got to know each other,' Jo said. 'No one can take them away.'

'I wanted to be his wife. I've never been a wife. I didn't mind not being a mother but it hurts, not being a wife.'

'I'm so sorry.'

'I wasn't marrying him for his money. I know everyone thought I was a gold-digger but I loved him.' Lucinda's voice cracked as she spoke. 'Money has never worried me. It comes and it goes.'

'Don't worry about money, Lucinda,' Jo spoke softly, 'we can sort everything out.'

'I was so happy.' Tears began to trickle out of the corner of Lucinda's eyes.

'And you'll be happy again.'

Jo reached out and held Lucinda's hand. She didn't know what to say or how to make things better. Lucinda was in shock and, as Jo knew only too well, it took time to heal the pain and grief that she was feeling.

'You're with friends.' Jo spoke softly as she watched Lucinda's eyes begin to close and drift into a restless sleep. 'Boomerville will always be here for you.'

Hugo lay on his bed and stared at the ceiling. It didn't seem possible. Only a few hours ago he'd been about to celebrate his brother's engagement but suddenly his world had been turned upside down.

Henry had always been the stronger of the two brothers, the backbone that Hugo relied on, with the wisdom that had driven their family business to success and allowed Hugo to play about with politics, in a career that he'd never had to work hard for. His life had been one long party if truth be told; any scrape that he'd found himself in had soon been remedied by his brother and over the years there had been many.

Hugo had never married and enjoyed his bachelor status, leaving Henry to find a wife and produce heirs, which had in turn given Hugo a family life. He'd had no objection to Henry hooking up with Lucinda, for his brother had been a widower for a long time and Hugo was pleased that Henry was having a bit of fun in his final days. But what was Hugo going to do now? Life without Henry seemed unimaginable and Hugo wondered how on earth he was going to carry on.

A knock on the door interrupted Hugo's thoughts and he sat up. 'Come in,' he said and wearily swung his legs over the side of the bed.

Andy walked into the room. He was carrying a bottle of whisky and as he closed the door he glanced at Hugo then moved over to the desk, where he found two glasses and began to pour.

'I know it's not yet lunchtime but I thought that you might be in need of a drink,' Andy said.

'Thanks, old boy, I appreciate that.' Hugo took a large swallow.

'Terrible news, I'm so sorry,' Andy said.

'A bit of a shocker.'

'You'll have to make a lot of arrangements?'

'What?' Hugo looked up. 'Oh yes, I suppose so. Funeral and all that.'

'Be heading off soon?'

'Yes, yes, I hadn't thought about it.'

'Given any more thought to the business you mentioned last night?' Andy wasn't sure whether Hugo had remembered telling him about the photographs and blackmail demand.

'What's that?' Hugo frowned. 'Oh, the photographs. Have you had a demand too?'

'Er, no.' Andy hid a smile. Hugo clearly thought that Andy had used the website in a similar manner and had no idea who his blackmailer was. 'Actually, I've closed your account down and cleared the laptop so there's no trace of you anywhere.'

'Good show.'

Hugo was distant and Andy wondered if Sir Henry's death had thrown the implications of the blackmail threat onto a backburner.

'But blackmailers don't go away.' Andy topped up their glasses. 'It doesn't really matter now.'

Andy was incredulous. Was Hugo saying he wasn't bothered about the photographs? Andy began to panic as he knocked back his drink and poured more. He knew that there was nothing he could do to put the pressure on if Hugo didn't cough up, for he had no intention of going to the press, who would insist he came clean with his source.

'You don't mind the press running a piece on you?' Andy asked.

'They'll never do that.' Hugo drank more of the whisky and his voice began to slur.

'I wouldn't be so sure.' Andy's hands were shaking. He had to convince the old fool that the threat was real. His blackmail scam was about to fall apart, leaving him with a big hole in his future income.

'No, they'll never do that.' Hugo lay back on the pillows and closed his eyes, alcohol and tiredness catching up.

'How can you be so sure?' Andy fought to control his voice; he wanted to grab Hugo and shake him.

'Because I shall pay it.'

'What?' Andy was staggered.

'Henry is dead. Everything comes to me and I sign the cheques now.' Hugo breathed heavily. 'Henry's son will get a lump sum and continue to receive a damn good income from the business, as he runs it, but he'll have to wait 'till I croak before he gets everything. It's a clause Henry and I agreed in both our wills.' Hugo's voice trailed off. He slumped further down the bed and with a final sigh, soon began to snore.

Andy stared at the man on the bed.

Hugo had fallen into a deep sleep and wouldn't be roused for hours. Andy grabbed the whisky and as he poured himself another drink, he began to laugh. It was unbelievable! Far easier than he'd ever imagined! This was only a down payment on a scam that could run and run. Andy could hardly believe his luck. Thank God Sir Henry had died. Hugo had plenty of life in him and would have total control of the family finances. This could keep Andy going for years!

It was time to start packing his bags.

Money from Kate was already flowing through his web of untraceable offshore accounts and he'd spent the night moving funds around. But any day now she would notice. He knew that Kate had been acting as a nursemaid for Lucinda but the old bat would wake up soon and Kate, wanting to return the ring, would come looking for him. He supposed he would need to placate her, feign shock and hurt and all that. He didn't give a stuff if she kept the ring; it was small change for the amount he was taking. But if she thought he was upset, it would justify his leaving and play right into his hands, giving him time to make his escape.

Andy studied his watch. Perhaps Kate was free now? He picked up the almost empty bottle and raced from the room. He'd smarten himself up, then go and find her. The sooner he made his getaway the better!

Kate sat in the lounge. There was no one about. Most of the guests, upset by the death of Sir Henry, had gone out for a walk or retired to their rooms. She smoothed her skirt over her knees and ran her fingers through her hair. She knew that she looked tired and dishevelled but in the cold light of morning, it was the least of her concerns.

The sooner she confronted Andy, the better. She'd spoken to him on the phone a few moments ago and asked if he'd meet her downstairs. Kate had discussed with Hattie how to break things off and give back the ring and they'd decided that it was best done in a public place, where there was no chance that he might become angry and hurt her.

Kate drummed her fingers on the arm of her chair and tried not to think about the way things had turned out. For tomorrow, she intended to go back to the schoolhouse. Back to her lonely life, with no man by her side to keep her company in her autumn years. She'd bitten the forbidden apple and tasted the glorious flavour of romance, but in a few short weeks it had all gone horribly sour and left a foul and bitter taste in her mouth.

She knew that she had a novel to work on and if she could keep going, there may be more writing in the pipeline. At least that was something to be proud of. Somehow she must stay optimistic. But the emotional turmoil that she'd experienced for so long when caring for her dad was back. Kate felt as though a knife had been driven through her heart and it physically hurt.

Had she really been so vulnerable when she met Andy? At such an emotional low ebb that she'd been so easily fooled into falling in love?

Kate reached into her bag and found the box that held Andy's ring and placed it on the table. She longed to throw it across the room and hurl it into the fire or scratch it across his handsome face, but she knew that she was being petty and must keep calm and dignified until it was over. She stared out of the window at the willow tree and wondered if the Shaman was watching. Her fingers were aching and the pain had come back.

She felt angry.

What a waste of time the Shaman was! Casting spells to make people better and curing evil, it was farcical and she wondered why she had been uneasy in his company. He was just a silly old man, an imposter bought in to spice up the courses and she wasn't going to spend another moment of her time in his presence.

She heard the door open and spun around.

'Kate, my darling, there you are.' Andy stood at the entrance. His face was distraught and he hurried across the room to sit by her side. 'Please can we talk about the future? You know that I can't live without you.'

Kate could smell whisky. There was a smell of sour alcohol and stale cigar smoke. Andy hadn't shaved and looked unkempt and as she recoiled, Kate knew that she no longer had any feelings for this man.

Thankfully, this was going to be easier than she'd thought.

James wandered down the corridor of the hotel and yawned as he pulled his coat around his shoulders and reached into a pocket for his scarf. The events of the previous evening had been exhausting: sitting through the night with Kate beside Lucinda, unable to talk so they didn't disturb the newly bereaved fiancée, yet needing to stay awake. When the mourners returned from the hospital, he'd had a large brandy and decided to snatch some sleep on the sofa in his studio.

He'd only just woken up.

His car was parked at the front of the hotel and as he reached the hallway he stopped. Hattie was by the Green Room. The door was closed and she was bent down with her ear against the keyhole.

'Hattie, what are you doing?' he asked.

'Shush!' Hattie held up her hand and indicated that James should keep back.

'You shouldn't listen at keyholes.'

'Belt-up James,' Hattie hissed. 'I can't hear a thing with you prattling on.'

'Then perhaps you should come away.'

'Oh, you don't understand.' Hattie straightened up and turned to face James. 'I'm keeping an ear out for Kate. She's talking to James Bond and I don't trust him as far as I can throw him.'

Hattie had caught James' attention. Mention of Kate stopped him in his tracks and he too bent down to the keyhole to listen. 'What's she saying to him?' James whispered.

'She's giving him the old heave-ho.'

'Breaking it off?' James straightened up.

'Snapping it in two if I had my way,' Hattie said, face darkening, 'before the evil shit lays one more finger on her.'

'What did you say?'

'Oh, you heard,' Hattie snapped. 'I'd have had him arrested but she wants to do it her way.'

James stood back. He took a moment to digest Hattie's comments. If he understood correctly, Hattie had just informed him that Andy had been physical towards Kate, who was now alone in the Green Room with the monster.

James removed his coat, scarf and glasses and handed them to Hattie. 'Hold these for one moment, please.' He opened the door to the Green Room and stood at the entrance.

Kate was sitting in a chair by the far window and Andy was on his feet towering over her. He didn't see James and as he made ready to exit the room, James heard Andy leave Kate with a parting shot.

'You'll regret it,' Andy snapped. 'Your final years will be lonely and isolated because you're a middle-aged matron whose looks are fading and no one else will have you. You'll wish you hadn't turned me down.'

Kate had seen James and as her frightened eyes darted towards him, Andy spun around.

'Oh, I see, your literary lover leaps in to soothe your pain,'

Andy said and began to march past James. 'Where's your glasses, four-eyes?'

James stepped forward and, with one smooth and alarmingly accurate shot, punched Andy hard on the nose, cracking his head back and sending him careering across the room.

'James!' Kate screamed.

'Bleedin' hell, James!' Hattie shouted and rushed forward to land a hefty kick in Andy's stomach as he lay writhing on the carpet.

'What on earth's going on?' Jo ran into the room and saw Hattie land the kick. Pete was close behind and Bunty, sensing tension, lurched herself onto Andy and grabbed the leg of his trousers.

'Get that bloody dog off me!' Andy yelled and kicked out.

'Bunty, off!' Jo screamed and tugged hard until Bunty released Andy's leg. 'Pete, help him to his feet.'

Jo looked around the room and looked questioningly at Hattie.

'It's a long story,' Hattie said.

James, who was rubbing his knuckles, stood back as Pete led Andy from the room. Andy's nose was red and he held a handkerchief to staunch the profuse bleeding. He swore under his breath as he glared at James and Hattie. 'I'll have you both for assault,' he hissed.

Jo stared at Hattie, then turned to Kate. 'Are you all right?'

'Yes, I think so.' Kate's eyes were wide and she seemed to look at James in a new light.

'You've got some explaining to do,' Jo said to Hattie.

Hattie held her arms out as James retrieved his coat. He knotted the scarf at his neck and replaced his glasses.

'If he wants to press charges you know where I am,' James said. 'It's time I went home.'

'He won't be pressing any charges.' Hattie reached for Kate's arm. 'I think Mr Mack will think twice about that.'

'Oh, I hope so,' Kate said. 'Thank you so much, James.'

But James had turned on his heel and was gone.

Chapter Thirty-Two

Sunday morning began with a thunderstorm as heavy black clouds swept in from the fells. Jo was woken by a menacing rumble as the heavens opened and stair-rods of rain ricocheted off the lawn. She wished that Pete was with her but he'd left early to attend a steam rally in Yorkshire and would be gone for a couple of days.

'Any room for a little one?' Hattie said, shoving the door of Jo's room with her bottom. She held a mug of tea in each hand, slopping the contents as she burst in. Bunty, who'd been snuggled on the bed, leapt down and began to lick at the carpet.

'Dismal day,' Hattie said and placed the drinks on a bedside table. 'The forecast is terrible for the next forty-eight hours. What rotten weather to be leaving Boomerville.' She pulled her housecoat around her body and dug in a pocket. 'Croissant?' she asked, revealing a fluff-covered pastry.

'No, thanks,'

'I'll organise Hugo's packing as soon as I'm dressed; we can't leave it all to the morning.' Hattie tucked into her breakfast.

'Have you booked his train?'

'Yes, he's on an early one tomorrow morning, direct through to London. Bob is going too. It made sense for them to travel together and Bob said he would make sure that Hugo got back safely.'

'That's kind of Bob,' Jo said. 'Will Hugo go to his flat?' She sat at her dressing table and began to brush her hair.

'I imagine so, then out to Hereford to sort out the funeral arrangements, which will be from Raven Hall, the family's country home.'

'What about Sir Henry's belongings? Hugo will never manage it all on the train.'

'We can send them on or take them when we go to the

funeral.' Hattie looked out at the deluge beyond the window. 'It would make Hugo's journey easier.'

The two women watched the storm. The trees in the meadow bowed as the wind howled and rain dashed against the glass.

'I think Kate will check out today,' Jo said.

'Aye, I wouldn't be surprised. James Bond hasn't been seen since last night but room service took whisky and a club sandwich up.' Hattie smiled. 'I bet the Porsche is packed and ready to go as soon as he's sobered up.'

'Do we know if he's all right?' Jo asked. Having learnt that James was the culprit who'd landed the crucial punch and Hattie merely followed up with a kick, she was anxious that charges weren't pressed against her employee at her place of business. 'It could be a problem for Boomerville if Andy involves the police. Is his nose broken?'

'Sadly, no,' Hattie replied. 'The housekeeper had a glimpse of him when she tried to clean the room and said he looked hungover but normal.' Hattie smiled. 'But I think he'll have a couple of shiners; she said his eyes looked bruised.'

'I don't know why you're looking so pleased.' Jo was cross. 'This could be serious.' She picked up a pot of face cream and, dunking a finger, began to smooth it over her skin. 'I feel terribly sorry for Kate, it's hard at any age to be let down in a relationship. I hope she doesn't think that was her last chance.'

'She's well shot of him,' Hattie said. 'I never liked him and there are plenty of men who would snap her up.'

'You're right, but Kate might not see it like that at the moment.'

'Well, maybe you should have a word and convince her otherwise, bang on about Pete turning up when you least expected it and all that sort of hopeful, happy-ever-after-ending stuff that you're good at. Give her hope.'

'You could say a few soothing words using your own love-life as an example.' Jo looked at Hattie's reflection in the mirror and raised an eyebrow. 'Or possibly not ...'

'I think my gallivanting days are numbered,' Hattie said.

'What do you mean?'

'Oh, I don't know, I look at you and Pete and sometimes think that I'd like to have someone around who wants more than a tumble or two. A bit of company that's cosy, with a pair of "his and hers" slippers by my fire.'

Jo stared at Hattie. She'd never heard her speak like this before. 'What are you saying?'

'I'm just making a point that it must be nice to have someone in your life who's there for breakfast, lunch and dinner.' Hattie was thoughtful. 'And possibly supper too.'

'A partner?'

'Aye, maybe, an older man who is comfortably off and not sponging, a man who would love and appreciate me.'

'Would you marry again?'

'Oh, who knows?' Hattie shrugged. She thought of her flings with Potter Paul and Harry the Helmet. The least said about her own affairs, the better. 'What are we going to do about Lucinda?' She sat on Jo's bed and swung her legs, then nestled into the soft pillows. Bunty jumped up and began to bury her nose in Hattie's pocket, her tail thumping as she found a stray crumb.

'Lucinda can stay as long as she likes.' Jo opened a drawer and rummaged until she found a bra and matching knickers, then shrugging off her nightie began to get dressed. 'Let her recover a little. She can take some painting classes when she feels up to it.'

'They'll be jolly, should attract a full class.' Hattie pushed Bunty to one side. 'Dark and deathly doodles, can you imagine her theme?'

'You're probably right, she may not be the best tutor to be teaching right now, but she could sit in on some of the other classes to take her mind off things.'

'Whatever.' Hattie sat up and slid off the bed. She picked up her mug and drained her tea then moved to the door. 'I'm going to get glammed up. I have a feeling we're going to have a busy day and I want to look my best.'

'I'll be over in a bit, after I've taken Bunty out.'

'See you later.' Hattie gave Jo a thumbs-up. 'Let's get this show back on the road.'

Kate was in her bedroom. She sat at the desk and stared at the pile of clothes on the bed. It seemed such a long time since she'd arrived at Boomerville and unpacked her belongings, storing them away in what was to become her home for the next few weeks. But now she had to empty the room, put everything back into cases and head back to the lonely life she'd come away from.

She felt an overwhelming sadness.

The euphoria had evaporated. All the joy that she'd known in having a new relationship had been snatched away. Kate had fallen in love and it had been glorious but then suddenly doubt had crept in and her trust had been shattered.

Kate went over to the window. It was dark outside, the morning as menacing as her mood where rain, turning to sleet, crackled off the gravel on the driveway below. Jo appeared from the side entrance of her house and ran after Bunty, who disappeared under the willow tree. Jo wrapped her raincoat around her body and peered from beneath the hood, urging Bunty to be quick. The dog scampered out and Kate watched Jo reach down to stroke her pet. Jo was smiling, despite the weather, as Bunty, devoted and trusting, wriggled playfully beneath her hand.

Perhaps I should get a dog? Kate thought, for clearly the love was reciprocal between owner and animal and not punctured with unforeseen pain.

Kate sighed. She must stop feeling sorry for herself. She had to gather her things and load up her car. There would be plenty of time in the weeks to come to mourn her broken relationship; right now she needed to get ready for her journey.

As she continued to pack she thought about James, who'd telephoned earlier and asked if he could take her for lunch. He seemed sad that she was leaving and wanted to see her before she set off on her journey. Kate had agreed. They could eat in the hotel where Sunday lunch was the best in the area. She picked up the phone and called reception.

'Good morning, Kate,' Hattie said in a bright and cheery voice. 'How are you today?'

'I just wanted to let you know that I'll be checking out today.'

'I'm very sorry to hear that. Are you sure you won't stay a little longer, help you take your mind off things?'

'No, but thank you, I need to move on. The whole place reminds me of Andy and the happy times we had here.'

'Well, if I could persuade you I would, but if your mind is made up ...'

'It is, Hattie, thanks.' Kate was about to put the phone down, then remembered her meeting with James. 'I'd like to book a table for two for lunch.'

'I think you'll find that it's already been reserved.'

'Oh?'

'James made the reservation just after he'd spoken to you.'

'Of course, thanks. How silly of me, naturally he would. I'll see you later.'

Kate hung up.

It would be good to spend time with James before she left. He'd been a great comfort when Lucinda returned to the hotel and helped Kate settle the dazed woman. In the hours that followed he'd provided a constant supply of refreshments and his presence had been reassuring. Kate had been glad to have him sitting beside her in the darkened room as Lucinda slept. James had been so inspirational in helping her to write and Kate felt sure that without him she would never have set about a novel. She stared out of the window where dark clouds hung low over the fells, shrouding them in a thick, damp mist.

She also knew that James had feelings for her.

Kate smiled. Had he really punched Andy?

Andy had antagonised James at every opportunity and although she would have never expected it of him, Kate was delighted that James had got his own back.

I hope Andy's face hurts like hell! Kate said to herself and, turning from the depressing weather outside, began to pack up her things.

Bob was also busy. He stood in Hugo's room and looked at the clothes and personal items scattered around and, pleased that he'd been given a job to do, set about packing Hugo's belongings into the leather cases that lay open on the bed.

'Damned good of you to help out,' Hugo said. He sat in an armchair nursing a glass of whisky. 'I can't seem to focus on things.'

Heavy rain lashed against the window as Hugo sipped his drink.

'It's the least I can do.' Bob reached into the wardrobe where Hugo's clothes hung to one side and Sir Henry's on the other. 'Hattie is going to make arrangements for your brother's things to be taken home. Don't worry about a thing, she'll take care of it all.'

'Fine woman,' Hugo said. 'Heart of gold under that heaving chest, make someone a first-rate wife.'

'All part of the Boomerville service, I'm sure.' Bob smoothed and folded, running his hands over cotton shirts and heavy tweeds, taking care to pack Hugo's finery. 'Do we know how Lucinda is today?'

'Taken to her bed, I hear.' Hugo poured more whisky. 'I'd better pay the gal a visit.'

'Would you like me to come with you?'

'Might ease the way. Would you mind old chap?'

'Not at all,' Bob said as he closed the final case and placed it on the floor. The last time he'd seen Lucinda was at the hospital. She'd been hysterical and it wasn't a pretty sight. God willing, she'd be zoned out on tranquillisers and unaware that she had visitors.

'Fancy a spot of lunch?' Bob asked.

'No appetite, old boy.'

'You might find you're tempted.' Bob walked across the room and took the glass from Hugo's hand. 'It's roast beef today, Yorkshire puddings and all the trimmings.' He placed his hand on Hugo's shoulder. 'Do you think you might try? It would help keep your strength up.'

'A roast. Henry's favourite.' Hugo's eyes began to mist as he eased out of the chair.

Bob helped Hugo to his feet and, with a last look around and satisfied that his work was done, led Hugo out of the room. 'We'll raise a glass of wine to Sir Henry as we dine,' he said and with a steadying arm guided Hugo down to the restaurant.

It was busy in the panel room as James and Kate went in for lunch. A fire blazed and they sat at a corner table close to the hearth, where they could enjoy the cosy warmth as the rain lashed down outside.

'It's wild out there today,' Kate said as James held her chair and waited for her to make herself comfortable.

'It certainly is. I think there might be flooding in the village if this keeps up. The river was very high as I drove over the bridge.'

They stared out of the window. Expanding pools of murky dark water lay on the patio as water gushed from downspouts struggling to cope with the deluge.

'I'm not looking forward to my journey home.'

'Do you have to leave today?' James flicked a serviette onto his knee.

'Yes, I think I should.'

'Have you seen anything of Andy?' James hated asking but was keen to know if Andy was still in residence.

'No. Hattie says he's holed up in his room.'

'I'd like to think that he'll be leaving. Surely he can't intend to stay on after the way he's behaved?'

'I have no idea what his intentions are and I don't intend to hang around to find out.'

A waiter appeared with their starters and both tucked in. Kate spread butter on a warm roll. She wasn't hungry but as soon as she tasted the creamy soup, her stomach craved for more. She hadn't touched a thing the day before.

'What will you do with your novel?' James asked.

'I'll get it finished and edited as you suggest, then try and find a publisher. Bob said he would help me.'

'Don't dismiss self-publishing; cream rises to the top and a high percentage of successful books are from authors who go it alone.'

'It certainly is a consideration.'

James had read Kate's work-in-progress and thought that the theme was strong. She'd created a cast that blended well, with plenty of suspense and a twist that would hold the reader to the final page. 'Did you know it would turn into a mystery?' James asked.

'No, not at all. It was a happy-ever-after romance that in truth was probably boring, but as I got going something seemed to possess me and the whole plot changed. I can't explain it.' Kate pushed her bowl to one side. She rubbed her fingers together; they seemed especially painful today.

'So Boomerville has been good for you?'

'Yes, I suppose it has, despite my stupidity.' Kate didn't want to discuss Andy but felt that the conversation was heading that way again.

'You weren't stupid at all,' James said softly. 'Your emotions were on the floor having dealt with your father's dementia for so long. I can't imagine how much that must have taken out of you.'

Kate stared into the fire and there were tears at the corner of her eyes.

231

'Andy caught you at a very low time and it was natural for you to respond.' James longed to take her face in his hands and kiss the tears away. He also wished like hell that she'd met him first instead of that bastard Andy.

A waiter cleared their bowls and Kate turned to thank him.

James looked at Kate and wondered if she'd absorbed anything that he said. He wanted to tell her that there were plenty of men who would stop in their tracks if she only looked their way, but her eyes were sad and she seemed defensive. If only he could tell her how he felt, that he adored her and always would.

'How's your hand?' Kate asked. She reached out to touch his knuckle.

'Fine thanks, nothing broken.' James felt Kate's finger run lightly across his grazed skin and once again resisted the urge to pull her into his arms. She'd recoiled the last time he'd attempted to hold her and this was no place for a scene.

'Andy was always winding you up, you must have bottled your feelings for some time.' Kate attempted a smile.

'Possibly.' James searched Kate's eyes for signs of encouragement. 'He was an annoying student who was always disrupting my class. I thought he was thoroughly dislikeable.' James sighed. 'I'm sorry to say that because you clearly felt differently.'

Kate looked away. How could she tell James that she was mortified with shame by the way she'd fallen so easily for Andy? She knew that James had feelings for her and under any other circumstances she'd have reciprocated, for James was a decent man. He was very attractive too. Not in a drop-dead-handsome way like Andy, but his charm and manner was appealing and Kate wondered why she'd never seen it before.

But it felt all too soon and her heart would not allow her to go from one to another.

Their main course arrived and as Kate helped herself to vegetables, she looked up to see Bob and Hugo come into the restaurant. They were guided to a table at the opposite side of the room.

'Hugo looks dreadful,' Kate said. The man seemed to have aged overnight, his brother's death weighing heavy.

'It was a great shock,' James said. Kate had diverted the conversation and his heart sank. He'd asked her to lunch to tell her how he felt in the hope that she would at least give him a chance but now he'd blown his opportunity.

Dessert was served and Kate asked James about Helen. He told her that he hadn't heard anything since she'd left for France.

'I hope you sort it out. Helen will have regrets if she doesn't enjoy her relationship with her sons.' Kate looked at James. 'I'm sorry, I have no right to comment on a parent's behaviour. I don't know what it is to be a parent.'

'Don't worry, you're saying all the right things.'

They'd finished their coffee.

'I must be making tracks,' Kate said. 'It's late afternoon already and I've got several hours of driving ahead. And I don't like the look of this weather.' She pushed her chair back and placed her serviette on the table. 'I have to go and pay my hotel bill.'

James stood too. 'Lunch is on me. I'll settle up and then see you off. Do you need a hand with your luggage?'

'That's kind, thank you.'

James watched Kate walk away and knew that his chances were fading. He determined that before she got into her car, he would tell Kate how he felt. After all, he had nothing to lose. He followed her through the restaurant and into the bar where a new group of boomers were chatting about their week to come. Hattie and Jo were in reception and both looked up as Kate and James approached.

'All set for the off?' Hattie asked cheerily and handed Kate her bill.

'Yes, I'll just sort this out.' Kate reached for her bag. She took a bank card out of her purse and handed it to Hattie as Jo took a payment from James for their lunch.

Outside, dark clouds collided as they rumbled in from the fells. Thunder roared and lightning streaked across the sky. They discussed the terrible weather as they waited for Kate's card to clear and Jo urged her to take care on her journey south.

'It says "insufficient funds",' Hattie whispered to Kate, sliding the card discreetly across the desk.

'What? There must be some mistake.' Kate was puzzled and searched for an alternative payment.

'Whoops, it's happened again.' Hattie did her utmost to be inconspicuous as Kate passed several cards to her but it soon became apparent that none were going to clear.

'But I don't understand?' Kate's hands were shaking as she fumbled around in her purse.

'Here, let me.' James handed Hattie a card to cover Kate's account.

'No, I couldn't possibly.' Kate pushed his card to one side. 'There can't be a problem. I have ample funds in all my accounts.'

Kate was becoming upset and Jo, sensing that new residents were within earshot and wishing to save any embarrassment, stepped in. She took Kate's arm. 'Let's wait a few moments, then try again.'

'I'll get my laptop and go online to check my account, there must be an explanation,' Kate said, but as she turned a crash of thunder shuddered through the building and the lights flickered in the hallway.

Suddenly everything went dark.

'That's the power off.' Hattie reached under the desk for a box of candles. 'By the look of this storm, it could be off for some time.'

'Oh dear.' Jo frowned. 'I think you're right.' She stared anxiously out of the window. 'I'm afraid to say it, but we could be in for a very long night.'

234

Chapter Thirty-Three

The lack of light was confusing and as a blanket of darkness fell on the hotel, Kate stumbled down the corridor with James in close pursuit.

'Kate, I'm fairly sure that the internet won't work in this storm,' James said. 'Come and sit down while we think what to do. You can't wander around in the dark.'

Kate held on to the banister at the bottom of the stairs. When she heard James, she stopped.

'And you can't possibly contemplate travelling.' James was firm. He took Kate's arm and without any protestations she allowed herself to be led into the Red Room. The fire cast an eerie glow that lit the room with dancing shadows as James found a sofa and they sank into the soft cushions.

'I must speak to the bank fraud line. There has to be an explanation.' Kate fiddled about in her bag. 'But my phone is dead.'

James dug in his pocket and produced his mobile.

He flicked it on and was pleased to see that he still had a signal. 'I must be on a different service provider. You can use mine. Have you got a helpline number?' He held out his phone so that it illuminated the number on the back of the card gripped in Kate's hand. 'Call now, while we wait for the power to come back.' He handed Kate the phone and she began to dial. 'You'll feel better when you've spoken to someone; they'll be able to advise you.'

'But will they be able to get my money back?'

James could barely see Kate's face in the shadows but he could sense her worry.

'I couldn't say,' he said softly. 'Let's keep everything crossed.'

Jo fumbled through the hallway. She wondered why on earth the emergency lighting hadn't come on from the back-up generator. It was now completely dark and, as the storm built, the torrential rain seemed to be getting worse.

She stood by a window and stared. The drains on the driveway were bubbling and as Jo looked up she wondered if the heavens were knocking on the roof, as an inescapable deluge fell from the sky. She could hear Hattie calling out to the residents as she guided them through to the Green Room and she went to join her, groping her way along.

'It will be safer if we keep everyone together in here,' Hattie said and shone a torch in Jo's direction. 'Grab this and give us a hand.'

Hattie pressed a torch into Jo's hand and together they found seats for the guests and settled everyone in. They placed candles in holders on the mantelpiece and lit them.

'It's quite spooky,' Hattie said as she turned and looked at the group, discernible in the flickering light, illuminated enough to make their skin waxy and eyes bright.

'I think we'd better do a roll-call and make sure that everyone is here,' Jo instructed. 'Can you get a list of names from reception?'

'I'm on it,' Hattie said and fumbled her way out of the room.

'Darling, what's happened?' Bob called out from the doorway, his voice excited. 'Will the power be off for long?'

'I hope not, but the last time there was a storm it was off all night.'

'Marvellous, we can sit by the fire and tell ghost stories.'

'Stories to pass the time are a good idea but perhaps not of the ghoulish kind.' Jo didn't want any heart attacks or sudden strokes to complicate matters.

'Leave it with me, I'll make sure everyone is entertained.' Bob waved his arms in front of his body and, scrabbling through the darkness, found a seat.

Jo went out to the hallway.

Where on earth was Alf? Her handyman was usually first on the scene when the weather threatened, checking the old place for leaks and damage and the generator was his favourite toy. He kept it in immaculate condition, always ready in case of emergency. With any luck, he'd be in the cellar working on it right now and very soon the lights would come back on.

Jo was uncomfortable in the dark and wished that Pete was with her. She remembered that Bunty was on her own in the house. Thunder and lightning didn't seem to bother the dog but Jo craved to hold the puppy in her arms. She shone her torch down the corridor and, with slow steady steps, set off.

Hattie stood on the back staircase. She held a lantern and fumbled to grab a rail for support as she put one foot carefully in front of the other and climbed. The lantern, left over from the Taste of the Raj evening, cast diamond shaped shadows that latticed the walls. The hotel was eerily silent, unlike the elements outside. Clouds crashed and thunder roared as wind and rain whipped furiously, shaking the old building to its core.

Hattie had checked on the residents and made sure that everyone was safe in the lounge but she'd been unable to find Hugo, Lucinda and Andy. Lucinda's room was empty, the bed unmade and the door wide open with no trace of the occupant.

Where on earth *was* she? Hattie knew that the artist was taking strong medication and she was worried that Lucinda might be confused and distressed in the dark. Hattie was determined to find her.

She didn't give a toss about Andy, but for safety's sake she knocked on his door and when there was no answer, used her passkey to enter the room. A cigar smouldered on a saucer, next to an empty glass. Hattie searched the room and poked her head around the bathroom door but Andy was nowhere to be seen.

She went over to the bed.

Two suitcases and a messenger bag were piled on the duvet, where a briefcase was open. A laptop lay in the briefcase, beside the messenger bag.

James Bond was planning to leave!

Hattie paused as she stared at the luggage and, a few minutes later, relocked the door and went in search of Hugo.

Hattie thought that Hugo was probably asleep. He'd had a substantial amount of wine at lunch and there was a good chance that he'd gone for a lie down, unaware that the power was off. She reached his door and knocked gently and, receiving no reply, turned the handle and crept into the room.

Loud snores echoed through the darkness and as Hattie's eyes focused in the gloom and she held her lamp out, she saw Hugo, fully clothed, asleep on his bed. She decided to leave him; he would take no harm in the dark and was probably exhausted, but as she turned she tripped on a rug and fell headlong into an armchair.

'Bugger!' Hattie cried out as her knee cracked on the wooden leg and upturned the chair, sending it careering into Hugo's bed. The bag slung across her shoulder became twisted and her lamp landed upright on the floor.

'What's going on?' Hugo sat up. He rubbed his eyes and tried to focus as Hattie emerged at the foot of the bed.

'Only me,' Hattie said cheerfully and plonked herself down. 'There's a power cut. I just wanted to make sure that you're all right.'

'Damned kind, old girl.' Hugo peered at Hattie. 'I thought my luck was in for a moment, don't fancy climbing aboard by any chance?' He patted the bed beside him.

'I'll pass,' Hattie said, pleased that Hugo hadn't completely given up on life. His brother may have died but Hugo wasn't one to miss an opportunity. 'Let's go downstairs, where we know you're safe. Just until the storm passes and the power comes back on.'

'We could go down to the pantry,' Hugo whispered and stared at Hattie.

For a moment, the years melted.

'I thought you'd forgotten,' Hattie said. She felt her cheeks burn as memories of their night of kitchen passion flooded back.

'Think about it every time I have a plate of cheese and chutney.' He smiled. 'Best night I ever had.'

Hattie was speechless. The old bugger! After all these years and he'd never said a thing. Flummoxed, she reached out to straighten the chair. But as she bent down to grab her lamp, a large brown envelope caught her eye. It was open and several photographs had tumbled out. 'What have we got here?' Hattie said, her eyes wide. She held the lamp over the pile and caught her breath as images came into focus. 'Bloody hell, Hugo, what's this all about?'

'Oh, good Lord, I can explain!' Hugo swung his legs over the side of the bed and scrambled over to Hattie. 'It's well, oh my goodness, I've made a terrible mistake.' Hugo sat back on the bed and, holding his face in his hands, began to cry.

'There, there,' Hattie said and put her arm around his shoulders. 'Tell me what happened.'

'But the pictures are pornography and you'll think I'm a pervert,' Hugo said between sobs, 'and the press will get hold of them and I'll be ruined.'

Hattie examined the photos. She didn't think Hugo was a pervert at all and as she carefully put the photographs back in the envelope, she smiled to herself. She rather admired the old boy for his spirit and as far as porn went, thought it quite mild. Hattie loved a bit of dressing up if it satisfied a sexual fantasy. Whatever turned Hugo on was, in Hattie's opinion, just fine. At least it showed that he still had feelings and wasn't dead from the waist down.

'Tell me all about it,' Hattie said suddenly, warming to Hugo. She wriggled her bottom up the bed and took hold of his hand. 'Don't dawdle with the facts, Lucinda's on the missing list and we need to find her.' As she made herself comfortable, Hugo began his tale.

Kate was in despair. She sat beside James and wracked her brains to try and work out what had happened to her finances.

She'd been on the telephone for what felt like ages. The weather was causing communication chaos and the line kept cutting off, but in the limited conversation she'd had with the bank's fraud team, their advice, other than telling her to inform the police, hadn't been optimistic.

Someone had definitely emptied her accounts. Now all she could do was wait for the investigations but meanwhile, she was stuck. With no money to even put petrol in her car and with the storm still raging, Kate would have to stay at Boomerville.

Jo kept popping in and out of the room to see if she could help in any way. She told Kate to try not to get anxious, that she could stay as long as she needed to and not to worry about settling her bill. Everything would be sorted out in due course.

Kate closed her eyes and thought about the questions that she'd been asked. Had anyone had access to her finances, her account numbers and passwords? Had she followed a responsible process to protect her account information?

She knew that she was on shaky ground.

Foolishly, she used the same password for her accounts and had written the information in her diary, which she'd kept in her handbag, where she kept her purse and all her cards. Kate was often forgetful. Only last week she'd left her bag in the Lemon Drop Café, when she'd had tea and cake with Andy and only remembered it when they got back to his car. Anyone could have poked around in the contents.

In summary, the bank had told her that if they suspected that a person had not done their part in protecting account information it was possible that the losses wouldn't be covered.

'So, what are your thoughts?' James asked. He'd listened to Kate's conversation, only moving to put a couple more logs on the fire and light another candle. 'Do you think it might be Andy?'

'No, I don't,' Kate said. 'He might be a total shit when it comes to not getting his own way in love, but he has plenty of money. I can't for one moment imagine that he had any need to go after mine.'

'I understand what you're saying, after all, Andy is still in the hotel. If he was guilty, one would think that he'd have checked out by now.' James sighed, he longed to pin this mess on Andy but it didn't make any sense. Kate was right, Andy may be a jilted lover and angry but he wasn't short of cash and had always made a show of how much money he had.

The wind outside howled and the wooden shutters rattled. They could hear the storm lashing against the sash windows. Kate felt as angry as the weather and wondered who the hell had hacked into her accounts. It was such a large sum of money and she kept asking herself why on earth she'd left so much in there. But it was too late now; it had gone and it seemed unlikely that she would get it back. Her anger was pointless.

'Will your life collapse without this money?' James asked.

Kate took her time before replying. 'No, I suppose not. I'm fortunate. I've no mortgage and have investments in other areas. I can only pray that the hacker hasn't got access to those.'

'Then you're not wiped out.'

'No, but it's so humiliating,' Kate said. 'It makes me feel sick and I feel violated and such a fool.' She sighed, weary with frustration for everything that had happened. 'I was so stupid not to protect my account information.'

Tears slid down her cheeks and James, distraught to see her crying, found the courage to reach for her hand. To his delight, Kate wrapped her fingers in his. After a few moments James put his arm around her shoulder and Kate lay her head on his chest, her eyelids drowsy with sleep. As the gusts and gales raged, the fire crackled and James soaked up the candle-lit atmosphere.

He turned and kissed the top of Kate's head.

Her hair was soft and smelt of freshly picked flowers and reminded James of sunshine and warm sunny days. He leant his cheek on her forehead and closed his eyes and in moments was sound asleep.

Hattie led Hugo along the corridor and told him that he must go to the Green Room, to join the other residents and wait until the power came back.

But Hugo was having none of it.

He wasn't going to let Hattie search around for Lucinda on her own in the dark, and said that it was his duty to accompany Hattie.

'You'd better grab hold of this then.' Hattie pulled her little rolling pin out of her pocket. 'If there's any sign of danger, use it.'

Hugo stared at the object and his eyes lit up. 'No, old girl, you keep a hold of that,' he said and whipped out Sir Henry's walking stick. 'My brother had multiple uses for this.' Hugo pulled the silver top off the cane and a blade glistened in the dark.

'Bleedin' hell, Hugo.' Hattie gasped and stepped back.

'Shhh!' Hugo whispered. 'There's someone coming.'

They'd reached the back of the hotel and could hear footsteps on the stairs. A faint light from the window cast a shadow along the wall. They could see a dark silhouette as the figure approached. Hattie gripped Hugo's arm and he turned and put his finger to Hattie's lips. Hattie felt her heart hammer as the figure got closer, a menacing object held high.

'Don't go any further!' Hugo yelled as he leapt in front of Hattie. He brandished the cane and the figure tumbled back onto the landing.

'It's only me,' a terrified voice squeaked out. 'I came to look for Lucinda.'

'*Bob!*' Hattie and Hugo hissed and both reached down to pull him back on his feet.

'I thought I could help,' a shaken Bob said. 'Jo told me that Lucinda is missing and the two of you were looking for her.'

242

He'd dropped the staff that he'd been carrying and groped around to find it. 'I brought my Shaman's stick.' Bob lovingly caressed the carved wood. 'If I bump into Andy, I'm going to use this.'

'Aye, well that's all well and good and you might have to,' Hattie said. 'But Andy is missing too and me and Hugo have formed a search party.'

'Oh, how exciting.' Bob had recovered. 'Can I join you?'

'Step right up, old chap, delighted to have you on board.'

The trio formed a line and with their weapons held high, they crept along the corridor, their shadowy silhouettes caricatured by the light of Hattie's torch as Hugo led them slowly down the stairs.

Chapter Thirty-Four

Jo sat in the Green Room and drummed her fingers along the arm of her chair. The storm continued to rage, like a thousand hounds wailing in the night, and she tried to appear outwardly calm but inside she was in turmoil.

Guests sat together and no one seemed able to speak, their fears growing, held prisoner by the terrifying weather.

Jo's anxiety was escalating by the minute.

She stood up and went over to the window, pulling a curtain to one side. Thunder rolled across the village rooftops and a streak of silver split the sky as the downpour pounded the countryside and water shimmered on the drive. Jo prayed that her guests didn't look out or sense her fear and she wondered where the hell Hattie had got to. She was tempted to go and find her but, if truth be told, Jo was too scared to creep about on her own in the dark and knew that she had to put a brave face on for the boomers, who were discussing the weather and lack of power, wondering how long it would last and if they were to be kept from their bedrooms all night. Bunty bounced around the room, tail wagging as she went from one group to another, enjoying strokes and cuddles in abundance.

Jo smiled with a confidence she didn't feel as she mingled, assuring them that the storm would soon abate. Earlier, she'd fumbled her way to reception and managed to find a pile of old blankets left by Hattie. The doggy smelling covers had come in useful again and she tucked the wool around the shoulders and legs of her guests. Despite the warmth of the fire, Jo sensed that their ageing bones were beginning to feel the creeping cold.

Hypothermia was all she needed.

The door opened and James poked his head into the room. He caught Jo's attention and she followed him into the hall.

Kate stood beside James. They both looked anxious.

'The weather is getting worse and it's flooding the drive,' James said.

Jo looked out at a lake of water where a howling wind whipped up crests of white.

'Oh goodness, I wish Pete was here.' Jo rubbed her forehead. 'I didn't realise that it was rising so fast. What on earth should we do?'

'Get tha' selves on a higher floor!'

A voice boomed out and they turned to see a flashlight swinging an arc of light along the hallway. A figure appeared. It was Alf, complete with rubber waders. 'The cellar is three-foot high in water and I canna contain it,' he said. 'The generator is sodden and wrecked.' He turned to James. 'There's sandbags in the store by the kitchen and we'd best get them piled against the doors. We haven't got long.' A damp roll-up hung off his lips and bobbed as he spoke.

Jo was relieved to see Alf but realised that the hotel was about to flood and with no lights they needed to move fast.

'Use this and get the guests upstairs, keep everyone together,' Alf instructed. He handed the flashlight to Jo and, reaching for a collection of battery-operated torches from the top pockets of his shirt, handed them to James and Kate. 'You come with me and get started on the sandbags.'

Jo grabbed the flashlight. If she wasn't careful, pandemonium would break out and she needed to keep everyone calm, but they had to know what was happening. She opened the door of the Green Room and stepped in. 'Alf has just advised me that there may be flooding on the ground floor and we should all stick together and go up to the first floor where we'll be safe.'

The guests suddenly saw the seriousness of their situation.

Many allowed themselves to be ushered upstairs but others, insisting on helping too, formed a human chain and these boomers began to assist James, Kate and Alf as they manhandled the sandbags and piled them around the ground floor doorways. The dark hampered their progress and, as they battled on, water poured over the carpets and rose at an alarming rate.

'It's no good,' Alf called out, 'get tha' selves out of here, we canna cope with these levels, it's rising too quickly.' He ushered everyone along the hallway and was the last to leave the ground floor as everyone gathered on the gallery at the top of the stairs.

They stared out of the windows overlooking the driveway and watched the waters rising.

Jo held Bunty in her arms and with telephone lines down, reached for her mobile to call the emergency services for the umpteenth time. The call was intermittent and when she eventually got through, the operator gave strict instructions to remain on the upper floors and wait for help to arrive.

But there was no telling when that might be.

The whole area around the hotel was now under water. The River Bevan had broken its banks and the road bridge in the village had been swept away. There was carnage outside where the flood raged, sending driftwood and rubbish thundering like a tsunami under the pressure of the worst storm seen in the county for decades.

Jo looked around. She'd expected to find Hugo, Hattie, Bob and Lucinda on the gallery and was dismayed to see that they were still missing. Hopefully, they would have the sense to stick together, somewhere safe. She saw that James and Kate had found bottles of water in the housekeeping store, which they were distributing with pillows and quilts. They worked together to help make everyone as comfortable and warm as possible.

Candle and lamp lights flickered in the rooms of the cottages and houses surrounding the village green and as Jo looked out, she could see people huddled in their windows. The village was elevated and fortunately not in the dip by the river, where the hotel was located. With any luck the flood wouldn't reach those properties but here, at Boomerville, they were in danger.

Jo began to pray.

She willed whoever was in charge above to ensure that everyone stayed safe and that help, in whatever form it might take, was somehow making its way to Boomerville. *Oh, where on earth could Hattie be?* Jo was now fearful for her friend and she turned to look at the guests, who clung to each other as they looked out at the storm. Jo wished that there was something she could do. She held Bunty tightly and as she nuzzled into the warm fur, she glanced over the banisters and down into the stairwell, where Alf stood on the bottom step.

The water had risen to his knees.

Alf looked up and their eyes met. Jo raised her eyebrows in question and as he gave a shrug in return, she realised that Alf had the fingers of both hands crossed. She turned to James and Kate and, kissing Bunty on her soft silky head, thrust the puppy into their arms.

'Where are you going?' Kate asked.

'I've got to find Hattie.'

'Not without me.' James turned to two ladies sitting together on the floor. 'Can you look after Bunty?' he said and placed the puppy in their arms.

'Nor me,' Kate said and grabbed James by the hand.

Jo hitched up her skirt and headed down the stairs until she reached Alf's side.

Alf took Jo's hand and turned to James and Kate. 'Follow closely,' he said.

Chapter Thirty-Five

Andy stood on the steps at the top of the garden and wondered how the hell he was going to get back into the hotel. He was soaked to the skin, despite his thick overcoat and the violent wind, which was almost knocking him over.

He'd run out of his room when he realised that the storm was getting worse and, in a panic, had jumped into the Porsche to drive it to higher ground. But now, with the vehicle parked at the top end of the courtyard and already a foot underwater, Andy knew that escape was impossible. It was inconceivable that the waters had risen so quickly and as he stared down the garden at the submerged lawn, he knew that the safest place to be was in his room, high above the rising water level, where he could wait for rescue to arrive. He had no choice but to make his way through the waters flooding the lawn and somehow get back into the hotel and up the stairs to safety.

A relentless gust almost swept Andy down the steps.

With his hair plastered across his eyes, he moved forward and began to make his way tentatively down the steps and through the water. The flood was up to his thighs and the lawn a muddy mass that sucked each footstep deep into the vortex of sodden ground. His progress was agonisingly slow and Andy's heart trembled as he battled his way forward. The conservatory door was closed, with sandbags piled against it, and the only way in was through a window. Andy pulled the drenched coat from his body and, wrapping it around his arm, smashed his elbow against the glass and reached in to lift a latch and push the frame to one side. He climbed up then dropped his body down into the water in the conservatory. His arm caught against the broken glass and blood swirled as a small gash appeared on his skin but at least he was in and, with difficulty, could drag himself through the pile of floating furniture and up to his room.

Moments later, he'd found the back stairs and, gripping the banister, pulled himself out of the water and fell into the corridor. He crawled gratefully along. Thank goodness he still had his key in his pocket, for Andy doubted that he had the strength to kick down the door. He tumbled into the room where everything appeared to be just as he'd left it and a bottle on the desk still held a good measure of whisky.

He held it to his lips and drank thirstily and as the whisky soothed his beating heart, he began to smile. Kate's monies were safely on their way to his offshore accounts and with the crisis that was taking place, no one would suspect or even be interested in investigating the circumstances leading to Andy's fraud.

Hugo's blackmail was well and truly in place and would be ongoing.

The old fool would cough up on a regular basis to an untraceable account, giving Andy a handsome source of revenue. He just had to be patient and hope that the storm would soon start to recede and rescue be on hand, then he would make his way to the nearest airport and get on the first available plane. In the meantime, he'd get changed out of his ruined clothes and be ready to get out of here.

Andy looked out of the window and wondered who would be first in, a rescue boat or a helicopter? But as he stared, he suddenly leapt back. Something was shooting through the dark sky towards him! An image swirling up from the waters began to materialise. It formed in to the face of the Shaman. His eyes glared like lasers, sharp and piercing and Andy felt pain stab his body. As if blasted by machine gun fire, he fell back on the bed, shocked and scared by the intensity. But as quickly as the image had come, it disappeared and slowly, the pain receded.

Andy closed his eyes with relief. The sooner he managed to get the hell out of this godforsaken crazy place the better.

Chapter Thirty-Six

Hattie, Hugo and Bob had given up on their search for Lucinda. They'd covered most of the hotel, but with the waters rising it had been impossible to get outside to the studios and they'd abandoned the hunt.

'I hope the old girl is safe,' Hugo said anxiously as he held Hattie's hand and helped her wade through the kitchen, where the sandbags placed against the back door were proving inadequate and water poured in.

Hattie wondered if she should be stocking up on food and glanced around to see if there was anything she could grab.

There wasn't a morsel in sight.

'Oh God, I hope we don't see Lucinda's body floating down the courtyard,' Bob wailed. 'Do you suppose she can swim?'

'Swimming won't be much help in this lot,' Hattie replied. 'She'd need an outboard strapped to her back to survive.' She'd spotted a shelf stacked with packets of biscuits and reached up to retrieve them. 'Give me a leg-up, Hugo,' she called out.

'I'd rather give you a leg-over,' Hugo said as he stood in the thigh-deep water and turned to Bob. 'Give me a hand, old chap? This is man's work.' Hugo and Bob struggled to lift Hattie and as they raised her above the water she reached for the biscuits but wobbled precariously when a voice shouted out.

'Where the hell have you been?' Jo appeared in the door by reception. Her face showed fear as she saw Hattie hanging off a shelf, steadied by Hugo and Bob. Alf appeared behind Jo, followed by Kate and James, sloshing their way into the kitchen. 'We've been searching for you. I thought something terrible had happened.' Jo rushed forward and grabbed hold of Hattie's legs. She held on tightly. 'For goodness' sake get out of here, before you all drown. Everyone is gathered upstairs in the front gallery and we're hoping that a rescue party will come soon and see us there.'

'I was just getting supplies,' Hattie said. She stuffed several packets of biscuits into her blouse and allowed herself to be helped down.

Forming a human chain, the party moved slowly and with Alf in the lead, made their way through the water and into the hallway.

'No sign of Lucinda?' Jo asked as they approached the main stairs.

'We can only pray,' Bob replied.

'Oh, this is just terrible, please God let her be all right,' Jo said as they helped each other up to the gallery. 'She was pumped full of sleeping pills and tranquillisers.'

'Aye, she may have fallen into the water.' Hattie shook her head. 'She won't last long in this lot.'

They reached the stairs and as they climbed up to join the group in the gallery, they stared out of the window. It had been an agonisingly long night so far and no one had any idea when rescue would come and how high the waters would rise. Boomers held onto each other and with arms interlinked and hands gripped in solidarity, they stood silently, urging the ordeal to end.

'Nothing we can do but wait.' Alf reached into a pocket of his waders and took out a tin of tobacco. He rolled a cigarette, which he stuck, unlit, onto his lips then looked out of the window and scanned the area below. 'Stick together here and hope that the waters don't rise this far.' He lifted the window and a blast of cold air shot across the group. They recoiled and pulled their blankets tighter. 'I think the wind has died down though,' he said and held his hand out into the night. 'The rain might just be easing.'

Hattie was distributing biscuits and held a custard cream out to Alf. She cocked her head to one side as she stood beside him and looked out. 'I think you might be right,' she said, 'the rain *is* stopping.'

'What's that sound?' Jo stepped forward and looked up at the sky. A faint stream of light could be seen heading through the pitch-dark cloud and in moments it beamed down, searching at the windows of the hotel.

'Bleedin' hell, it's a helicopter!' Hattie snatched back the custard cream.

'Look, there's something down there too.' Jo leaned out of the window and pointed at a canoe-shaped craft, racing through the water below.

'Holy smoke, it's the Shaman!' Hattie leaned out of the window. 'Oi! Namaste!' she screamed, 'Over here, mate!'

The Shaman sped through the water. He wore a sleeveless coat of rainbow colours and his hair, loose and free, blew around his face. The muscles in his naked arms pumped a long paddle and steered towards the window. Hattie waved wildly as she watched him spin the vessel around and throw a rope.

'Our saviour!' Hattie shouted as she stared at the craft and leaned over the sill to catch the rope.

'Tie it to the top of the guttering,' Alf instructed and reached out to assist.

Hattie thrust the rope into Alf's hands. She shook her head as she watched the Shaman steady his cargo. In the bottom of the craft, a figure lay hunched. Bedraggled and damp, but very much alive, Lucinda looked up and waved when she saw Hattie.

'Oh, thank the Shaman and all his spirit guides,' Hattie yelled at the group behind her, 'he's only gone and found Lucinda!' There was a thunderous cheer as everyone crowded around, hoping to catch a glimpse of their homecoming queen.

'Is she all right?' Jo asked anxiously and squeezed next to Hattie on the sill.

'Aye, looks a little damp and seems to be covered in white stuff, but otherwise she's very much alive and well.' Hattie peered through the gloom and studied Lucinda. The dusty white marks on Lucinda's black woollen coat looked familiar and Hattie was sure that there were finger imprints across the artist's chest.

'Are you sure?' Jo said.

'Alive and well and forming a cast if the damp mixes with the clay on her clothes.' Hattie had a good idea where Lucinda had been found. The loft above the pottery studio was a cosy retreat, as Hattie well knew, for she'd spent many an afternoon in there.

'What's that yellow dingy?' Bob clasped his hands and everyone turned. His eyes lit up as he saw a large inflatable rescue boat surging towards them. 'They've mobilised the army!' Bob swooned as the sturdy crew came into sight. 'I can't wait to tell Anthony ...'

'Women and children first,' Hattie said as the group threw their blankets aside and hugged each other. Many were sobbing with relief as they held hands and watched the rescue parties arrive.

Suddenly, out of the blue and without any warning, Andy appeared.

'I hope there's no pecking order here!' he shouted as he shoved his way through.

The celebrations ceased and everyone stopped to stare at the newcomer.

Immaculately groomed and wearing smart warm clothes, he carried a single suitcase with his messenger bag strapped across his body.

'You can give the rest of my luggage to charity,' he said to Hattie, and pushed her to one side to look out of the window.

'Not so fast, sunshine,' Hattie said. 'You can wait your turn.' She grabbed the sleeve of his jacket and tugged hard.

'Oh, just let him go.' Jo stepped forward and took hold of Hattie's arm. She didn't want any violence to break out again. 'We must all get out of here safely.'

'The sooner he's out of my sight the better,' Kate said.

'And mine.' James put his arm around Kate.

Hattie moved back and went to stand by Hugo. They looked at each other and he handed her a bag. Bunty began to growl and, pouncing forward, barked at Andy.

'Call the hound off,' he said and kicked out.

Shouts could be heard from outside as light from the

helicopter flooded the front of the hotel and more boats made ready to rescue the stranded guests.

'Have a good life!' Andy snarled and moved towards the window.

'Haven't you forgotten something?' Hattie called out.

Andy spun around. His eyes widened in horror as he stared at Hattie.

'You won't get far without this,' she said and reached into her bag, 'and as soon as we let the authorities examine the hard drive, your scamming days will be over.' She held Andy's laptop in her hands and jiggled it, teasingly.

Andy gripped his messenger bag, where his laptop was secured.

'No good looking in there,' Hattie said. 'I whipped it out when you went wandering.'

'You bloody bitch!' Andy shouted and lurched forward to try and grab the laptop. But Hattie was too quick and she threw it in Bob's direction, who in turn threw it to Hugo.

'I think you've been rumbled, old chap,' Hugo said and, with a grin, threw it back to Hattie.

'It's not rocket science to work out who the traitor is amongst us,' Hattie said, 'and I have every confidence that this laptop will contain all the evidence we need.'

Andy looked from one to the other.

Alf reared up. He was menacing as he stepped forward and together with James, blocked Andy as the rest of the group gathered behind them. They saw a look of fear and resignation in Andy's eyes as he was backed towards the window.

Unexpectedly, as quick as a flash, he turned and clambered onto the sill.

The rescuers called out for Andy to jump down.

Without another word, Andy launched his body into the air and took flight and, as the helicopter illuminated his leap, everyone gasped as he vanished into the dark and dangerous water below.

Andy Mack, the conman, had disappeared.

Chapter Thirty-Seven

Several months after the worst flooding ever known in the county of Westmarland, life began to return to normal for the inhabitants of Kirkton Sowerby. Nature had waved her magic wand over the waterlogged soil that had been deposited on the village green and in its place a carpet of bluebells swayed beneath the glow of a warm spring sky.

It had taken weeks for the bridge connecting the village to the main road to be repaired, separating children in the outlying areas from their school and workers from travelling to their businesses. Most of the village had been saved from the distress of flood damage and with houses and cottages sitting on higher ground above the River Bevan, only a few homes had needed repair.

As tulips and daffodils burst through borders dotted around the hamlet, the night of the storm and the village's lucky escape became a memory that would be talked about in the King's Arms for many years to come.

But across the road at Boomerville, a different tale was told.

The hotel had suffered badly. The ancient structure had been rocked and, despite standing strong in the heavy wind and gales, the gracious manor house was waterlogged and the contents severely damaged when the river broke its banks and flooded through the grounds. No one had ever seen anything like it in such a short space of time and Boomerville seemed to have taken the very worst of the weather that night.

The water level had reached waist-high throughout the building, destroying everything in its path. Carpets, curtains and Jo's beautiful antique furniture were ruined as it floated about with debris brought in from the storm. In Sandra's kitchen, the equipment had smashed as the water wrenched it from the walls, and outside in the courtyard the studios had taken a severe battering too.

In the garden, however, Mother Nature had intervened and now, signs of recovery showed beneath the walls, as the rich green of herbaceous plants peeked through the dark earth alongside crocuses, violets and colourful wallflowers.

Hattie and Jo strolled arm in arm on the newly gravelled path leading away from the meadow, where smoke puffed from the recently re-erected tepee. The gypsy caravan stood proud as Alf, cap at an angle and roll-up in place, applied a last coat of paint to dry in the sunshine.

Bunty trotted along behind. The growing dog was playful and rolled her ball for Alf to throw.

'I hope that we're back in business soon,' Hattie said as they walked towards the hotel and gazed at the old buildings. 'What a calamity it was, being flooded out so soon after opening.'

'I fear it's going to be some time before we can re-open the doors to the public,' Jo replied. With the fells as a backdrop and bathed in a soft light, the house stood proud and Jo felt her heart swell as she looked at the property that had been both her home and business for the best part of her life.

She'd wept when the storm subsided and the waters drained away, leaving devastation that she'd never envisaged on the day when the rain began to fall. Together with Hattie and Pete, she'd wandered through the ruined rooms and wondered how on earth they would ever get back on their feet. But Jo was made of strong stuff and with a stoical Hattie refusing to be downcast and Pete as practical as ever, they made a plan to bring Boomerville back to life.

They set about the clean up.

Help had soon arrived and with many pairs of hands volunteering to set-to and get stuck in, progress was slowly made. The rooms upstairs were undamaged and beds were available for those that needed them, whilst downstairs everywhere had to be gutted. Broken and ravaged furniture was piled high on the driveway alongside sodden carpets and damaged rugs. In time, when the bridge was repaired and the road re-opened, skips arrived and were piled high. Floors and walls were scrubbed and disinfected and windows and doors repaired.

'The plaster has to come off in most of the reception rooms,' Jo said, with a deep sigh.

'Aye, the electrician says the same in the restaurant too,' Hattie agreed.

'It could be months before the work is finished. What's going to happen to our boomers?'

'They'll still be there, chomping at the bit to get back,' Hattie said. 'You'll soon have the place full and firing on all cylinders again.'

'Lucinda has been a great help,' Jo commented as they continued along the path.

Lucinda had moved out and into the loft above the pottery studio, freeing up her room in the hotel. She'd had no hesitation in helping during the weeks following the storm and said that it was therapeutic to work hard. It helped to heal her broken heart. Hattie was sure that Lucinda was overcoming her grief with other aids and that Paul was now part of the healing process, but she kept her thoughts to herself.

'It was wonderful to have Bob and Anthony here too.' Jo smiled as she remembered the arrival of her much-loved friend and his partner, who'd both taken time out to assist.

'Aye, it was the talk of the village.' Hattie smiled. The pair had arrived, top to toe in leathers, helmets and boots, on Anthony's Harley-Davidson. They could be seen during the day zooming around as they fetched essential supplies, and at night held court in the King's Arms, regaling locals with back-stage tales of the theatre and London celebrity life.

They'd reached the top of the steps and stopped when they saw a man and a woman standing by an open window. The couple leaned out and waved.

'Good to see that James and Kate finally got together.' Jo smiled and returned the greeting. In the last few weeks, when people had turned up on her doorstep and offered to help, James and Kate had been the first to volunteer.

Kate hadn't gone back home after the flood. She'd been adamant that she would stay on to assist. James too had started work on the storm damage and the couple were together every day. With hot meals, cakes and snacks arriving from the kind folk in the village, the community feeling was strong and they all pulled together. Jo's team was boosted when Alf and Sandra got stuck in alongside staff and villagers and everyone had their makeshift picnic meals together and bonded as they toiled from dawn until dusk.

Whether it was the physical work in close proximity that drew Kate closer to James was anyone's guess, but the couple became inseparable and Jo and Hattie watched love blossom once more at Boomerville.

'It was a pity about Andy Mack,' Jo said as they headed down the steps and across the lawn.

'Not in my book,' Hattie snapped. 'Bleedin' good riddance to him if you ask me.'

'I'm so glad that James and Kate have named the day,' Jo said.

'It's going to be a wedding with a difference, that's for sure.' Hattie grinned. 'I can't wait!'

Kate picked up a sponge and plunged it into a bucket of hot soapy water. She wriggled her fingers to create a lather and, gripping the soggy mass, wrung it tightly.

Her fingers were pain free.

There was no discomfort or ache and as Kate lifted the bucket away from the tap, she realised that she felt absolutely fantastic in every aspect of her life.

Who would have thought that this could happen after ending her relationship with Andy? She'd believed her heart to be broken and had lost most of her money but a terrible flood had bonded her to Boomerville, within hours of her plans to return home. And what would home have been for her then? A lonely old house to rattle around in with memories of her poor father haunting her for the rest of her days.

Instead, a miracle had happened. On the day of the storms, the floodgates had literally opened for Kate and her life had magically changed.

Her miracle was called James.

As one of the last to leave the hotel, James had helped Kate into a rescue craft and as it forced its way through the thundering water, she'd glimpsed the tail-end of a canoe, gliding further upstream. The Shaman stood tall as he paddled and Kate was sure that he'd held up his hand and acknowledged her before disappearing into the darkness. They'd learnt later that he'd been searching everywhere for Lucinda and found her on the upper floor of the pottery studio, where he'd helped her down and into his canoe.

Kate had been subdued as they sat in the boat and as James put his arm around her shoulders, she remembered the Shaman's words.

There is a power amongst us that threatens!

She wondered if that threatening power had manifested in the form of Andy Mack. The Shaman had been warning them all. He certainly seemed to protect and help and Kate had no doubt that he had healing powers too.

When Andy jumped from the window, they'd all held their breath. He'd leapt far away from the boat below as if purposefully leaping to a certain death. Kate knew that Andy couldn't swim and with his heavy clothing and the vicious current, he was certain to be carried away.

There'd been no news while they waited at the emergency centre and several days later they were allowed to go back to the hotel. Kate made her mind up that she was going to stay on and help with the aftermath of the storm. She hoped that she'd have word of her missing money but didn't expect much joy on that and, meanwhile, knew that there was a lot of hard work to be done helping Jo and Hattie.

James had no hesitation in assisting too. He'd immediately offered his services and within a day, he'd moved into Kate's room.

They'd been inseparable ever since.

Kate wondered why it had taken so long for her to see that James was a wonderful man. She knew now that she must have been terribly vulnerable when she arrived at Boomerville, which would explain why she'd fallen into a relationship with Andy that had been mostly in the bedroom and was without any depth. She hadn't seen Andy for what he really was.

A gigolo.

A man ultimately supported by a woman to be her escort or lover. But this particular gigolo had also been a crook and Kate had been foolish. One day she might write about it in a book and use her experience as research for a story that few would believe was fact.

But in the meantime, her own unfolding story was something she was looking forward to.

'Come on slowcoach,' a voice called and Kate looked up.

'I didn't see you there,' Kate said.

'What are you smiling at?' James asked. He reached out and took the bucket then leaned in and kissed her, closing his eyes as their lips touched. 'We've almost finished,' he mumbled, 'and then we can go to our room.'

'Not until the kitchen is spick and span.'

They found Sandra standing by a new stove. She looked puzzled as she studied an instruction book and fiddled around with the dials. Alf stood close by and poured boiling water into a teapot, from a sparkling urn.

'Does tha' fancy a cuppa?' he asked.

'Two sugars for me,' James replied, 'but Kate is sweet enough.'

'Is that a sick bucket you're carrying around?' Alf shook his head. 'Tha'll not be so sentimental once tha's married.'

'Aye, all that stuff soon wears off,' Sandra mumbled. She was distracted as she pressed a button and the cooker sprang to life. 'Induction hobs!' She cursed as she placed a pan cautiously down. 'More like corruption hobs. What was wrong with good old Calor gas?'

'Your kitchen is now state-of-the-art.' Kate ran her sponge over the new tiling. 'You have the flood to thank for that. Thank goodness Jo made it her first priority and you're up and running again.'

'A kitchen is the heart of the home,' James said as he polished a stainless steel table.

'All new-fangled gadgets.' Sandra's eyebrows raised as the soup in her pan boiled in seconds and bubbled up the sides.

'I'm so glad that it's all ready for our wedding.' Kate looked at James. 'Fully operational, just in time.'

'I'm leaving that to Hattie,' Sandra mumbled and put the pan on the table. 'She says she's got the catering sorted and it's going to be a surprise.'

'It's all in her capable hands and we know that she'll do a great job.' Kate smiled and together with James set-to and continued with the final clean of the kitchen.

Alf glanced at Sandra and shrugged his shoulders. The pair silently wondered if the couple beside them would still be smiling when they found out what Hattie, their wedding planner, had prepared for the day.

Only at Boomerville! their look seemed to say.

Chapter Thirty-Eight

Andy sat on a rock-hard bed and stared at the paint that was flaking on the walls of his cell. It was pale yellow in colour and reminded him of the studios at Boomerville. But unlike the fresh new shade that enhanced the walls, this paint was cracked and dingy and hadn't been replenished in years.

He longed for a cigar and a glass of whisky, but the luxuries of life had been left on the other side of the prison door when it closed, firmly behind him. Now he was lucky if he could manage a roll-up and a tin mug of builder's tea.

His money had been confiscated and his accounts suspended. He'd refused to co-operate with the fraud squad but couldn't prevent his computer being forensically examined and there was every chance that the experts would be able to trace some of his web of deceit.

Several other skeletons had come out of his closet and a string of women, buoyed up on learning of his arrest, came forward to make their complaints and now a further list of charges had been filed. The way things were going he was looking at the business end of a very long stretch.

Andy lay back on his granite-like mattress and contemplated his future.

Would life have been so bad if he'd gone straight? He'd a sharp brain and quick wit and combined with good looks, he'd mingled in influential circles. But his desire to deceive and connive had been great and his greed was as big as his ego. He wondered what life would have been like had he spun Kate a hardship tale and settled down with her in suburbia? But it wouldn't have been enough for a man who'd always thought on his feet and kept them moving when sense and practicality came knocking on his door.

Now he would never know.

The chances of him being in a position to scam his way out of his current situation were non-existent and it was with the heaviest of hearts that he grabbed his paper-thin pillow and turned angrily on his side.

He should have died when the waters swirled over him.

Andy closed his eyes and shuddered as he remembered jumping from the first floor window. He'd been convinced that the rescue craft was beneath him. It was a big boat with plenty of room and many pairs of willing hands reached out to safely assist his fall. If only he'd managed to land into it and get to an emergency shelter. He could have slipped away before the shit hit the fan and the police caught up with him. With his numerous passports and the money that he still had, he could have slipped out of the country and started again.

But inexplicably, as though a mystical magnetic force was at work, he'd flown into orbit and bypassed the boat and his flight sent him cascading helplessly into the swirling black waters. As the current started to drag him away, he'd felt a wooden paddle poke his body and he'd held on tight.

He couldn't remember what had happened after that but the next time he regained consciousness, he was lying in a tepee with his hands and feet bound and the Shaman standing over him.

'He's all yours, Harry,' someone had said and Andy was conscious of a woman close by. He'd also made out the shape of a uniformed policeman who leaned in, poked him with a truncheon and read him his rights. The Shaman held the flap on the tepee and the policeman and woman moved away.

Andy was vaguely aware of their conversation as they were ushered outside.

'Good to see you again,' the policeman said, 'and if you fancy an hour or two with my truncheon next week, give me a bell.'

Andy had slipped into oblivion and the next time he woke, he was incarcerated.

Now, as he lay confined to the four walls of his own personal hell, he wondered what he would do to count the days off while he served his sentence.

A book from the prison library lay on the table beside his bed and he glanced at the words on the spine. It was a tattered old copy of a James Bond novel and he read the fading title.

Tomorrow Never Dies.

But for Andy Mack, tomorrow was already dead.

Chapter Thirty-Nine

Hattie loved a wedding. There was no finer day out in her opinion and this particular day was going to be very special. Several months after the flood, Boomerville was re-opening its doors and James and Kate were to be married in the church on the village green, followed by celebrations at the hotel arranged by Hattie, their wedding planner.

The hotel was still far from ready to take guests but the kitchen was operational and Hattie had arranged a catering service to help Sandra prepare for the wedding meal.

Kate and James were delighted to let Hattie make all the arrangements.

A marquee had been erected and an events company hired to furnish and decorate the structure. Boomerville staff were back in their uniforms and there was much excitement as finishing touches to the preparations were made.

Hattie sat in her bedroom at home in Marland and fiddled with the corsage she'd chosen to match her outfit. She was thoughtful as she stroked the pretty pink roses, remembering everything that had happened to lead up to this day.

Thank goodness Andy Mack had been arrested.

It was a funny old world and the gods moved in mysterious ways. Hattie was pleased that their own Shaman had captured Andy and thanked the day that she'd suggested to Jo that they bring the Shaman down off his hillside to run classes at Boomerville. Her instincts had been correct about Andy the con-man and with the Shaman's help, and Hattie's call to Harry the Helmet, Andy had ended his scamming days in the Shaman's rural tepee. From there he was taken to Marland police station and held behind bars as a guest of Her Majesty's Prison Service, awaiting trial.

Hattie hoped that he'd receive a very long sentence.

The trip to Hereford for Sir Henry's funeral had been memorable. It had been a beautiful winter's day with a crisp frost underfoot as the procession made their way from the Mulberry country home, where Henry and Hugo had grown up, to the quaint little church in the village. Hattie, Jo and Pete were joined by Bob, James and Kate and they walked together behind relatives, friends and workers from the cider factory. Guests from Boomerville who'd known Sir Henry had come along too.

Dressed formally in black and carrying a top hat, the funeral director walked in front of the hearse. The cortège slowly followed as they made their way through the village to the overflowing church. Sun beamed through the windows onto Henry's flower-laden coffin, where his silver cane lay on a mass of lilies and gardenias, and Hattie could still remember the overpowering smell of the blooms.

A wake was held at Raven Hall, the family home, where Hugo was the perfect host. It was a poignant day with fond recollections of Henry from his youth to his dotage. Lucinda was very subdued. She wore her engagement ring and was dressed in a smart wool coat. The black fabric emphasised her pale skin and she seemed frail as she moved amongst the mourners. At Jo's invitation, Lucinda would move permanently to Boomerville and would take up her post as artist-in-residence when the retreat opened once more.

Hattie looked up and studied her reflection.

She'd selected her outfit with care. The dress had a firm foundation with Lycra in all the right places and was overlaid with a layer of salmon-pink lace. A crown of roses, matching her corsage, lay on the dressing table. Hattie knew that it was over the top but she wanted to feel special and with handbag and shoes matching the ensemble, she thought that she'd chosen well.

Jo had wanted Hattie to stay at Boomerville the previous evening, but with guests arriving for the wedding, Hattie insisted on all rooms being made available. Hugo was back in his suite and Bob, who'd arrived with Anthony, was staying in Jo's spare room.

Hattie looked at the clock on the bedside table. Kate and James were getting married at two o'clock and although it was only ten, Hattie had much to do.

She picked up the corsage.

'Happy wedding day, everyone,' she whispered and pinned the flowers to her chest.

Jo stood beside Pete and pinned a single rose to the lapel of his suit. She tweaked and pulled at the fern surrounding the petals, until she was satisfied that the bloom was perfectly in place.

'Is she coming too?' Pete looked down at Bunty who was asleep in her box and snoring softly. She wore her fancy pink collar with a matching bow.

'No, I wouldn't dream of taking her to the church.' Jo smiled. 'I walked the paws off her earlier and she'll doze until later.'

She picked up a wrap and Pete draped the silk fabric over her shoulders.

'You look beautiful,' Pete said as he admired her outfit. The knee-length dress with matching accessories was perfect for a spring wedding.

'We'd better go, I don't want to be late.' Jo picked up a hat and carefully placed it on her head. She looked at her reflection in the mirror over the fireplace. 'Thank goodness we got this room done up in time for the wedding,' she said as she turned and took Pete's arm.

'Aye, it will serve well as a makeshift lounge for your guests.'

The downstairs area of Boomerville was still recovering from the flood and with electrics under repair and re-plastered walls drying, they were months away from completing the renovations.

But no one seemed to mind.

The bedrooms were warm and cosy and guests attending the

wedding were perfectly happy to stay in the half-finished hotel, with any overflow accommodated at the King's Arms.

'Look,' Jo said as they crossed the road to the church, 'everyone has come out to see the happy couple.' She waved as she recognised villagers and local folk who stood in the sunshine waiting for the bride to arrive.

Pete escorted Jo into the church. It was full to capacity with friends and family and as they slid into their seats, Jo gazed at the beautiful flowers and ribbon-decked pews and felt her heart overflow with pleasure.

Her first wedding at Boomerville.

She saw James standing at the front of the church, beneath a stained glass window. Tom and Jack were by his side and as light poured through the multihued glass, the family likeness was clear. They all looked handsome in their wedding suits and appeared relaxed as they chatted and joked. Jack kept glancing at a woman a few rows back and Jo recognised a heavily pregnant Desiree.

'I wonder how things are with Helen?' Jo whispered to Pete.

'The gossip I heard earlier is that she's in rehab and making progress.'

'I hope she sorts things out, especially with a grandchild on the way.'

'Where's Hattie?' Pete asked. He studied the faces around them but Hattie was nowhere to be seen.

'I don't know. I can't see Anthony or Hugo either.' Jo was fretful. 'I wonder what on earth can have happened to them.'

Moments later, she sighed with relief when she heard the sound of a familiar step as heels sped along stone slabs.

'Sorry we're late,' Hattie whispered. Hugo and Anthony were with her and they escorted her to her seat.

The organist began to play and as the familiar chords of *The Wedding March* began, Pete took hold of Jo's hand.

Everyone got to their feet.

James' face was a portrait of joy as he turned and looked down the aisle.

His bride had arrived.

Kate waited on the steps at the doorway to the church and gripped her bouquet. She turned to her Matron of Honour who fussed around with the veil. Lucinda, conscious of her responsibility, was attentive and thorough as she knelt down to make sure that the fishtail hem of Kate's floor-length silk dress flowed in a neat line and would match her own shorter version. Satisfied that the bride was perfect, Lucinda took her place behind Kate and they entered the church.

Kate's heart was pounding as she stepped forward and she wished that her parents were alive to be a part of this day. But her feelings were of pure happiness and elation as she reached out to take Bob's arm. Her new friend, resplendent in his formal wedding suit, beamed as he proudly prepared to carry out his duty and give Kate away.

Bob nestled Kate to his side and patted her hand.

'You look beautiful, my darling,' Bob said. 'Are you ready?'

They heard *The Wedding March* begin and, as they started their slow walk down the aisle, heads turned. Many had tears in their eyes, for Kate was a stunning bride.

She'd never in her all wildest dreams thought that this day would actually come and that a man as wonderful as James would be waiting to place a ring on her finger and give his simple oath that he would love and honour his new wife.

'Till death do us part.

Kate looked up and saw James at the altar. He stood proud and tall beside his sons and wore a look of elation that matched her own. His expression spoke of the love he felt and she choked back a tear as she felt Bob grip her tightly. As James stepped forward and Bob stood back, nodding with pride as he watched James take Kate's hand, Lucinda reached for the bride's bouquet.

Kate looked into James' eyes and knew that her life was going to be everything that she could ever have wished for, and when the vicar pronounced them man and wife, she held him tightly as the congregation cheered.

The couple kissed and sealed their union.

Outside, villagers clapped as the newly-weds stepped into the sunshine to be showered in a blizzard of confetti. Cameras clicked, and when the photographer was satisfied that he'd captured the moment, James and Kate were guided to a waiting vehicle.

'Hop up!' Willie called out. 'Mind tha' step.' He was suited and booted and grinning like a Cheshire cat as he took Kate's hand.

The coach from William's Wheels looked splendid and gleamed with polish and shiny ribbons. Huge bows draped around the paintwork.

'Henry would have liked that,' Hugo said. He stood with Hattie as they watched the couple wave to the crowd and climb aboard. 'One of his favourite vehicles.'

The words *Just Married* appeared on a board in the back window and cans, tied to the rear, clattered as the vehicle pulled away. Willie was taking the couple on a tour of the village to give guests time to walk over to the hotel, where they were met by staff who took them through the decorated courtyard and into the marquee on the lawn. A band played and champagne was served before everyone took their seats.

Excited chatter ceased as the bride and groom, reunited with their guests, entered and everyone stood to applaud as James and Kate, holding hands and faces smiling, made their way to the top table.

'Everything ready?' Hattie put her head around the kitchen door.

'Aye,' Sandra replied. 'Me, Biddu and the boys are ready to rock.'

Sandra wore a sari, borrowed from Hattie, and a tall chef's

hat. She led Biddu and his staff from the Bengal Balti into the marquee. They carried platters laden with delicacies.

'Ladies and gentlemen,' Hattie announced. 'Biddu's Bridal Bash is about to begin and the wedding meal is served.'

There were speeches at the end of the meal. Tom and Jack, as joint best men, stood to congratulate their father and thanked him for being such a great dad. They welcomed Kate into their family. Bob, having had the honour of giving the bride away, told a few jokes and reminded the boomers of some of the happier times that had brought the couple together, carefully evading any mention of Andy. He was humbled to be part of such a fabulous day and, glancing at his partner, said that he hoped that James and Kate would be as happy as he was with his own dear Anthony. James stood up to make a speech and said that marriage was more than a ring or a piece of paper, it was the beating of two hearts, a blessing and a bond between soulmates. Many dabbed at their eyes as James looked lovingly at his wife.

Hattie rattled a spoon against a glass.

'As we draw to the end of the meal, I'm instructed to tell you that there is much more to come.' Guests cheered and Hattie held up a hand. 'There's dancing to follow and Sandra and Biddu will keep the food going all night. Samosas 'till sunrise!'

A toast was made to Sandra, Biddu and the chefs.

Hattie continued, 'If you'd care to walk through to the meadow, you'll find entertainment by our resident Shaman and James and Kate both hope you'll enjoy taking part.' She glanced at her watch. 'It starts in thirty minutes, so please don't be late.' Hattie's eyes searched the room. 'Let's thank Jo, for without her Boomerville brainwave, we wouldn't be here today.'

Jo raised her glass as guests applauded.

'To all the people who helped make this happen,' Hattie said, drawing her speech to a close, 'have a truly marvellous evening and I hope from the bottom of my heart that everyone is as happy today as I am.'

Jo and Pete linked arms as they looked up at a full moon unfettered by clouds, shining brilliantly over the countryside below. The River Bevan wound its innocent way through the valley, a silver snake that gave no indication of the danger of nature when roused. Twinkling lanterns lit the meadow and a campfire burned brightly in front of the tepee, lending heat to the cooling night.

The wedding guests stood in a circle as they waited; their expectant faces were cast in an orange glow as flames flickered and sound of sitars floated magically in the air.

Suddenly, a drum began to beat and the flap of the tepee was flung back.

The Shaman appeared.

His hair was parted in two beaded plaits and he wore a sleeveless coat of leather, trimmed with fur. His weatherworn skin shone and the guests leaned in to study drawings on his muscular arms and neck. He was an imposing figure who commanded respect.

With eyes closed, the Shaman began to chant.

'What's going on?' Jo whispered and she nudged Hattie's arm. The Shaman was now dancing, forming a circle around the fire.

'Shush,' Hattie said, 'you'll see.'

Two figures stepped out of the tepee and the Shaman turned towards them. He beckoned them forward into the moonlight.

'Oh, good Lord!' Jo exclaimed.

Lucinda, still in her fishtail dress, stepped barefoot into the circle and turned to the man by her side. Potter Paul smiled as he took Lucinda's hand.

'It's a shamanistic wedding,' Hattie whispered.

'What on earth?'

'You obviously didn't see that coming.'

'I had no idea at all.'

Jo and Hattie watched the proceedings that followed and as things drew to a close and Lucinda and Paul hugged, the Shaman stood back and everyone applauded.

'Is it legal?' Jo asked.

'Haven't a clue but who cares? Kate and Lucinda have become good friends and Kate wanted Lucinda to be a part of her wedding day.'

'It's a cabaret with a difference.'

'Aye, and there's a little bit more …'

Hugo walked into the circle. He carried a box in his hands.

The Shaman called Hugo forward and as Lucinda and Paul stood back, the guests watched the Shaman take the box and open it. He scattered the dusty contents onto the fire.

Sparks exploded into the sky and cascaded like fireworks into the darkness. There were gasps as the display unfolded.

'What on earth is in that box?' Jo hissed at Hattie, hoping that the glowing debris falling onto the meadow didn't set light to the gypsy caravan.

'He would have wanted to go out with a bang,' Hattie said as she watched the fire crackle and flames shoot up.

'No.' Jo's eyes were wide. 'It's not what I think it is?'

'Heading to heaven in style.'

Hattie stepped into place alongside Hugo. She took his arm as they stared at the sky.

'Damn fine show,' Hugo said and gripped Hattie's hand.

'Sir Henry will be pleased.' Hattie leaned into Hugo.

'His ashes scattered on his fiancée's wedding day.' Hugo stared at the brilliant blue flames. 'He wanted Lucinda to be happy.'

'As happy as us?'

'No one could be that happy.' Hugo took Hattie's face in his hands and kissed her tenderly.

Jo, who was watching Hattie and Hugo, was dumbfounded.

Shocked, she turned and stared at the circle by the fire, where James had his arm around Kate, Paul held Lucinda and now Hugo was kissing Hattie. In disbelief, she wondered if the Shaman had thrown some of his herbs on the fire.

What on earth was going on?

'Are you all right, darling?' Bob stood beside Jo and reached for her hand.

'Am I seeing things?'

'What you're seeing is what you created,' Bob said. 'You wanted everyone to be happy and fulfilled and here's the evidence. It doesn't get better than three Boomerville weddings in one day.'

'*Three* weddings?' Jo gaped at Bob. 'What do you mean?'

'Hugo and Hattie were married at Marland registry office this morning. Anthony was a witness.'

'Oh my goodness, why on earth didn't Hattie tell me?'

'She knew that you'd make a fuss and want something big and grand for her and she didn't want to spoil Kate's day.'

'But we could have made plans, had a wedding when the hotel re-opens,' Jo stuttered. 'I would have loved to prepare for it and give them the wedding they deserve.' She had tears in her eyes. 'Hattie is my best and dearest friend.'

'How much time do you think Hugo has?' Bob spoke softly. He took Jo's hand and looked into her eyes. 'His brother has just died and he knows his days are numbered. They want to be together and make every moment count as a couple, from now on.'

'Oh, Bob, of course.' Jo nodded her head. 'You're right. I didn't think.'

The lump in Jo's throat refused to go away as she stared at Hugo and Hattie. She was deliriously happy for her friend, who had become more like a sister as the years had passed.

Hattie looked up and, seeing the tears pour down Jo's cheeks, ran over to embrace her friend.

'Oh, Hattie, I'm so happy for you,' Jo cried.

'Are you really?' Hattie was crying too. 'I thought you might be mad at me.'

'How on earth could I be cross, I think it's bloody marvellous!' She hugged Hattie tightly. 'I must be blind.'

'Aye, as blind as I've been all these years.' Hattie smiled. 'I've always loved the old fool but I just didn't know it 'till the flood. He's my hero in every way.' She looked lovingly at Hugo who was standing by the fire, shaking the Shaman's hand. 'We're going to make the most of our days together and travel the world. I'm so sorry to be leaving you but I'll be back for visits.'

'But what on earth am I going to do without you?' Jo looked searchingly into Hattie's twinkling eyes.

'You'll manage, Jo.' Hattie spoke softly. 'You built Boomerville and created all this.' She spread her arms wide. 'It's all your doing.'

'Happy wedding day, my dearest Hattie.'

'Oh, my lovely friend, Jo,' Hattie replied, 'Happy Boomerville. The place where all your boomers will soon bloom once more.'

They each reached for the other's hand and smiled.

'At the Best Boomerville Hotel.'

Chapter Forty

Three years later ...

Kate Bryne stared at the shelves of books as she stood in the hallway of her home.

She'd read them all.

The book that she'd enjoyed the most was a paperback. The cover was eye-catching and the pages well turned. *The Deadly Dating Game* by Kate Bryne was a bestseller and, apart from her husband, the pride of Kate's life. Two more books had followed since its publication and were selling worldwide. Kate's agent, whom she'd met through Bob and Anthony, said that she was a publisher's dream. A prolific author with a fresh and sensitive feel for her writing.

Kate had never been happier.

She went into the kitchen and stood by the window. In the garden, James was feeding the ducks. A black Labrador scampered about beside him and a toddler wobbled across the lawn. James stooped down to scoop the little girl up and held her high in the air. Her cries of joy were music to Kate's ears as she waved at Jack and Desiree, pregnant once more, who were lazing in the gazebo nearby.

A paper lay on the table. James had folded a page back to fall open at the business section where he'd highlighted an article for Kate to read.

Boomerville was booming.

Jo Docherty was expanding her business and the journalist explained that Boomerville was a concept with a difference, where people of 'a certain age' were flocking to its doors.

She watched James play with his grandchild and remembered the day that she'd seen Hattie's advert and decided that it was time to do something positive with her life.

The people she'd met at Boomerville were good friends now. Jo, Pete, Bob, Anthony, Lucinda, Paul, and Hattie and Hugo too. Kate knew that she'd learnt a difficult lesson when she'd foolishly fallen for Andy. She'd lost a great deal of money, but mercifully, some had been returned. Boomerville had been the best thing that had ever happened to Kate.

For in James, she'd found The One and he was everything she could have wished for.

Boomerville had picked her up when she was down, taught her how to write and how to love and how to make friendships in later life, when she thought that she may never have another friend. She closed her eyes and thanked whatever path had steered her to the people and courses at Boomerville.

It was never too late to begin again.

Her mother's words no longer haunted Kate and with a sigh of pleasure as she watched her new family, she whispered, *'Somewhere in the universe, there is someone who will love us, understand us and kiss us and make it all better.'*

Thank You

Dear Reader

Thank you so much for reading *The Best Boomerville Hotel*. I hope that you enjoyed the exploits of Jo, Hattie and the guests at the hotel and are as happy as I am with the outcome.

Hotel Boomerville is a figment of my imagination but the building is based on reality. I owned a hotel in beautiful Cumbria and if I had the property today I would recreate it as the retreat described in the book. Writing this story has proved to me that it doesn't matter what age you are, it is exhilarating to go out of your comfort zone and tackle new experiences.

Reader feedback helps an author and I'd love to know your thoughts on *The Best Boomerville Hotel*. I would be thrilled if you would take a few moments to share them by way of a review.

Please feel free to contact me on Twitter: @CarolineJames12 or through my website, www.carolinejamesauthor.co.uk

Happy reading and warmest wishes,

Caroline x

About the Author

Caroline James has owned and run businesses encompassing all aspects of the hospitality industry, a subject that features in her novels. She is based in the UK but has a great fondness for travel and escapes whenever she can. A public speaker, consultant and food writer, Caroline is a member of the Romantic Novelists' Association and writes articles and short stories and contributes to many publications.

Her debut novel, *Coffee, Tea, The Gypsy & Me* is set in North West England, at the time of a famous gypsy horse fair. The book went straight to number three on Amazon and was eBook of the Week in *The Sun*. In addition to *Coffee, Tea, The Gypsy & Me*, Caroline has self-published several other novels.

In her spare time, Caroline can be found trekking up a mountain or relaxing with her head in a book and hand in a box of chocolates.

The Best Boomerville Hotel is Caroline's debut with Ruby Fiction.

Follow Caroline:
www.carolinejamesauthor.co.uk
Twitter: www.twitter.com/CarolineJames12
Facebook: www.facebook.com/AuthorCarolineJames/

Introducing Ruby Fiction

Ruby Fiction is in imprint of Choc Lit Publishing.
We're an independent publisher creating
a delicious selection of fiction.

See our selection here:
www.rubyfiction.com

Ruby Fiction brings you stories that inspire emotions.

We'd love to hear how you enjoyed *The Best Boomerville Hotel*. Please visit www.rubyfiction.com and give your feedback or leave a review where you purchased this novel.

Ruby novels are selected by genuine readers like yourself. We only publish stories our Tasting Panel want to see in print. Our reviews and awards speak for themselves.

Could you be a Star Selector and join our Tasting Panel?
Would you like to play a role in choosing which novels we decide to publish? Do you enjoy reading women's fiction? Then you could be perfect for our Tasting Panel.

Visit here for more details ...
www.choc-lit.com/join-the-choc-lit-tasting-panel

Keep in touch:
Sign up for our monthly newsletter Spread for all the latest news and offers: www.spread.choc-lit.com. Follow us on Twitter: @RubyFiction and Facebook: RubyFiction.